Imagine . . .

Returning to historical incidents through time travel—where reality TV takes on entirely new dimensions . . .

Facing an ancient evil that has been unleashed upon the world.

What you would do if ancient statues across the globe started mouthing a code—which you deciphered as a countdown to an unknown event happening in just eight days from now?

The possibility of mummified cells being used to regenerate people long dead?

Suppose . . .

All creative genius resides in certain neurons—that can be ripped out and sold to the highest bidder.

The greatest symphony of all time has been composed, but the orchestra is out of this world.

A military experiment to see into the future reveals more than anyone wanted to know.

Dream . . .

That man has been the only sentient life in our galaxy, until one day, on a frozen moon . . .

Being able to instantaneously traverse the galaxies by means of the Span.

Awakening to find yourself in another body, in another city, on another planet—and have no idea how you got there.

Wonder . . .

How handcrafted glass art is both beautiful and irresistibly alluring—especially when enchanted with magic.

What would be the outcome if man's technology finally turned on him?

Will man's journey to space always be opposed?

What Has Been Said About the
L. RON HUBBARD
Presents
Writers of the Future
Anthologies

"The Writers of the Future Contest exists to give new, talented writers the big break they need. If that's you, then you can't afford to turn this opportunity down. Buy the book; enter the Contest; take a chance on yourself. The future could be brighter than you ever imagined."

—Sean Williams, Author
Writers of the Future Contest winner and judge
NYT bestselling author, Australian Ditmar and
Aurealis Award winner

"It's been four years since I was in *Writers of the Future.* But I'm still in contact with my anthology mates. We talk about writing and help each other out, sharing contacts and giving advice.

"My first book hit the shelves with a back cover full of Hugo winners and *New York Times* bestsellers: Terry Brooks, Tad Williams, and of course, Kevin J. Anderson. The reviews have been ridiculously good, and I've won the Quill Award for best SF/Fantasy/Horror. We've sold the foreign rights to the book in a dozen countries.

"But it all started when I won the Writers of the Future

Contest. They were my first publication. My foot in the door. Without them, I can honestly say I would not be where I am today.

—Patrick Rothfuss, Author
Writers of the Future Contest winner

"Looking back now it is easy to see that winning the Writers of the Future was a watershed moment in my career. I entered the workshop wrapped up in insecurities, sure that I was an impostor about to be found out at any moment, and left with the confidence that I had the drive to turn my ambition and talent into a career. The best way to explain it is that the Writers of the Future lit a fire under my backside. I've been a full-time writer for the last three years, have published six novels, edited three anthologies and sold somewhere in the region of 750,000 words at pro rates (over a million if you count translations) since winning back in Volume XIX.

—Steven Savile, Author
Writers of the Future Contest winner

"L. Ron Hubbard's Writers of the Future anthologies are a road map—they show the future of science fiction by showcasing tomorrow's writers today. These are the best of the next generation, and their stories are a heck of a read. But they also point the way to the writers who are pushing to come next. My own achievements in Writers of the Future opened a path of success that I'm still exploring—if you want to follow that path, read the book, enter the Contest, grow with the winners."

—Jay Lake, Author
Writers of the Future Contest winner
John W. Campbell Award winner

"Winning the Contest was my first validation that I would have a career. I entered five times before winning and it gave me something I could reach and attain. It kept me writing and going for something. Reading the anthology is important. Writers of the Future is a market and you have to KNOW your market if you are going to submit and win. I had the first four volumes of *Writers of the Future* and just read them over and over before I won and was published in Volume V."

—K. D. Wentworth, Author
Writers of the Future Contest winner and judge

"Prior to L. Ron Hubbard's Writers of the Future Contest starting, there was no field which enabled the new writer to compete with his peers—other new writers."

—Kevin J. Anderson, Author
Writers of the Future Contest judge

"These stories push the boundaries—entertaining, creative and greatly varied. A feast for short story lovers."

—Gregory Benford, Author
Writers of the Future Contest judge

"This Contest has changed the face of science fiction."

—Dean Wesley Smith
Author and Editor

"L. Ron Hubbard's Writers of the Future Contest and the *Writers of the Future* anthology represent not only the premier showcase for beginning writers in the field of speculative fiction, but also a wonderful teaching tool for aspiring authors."

—John L. Flynn, PhD
Professor of English and Modern Languages
Towson University, Maryland

L. Ron Hubbard PRESENTS
Writers of the Future

VOLUME XXIII

L. Ron Hubbard PRESENTS

Writers of the Future

VOLUME XXIII

The year's thirteen best tales from

the *Writers of the Future*

international writers' program

Illustrated by winners in

the *Illustrators of the Future*

international illustrators' program

With essays on writing & illustration by

L. Ron Hubbard / Kevin J. Anderson / Judith Miller

Edited by Algis Budrys

GALAXY PRESS, LLC

Art and Communication: © 1979 L. Ron Hubbard Library
Primetime: © 2007 Douglas Texter
The Sun God at Dawn, Rising from a Lotus Blossom: © 2007 Andrea Kail
The Frozen Sky: © 2007 Jeff Carlson
The Stone Cipher: © 2007 Tony Pi
Obsidian Shards: © 2007 Aliette de Bodard
Ripping Carovella: © 2007 Kim Zimring
If Only I Had the Time: © 2007 Kevin J. Anderson
Our Last Words: © 2007 Damon Kaswell
Saturn in G Minor: © 2007 Stephen Kotowych
By the Waters of the Ganga: © 2007 Stephen Gaskell
Pilgrimage: © 2007 Karl Bunker
Here's the Thing . . .: © 2007 Judith Miller
The Gas Drinkers: © 2007 Edward Sevcik
The Phlogiston Age: © 2007 Corey Brown
Mask Glass Magic: © 2007 John Burridge

Illustration on page   28: © 2007 Randall Ensley
Illustration on page   83: © 2007 Yuliya Kostyuk
Illustration on page 106: © 2007 Bogdan Stetsenko
Illustration on page 154: © 2007 Lars Edwards
Illustration on page 198: © 2007 Marcus Collins
Illustration on page 255: © 2007 Artem Mirolevich
Illustration on page 277: © 2007 Amelia Mammoliti
Illustration on page 312: © 2007 Randall Ensley
Illustration on page 328: © 2007 Artem Mirolevich
Illustration on page 371: © 2007 Peter Town
Illustration on page 390: © 2007 Geir Lanesskog
Illustration on page 459: © 2007 Bryan Beus
Illustration on page 507: © 2007 Lorraine Schleter

Cover Artwork: Cosmonaut © 2007 Stephan Martiniere
Interior Design: Jerry Kelly

ISBN: 978-0-7394-9104-1
Printed in the United States of America

CONTENTS

INTRODUCTION by *Algis Budrys*   1

PRIMETIME
by *Douglas Texter*   5
    Illustrated by Randall Ensley

THE SUN GOD AT DAWN,
RISING FROM A LOTUS BLOSSOM
by *Andrea Kail*   41
    Illustrated by Yuliya Kostyuk

THE FROZEN SKY
by *Jeff Carlson*   91
    Illustrated by Bogdan Stetsenko

ART AND COMMUNICATION
by *L. Ron Hubbard*   143

THE STONE CIPHER
by *Tony Pi*   149
    Illustrated by Lars Edwards

OBSIDIAN SHARDS
by *Aliette de Bodard*   191
    Illustrated by Marcus Collins

RIPPING CAROVELLA
by *Kim Zimring*   225
    Illustrated by Artem Mirolevich

IF ONLY I HAD THE TIME
by *Kevin J. Anderson*   259

OUR LAST WORDS
by *Damon Kaswell* 265
    Illustrated by Amelia Mammoliti

SATURN IN G MINOR
by *Stephen Kotowych* 291
    Illustrated by Randall Ensley

BY THE WATERS OF THE GANGA
by *Stephen Gaskell* 315
    Illustrated by Artem Mirolevich

PILGRIMAGE
by *Karl Bunker* 353
    Illustrated by Peter Town

HERE'S THE THING . . .
by *Judith Miller* 379

THE GAS DRINKERS
by *Edward Sevcik* 385
    Illustrated by Geir Lanesskog

THE PHLOGISTON AGE
by *Corey Brown* 421
    Illustrated by Bryan Beus

MASK GLASS MAGIC
by *John Burridge* 463
    Illustrated by Lorraine Schleter

THE YEAR IN THE CONTESTS
by *Algis Budrys* 515

CONTEST INFORMATION 521

Introduction

BY ALGIS BUDRYS

When L. Ron Hubbard first announced a contest for aspiring writers that would not only have their work selected by top names in the field of science fiction and fantasy, but would then also see the winning stories published in a book dedicated to these winners, fans of SF were about to discover an exciting new source for great reading—and one that has remained so to this day. Other anthologies published since the Contest launch are for established writers and do not provide the all-important opportunity for beginning writers to make their break into publishing. And as the magazines with their demand for short fiction continue to die away, the newcomer has found an even more difficult task in getting that first all-important career start.

I was very familiar with L. Ron Hubbard as one of the most famous writers of the time. Having seen him once at a science fiction convention in New York City, where he was a surprise speaker, I witnessed firsthand the incredible effect he had on the con guests—including myself. Everyone went quiet and simply whispered to each other, "It's him—it's Hubbard." So when I was invited by his literary agency to come on board as the coordinating judge and editor for a new contest being sponsored by Hubbard himself, I gladly accepted.

Having been an editor for most of my adult life, I have been able to introduce the likes of Robert Reed, Nina Kiriki Hoffman and Karen Joy Fowler to the pages of this series of books.

1

I knew the importance of getting that first break—especially if science fiction and fantasy were going to continue seeing an infusion of new vitality that the pulp magazines had previously been the source for.

My first order of business was to put together a panel of judges worthy of such a program, and I think you will have to agree with me that, from the beginning our judges have been first-rate. While not all of them are with us today, their contributions to this Contest along with their works continue to live on. Over the last twenty-three years, our Writers' Contest judges have included Kevin J. Anderson, Doug Beason, Gregory Benford, Ben Bova, Ramsey Campbell, Orson Scott Card, Hal Clement, Brian Herbert, Frank Herbert, Nina Kiriki Hoffman, Eric Kotani, Anne McCaffrey, C. L. Moore, Larry Niven, Andre Norton, Frederik Pohl, Jerry Pournelle, Tim Powers, Robert Sawyer, Charles Sheffield, Robert Silverberg, Theodore Sturgeon, John Varley, K. D. Wentworth, Sean Williams, Jack Williamson, Gene Wolf, Dave Wolverton and Roger Zelazny. And just this year, I am happy to announce Rebecca Moesta as our most recent judge.

As L. Ron Hubbard knew only too well the importance that illustration played as the complement to a good story, a few years later saw the launch of the Illustrators of the Future Contest with Frank Kelly Freas as its coordinating judge. Kelly had originally met Hubbard in John W. Campbell's office many years earlier. After multiple meetings and witnessing Hubbard's ready willingness to help struggling young writers, Kelly commented, "(Hubbard) was a gentleman as well as a literary force, with the capacity to make an acquaintance feel important and a friend seem cherished."

And as has been done with the judges for the Writers' Contest, a similar list of top names in the industry came on

2

*board in support of a contest giving the aspiring artist a chance
for a career boost in the very competitive field of illustration.
Throughout the history of the Illustrators' Contest the judges
have been Edd Cartier, Vincent Di Fate, Diane Dillon, Leo
Dillon, Bob Eggleton, Will Eisner, Frank Frazetta, Frank Kelly
Freas, Laura Brodian Freas, Stephen Hickman, Judith Miller,
Shun Kijima, Jack Kirby, Paul Lehr, Ron Lindahn, Val Lakey
Lindahn, Moebius, Sergey V. Poyarkov, Alex Schomburg,
H. R. Van Dongen, William R. Warren, Jr. and Stephen Youll.
And I am equally as happy to announce Stephan Martiniere
as our newest illustrator judge.*

*And now, with over five hundred winners between both
Contests in their twenty-three years, I am very pleased to be
able to point to their success. They have proven and continue
to prove themselves as L. Ron Hubbard knew they would from
the start, when the Contest was established and these words
were printed in his introduction to* Writers of the Future
Volume 1:

A culture is as rich and as capable of surviving as
it has imaginative artists. The artist is looked upon
to start things. The artist injects the spirit of life
into a culture. And through his creative endeavors,
the writer works continually to give tomorrow a
new form.

In these modern times, there are many
communication lines for works of art. Because a
few works of art can be shown so easily to so many,
there may even be fewer artists. The competition
is very keen and even dagger sharp.

It is with this in mind that I initiated a means
for new and budding writers to have a chance for
their creative efforts to be seen and acknowledged.

3

*Today, the Writers of the Future Contest is so well known
and respected by editors that winners automatically see their
submissions taken out of the slush piles and placed for immediate
reading. And I have been told that it has now gotten to the
point, with the number of quality stories being submitted to the
Contest, that even finalists are finding their work considered
an editorial "must review."*

*Fans can find the works of the Writers' Contest winners
in all genres of fiction with over three hundred novels and
three thousand short stories published (at least that's what
we know of) and its Illustrators' Contest winners, equally as
impressive, with thousands of their illustrations published.*

*So turn the pages and let this year's winners take you to
places you have never been, with sights you have never seen,
to meet people you have never known in* L. Ron Hubbard
Presents Writers of the Future Volume XXIII.

Primetime

written by

Douglas Texter

illustrated by

RANDALL ENSLEY

ABOUT THE AUTHOR

Douglas Texter's parents seemed to know what makes a writer. Every birthday they'd give him books. He grew up liking literature, history and politics (he spent five summers canvassing for different causes).

Douglas had done quite nicely in academia (he's a doctoral student in English), writing entries for the American Movie Classics Companion *and back cover copy as an editor. Five years ago, he started writing science fiction and satire. He's enjoyed writing about heroes, combat and strange choices ever since. Douglas says he's been lucky—even his canvassing has helped him: "Keep knocking on doors because for every one yes, you get ten nos, but those yeses: they are so sweet." A Writers of the Future quarter-finalist in 2004, he hopes this win will help cut down the nos and make it easier to get to yes.*

ABOUT THE ILLUSTRATOR

Randall Ensley was destined to draw outer and inner space. Born in Melbourne, Florida where his father worked at Cape Canaveral (now Kennedy Space Center), Randall became a "fanatic" about astronauts, space travel and science fiction. Soon he was drawing images of stories he was reading and flights he was hearing about. He credits great pulp illustrators like Virgil Finlay as major influences, as well as heaping doses of TV's Lost in Space, The Herculoids *and Robert Heinlein.*

Randall first learned of the Illustrators' Contest years ago from former winner Frank Wu through an e-mail exchange. In 2004, he met Wu at Boston's WorldCon, where Randall received a Judges' Choice Award for his illustration "Final Frontier." But Randall was still not sure if he was eligible until he contacted us directly this year. He hopes his appearance in these pages will open doors to interior illustration projects, his true artistic desire. Randall lives in Connecticut with his wife, Pam.

Primetime

I popped in three hundred feet above No-Man's Land near La Boiselle and did a quick equipment check: anti-grav unit and maneuvering jets functional. Invisibility shield and soundproofing on. Sensory body-webbing okay. My nose filter picked up the acrid smoke from the English artillery barrage that had just ended. The chronometer readout inside my goggles showed that the techies had put me exactly when I was supposed to be: 7:24 on the morning of July 1, 1916. Through the miracle of tape-delayed coverage, two hundred million viewers in vid-web suits would soon witness the start of Sir Douglas Haig's tragic adventure.

I was six minutes away from H-Hour as a light rain sprinkled Rawlinson's Fourth Army below and in front of me. A stream of Tommies in washbowl helmets and puttees flowed up the muddy duckboards from the rear. The first-wave troops reclined against the mud walls of the trenches and salients, ready for Haig to send them over the top. The whole scene was eerily quiet.

Then the voice of my producer, Paul, buzzed in my right ear.

"Alex, let's check your goggles' telescopic function.

We want the folks to be able to see all the action at the Somme."

The action. What he meant, of course, was the slaughter.

In living color. With full auditory and olfactory accompaniment. If my timing was right, I might even give them the thrill they were all looking for: the ability to touch death from the comfort of their own twenty-fourth-century living rooms.

I zoomed in on a duckboard. A green English leg wrapped in a mud-caked puttee came into my field of vision. "Focus on that, Alex. I'll check color, too."

After a few seconds, Paul said, "You're fine. 5:10 until H-Hour. Line up a mark. Hey, Alex," he added, "try not to screw up. Vinson's watching the feed today. Rumor has it that the Network wants a team for something big. Past-First! is losing some leverage at the Historical Coverage Protocol Renegotiations."

Something big. Exactly what I wanted. I had been covering second-banana wars and police actions for eight years, since I had gotten my history degree from Penn and joined the Network.

I had been floating in a standing position. After flipping over onto my stomach, I dropped to about three feet above the ooze and jetted slowly toward the British lines. When I reached the rows of sandbags, I raised myself five feet and hovered. In front of me stood a squad of about a dozen Tommies.

I panned them. First, an old, heavy-jowled sergeant, his face and chevrons covered in mud. "Nah, too ugly," I said. "Nobody will want to watch him die."

I looked at five more. Paul and I vetoed them all. With

time running out, I hit the jackpot: a lance corporal, probably twenty. "There he is," I said, zooming right up to him.

He wrote in his journal. Blond bangs peeked out from beneath his helmet. He was thin, and bags hung under his eyes. He looked so tired and so very resigned. After finishing writing, he unbuttoned his tunic. As he lifted the journal to tuck it in, the name written on the front cover popped into view: "David Smith."

"Did you catch that?" I asked Paul.

"Got it," Paul said.

"Yep," I said. "Beautiful face and a name to go with it. This guy's a keeper. Get Research to see what they can get on him."

"Done," Paul replied. "Meanwhile, in case you haven't noticed, you have fifteen seconds. Get your ass up."

Paul didn't have to tell me twice. Still floating on my stomach, I jetted up twelve feet and simultaneously started reversing so I could give viewers a relatively wide-angled shot.

When I reached my safe perch, whistles sounded and Tommies climbed up over the sandbags. Upon righting himself, one soldier dropped a soccer ball and kicked it toward the German lines. Laughter erupted from his fellow soldiers.

"That's fantastic," Paul said. "Now get back to Smith."

"Right," I said and zoomed in on my Tommy. He had lost his footing and slid back down into the trench.

"Wonderful," Paul said, with a hint of annoyance in his voice.

"Yeah," I said. "People hate klutzy fallen heroes."

Smith made it out of the trench on his second try. After sinking slightly into the mud, he ran ahead and fell in step with the other Tommies.

I backed up slowly, keeping pace with the advance. "Piece a cake, lads," a decidedly Scottish sergeant said. "Lek I told ya, we'll be in Berlin bah noon."

Smith's mouth moved. But I couldn't quite hear what he was saying, so I boosted audio intake. You never know. Something a subject says could jack up ratings.

Devil's in the details.

"We're not going to make it," Smith said. "End it quickly, please." Smith half-whispered this, over and over, like a mantra.

As he finished his third refrain, the German gunners opened up.

Ta, Ta, Ta. It was a perfect staccato.

"Great catch. Nice timing," Paul said.

The Maxim guns methodically mowed down the Tommies, who marched in step toward the wire. Bullets tore into Smith's tunic, right above his waist. Jets of blood spurted out.

"Red picked up just right," Paul said.

Amazing. With at least four slugs in him, Smith was still on his feet, staggering.

"Come on, fall back, not forward, you bastard," I said. "Don't screw up my shot."

"Perfectionist," Paul said. I could almost see his grin spreading across the four-hundred-year void.

"Hey, everybody has a role to play," I said. "Tommy's is easy. All I ask is that he does it right."

I got my wish. The weight of Smith's haversack pulled him back.

"The gunners have moved on," I said. "I'm going down to see if I can get a little somatic feedback. Open the flow. Let's get the money shot and then I'm outta here."

"OK, flow's opened," Paul said. "Pop-out in fifty-eight seconds." Whistles sounded again. "Second wave's over the top, Alex," Paul said. "Be careful. The gunners will do a second sweep. You'll be able to tell how close they are by the English bodies collapsing."

I dropped down and moved forward. In front of me a wave of about ten thousand soldiers advanced.

I jetted to Smith and hovered over him, putting a hand on his chest. The blood was hot, souplike. When he felt my touch, he lifted up his head and said, "Oh God, let this end."

"Great audio, Alex," Paul said. "Thirty seconds to pop-out."

The angry staccato again: *Ta, Ta, Ta.*

Paul's voice chimed in: "Gunners have opened up. Look up, Alex."

I lifted my head. Far to my right Tommies dropped like marionettes with their strings cut.

"Alex," Paul said, "if the gunners get too close, break contact and get above the firing zone until pop-out. Twenty-six seconds."

Break contact? Was he kidding?

I wouldn't do that for anything in the world. This was the shot that was going to get me what I wanted: primetime. The somatic feedback would drive the audience absolutely berserk.

Smith's hands were balled into fists. If only he would die within the next . . .

"Fourteen seconds until pop-out. Look up, Alex."

About ten yards to my right, a marionette fell.

Smith lifted his head again. His breathing became shallow.

"Ten seconds," Paul said. "Fire's too close. Break contact and emergency ascent. Eight seconds."

A world of time. Smith was going to go. I knew it. A death rattle came out of his mouth. The closest still-standing marionette was now about four yards to my right. Bits of dirt flew into the air.

"Four seconds. Up, NOW!" Paul said.

"No way," I said. "I'm getting the money shot."

David Smith gave up the ghost with a second and a half to go. A fountain of dirt rose practically in front of me. I could feel the heat from the rounds flying past.

Then the white flash. Pop-out.

After getting what I came for, I was on my way back to the twenty-fourth century.

When I popped back onto the pad in the Network Time Sat after about twenty minutes in the flow, Paul was waiting for me. Perspiration darkened the armpits of his baby-blue jumpsuit. I had made him sweat.

Before I could even step off the pad, he was all over me. His hands slashed through the air. I thought he was going to karate chop me.

"What the hell are you doing?" he said. Spittle flew from his lips. "God damn it! That was too close. I'm producing, so I call the shots. I told you to ascend. Do you have any idea what would have happened if you had gotten hit and I couldn't pull you back?"

I knew. I knew only too well.

Paul would have turned around to the techie two rows behind him, Sarah. She was a beautiful brunette, about twenty-five years old, one of those *wunderkinder:* class of 2344 Harvard-Yale Combined. If a producer ever said, "Terminate," Sarah, or somebody like her, would spring into action and vigorously enforce Network policy.

Sarah was hooked into a three-way audio link with the producer and one of the Network vice presidents Earthside. Once the producer said "Terminate" and the VP confirmed the order, the five-second countdown would begin.

When it ended, all three—Producer, VP and Sarah—would again say, "Terminate."

Poof. Ashes to ashes. Dust to dust.

Somebody made part of the detritus of another time.

So, I knew. Trust me. I knew.

I patted Paul's shoulder, hoping that I could get him not to chop me. "Relax," I said. "I know what I'm doing. I got the money shot. We're going to get a rating of at least forty when they run the program."

Paul cut the judo moves and dropped his hands to his side. His face went blank for a second. Then he sighed. "Fifty-two, actually. The Network focus group projected it a point higher than the Bastille."

"Really?" I had outdone myself. "See, I know what I'm doing."

"Yeah, Alex. You've got it all under control." He shook his head and sighed again. "Well, I do have some more good news. Vinson's on the satellite, and he wants to see you."

Vinson. The Big Brass. The biggest.

Vinson was the Network president. And he had been the very first correspondent, when World Gov had allowed the Network to use time-travel technology. Something of a living legend, Vinson almost never came on the satellite. He spent most of his time representing the Network at the World Court and the Trans-Solar-System Council.

"Vinson wants to see me?" I said.

"You and Will Franklin," Paul said. I could hear the disappointment in his voice. In any organization, access is money. And Paul's account had come up short.

I touched Paul lightly on the shoulder. "Next time, man," I said.

"Sure," he said. He nodded and smiled with forced good cheer. We both knew that there wouldn't be a next time. Paul realized something that it took me a while to get. The Network had been monitoring our transmissions while I was back in France. Paul told me to ascend. I disobeyed. Someone way up in the chain of command had agreed with me, not Paul.

So, I was heading up alone.

Well, not alone, actually. In the company of Will Franklin, sort of my rival. Will specialized in French history. He had done a credible job with the Norman Conquest and gave some great feed on Charlemagne. But his real gig was the French Revolution. He loved it. And, judging from his ratings, it loved him. Jesus, he had gotten some good shots. Heads landing just right in the basket. And the bathtub scene was just tremendous. He almost blew it, though, when his watch had fallen off

14

and dropped next to the tub. Marat didn't see or hear it. Thank God it had landed on a towel. Muffled the sound. Right after that scene, the Network had come up with a new rule: all jewelry off before pop-in.

Thinking of Will's watch, I smiled and shook my head. "When does Vinson want me?"

"Tomorrow morning at eight," Paul said. Then he simply stood still. It was as though he were waiting for me to say something, to invite him along.

"Well, I better get going," I said. "I'm tired. I want to get cleaned up." David Smith's blood was all over my jumpsuit.

"Hey, put in a good word for me."

"You know I will," I said.

We both knew I wouldn't.

"OK, then," Paul said. "Have fun and tell me what the big guy's digs are like."

"For sure," I said. Then I walked out of the pad room, on my way to primetime.

At a few minutes before eight the next morning, I ran a hand over my dress clothes, trying to smooth out the wrinkles. I stepped into the beige-walled elevator and said, "Executive Suite." The phrase almost tripped over my tongue. The doors swished shut, and a computer voice said: "Identify." I lifted my eyes slightly so that the computer could scan my retinas. A little red laser zapped my eyes.

"Identification complete. Davis, Alex. Specialist in twentieth-century armed conflict. Grade One Unassigned."

Weird. I was a Grade Two, and I had been working with Paul for almost five years. "Computer," I said, "Grade and assignment inaccurate."

"Grade level accurate. Promotion processed 12:43 AM satellite time. By order of Vinson, James, Network President. Assignment pending conference."

Jesus, the execs move quickly.

The elevator doors shut, and I headed up. Vinson's office was only three decks above the pad room and five above my quarters. But there's a huge difference between geographic and political distance. Executive Country might be physically close to where I lived and worked, but it was galaxies away in any real sense. As the elevator rose, I noticed that my palms were damp. Although this was exactly what I had always wanted, I was a little nervous. It's odd. I could handle live rounds flying past me in the charnel house of history, but a meeting with a poobah of the present still struck fear into my heart.

The elevator doors opened: Executive Country.

The space was large and Spartan. Real wood floors, shiny, without a scratch on them. Power is often very plain. Requiring no trappings, it is what it is. Directly in front of me a set of double oak doors, about twelve feet high and no knobs. The only way in was through an invitation from the inside.

Typical.

Above the doors was the Network's logo: a black outline of a man on horseback, with a giant eye above.

To the right of the door was a small wooden desk. A blond-haired woman, about thirty, sat behind it. "You're

thirty-five seconds late, Mr. Davis. Mr. Franklin is already
in with Mr. Vinson. He doesn't like to be kept waiting."

She paused and then added: "Even by excellent
correspondents." Her manner softened. "Congratulations,
Alex. The Somme feed was impressive. I'll let him know
that you're here." She pressed a button.

"Thanks," I said. I stood and rocked slightly on my
heels. After about a minute, one of the oak doors opened.
A tall black man who had to be about seventy strode
confidently out. Christ, he didn't look a day over forty.

He was dressed in a tight-fitting black T-shirt and
pleated gray pants. There wasn't a spot of gray in his
close-cropped hair. I walked forward to shake his hand.
His grip was astonishingly strong for a man of his age.
He smiled. It seemed genuine. His sparkling brown eyes
bored into mine.

"Welcome, Mr. Davis," he said. "Thank you for
accepting my invitation. Come in. Mr. Franklin is already
waiting for us." He put an arm around my shoulder and
guided me into the office. The door swung shut behind us.

Vinson's office. Hooh boy. Utterly spectacular. Three
walls and the ceiling itself were transparent. A greenhouse
in space. Below and on a right angle was the Earth.
A hurricane swirled off the coast of Guiana. In the
distance, transport tugs dragged mineral barges in from
Mars. Smaller satellites danced by us, their marker lights
winking and blinking.

Will sat on one of two straight-backed wooden chairs in
front of a large ebony desk. Like that of most executives,
Vinson's desktop was immaculately clean. There was
a green leather-bound blotter and a laptop. Vinson did

make one concession to whimsy. A feather quill and ink jar sat on the desk.

Vinson deposited me in the chair next to Will and walked slowly around his desk. While Vinson's back was to us, Will and I did a little pantomime. I lifted my left arm as to indicate I was looking at the time, and I tapped my left wrist with my finger. Will, the consummate professional, shot me the bird. Both of us watched Vinson, of course. By the time he turned to us, we sat at attention, our hands in our laps.

After sitting down in his own high-backed chair, Vinson put his elbows on the desk and laced his fingers loosely together. He smiled, warmly and generously, as if smiles were some kind of emotional capital and that he wanted to prove that he had plenty of them to go around.

"Gentlemen, I believe you know each other."

We nodded.

"Well, then, I'll be brief. It hasn't been made public yet, because of a gag order." He stopped and motioned to space. "When it is, I'm sure that my office will be surrounded by Past-First! activists trying to hang banners."

That was Vinson, the consummate dramatist. Not telling us what "it" was, creating tension.

"I'm pleased to tell you that for the last three weeks, I've been representing the Network at a World Court closed-door session. We've been renegotiating the Lisbon Historical Coverage protocols." He darted his head back and forth quickly as if to make himself look slightly conspiratorial. "The Japanese Past-First! coalition fell apart yesterday."

Will said it for both of us: "Hiroshima's open?"

Vinson beamed. "Yes," he said. "The Network projects the highest rating ever." He paused for effect. "Especially since we're going to do a double pop-in."

"Has that ever been done?" I asked.

"No," Will said.

"Mr. Franklin is correct," Vinson said. "But such a historical event requires special coverage. We're going to do two pop-ins. One right above the *Enola Gay* before the detonation, and then we'll pull the correspondent out and put him in the city two minutes after."

"Well, anything's doable, once you know how," Will said.

Vinson said, "I like the way you think, Mr. Franklin. I like it very much." He smiled again. "Gentlemen, I'm not going to waste any time." He sat back in his chair and made a sweeping motion with his right hand. "The Network is already designing the promos. We'll be going on primetime live in sixty days. Tomorrow, I'm calling a meeting of senior creative people to start thinking about what we want to accomplish and how. The upshot is that I need a producer/correspondent team. Are you both interested?"

Simultaneously, we said, "Yes." Our backs were ramrod straight. We were going to be a part of the biggest broadcast event in history.

Vinson said, "So, which one of you is going to ask the question?" He was teasing us.

"I will," Will said. "Who covers and who produces?"

Vinson shifted in his chair. Leather sibilantly creaked. "Mr. Franklin, I said a moment ago that I like the way you think. And I do, very much."

I winced. Will was going to cover.

19

"Thank you," Will said. Now I wanted to give him the finger.

Vinson said, "You think like a producer. In fact, as of this moment, you are a senior producer. Elizabeth will have the paperwork for you to sign. Congratulations, Will."

If Will was disappointed, he never showed it. "Thank you, Mr. Vinson. I'll endeavor to live up to the Network's standards."

"I know you will. I wouldn't have promoted you if I hadn't thought that the case. Now, if you could excuse us, I need to talk to Alex alone for a few moments." Will stood up and turned toward the door.

I was giddy. I had just been given the most important assignment that the Network had to offer.

I heard the oak door swing open.

Vinson and I sat silently for a second, waiting for the door to shut. I looked out those amazing windows. Another tug pulled a barge toward one of the industrial space stations on Earth's far side. The door shut with a click.

"So, how are you feeling, Alex?" Vinson asked.

"Stunned. Why did you pick me? You said that you like the way he thinks."

"I do. He thinks like a producer."

"What do you mean?"

"Did you ever ask him about how he decided on the Bastille shots?"

"No."

"Of course you didn't. You probably assumed he did it the same way that you captured the final struggles of Corporal David Smith yesterday at the Somme."

"What do you mean?"

"I asked his producer to ask Will about his coverage in France. He analyzed past viewer responses and then acted on the analysis."

"All very rational," I said.

"To be sure. That kind of thinking will make him an excellent producer, with consistently high ratings on his shows." He paused. "Let me ask you a question, Alex. Why did you disobey your producer's orders? You flouted protocol and put yourself in direct danger. You could have caused a historical incident. That we don't particularly like."

I opened my mouth to explain.

He held his hand up, palm outward. "I'm not accusing, Alex. I'm simply stating fact. It's also a fact that you got the Network an incredibly high projected rating." He smiled. "That we do like. So, why did you do it?"

"Because it felt right."

Vinson smiled again. "Because it felt right." He sighed. "Tell me what you felt so I can make sure that I didn't make a mistake."

I held my breath for a second, thinking very quickly. I exhaled: "Well, I felt that David Smith was one of the loneliest and most lost people in the world. He was trapped, like most of us are from time to time, in a situation he couldn't get out of. People could relate. His story is everybody's. His death was a tragedy."

"Did you feel anything else?"

"I also felt that he had a pretty good jaw line."

Vinson chortled. "Well said, Alex. Well said, indeed. I've picked the right person."

"I hope so," I said.

Vinson nodded. "I tend not to make mistakes. I can't afford to. Alex, when we go in, I want you to keep feeling. Mr. Franklin will do the thinking, give you general guidelines. But don't get trapped in rationality. In our line of work there are definite limits to formal reasoning and calculation. Part of being a good correspondent is knowing when to break the rules. If a shot feels good at Hiroshima, take it. I'll back you. Sometimes one good gut reaction is worth months of careful planning."

I nodded. That was what I had always felt.

Vinson stood and walked around the desk. I stood as well. "Mr. Davis," Vinson said, "it's been a pleasure talking to you. But I'm due on a shuttle. We'll meet again in two days with the entire creative team. Meanwhile, get some rest and start reading about Hiroshima. Get a feel for it."

Under the cold, eternal stars, we left Executive Country, and I began my descent into history.

I popped in thirty-five thousand feet above the Otta River, five-fingered and muddy. It was 8:10 Japanese time, on the morning of August 6, 1945.

Free-falling through a cloudless sky, I did a quick equipment check: oxygen on. Goggles functioning. Jetpack okay. I rocketed toward three silver slivers about four thousand feet below and in front of me.

The *Enola Gay* and its escorts, *The Great Artiste* and *No. 91*. Right on schedule. The voice of my producer, Will, buzzed in my right ear: "Alex, we're going live in five, four, three, two, one." Driving music of the opening sequence, an old song from the twentieth century: "Ride Like the Wind."

"You're now seeing for nine billion," Will said. "We'll be on the Trans-Solar-System linkup in thirty seconds." Then he delivered the old producer line: "Try not to screw up."

"Don't worry, I left my watch at home."

Another voice chimed in: Vinson's. "How's it feel, Alex?" I knew that Vinson sat in a chair rigged up right behind Will.

So, how did it feel?

Unbelievable.

Adrenaline raced through my body. I hurtled at five hundred miles an hour toward a plane about to unleash Armageddon, or at least all the Armageddon that one hundred thousand people could handle. More than that, I was at one of the major intellectual turning points in the history of my species. After the bomb, almost everything else of real importance was small—the computer, the internet, genetic engineering, microbiology, cloning, the human-development movement, the discovery of the time flow.

Of course, the members of my audience weren't primarily interested in the intellectual implications of all this. They wanted a big boom.

And I was going to give it to them—in spades.

"Alex," Will said, "pan the city before you get to the ship."

I looked down. Six miles below, Hiroshima awoke from its summer slumber. Anybody gazing up would have thought they were simply seeing the control ships for the massive B-29 raids that always formed up a little north of the city. Below sat the green checkerboards of the parade grounds of the Second Imperial Army, ostensibly the mission's target. Below also squatted the intricately latticed Hiroshima Castle, where ten very unlucky American POWs were about to be burned alive along with their captors. Irony. Kill the people you're trying to save.

I turned back to the ships. God, they were majestic. Aloof, proud, sleek.

In the distance sat the T-shaped Aoi Bridge, the aiming point. I had to hand it to Will. He called the shots like clockwork. Together, we had read almost everything ever written about the destruction of Hiroshima, including a story in which the city was never bombed at all. Some peacenik bombardier dropped Little Boy in the water. A big splash but everybody walked away alive, much to Truman's consternation. That wasn't going to happen here. This was the real deal, a very different kind of lucky strike. . . .

Will's voice buzzed: "Alex, close with the *Enola*. We're hooking into the Allied communications net."

I streaked past *No. 91* and *The Great Artiste*. My target was the underside of the *Enola*. Coming in a little to the left of the ship, I could see the giant "circle R" on the tail fin. I also saw the young, angular face of the tailgunner, Bob Carron. He was smoking a cigarette and sitting in front of the dual fifty-cals. They hadn't been needed on this trip. The Zeros that had menaced Allied bombers for three years were gone, their pilots either burned alive or sitting at the bottom of the Pacific. Except for the occasional kamikaze, the Japanese air force was finished, washed up.

All of a sudden my left ear hurt. Static crackled, and then there he was: the Old Bull himself, Paul Tibbets.

We caught Tibbets in midsentence: ". . . on your goggles and place them on your forehead. When you hear the tone, pull the goggles over your eyes and leave them there until after the flash." By the time Tibbets finished his instructions, I had reached the back of the plane. Stubbing out a cigarette with one hand, Carron picked up his goggles with the other.

I zoomed under the *Enola*.

Will's voice again: "OK, Alex, bomb bay doors open in fifteen seconds. Hook on." This would be tricky. I was now moving precisely at the speed of the *Enola*. The plane flew about five feet above me. I carefully maneuvered upward, making sure that I didn't accidentally get sliced and diced by the propellers. The magnet on the rear of my jet pack clunked onto the hull. I was hitching a ride on one of the most famous aircraft in history.

A vibration, and the bomb bay doors snapped open in front of me. I looked down. We were even with the Aoi Bridge. "Alex, get ready," Will said. I pictured Ferebee peeking through the crosshairs of his Norden bombsight.

Then the tone. High and clear, it dissolved my mental image of the bombardier. I stared ahead into the clear blue Japanese sky in front of me. The cold kissed my cheeks. Then the tone stopped. A lurch. The ship shot up almost vertically. Little Boy—the deadly dream of Szilard—descended slowly, almost majestically, from the bomb bay. The bomb was green and had a square tail fin. For a second, it floated in front of me.

Almost immediately the *Enola* banked hard to the right. The four Pratt & Whitney engines screamed as Tibbets gave them full throttle. The Old Bull was putting some distance between himself and "the gimmick."

He knew generally what the atomic bomb was, and he had seen the Trinity films, but he wasn't quite sure what was going to happen. Hell, a month before, Robert Oppenheimer and Enrico Fermi bet about whether the test explosion would set the atmosphere on fire.

Will spoke in my right ear. "Reposition yourself and then zoom down on the city, Alex. See if you can get us a face." I was looking forward, and the explosion would be behind me. So, I turned myself one hundred eighty degrees. Hiroshima receded in the distance as the Old Bull took us back out to sea.

I zoomed down and down and down.

I was looking at a small street, empty save for a horse-driven delivery cart. A small man sat in the driver's seat. He looked up. A natural reaction. The fire bombings of Tokyo and dozens of other towns had made the Japanese used to watching the sky. They were being destroyed city by city.

The Allied strategy had been to burn Japan to the ground and finish the war.

But strategists forget what it always comes down to: people just trying to get along. This poor slob squinted against the soon-to-set sun of the Japanese Empire. Trying to get by. Like David Smith and like everybody else.

I did a close-up. He was about fifty or so. Beads of sweat trickled down his forehead. His hair was thinning. Holding the reins in his right hand, he wiped his face with his left.

My reverie was shattered by Will's voice: "Forty-five seconds until detonation, Alex. Pull way back. It's almost time for the fireworks."

"OK," I said. "Hey, when we do the next pop-in, put me down next to this guy. I have a feeling about him."

"Right," Will said, "but there's probably not going to be much left. He's only 2.5 miles from the epicenter. Thirty seconds. Sweep the sky. I want a sense of calm before the storm." The music changed. *Also Sprach Zarathustra* played.

I panned the beautiful sky.

And then the firmament broke apart.

Even with my goggles on, the blast was blinding. I had to close my eyes for a second. Luckily, the camera captured the whole thing. When I opened them, I saw the mushroom cloud. Dark. Beautiful. Terrifying. Below me, Hiroshima simply ceased to exist. Gone, in a blink of an eye. In my left ear, Carron's voice: "Holy Mother of God! What have we done!"

In my right ear, Will's voice: "Nice capture. We passed eighty-five. A hundred million more viewers tuned in. We even got seven million seniors. Good job, Alex." I always had trouble with that demographic.

A wave of shimmering, compressed air came at us. Carron saw it, too. "Jesus Christ, Colonel. Get us out of here."

Will's voice again: "Shock waves in twenty seconds. Flow's open. Pop-out in sixty. On my mark. Now."

Tibbets' voice buzzed in my left ear. I had to hand it to him. He was one cool customer. Without any indication of stress in his voice he said, "I'm doing my best, Bob. Batten down the hatches, everybody. The ride's going to get a little rough." A little rough. The man had just nuked a city. And it was as though he were announcing a bit of turbulence on the descent into Cancun.

27

RANDALL ENSLEY

Will's voice: "Two seconds to shock wave, Alex."

It hit, like a tidal wave. The plane shot forward. My shoulders felt like they were going to rip off.

Then Carron screamed into the microphone. "Another wave. Oh, damn."

This wave was less fearsome than the first. After regaining his composure, Carron said, "Colonel, I want to take some pictures. Can you bank the ship about ten degrees so I can get a better shot?"

As the *Enola* dipped its left wing, Will's voice chimed in. "You better take some shots, too, Alex. Give me the city. Pop-out in twenty."

It was like watching bubbling molasses rolling out of a black, evil cloud. Buildings, people, even the earth itself melted.

I thought about the poor slob on his cart. Will was right. He had probably been vaporized.

Poof. Ashes to ashes. Dust to dust. Then the white flash. Pop-out.

In retrospect, it was the second pop-in that screwed everything up. I had to take equipment off in the flow. Never did that before. I didn't need the jetpack or oxygen tanks anymore. The maneuvering thrusters and the anti-grav unit were going to be enough. Anti-grav supports about two hundred pounds. I'm one hundred and fifty. The jetpack weighed almost as much as I do. So the pack had to go back to future ahead of me.

I had ten seconds in the flow before the second pop-in. I unstrapped the pack and oxygen tank and pushed them toward my feet. But something caught on my leg, gashed it. After wincing with pain, I had only two

29

seconds to give the pack a swift kick toward the future. So, I was already hurting before I popped in.

"I'm wounded," I said the second after the white flash.

"How badly?" Will asked.

"My leg is bloody, gashed it on the pack in the flow. But I'll make it."

Another voice in my ear: Vinson's. "Are you okay, Alex?"

"I'll be fine," I said, trying to sound optimistic.

I had popped in twelve feet above the ground, about two minutes after the blast. Most of the city was gone. Will had honored my request to be put in as close to the old man as possible. I didn't expect to actually see him. But both the old man and I had gotten lucky, luckier than either of us had a right to expect. Bleeding and stunned, he sat against the wall of a white, thick-bricked building. Debris fell through the air.

"I'll be damned," I said.

"Get a close-up of his face," Will said. I zoomed in. Pain there, of course. But also utter confusion. There was no paradigm for what had just happened.

The blast had been like a river, rolling through the city, sweeping away everything in its path. Occasionally, though, the river met with something more solid, something it couldn't sweep away, like the bank building that the old man's horse and cart had been in front of during the explosion.

I did a double take. There was the old man, dressed in sandals, light brown pants, a kind of ballooning white shirt and a black vest. The blast had been almost surgical. But in front of the cart was nothing. The long wooden pieces connecting the horse to the reins were singed and ended about two feet in front of the cart.

30

Will caught on quickly. "Hey, where's the horse?" he asked.

"I don't know." Debris flew around me.

"Take a fast look around for it, at least the body."

"More pathos, right?"

"Yeah, kids love horses. We'll get the under-twelves that way."

"Right," I said. I zoomed forward, looked both right and left. No horse. Probably swept away by the blast. Then I looked down.

"Hot damn," Will said quietly. "You just brought our ratings up."

There was the horse, or rather the outline of it, burned into the ground.

"Jesus," I said. The blast must have flipped the horse over onto its side and then seared it into the asphalt.

"OK," Will said, "see how the old man's doing. Maybe he can get up and do something for us."

And then all hell broke loose. A piece of debris nailed me square in the back. Everything went down: the maneuvering jets, the invisibility shield, the anti-grav unit, and, worst of all, the transponder they use to bring me home.

"Uhh," I said. I was only five feet up, floating in a standing position, but I fell quickly. I dropped down and landed on my feet, hard. My right ankle buckled, and I crashed down on my side.

The old man looked at me. I realized something. I was dressed in a tan jumpsuit, quite similar to the ones that the B-29 crews wore. Who would he think I was?

Will's voice buzzed in my right ear. But he wasn't talking to me. He was beginning a litany I had never

31

heard before but understood only too well: "Level three emergency. Invisibility breached. Capability to retrieve correspondent compromised." I knew that Sarah would be inserting the key into the slot of the plastic cover. The network VP Earthside would be sending out an automated message to the Board of Directors.

All of a sudden Vinson's voice chimed in. I heard genuine concern. "Alex, can you hear us? Are you okay?"

"Broken ankle." I pulled off the pack and stood up. Oh God, it hurt.

The old man's sadness changed to a look of hate. The tears stopped, and his face quivered. He stood up. God, he was fast. His hands balled into fists at his side, like David Smith's at the Somme. But the cause was anger rather than pain. He shrieked at me in Japanese. I could tell he thought I was a pilot.

As the old man screamed, an entirely different kind of drama played itself out in the future.

Will's voice again: "Correspondent and subject interacting. Recommend termination."

The VP: "I concur. Begin termination sequence."

Then Sarah's voice: "Confirm termination."

Will spoke to me directly. "Sorry, Alex. We can't get you back. You know I have to do this." Then he stopped speaking to me, and he said, "Prepare to terminate on my mark. In five."

On the next number, the VP's voice joined Will's: "Four."

On the third, Sarah's voice: "Three."

A chorus of voices: "Two."

"No!" I shouted, not really knowing whether I addressed

the man who wanted to rip my throat out or the producer who was going to turn me into dust. At the last second, I remembered something Vinson had said during our meeting. "Back me!" I shouted.

Three voices: "One."

I now knew what David Smith had felt. Utterly alone, beyond help, knowing you're not going to make it. I muttered what I thought were going to be my very last words in the past or the future.

"End it quickly, please," I mumbled.

I closed my eyes, waiting for whatever fate was in store.

Then a new voice. Vinson's: "Override termination."

"Authority?" the VP said.

"Vinson, James. Network President."

"Termination override granted, Mr. Vinson," the VP said. "You know that I must now inform the Network Board of Directors." He paused and said, with almost a note of guilt in his voice: "I'm just following protocol, sir."

"Yes, I know the protocol. I wrote it."

In my right ear buzzed a conversation about my fate.

Will: "Mr. Vinson, we can't get him back."

Vinson: "Yes, we can."

Will: "How?"

Vinson: "This is a day of firsts for the Network. We're going to perform the first rescue. Mr. Franklin, get down to the pad. Suit up. Take somebody with you. You're going to bring Mr. Davis home. In front of the biggest audience ever." Vinson paused and said, "Alex, we're backing you. Help is on the way."

He then spoke to the audience: "Ladies and gentlemen, this is James Vinson, Network President. One of our best correspondents, Alex Davis, is trapped in the past. Like you, the Network takes care of its own."

Then he addressed Will. "Pop-in without the invisibility shield. The subject already knows we're there. But he thinks Alex is a pilot. There's so much chaos that a little more will be par for the course." He spoke to me: "Alex, they're going to come in a little to your right. I want you covering them. We'll split the screen three ways."

I had gone from covering an event to being the event. But I had a more pressing problem at that moment.

The old man charged me. He was twenty years older than I was, but I was dazed. With the strength that only rage can fuel, he rammed me headfirst in the stomach. I went over on my back. Smelling the rice wine on his breath, I winced in pain.

I still had my goggles on. Everybody back home was picking this up. And I do mean everybody.

Vinson chimed in: "Alex, our ratings are now off the indicators."

That was gratifying, but I was in a little trouble. The old man sat on my chest. With one hand he grabbed my throat. With the other he searched the ground for something. A rock.

"Oh, damn," I said.

"Mr. Davis," Vinson said, without a trace of stress in his voice, "I suggest very strongly that you bean your subject before he kills you. Your death would be rather pointless and might bring down our ratings."

"I'm doing my best," I said. The old man, spittle flying

from his lips, screamed at me. His right hand grabbed a rock at the same moment that mine did. My rock found his temple. His found mine.

I saw stars. The old man slumped off my body. Unconscious but still breathing.

"Well done, Mr. Davis," Vinson said. "Our ratings continue to be unparalleled." Then he paused and said, "How's it feel, Alex?"

How did it feel?

Unbelievable. I was in one of the biggest hellholes in human history. Debris flew around me. Mini-firestorms swept the city. I smelled burned bodies. And some survivor of all this mess had just tried to kill me. I remembered an old expression that American soldiers had used in the Second World War: FUBAR.

"Alex," Vinson said. "They'll be popping in in about twenty. Get ready. I want a shot of this. It's the first time that anybody's seen a pop-in. Including me, actually." Excitement laced his voice.

I watched the old man shake himself awake as debris fell on us.

Then Vinson's voice: "Pop-in in five, four, three, two, one."

And, my God, there they were: Will and Paul, floating about twenty feet in the air, covering me as I covered them. They dropped down and jetted toward me.

Vinson narrated: "Ladies and gentlemen, this is one of the oldest scenes in history: the rescue. Comrades taking home one of their own."

They reached me. Paul said, "Well, Alex, I see you still have everything well under control."

I arched my eyebrows. Will said, "Alex, I didn't want to burn you. I was just following protocol. You would have done the same thing."

No, I wouldn't have. Not now. But I didn't want to rub it in.

They picked me up, put my arms on their shoulders, and all three of us rose. "Flow's open," Vinson said. "Pop-out in sixty."

We went up to about twelve feet. I looked around. Light debris wafted on the currents of warm air. Wails of human misery all around us. Fires burning out of control. Blocks full of rubble. The old man was groaning.

Then, Vinson's voice. "It's time to come home, gentlemen. Five, four, three, two, one."

The white flash. After getting what we came for, and more, we were on our way back to the twenty-fourth century. Pop-out.

Epilogue

An absolute mess, I spent about three weeks in the satellite hospital. Tendon damage in my leg, a broken ankle, a nasty concussion, face lacerations and even a bit of radiation sickness. The docs pumped me full of neo-chemo treatment.

One afternoon, Vinson came by to see me.

"Mr. Davis," he said, "glad to see that you're still with us."

"Me, too, Mr. Vinson," I said. It was only the truth.

He sat down next to my bed and touched my shoulder

lightly. "I have good news for you, Alex." He beamed. "Although Past-First! was a bit upset by our coverage, the board was absolutely tickled by the 99.999 rating you sustained for approximately three minutes. On my recommendation, you're getting your own weekly show. You'll cover and produce, call your own shots." He paused and coughed. "As long as you keep your ratings up, of course." He stayed five minutes and then caught a shuttle to Mars for a meeting of the Trans-Solar-System Council.

That's Vinson: the bottom line always in the background. When he told me about the promotion, I considered turning it down and resigning from the Network. After all, the man now promoting me had almost allowed me to be turned into dust. Talk about double-edged swords. But I did accept. For two reasons. First, I've learned never to turn down a promotion. I move forward, not back. Second, I now had a real reason—not just glory seeking—for wanting to have control over my own coverage.

The Research Department had dug up David Smith's Somme journal from the Imperial War Museum in London. With Mussorgsky's *Pictures at an Exhibition* playing softly in the background in my hospital room and Ecuador passing below outside the portal, I had read through it. Mostly what I had expected: the banality of basic training, the horror and strange exaltation of combat. David's first sexual encounter with a prostitute in Soho during a rest leave. And then, I reached the last entry, the one he had finished when I saw him:

37

I write for what I know in my heart is the final time. Sergeant McQuaig has repeatedly assured us that we will be in Berlin by noon. But then Sergeant Jones said that we would be home by December of 1914. And Sergeant Sassoon said that Fritz would scurry back to his hole six months ago. Jones and Sassoon have been dead for months, and the new sergeant and I are the sole surviving original members of the platoon. I think that we too shall be gone soon.

Last evening, with the glow of the evening sunset behind me, I looked into the trench glasses and saw—through a small break in the wire—the faces of two of my so-called enemies. One had a horrible scar on his cheek and the other looked like a teacher of mine. These men mean me no harm. Haig and Asquith are my true foes.

Our chaplain came by last night after sunset stand-to and told us that God wants us to fight on, to do His work. If this is so, then His work is butchery and I want no more of it. If I could flee, I would. But I would be found, and I suppose that I would rather be shot by Fritz than by Tommy.

To those in the future who may read these words after I am gone, I ask only that you find some way to prevent this kind of tragedy from happening again.

Before I close, I want to say that for the last several minutes, I've had an odd sensation, as if some presence were observing this, watching me. But I know that's only a feeling, one produced by fatigue. There's nothing out there but Fritz and death.

The barrage has lifted. H-Hour approaches. I must go to whatever fate awaits me in No-Man's Land.

I cried when I finished the entry. David had somehow known that I was there. And, indirectly, he was asking for my help. I couldn't do much. But I could do something. I figured I owed him. His death—which I had been so callous about—had literally gotten me to primetime. Now that I was there and had finally felt in Japan what he had felt at the Somme, I wanted to help.

I'm no devotee of Past-First! The past only gets its meaning in the present. And I know my audience and myself well enough to realize that people will always want big booms. They're exciting. But they want something else, too. Maybe "want" isn't the right word. Maybe "need" is better. The booms only make sense in a larger context. And on my show, I'd quietly go about giving it.

I closed David's journal and vowed that I would bring a different side of history, a human side, to primetime.

The Sun God at Dawn, Rising from a Lotus Blossom

written by

Andrea Kail

illustrated by

YULIYA KOSTYUK

ABOUT THE AUTHOR

Andrea Kail began pretending to read at a very young age to keep up with her much older, much smarter, brother. However, once she discovered that the whole reading thing was actually "kinda cool," she promptly stole all his Lord of the Rings *books and has never given them back. Reading quickly led to writing, which eventually led to the Dramatic Writing Program at NYU's prestigious Tisch School of the Arts. Since graduating, Andrea has worked in New York's film and television industry, a career that has spanned two decades and led to her current job as Script Coordinator at* Late Night with Conan O'Brien.

Wishing to return to her speculative fiction roots, Andrea enrolled in the Odyssey Writing Workshop in 2004 under the tutelage of World Fantasy Award-winning editor Jeanne Cavelos. Born and raised on the Lower East Side of Manhattan, Andrea still lives in that neighborhood along with her uber-supportive husband, Michael, to whom this winning story is dedicated.

ABOUT THE ILLUSTRATOR

Yuliya Kostyuk, a citizen of the Ukraine, now lives in Germany working for a video gaming company. Ever since she was a young child, she wanted to be an artist and illustrator. She loves creating artwork on the computer, but also enjoys working in other mediums as well and wishes to realize her dream to be a full-time artist/illustrator.

The Sun God at Dawn, Rising from a Lotus Blossom

Mr. Abraham Lincoln
Smithsonian Institution
National Museum of American History
1400 Connecticut Avenue, NW
Washington, DC 20004
United States of America

12 February 2168

Dear Sir,

I hope you will forgive the impropriety of this personal letter sent without the benefit of previous acquaintance, but I feel compelled to write you in order that I might, indeed, introduce myself, and also so I might render to you my personal wishes for your hale and happy birthday. And, as I am scheduled to go on display in just a few days' time, I would additionally like to express my genuine and incalculable pride that I am soon to be joining your illustrious ranks.

I do not know what, if anything, you have heard of me in the media—I myself am never exposed to such things and know not what they say—but I have led a quiet life thus far, one much devoted to the study of my impending duties and, to better acquaint myself with my peers, of the other personalities currently on display.

I must admit that the latter has been a humbling endeavor.

Chopin, Michelangelo, Czarina Catherine—so many great and talented people to measure myself against. And yet, sir, of all the biographies I have been researching, yours is the one which impressed me most of all. Your humble beginnings and your determination to learn in the face of all obstacles struck a deep chord within me. And your eloquence, your integrity, your steadfast and erudite devotion to freedom for all peoples despite hardship, war and criticism—truly I do not think there is another man in history that can match you.

Which makes me quite determined, sir, to emulate you in all things, right down to your expressed inclination for handwritten correspondence, in order to, as you say, 'keep a true and genuine connection to the past.' My mentor, Dr. Fouad, is quite of the same mind on such things. Dr. Fouad is the curator of the Museum here in Cairo. He, also, believes that I should live as my prime did, or as close to as possible and, no doubt, would chastise me for not employing the use of a scribe in the writing of this letter. I enjoy writing, however, and so, if you would be so generous as to keep my secret, I will continue to draft my own correspondence, with only you and I to know the truth.

Again, please forgive me if, in the fervor to express my admiration, I have inadvertently offended you with any ill-timed or unwanted correspondence. If so, perhaps you will be kind enough to allow my youth and inexperience to buy my pardon? I hope that you will.

Signed,
Your admirer in all things,

Tutankhamun

3 April 2168

Dear Mr. Lincoln,

I cannot express my gratitude—indeed, my utter relief—at the receipt of your letter of 23rd March. While I did not think you would completely ignore my overture, I must admit to being worried that I had somewhat overstepped the boundaries of polite address. And as you yourself so hilariously illustrated in the story of your treatment at the hands of the Bonaparte, one can never be sure of one's reception, even amongst peers.

I am equally gratified, I confess, by the extended hand of friendship and the warmth of your welcome into this august fellowship of ours. To be counted amongst such men of history, vision and accomplishment is no easy burden, especially for one so young and inexperienced as I am, and yet the kind and generous tenor of your words made me feel so very much a part of something greater than myself that I vow I shall strive to be worthy of the honor.

As you so kindly inquired, here are my particulars:

Until my installation in the Museum this February past, I lived in the household of my mentor, Dr. Fouad. Dr. Fouad is also my teacher, instructing me in my heritage and in the long and glorious history of my country, and under his tutelage, I have learnt how to perform the various tasks that are part of my duties here at the Museum.

I also study daily with Dr. Sweeney of Oxford University, who teaches me languages, of which I have mastered Arabic (of course), English, French, Spanish, German, Italian, Greek and Hindi. A modest eight to your twenty-four. However, Dr. Sweeney assures me that I shall soon add more as I am 'linguistically gifted.' Is that not a pleasing phrase? I find it to be so, as I find much of your English to feel and sound musical on the tongue. Such fun and bizarre pronunciations, too. Thur-oh or thur-ah for thorough? Kawf for cough? And the absence of gender! Well, I cannot say that I understand it at all, but I enjoy it just the same.

And so that brings me, again, to this past February when I turned nine (our birthdays fall within the same week!) and was formally installed in the new exhibit. *The Living Pharaoh* it is called, and they've built a palace reconstruction to house it—to house me, really—and annexed the whole of it to the Museum.

It was strange, at first, moving from Dr. Fouad's small home to this airy, cavernous place. Despite the palace they have built and despite the guards that roam the halls, the Museum is dark at night and full of dead things, and I must confess to being greatly affected and reluctant to stay alone. But Dr. Fouad detailed for me the Museum's and his own quite sizable personal investment in my creation and vigorously explained that, as I am a man now and a king, too, in some respects, I must endeavor to behave as such. And, from time to time, men—and especially kings—must do things they would rather not. This was one of those times. And so I stayed. And indeed, after a period of acclimation, all is now well, though I must admit that I had some help in my adjustment, and that help was named Hanifa.

Hanifa is Dr. Fouad's daughter. She is fifteen and terribly clever. She grew up in the Museum due to her father's work, and so she knows all the guards and the best places to hide as well as how to sneak in and out without being caught by the cameras. And in the beginning, when I was so horribly lonely, Hanifa would come and stay with me at night. Her presence made the world of difference, and I am glad that I have such a friend—a sister, really—who cares so for my happiness.

And so, over the past months, I have settled into my new routine: I arrive in the throne room at eight AM and receive 'ministers' and 'ambassadors' whilst the tourists stand beyond the glass listening to the prerecorded guides. Then I lunch in private, often with Dr. Sweeney. Then I either go back on display performing various other pharaonic activities or I give private tours to more important guests—foreign officials and diplomats and the like.

And that is the long and the short of it, for now, sir. Once I have more responsibilities, I shall relate them to you.

On a truly personal note, I would like to request an indulgence, if I may. In my first letter, I operated under the assumption that if I used my cartouche as my signature, that perhaps it would lend more weight to my words. I feel foolish, now, thinking I needed such bait. For you see, when I was just a babe and learning to speak, I had trouble pronouncing my name, and so it was never used. But, too, Hanifa thought the truncated 'Tut' was simply not dignified enough. So instead, she called me Ghazi, after a favourite uncle, and the name has stuck. Only those closest to me call me so, and I would ask, sir, that you do the same, for indeed I second your hope that we are to be great friends.

> Sincerely,
> Ghazi

30 June 2168

Dear Mr. Lincoln,

I wish to thank you for your last letter for two reasons, the first being your introduction of the word 'quotidian.' Such an excellent word! And so very useful as well. I have managed to employ it in my dialogues several times in the past month to great effect and even once in a tour I conducted for a senator visiting from your country. I believe he was greatly impressed.

My second reason for thanking you is for making me aware that I am fashioned to be proficient in languages. I asked Dr. Sweeney, and he confirmed that, yes, language skills are standard genetic design for us, though he did seem to be of the opinion that Dr. Fouad would be angry if he knew I was aware of it. For the life of me, I cannot understand why.

But despite that, I think it quite a remarkable accomplishment, and quite clever, as well, considering our intended purposes. For we—you & me & all the others—are, in effect, ambassadors for our countries & for our cultures, and as such, communication is our stock in trade. And I, for one, am quite proud of my trade.

And now, though you have been so very indulgent, Mr. Lincoln, I hope that you will indulge me further still. I have told you of my life, and I wish, now, that you would tell me of yours. What are your duties? What were your experiences when you first took on the mantle of your service? I ask in order that I might ascertain how a truly great man handles the burden of this trust we are both a part of, as I believe there is much I can learn from you.

Again, thank you for being so tolerant of my curiosity.

With all my respect,
Ghazi

13 September 2168

Dear Mr. Lincoln,

I must say, sir, that your roster of events & activities is quite impressive indeed. Would that I had so many public engagements, so many speaking events. I come into contact with people only through my private tours, and those are given mainly to government officials, et al & are very highly regulated for reasons of which I am not entirely certain. However, Dr. Fouad has assured me that in time, more public events will be scheduled, and I confess that I look forward to those a great deal.

And yes, I believe you are right when you say our experiences will likely differ greatly. One, because our cultures are so divergent, and two, because you, in fact, are a third generation and have your routines down, whereas I am a first, and we here in Egypt are, to use your American slang, still 'playing it by ear.'

As always, your admirer,
Ghazi

18 November 2168

Dear Mr. Lincoln,

I hope this letter finds you anticipating a very happy Thanksgiving holiday. I wish you great joy of your turkey & your cranberry dressing, and I also wish the football team of your choice great success in the day's contest.

Allow me to say once again, sir, how greatly impressed I am by your accomplishments. It is not every man, nor even every country's leader, who can lay claim to promulgating a national holiday, especially one that has lasted so long & speaks so much of your country's traditions & of family & of faith.

I do therefore invite my fellow citizens in every part of the United States. And also those who are at sea and those who are sojourning in foreign lands, to set apart and observe the last Thursday of November next, as a day of Thanksgiving and Praise to our beneficent Father who dwelleth in the heavens.

In copying that out, I was struck again by how rich is your prose in reference to god. Or perhaps I should clarify and say one, singular god. You would think this would not come as an oddity to me, the product of a country & a people as steeped in our religion as is

Egypt. However, I was raised as an ancient, you see, not a Muslim, and my gods are the oldest gods: the gods of the sun & of the moon, of the earth & the sky, of animals & of rebirth & finally, of death & an eternal & glorious afterlife.

I cannot speak of such matters with Dr. Fouad, for he is not a spiritual man, preferring to talk, rather, of money or business and such. But I consider it passing strange that of all the pharaohs, of all the great pyramids & the secret burial chambers, the false doors & the hidden corridors & of all the great curses & of all the prayers said by all the thousands of priests of Ra, that I, Tutankhamun, am the only one to achieve a true & lasting afterlife.

Perhaps I truly have become a god, then? Perhaps upon my death Anubis led me here to this future? I do not know. But it is an odd thought, don't you think? Odd & somewhat humbling.

Again, I wish much joy to you on this quintessential American holiday & allow me to hope that, your schedule permitting, you will find the time to write again.

Always your servant,
Ghazi

17 February 2169

Dear Mr. Lincoln,

I can barely find the words to thank you for your magnificent gift! A scooter! Even the name is fun!

How very generous a friend you are, sir, to think of me on my birthday & to go so far out of your way to find me something that I most certainly did not have.

In fact, I must admit to not knowing even what a scooter was until Dr. Sweeney showed me. And a good thing he was with us, too, because he also had the knowledge of how to put it together. We did have some trouble finding a wrench at first, but once that was accomplished, Dr. Sweeney had it assembled in a trice.

How fast I went! I wish you could have seen. I raced the scooter up & down the marble corridors of the palace, in & out between the columns of the hypostyle hall & then out into the garden where I led the guards on quite a chase before they finally caught me. And how we all laughed when they did!

And I must thank you for this, also: that you made a festive occasion out of a somewhat lackluster celebration. Indeed, a lackluster few days. You see, Dr. Fouad is currently on a speaking tour & is not expected home for some weeks, and for the span of his absence, my duties have been curtailed. I am not certain why, but Dr. Fouad feels it is appropriate, and so that is that.

In any case, we had a small party amongst ourselves: me, Dr. Sweeney, Hanifa & my guards Atef & Kamal. We hung zeena all about the reception room & ate cookies & gateaux & sesame sticks that Hanifa had made. As a gift, Hanifa gave me a painted crocodile on a string that snaps again & again when you pull it. From the guards: a football to kick about in the garden. And Dr. Sweeney gave me an excellent new senet board inlaid with real ebony & challenged me to a game. (Dr. Sweeney is a fine senet player, but not so good as I am.)

But your gift was truly a sensation. I do not remember

when last I had so much fun. Believe me that your injunction to remember that I am still a boy has gone well heeded.

> Your devoted friend,
> Ghazi

> 15 May 2169

Dear Mr. Lincoln,

I apologize for having taken so long to reply to your last letter, but I feel the need to relate to you an incident that has occurred, and I hope that you will not judge me too harshly, as I am greatly in need of your guidance.

The evening Dr. Fouad returned from his European engagement, we dined together to discuss the reinstatement of my regular schedule. And I told him, over dinner, of my birthday celebration & of the fun we had despite his absence & of the gifts I had received, & quite suddenly Dr. Fouad was very, very angry—angrier than I had ever seen him in my life.

And the source of his anger? Can you guess it? Your scooter! Such a thing is neither ancient nor Egyptian, he said & I am likely to break my neck on it & what right had I to risk my life for such childishness? And so saying, Mr. Lincoln, he took your gift away and forbade me from contacting you again. I do not know when I have been so sick at heart! I confess, I cried the entire night until sleep took me.

Hanifa, when she discovered what had happened, was furious. She, also, was angrier than I had ever seen her. I asked her not to interfere & extracted a promise from her that she would not, but later that night, she woke me from my sleep. She had the scooter, had found it in the refuse pile where her father had tossed it, and she took it & returned it to me.

And so I am conflicted. Mr. Lincoln, though I do not approve of purposely defying Dr. Fouad, contrarily, I cannot imagine never writing to you again. And I must admit that I was quite happy to see my scooter. Your gift truly meant so much to me, sir, not only for itself, but also as a symbol of your friendship. Would it be so awful, then, if I were to continue with our correspondence? If I were to keep my scooter? I do not know. Please, if you have any advice, it would be greatly welcomed.

Sincerely,
Ghazi

Post Script:

Atef has agreed to post my letters for me now & to receive yours in return. His address is as follows:

Mr. Atef Fahmi
256, El-Makrizy St., Heliopolis,
Cairo 13148
Egypt

8 August 2169

Dear Mr. Lincoln,

There is, of course, no reason for you to apologize, sir. I, in fact, should be the one extending apologies for putting you in the awkward position of sending letters to a strange address & having to endure a scolding at the hands of Dr. Fouad.

I am eternally grateful to you for bearing it as well as you have done & not taking what would most likely be a rightful grievance to your government officials. I would be appalled to think that I had been the cause of an international incident.

However, I thank you for your concern, and I wish to assure you that I am much more sanguine about the situation than I was in my last letter. Dr. Fouad believes this issue to be closed & believing such, will not broach the subject again, nor allow it to be broached by any other.

And so, you see, we continue on with our lives as if nothing had happened. And indeed, it seems as if nothing did happen, really, except that I may not bring out my scooter when Dr. Fouad is in the Museum nor have your letters about where he can come upon them. He need not ever know, and no one, not Hanifa, nor Dr. Sweeney, nor the guards about the Museum, will tell. It is not so great a sacrifice, nor so heavy a sin, don't you agree?

Again, thank you for the grace with which you have dealt with us. I would be forever heartbroken should this in any way impair our friendship.

> Your friend,
> Ghazi

21 December 2169

Dear Mr. Lincoln,

At last, I made a trip about the city, à la the great Heb Sed processions of my ancient ancestors! What a glorious experience!

Even though they had planned it for months, I did not know about the excursion until President Hamouri & Dr. Fouad told me a few days beforehand. I was so excited I could barely sleep that whole week!

Regular viewing hours were cancelled on the day, but even so, my excitement would not allow me to lie abed past the first stirrings of the sun, and so I rose and dressed myself in the most kingly garments I own. I could barely sit still for the stylist to apply the kohl to my eyes, which greatly exasperated Dr. Fouad, and yet, when it was all done, even he was pleased with my appearance, I think. Truly, I looked like a pharaoh, and I felt like one as well!

I could tell by the noise that, outside, crowds had begun to gather, and when all was ready, I exited through the lower hall of the palace & there, in the courtyard, was a chariot, all of gold & lapis. Painted, of course, not real inlay, but a golden chariot nonetheless & pulled by a pair of fine white Arabians. And at the reins was poor Atef, dressed in his ancient soldier costume & looking none too pleased to be driving about the city in such a get-up. I covered my mouth so that he would not see me laugh.

Out into the streets we drove, into the crowds, and on each corner, people, four or five deep, waving fronds & cheering as I passed. Tourists, yes, to be sure, in their odd holiday clothes, with their cameras, snapping pictures & sweating, unused to the Cairian heat. But, also, I saw my own people, Egyptians, and they, too, were cheering!

The trip lasted so short a time, only a few minutes

THE SUN GOD AT DAWN

it seemed to me. I know it must have been longer, two miles we traveled, or so I am told, but when we reached the Museum again, I could hardly remember what had happened, or all I saw & did.

I truly do not have the words to describe how the crowd made me feel, how much I enjoyed the adulation, the singing, the throwing of flowers, and I can only imagine what the pharaohs of old, pulled in chariots of real gold through the dusty streets of Amarna & Thebes & Memphis, felt. Truly as gods, I suspect.

Sincerely,
Ghazi

19 -го февраль 2170

Дорогой Г-н Lincoln,

С рождеством и новым годом Вас, сэр. Приношу свои извенения за запоздавшие поздравления. В последнее время я был довольно занят. Как вы уже заметили, я учу русский язык! Я нахожу, что он мне нравится столько же, сколько и английский. Изумительный язык – настолько резкий и гортанный – очень подходит для бранной речи. Alas, Dr. Sweeney will not teach me *those* kinds of words.

And so the reason I am learning Russian now is because the president of the Federation himself is coming to Cairo for an official visit, and I am to play Museum host & tour guide! And there will be a press conference (my first!) with members of the media from all around the world. I believe I will have a chance to test all my languages. I am so very excited!

I must return to my studies. Dr. Sweeney is drilling

me on idioms this evening. I will write you immediately after the visit to give you a full accounting of all that has gone on.

Your friend,
Ghazi

9 April 2170

Dear Mr. Lincoln,

Have you heard the news? By the time you read this, you will have. I am not quite sure what has happened, and I greatly need your counsel.

The Russian president arrived with his family, and I greeted them with all official rites & courtesies. I showed them some of the pharaoh's rituals, and I gave them a tour of the Museum & the palace. It went very well.

And then the press conference, and it was all so exciting: the large room with the tables, the sea of reporters stretched out before us, interested in us, in me.

Dr. Fouad was not happy; I could see that from the outset. I do not think he wanted the press conference, didn't want me around all those modern things, but I believe President Hamouri arranged it, and so he could not argue.

In any case, the questions began: about the Russians' trip, about the tour, how we all got along & etc. And everyone listened to what I had to say, and they wrote it down. What a heady feeling that was!

And then a reporter stood & asked me a question & I remember exactly his words. He said, 'How do you feel, Your Majesty, about the threats to your life?' And before I could speak, before I could even contemplate what he had said, Dr. Fouad, just like that, ended the press conference & motioned the guards to take me out. The room became a cacophony of shouted questions & yelling & such. It was utter chaos. I did not even get a chance to say a proper goodbye to the Russians. I am sure they were offended.

And now I am here alone with no one to talk to. Dr. Fouad has not come to see me & explain what has happened or what that man meant. Hanifa has not come, either, most likely prevented in some way, and that in itself is disturbing. And Atef & Kamal stay outside the doors & let no one in. They have been ordered not to talk to me either, though I hope, still, to be able to persuade Atef to post this letter.

I do not understand, sir, and I appeal to you to tell me what has gone on, what the significance of that man's question is. Why would anyone want to threaten my life?

Sincerely,
Ghazi

4 May 2170

Dear Mr. Lincoln,

Thank you so much for your upfront & forthright reply. You cannot imagine, after the events of the past few weeks, how refreshing it is to have someone be truly honest & open with me.

I understand now so much more than I did, and, yes, I agree, it is much better to see truth in the clear light of day than to linger in the shadows of ignorance. However, with this newfound understanding has come an attendant sorrow.

I had no idea, sir, none at all, that there were factions

opposed to our existence, nor that they were willing to go to such violent lengths to achieve their ends. No doubt Dr. Fouad intended to keep me ignorant of such malice, and I do not fault him for it, not really. He is trying to protect me, I suppose, though his methods are not all that I could wish.

The day after 'the incident,' as Hanifa has come to call it, I awoke to find all my morning duties cancelled, and I sat upon the divan in my bedchamber, not sure what I should be doing. I am unused to idleness, and I do not like it in the least.

When Dr. Fouad finally arrived—well past midmorning—I was overjoyed, not only because I assumed he would bring me an explanation for the goings-on of the previous evening, but because I wanted so desperately to have someone to talk to.

I quickly found myself quite mistaken on both counts.

Without preamble, Dr. Fouad announced that I was to listen only & then proceeded to inform me that the reporter was mistaken. My life, he assured me, was in no danger; no one was threatening me. He asked if I understood, and, not knowing if the injunction to stay silent was still in effect, I merely nodded my head. He returned the nod, told me I would be resuming my duties the following day & left. And that was that.

I knew straightaway that I did not believe him.

It is a shocking thing to realize, suddenly, that you do not trust a man you have known your whole life, a man as close to you as a father.

I longed to speak with Hanifa.

She came, finally, late that night, and I have never been so delighted to see anyone. It was as I had suspected: she had not come before because her way into the Museum was blocked by police.

Yet after I had related to her my fears that her father had lied, she expressed no surprise. In fact, she readily agreed that it was so, told me that she knew for a certainty that he was lying because she had seen the threatening letters herself!

I was, you may say, astounded. Not only had Dr. Fouad lied to me, but Hanifa was his co-conspirator!

A charge she denied, and, yes, perhaps it was a bit unfair, but still, I wish someone had consulted me, had informed me of these facts which bear so heavily upon my very life!

To her credit, Hanifa apologized profusely. It was, she said, only out of a desire not to upset me & because the information came to her by a rather underhanded method—she had snuck into her father's office where none of us are allowed unsupervised & there found the letters amongst the papers on his desk.

And so I have told her I forgive her, and I have. I love Hanifa & would not quarrel with her.

Yet after all of this, I still do not understand why anyone would be so opposed to us. You say poverty, Hanifa blames ignorance, and I suspect you are both correct, but who knows where the whole truth lies?

However, I have conceived a hope, sir, that perhaps we can convince these people that we are not, after all, abominations. That we are, in fact, as human as any other men. Perhaps I am being naïve, but do you, sir, believe this is possible?

Sincerely,
Ghazi

10 August 2170

Dear Mr. Lincoln,

I have a confidence I wish you to keep, and I hope you will not tell a soul nor chastise me for concealing such a thing from the authorities. The secret is not mine, you see, or perhaps I should say it is not wholly mine.

The evening of this Wednesday past, Hanifa came to my rooms through her usual methods, and, of course, I was delighted to see her. However, this night she was not alone. She brought a man with her, a friend, she said, from university. I was, of course, surprised because she had never spoken of any such friends, and I had assumed that Hanifa always kept me abreast of all things concerning her life outside.

He gave me the Arabic greeting & introduced himself as Khaled. He was tall & dark with the full beard of a Muslim, a very imposing man. Hanifa seemed nervous, the first I had ever seen her so, and she talked quickly of how this friend could help me to understand the reasons why my existence was opposed by so many.

I was, to say the least, skeptical. I did not see how a stranger, friend to my friend or no, could do this, when those that I loved & trusted could not seem to make it make sense for me. Yet I held my tongue; I love Hanifa & would not disappoint her, & so, for her sake, I invited this man to talk.

And he spoke to me of religion & of politics, of centuries of conflict, of war & oppression & of rich men & of poor men & of all the many strata in between.

I must admit that he was exceedingly articulate, and,

after a time, I understood why Hanifa gazed at him with such fire in her eyes. Yet, what I understood also, what became so very clear to me, was that it truly is all so very foolish, all these things that make one man hate another.

I know you feel this way as well, sir. Perhaps that is because, indeed, we *are* somewhat different from others in that we trace our origins back to science, not an almighty or an act of procreation. And perhaps now, by gene & precept, we are above such petty hand flapping that makes other men so very unreasonable. I do not know. All I know is that I wish to do something about it. I do not know what, but I pledge to you, sir, that when I am grown, I will do my best to erase such intolerance & blind hatred. An ambitious goal, and one I whisper only to you, for I know that you will never mock my aspirations.

Sincerely,
Ghazi

16 November 2170

Dear Mr. Lincoln,

I met a prince of England today, a boy named Edward. He is my age or thereabouts.

Initially, I was quite excited by the prospect. It had been arranged that I would give him & his family a tour of the Museum, talk about my heritage & the history of my country, etc. . . . not much different than any other special visitors, though it was special to me because it was a boy my age, a peer. Things, however, did not go exactly as I had anticipated.

63

The prince did not talk much, and I attributed this to a natural shyness on his part. Though I do not suffer from this condition (I expect I am genetically predisposed towards extroversion???), I sympathized with Edward, and so I chatted a great deal to compensate for his silences. Everyone seemed greatly pleased. But then after the photographers had all gone away & Dr. Fouad & the president had taken the king & queen into a reception room for tea, I was alone with the young prince.

I understand you have met him as well, and I am compelled to ask you, sir, how you found the boy, because, though I am loath to admit it, upon closer acquaintance, I must say I did not like him at all.

To begin, I soon discovered that he was not in the least shy. In fact, in private, the boy was outright rude. He mocked the shape of my head. He criticized my clothes & my crown, told me he had a much finer one at home, said that he would be a legitimate king someday, not some pathetic museum piece.

And then he asked me a question for which I still do not have an answer. He asked me what I was famous for. What is one expected to reply to that? He said in his museum at home, they had Lord Nelson, and he was famous for winning a great battle. And he'd met Bonaparte who was famous for being defeated at that great battle. But what was I famous for? What great battle did I win? What did I do to deserve a second future?

And though I have pondered this question the entire day, I must admit that I have yet to find a satisfactory answer. What *did* I do? What right do *I* have to be reborn when there are so many more deserving pharaohs resting within this very building? Rameses the Great who defeated the Hittites; Tutmosis III, the Napoleon of Ancient Egypt; bold Hatshepsut who dared to attach the beard to her likeness. Why not these? Why me?

When I told Hanifa, she scowled & said that all English are like this: arrogant & full of their own importance. But I have never found this to be so with any of the other Englishmen I've encountered during my duties, nor has Dr. Sweeney ever seemed so to me. In fact, when I told him of this incident, he became quite angry. He called the boy an ill-mannered lout & apologized for his countryman, and I thought that quite well done.

And so, in the end, I find myself utterly dejected and confused. Tell me, sir, since you have a benefit of years that I do not, was this boy right? Am I out of my league? Am I treading in footsteps I have no right to follow?

> Sincerely,
> Ghazi

3 January 2171

Dear Mr. Lincoln,

Thank you so much for your letter. I am quite gratified—relieved, even—to learn your impression of the boy meets my own, and I appreciate your kind words of support.

Yes, I have posed my questions to Dr. Fouad (without relating the particulars of the incident, of course). According to the doctor, I am an icon; I am the embodiment of my country's history; I am what people think of when they think of Egypt, which is why I am here & the others are not. So, though I won no great battles & made no great strides, this, at least, is something Dr. Fouad says that I can point to with pride: that my legacy survived where so many others did not. And yes, when I think on it, I am proud of that.

As for the other matter, yes indeed, you do speak quite a lot of good sense. And I agree that it is wrong to condemn a whole people on the actions of just one representative. Not all men are the same, and you are right that I should judge them on their individual actions, not on other people's intolerances.

I do not know why Hanifa suddenly dislikes the English so. She has never displayed such a prejudice before, and she has always treated Dr. Sweeney with seeming great affection. It is a puzzlement, indeed.

And no, sir, you need not worry that I dwell on this incident overmuch. A mere evening of melancholy prompted me to write the dolorous letter you received previously. I assure you that I am quite my old self once again.

> With many thanks &
> great affection,
> Ghazi

21 March 2171

Dear Mr. Lincoln,

Khaled & Hanifa came to my chambers last night, as they have been doing often these past few weeks. They bring me news of the city, and we discuss politics & religion & such. It is all quite stimulating. I have always loved learning, but no one has ever challenged me as much as Khaled does.

Last night's discussion concerned humanity & its nature. Khaled tried to convince me that a true human—a true *man*—is willing to give his life for a cause; that martyrdom is the ultimate test of humanity & of manhood. I disagreed & argued that a test of true humanity is not one's ability to take life, but to save & to nurture it. He countered that, in the end, the acts of a martyr do indeed save lives, and that the martyr braves death for the greater glory of his brothers, thus transcending humanity. A specious argument, I believe, yet even so, I do not think that I prevailed; Khaled is quite the talented debater.

But then after we were done & had agreed to disagree, he said something quite extraordinary. Khaled said that he was surprised by how truly human I was. He did not think I would be so, and when Hanifa proposed a meeting, initially, he had been opposed.

I do not quite know what to make of this confession. Should I be flattered? Insulted? I am unsure. Perhaps I shall resolve to think neither one nor the other, the better to preserve the peace.

Ghazi

26 June 2171

Dear Mr. Lincoln,

At long last, another procession through the city.

I will admit that I was quite nervous for this outing, as it was the first since I learnt that there were factions who would see me dead. And indeed, the crowd did not seem as welcoming, the sun not as warm, the garlands not as bright. A function of my nerves? I suspect so.

From the moment I stepped foot inside the chariot, a knot formed in my belly the likes of which I have never felt before, and it did not desist, even after we began riding about the streets. Oh, there were as many people as always, cheering & waving fronds, and Atef & Kamal & all the other guards were their usual alert selves. But still I could not help it: I looked at every man, woman & child askance.

The tourists, of course, all wore their sunglasses so I could not see their eyes, and this bothered me. Then, even the faces of some of my own people took on a sinister cast, and I had quite determined to ask Atef to turn the chariot about & return to the safety of the palace when out from the crowd pressed Khaled, grinning at me & waving a frond above his head. I smiled. And then I laughed. And Khaled laughed, too. I did not ask to go back.

A strange story to relate, and I am still unsure of its meaning. But this I know: today I have faced down a demon, and I have triumphed. Are you not proud of me?
Ghazi

17 September 2171

Dear Mr. Lincoln,

I write to you of a dream I had last night, of which I have told no one, not Dr. Fouad nor Dr. Sweeney nor Khaled & most definitely not Hanifa, though she is my closest friend & confidant.

In my dream, I lay upon the couch here in my bedchamber, a breeze blowing the linen hangings back into the room like white wings. The sun sprawled lazily on the western horizon, its orange light sparkling across the Nile below my terrace. I wore only a *shendyt,* the cool air from the river a million gentle fingers across my bare skin, the breath of crushed lotus an opiate to my senses. And, still, I felt alive, more alive & awake than I have ever felt before.

Then Hanifa came, though it did not resemble her in the least. This person was more womanly than any I have ever known, more beautiful than I have ever seen, but I knew, the way one knows in a dream, that it was she, Hanifa.

And this woman who was & was not Hanifa, she smiled, and she walked to me, and I rose to meet her. She said no words, yet brushed her lips against mine. I grew restless & hot, though the cool breeze from the Nile still fluttered the curtains. I pressed myself to her, felt sensations I have no words for. I placed my arms about her, held her to me. Drums thumped upon the Nile, the sound carried up & outward by the water, beating in time with my heart. I pressed my face to her neck & the smell of the lotus flower enveloped me & I realized that she was the source of it; she was the crushed flower giving forth its scent.

I became dizzy, and the room spun. It became hard to breath. My body felt rigid & liquid all at once, and soon I could stand it no longer, and then, like a shot, I sat up.

I was alone, awake in my own bed, the linen sheets clinging to my damp skin, my breath ragged in my throat.

I do not know what to make of such a dream, sir. I

have never had one so strange before, and I must admit that I felt somewhat ashamed when I saw Hanifa the next day. It is all very odd. What do you make of it? Have you ever had such a dream?

Sincerely,
Ghazi

22 October 2171

Dear Mr. Lincoln,

Thank you for your insight. I feel somewhat foolish, now, for not having guessed as much myself, and for bothering you with such frivolousness. Well, I suppose it only goes towards illustrating exactly how human we are. If only I had the courage, I would send the evidence to those who would call us abominations.

Regards,
Ghazi

28 February 2172

Dear Mr. Lincoln,

I have seen my corpse today.

I tell you, sir, that you are lucky that yours is out of reach, for I have discovered it is indeed a fearsome thing to bear witness to one's dead self. How did this come about? I will tell you.

Last night Khaled and Hanifa visited, and we talked of history, Egyptian history, a subject about which I did not imagine there was anything else I could learn, and yet, Khaled surprised me.

Did you know, Mr. Lincoln, of the servitude my people suffered under foreign rule? Of how we were made second-class citizens in our own lands, in our own culture? How much of my country's wealth was taken by the English and other looters? How much of my ancient history has been pillaged to grace the museums of London or Paris or New York? Khaled showed me on his computer the extensive 'collections' in these so-called bastions of culture. Collections, indeed! Stashes, they should be called, their museums merely elegant buildings made to house their plunder, their archaeologists nothing more than crooks and swindlers and tomb robbers. At least the men who stripped the pyramids in antiquity were honest thieves. They did not lay grand claims to preservation; they did not call themselves saviors of culture.

And I looked and I looked and when I could take it no longer, we spoke of my own tomb. I have known for quite some time the story of its discovery: the hints of a long-lost boy king, Carter's years of fruitless digging, Lord Carnarvon nearly at the end of his patience. How could I not know it? But, oh, there was so much more. So much I was not told. So much deliberately kept from me.

My body is housed in the Museum now, did you know this? All the mummies were moved from the Valley years ago due to the depredations of 'archeologists' whose methods brought about the extensive water damage that has made the final resting place of so much royalty completely unviable.

And so they rest now, those kings, not in their silent, stone tombs, but in sliding glass trays, packed in cotton, under special lights, pulled out from time to time and poked like dead animals upon the road. Down into these rooms we went, to the lonely, dark place where little-known kings and mummies too delicate to display sleep. To the room that also holds me. And there—there I was.

Tutankhamun.

He is smaller than I am. The mummification process, I know, but I was unprepared for how fragile, how desiccated he would be. I was also unprepared for his condition. This they never told me: that to remove the precious objects from the body, which were stuck fast by the hardened embalming resins, Carter cut the mummy to pieces. The arms and legs were detached, the torso cut in half. The head was severed; hot knives were used to remove it from the golden mask to which it was cemented by resin.

Me. My head. My body. Carved up like a holiday feast.

I have never been so angry, and, truly, I do not know how I will go on with my duties when everything I have been told is a lie, when everything I have ever believed is suspect. And how may I look Dr. Sweeney in the eye, now, when all I see is the avatar of so much misery and destruction?

Indeed, I begin to suspect that Khaled has been in the right all along, that his path is the true one.

No doubt you will chastise me for this polemic, try to reason with me, enjoin me to make some kind of peace. But I cannot listen. No. No, I cannot do it. Much though I regret the sentiment, your brand of prudence, sir, would not be welcome at this moment.

3 March 2172

Dear Mr. Lincoln,

As you wrote, sir: *Beware of rashness. Beware of rashness, but with energy and sleepless vigilance, go forward.*

Perhaps I should have reviewed this admonition before I penned my earlier missive.

Sir, allow me to apologize unreservedly for the ungracious words and splenetic tone expressed in my letter dated 28 February. I cannot begin to articulate my chagrin when, in a calmer frame of mind, I recalled what I had written. I hope I have not given any lasting offense; I pray you will chalk it up to the hot blood of youth, and not to any kind of true or permanent enmity.

I assure you, Mr. Lincoln, that I am dedicated to, as you so succinctly and elegantly voiced, *do all which may achieve and cherish a just and lasting peace, among ourselves, and with all nations.*

Again, my humblest apologies.

With eternal respect and affection,
Ghazi

11 April 2172

Dear Mr. Lincoln,

I cannot begin to thank you, sir, for your charity. Yes, it is said that forgiveness is a divine trait, but not many men who had been so sorely abused would deign to forgive so readily and so generously.

I do not know what I have done to deserve such unmitigated understanding and friendship.

Again, thank you.

With respects,
Ghazi

21 August 2172

Dear Mr. Lincoln,

I believe I said that I would not trouble you with the frivolities of my dreams again, but this one bears discussion.

In this dream, just as before, I lay upon the couch in my bedchamber whilst the wind blew back the curtains. It was evening, and the Nile was alive with silver light. Again I inhaled the scent of the crushed lotus. I turned to view the door & there, once more, was Hanifa.

The restlessness grew upon me even before she had crossed the room into my arms. The sweetness in the air was overwhelming. Her lips were as soft as petals, her arms about me like iron bands. Drums beat upon the water again, stirring me, urging me on.

Then, like a crack of lightning to my skull, a blow from behind. I fell & lay bleeding upon the cold, stone floor, yet still Hanifa smiled whilst my life's blood pooled about my head.

It is foolish to be frightened by dreams; it is childish to wake crying. And yet I did, and now, hours later, I still cannot shake the feeling of melancholy which has descended upon me. Do you know what such a vision means? Do you suffer much from your dreams, sir?

Ghazi

7 October 2172

Dear Mr. Lincoln,

Thank you, sir, for your concern. No, I did not tell Dr. Fouad. I never spoke of the other dream, nor do I wish to, and it seems foolish to speak of one without mentioning the other.

However, I believe, now, that it was all a great deal of nothing, and I am, I assure you, quite recovered from its frightful effects. It was only a dream after all, only a stray thought woven inside a nonsensical story. I shall bother you no more with it.

Sincerely,
Ghazi

31 March 2173

Dear Mr. Lincoln,

I am so chock full of secrets that one day I imagine I will simply burst apart, and all the confidences I keep will come spilling out from me like silvery fish upon a wooden dock.

Dr. Fouad called me to his office last evening. Dr. Fouad rarely receives me in his office. In fact, he rarely receives anyone there at all, preferring to preserve his privacy, or as Hanifa calls it, his secrecy. It is an imposing room, small yet full of papers & cabinets & books of all sorts & types & levels of disrepair. Something was amiss, I knew, and not only because of the unusual summons.

Though Dr. Fouad's mien is always serious, the one he wore last night was especially so. Troubled is how I would describe it, though I do not believe that I have ever really seen him so in the past. Angry, yes. Irritated. Imperious. But never troubled. He paced for several minutes behind his desk strewn with papers & files, up & down, up & down, looking for all the world as if he were trying to form his question. And when he did form it, he asked it, point blank & without patina: to my knowledge, were there or had there ever been any others in the palace or the Museum at night?

I do not know what expression I wore at first. Shock, perhaps? Surprise? I do not know. I think my mouth opened once or twice but nothing came of it. Finally, I cleared my throat. No, I said. Just that. No.

Dr. Fouad appeared to believe it, for he nodded only once & released me to my leisure.

I have lied to him, Mr. Lincoln. I have never outright lied to my mentor before. Yes, this letter is, in effect, a lie. This I know. But a lie of omission, not commission. I know, I know you shall say that I should not have done. I know you shall say I must tell all, make a clean breast of it, wash my hands of the whole affair.

And yet . . . and yet.

The secret of Khaled is also Hanifa's, and how shall I face her again should I betray that trust? It is a conundrum I cannot untangle, and I am left quite at odds.

Ghazi

5 April 2173

Dear Mr. Lincoln,

I wonder if perhaps you aren't right, sir, that I should not be keeping this secret from Dr. Fouad.

Hanifa & Khaled came to my bedchamber last night, and I told them of Dr. Fouad's suspicions, and to my great astonishment, Khaled insisted that Hanifa leave with him & not come back.

She said no, of course, whispered that she still had facts

to root out for him, argued that her position was crucial to the cause, whatever that may mean. And though Khaled disputed her many points, still she remained steadfast in her resolve to abide.

But it was, to my discerning eye, a reluctant no. And the way she looked at him—I had assumed before that it was merely admiration for his erudition, for his oratory style that made her eyes so bright when he speaks. But now . . . now I have a suspicion that that is indeed not the case.

I tell you, I cannot like it. I cannot like how readily he believed she would leave her family at his word. I cannot like his over-familiarity.

Should I tell Dr. Fouad, then, that he has been here? I suspect Hanifa would never forgive me. I could do it under a cloak of anonymity, I suppose, but to be so underhanded . . . no. Best to do it honestly or not at all. I am thinking only of Hanifa's safety, am I not?

Ghazi

17 March 2174

Dear Mr. Lincoln,

My apologies for being so long absent. I am sure you know what has happened, of the 'cowardly attack' as the media here has named it.

I am perfectly fine. I was not injured in any way. And I am sorry that so many of your urgent letters went unanswered and for the worry that caused you. I only wished to be undisturbed for a time. I cannot truly explain it, but I hope you can understand, nonetheless.

We were on another chariot procession through the

city in a place where the streets grow quite narrow. They were jammed that day with people three or four deep. We had just reached the Midan Hussein, a more open plaza where the sun could shine down on us and the air could circulate. I looked about me, at the startling blue sky, the silver domes of the Mohamed Ali Mosque shimmering in the distance, at the sea of faces, waving fronds and cheering, and the tourists, so conspicuous in their dress and their paraphernalia. And I smiled, as I do, because indeed I love these trips.

And there on the edge of the crowd, where I have seen Khaled stand and smile and wave like the rest, I saw another man, a man darker of aspect, who was not smiling, who was not waving a frond or cheering. I caught his gaze and a cold frisson gripped me, the kind of cold that is not felt here in the desert. The man pressed forward into the sea of people, and he clenched his fist, and as he did, the crowd surged, and I lost the sight of him.

Then there came a loud concussion. I was thrown back, down to the ground, and I lay there for several heartbeats staring at the blue, blue sky above. My ears did not seem to work right, as if I were floating just beneath the surface of water. So I shook my head, and after a moment, I could hear again, though I soon wished that I could not.

The screaming of the horses was a horrific sound. Then I saw them, rolling on their sides, broken and bleeding and tangled in the traces. People were screaming as well, and I saw them running with blood upon their hands. I saw tourists lying in the street, missing limbs and faces and gods know what else. I saw blood fill the cracks in the pavement like rainwater. And then my guards carried me from the carnage, and I saw nothing more.

And that is that; I will speak no more of it.

A month passed before Hanifa brought Khaled to me. I did not want to see him. Hanifa pleaded, but no, I would not do it, I would not face him. I turned to look at the wall. So he sat upon the edge of the room, talking into the air.

A mistake, he said. Not meant for me, he said.

I did not care. I wanted only to be alone. He spoke, then, of the civil war that left Egypt a wounded battleground, of the dictator that replaced a dictator that replaced a dictator and called it democracy. He spoke of the struggle of the poor against the powers of money and corruption. He spoke of victims and of symbols. He spoke of me, of my life and my existence. I am a victim, he said, and a symbol, as well, of money and of power and of the oppression of the true people of Egypt. And then, in his best sideways fashion, he said I had the power to change all of it.

As if this would convince me to be part of his cause! As if I wanted his sort of glory! As if I could do such evil as this!

I could listen no more and put my hands over my ears, and so he left, and I have not seen him since, though Hanifa asks and asks.

Dark dreams have come again. I do not want anyone to see me cry.

Ghazi

12 June 2174

Dear Mr. Lincoln,

I appreciate your concern & your offer of help. Thank you for listening. It lightens my burden to speak of these things.

Two nights past, I dreamt I stood upon the west bank of the river, the soil beneath my feet black from the flooding, and in the distance women sang a lament in the old tongue, though I could not pick out the words.

And then I hunted wild bull in the waving grasslands beyond the delta. The animal came at me, snorting, the ground trembling beneath its heavy tread, and though I tried, I could not heft my spear. My arm was leaden, stuck to my side. The animal came nearer, and I strained against my invisible bonds, but to no avail, and it gored me where I stood. I lay upon the ground bleeding from the wound, crying for help, but none came. None came. And the women only sang and sang.

And I woke thus, crying like a child. I have told no one of these dreams, Mr. Lincoln. No one but yourself, knowing that you will keep my secrets. Knowing that you are my loyal friend.

Sincerely,
Ghazi

9 October 2174

Dear Mr. Lincoln,

Sir, I assure you there is no need for you to be so troubled as all that. In fact, I believe that you are more unsettled on my account than I am. Knowing your caring disposition, I realize now that I should never have burdened you with my nonsense. And, of course, it *is* just that: nonsense.

You worry for me overmuch. Do not, I beg of you. All is well enough.

> With affection,
> Ghazi

26 February 2175

Dear Mr. Lincoln,

Perhaps Khaled was right. Perhaps I am indeed become a symbol.

We traveled to Abu Simbel today. The Nile was placid, our voyage down smooth. My guards no longer wear their costumes. Instead they wear uniforms & armour & guns, glittering & black in the desert sun. There is no need for this trip other than to prove they can do it, that I am not a prisoner of fear. They have cameras staged along the banks of the river to capture our journey, to make sure the world knows it is safe for tourists here. And I must smile & wave, a trained dog before its audience.

But despite their efforts, the crowds are gone now, and with them the cheers, the adulation, the palm fronds waved for the visiting deity. No one is allowed near me any longer except those I already know: Dr. Fouad, Dr. Sweeney, Hanifa. But in Hanifa, there is no comfort, there is only the question in her eyes, and I cannot answer.

I felt small at the feet of the colossi. So massive, those stone giants, proclaiming the greatness of Rameses loud enough so even the gods could hear. There are no such statues for me. I was the king lost so thoroughly even the thieves could not find me. Such a noble story!

No, Rameses was a real pharaoh, a man who deserved to be made again, though instinct tells me that he would not have stood for remaining this impotent puppet they have made of me. Perhaps that is why I was chosen; perhaps they thought I would be satisfied with less. Or perhaps they designed me to be placid and accepting, designed us all to be so. Who is ever to know? All I do know for certain is this: that Rameses was the man to be resurrected, not Tut, the accident of history.

When we returned to the Museum, Hanifa insisted on speaking to me of Khaled, said she wished for me to see him, to speak with him again. I refused, and I said to her things I should not have, things I will not repeat. And then I told her that I hoped she would leave with him, because I wanted never to see her again. She fled my room with tears in her eyes, and I immediately regretted my words & wished I could retract them. But I could not.

I wax melancholic. It is time for sleep. Perhaps tomorrow will bring brighter & better things.

Ghazi

19 July 2175

Dear Mr. Lincoln,

I ventured down to the Royal Mummy Room last night and stood amongst my ancient ancestors, my brother kings. There was Rameses. There Tutmoses. Akhenaten. Amenhotep. All with their pictures displaying how they

YULIYA KOSTYUK

appeared in life. I was reminded of that prince—so long ago it seems now—the one who asked me what I was famous for. I did not know how to answer him then. I still do not.

I left there quickly. I have enough to make me sad without inviting it myself.

Have you finally tired of your little friend, Mr. Lincoln? I have received no letters from you in some time. I miss them, truly.

Ghazi

12 December 2175

Dear Mr. Lincoln,

Has something happened? It has been months since your last letter. Have I offended you? Do you wish me to stop writing? I hope that is not the case. Please, sir, send a note so that I know that we are still friends. I value your company & your counsel, distant though they are. I did not know how much until I was deprived of them.

With respect
& admiration,
Ghazi

31 January 2176

Dear Mr. Lincoln,

I do not know if you will get this letter or if you've received any of the letters I've sent in the past few months. I write now in the slim hope that I may have the opportunity to post this at some future time.

Hanifa is gone, and I feel as if the world has come to an end.

Dr. Fouad summoned me to his office, early, just after I had risen. Hanifa had decamped, he told me. She had chosen a man over her family. She had chosen shame, and I was not to mention her name again. Ever. Then I was dismissed & that was that.

When I returned to my rooms, I found that all my guards had been replaced with men I did not know. I have been taken off display & confined to my bedchamber for I do not know how long.

She is gone. They are all gone. And now I am alone.

How could Hanifa abandon me? How could she leave without even saying goodbye? How could she choose Khaled when I need her so? I did not mean it when I said I wished her gone. Not truly. I do not know now if I will ever see her again, and it is a thought I can hardly bear.

Ghazi

27 March 2176

Dear Mr. Lincoln,

I understand now, sir, why I have not heard from you. You, I would guess, do not have a similar knowledge. Allow me to shed light upon the situation.

Last night I was awakened from a restless sleep by Hanifa, and I was so happy to see her, I simply held her for a full five minutes. She had repented, I'd hoped, come back for good. But no, she said, only to see me and even that could be but a brief visit.

They had intercepted our correspondence, she said, and that is how Dr. Fouad learned of Khaled, how she'd come to be shunned. My fault, though Hanifa says no, because when her father came to confront her with the evidence, he discovered her reading his personal files, the ones he locks away and lets no one else see, and that alone would have meant her exile. So she does not blame me. They did not know everything, obviously, or else she would not have been able to get in through her back door, but they knew enough, which is why I am no longer receiving your letters.

And then she began to speak in strange and ominous hints, of things she says she cannot tell me, things she says I must discover for myself.

In her father's office, there is a cabinet, locked, and inside this cabinet are files—files containing information about me. She gave me the combination. She did not tell me to go there. She did not say 'must' or 'have to.' She said only this: that it was there, and that I had the choice. And with tears in her eyes, she kissed me, and she left. I do not know if I shall ever see her again.

Will I go down to the office & open the cabinet? I do not know. I have kept the paper with the key code close to my heart. I have meditated over it late into the night, after everyone has gone & the doors are locked & only the nameless guards are left to wind their way through the dark & empty corridors of the Museum.

I have prayed, to Ra & to Osiris & to Isis. I have prayed to Jehovah & to the Christian god & to the god of the Muslims for guidance. But none has given me an answer.

The decision is mine to make. I do not know what I shall do. I long for your sage advice.

Ghazi

14 April 2176

My Dear Mr. Lincoln,

This letter is my farewell and the last you shall be hearing from me. And of the things of this world I will miss, this grieves me most of all, for I find that I have come to rely greatly upon your kindness and your boundless generosity. Your wisdom has been a great boon to me, though perhaps I did not listen so well as I should. Yet above all these, I have been most proud, sir, simply to call you my friend.

Mr. Lincoln . . .

Abraham.

Though you have called me Ghazi for years, only now, at the end, do I feel able to lay claim to the honor of referring to you in so familiar a fashion. It was never any lack of affection that fettered me, of course, only that I never felt equal to you, sir, and tended to look upon you more as a child might look upon a father rather than a man upon a peer. I hope you take the sentiment with the love, affection and honor in which it was meant. And I hope that you, in your wisdom, do not judge me so harshly as perhaps I now deserve.

You cannot understand, my dear, dear friend, what it means to be a working-class king. You do not come from such a country. Your society has never known monarchs, and your gods have never walked amongst you. And you personally, Abraham, have already lived a life so full of accomplishment as to never need to wonder if your deeds will be remembered. That proof is in your very existence. I have no such laurels, recent or ancient, to rest upon. I have no past, and my future, such as it is, is set as stone in the pattern of my genes.

For you see, I have ventured down into Dr. Fouad's office. I have unlocked the cabinet. I have seen all the contracts and read all the reports, and now I know the truth. Now I know what it is that I am.

An experiment. A 'limited test run.' An attempt to justify the cost. And if the tourist money came, if it proved to be enough, then . . . then the government itself would invest in a new creation. A new Tut. A real one. One that would last longer, stay young.

And as for me? What is to be my fate? It is this: that no matter the outcome, no matter the success or failure of the experiment, I, Ghazi, am designed to expire, just as my prime did, in my nineteenth year. For who indeed wants to see a boy king at fifty-five? Surely, that is not what the tourists pay good money for.

Oh, there will be no pain, of course. They are not monsters, no. No, for me there will be only a night like any other and a simple and gentle fading away, down into an endless sleep.

Two years, my friend. I have but two years left to live. Do you blame me that I choose to spend them no longer as a eunuch? I hope that you do not, and I hope that, in the passage of time and the soft light of remembrance, you forgive me for the course upon which I now, this night, shall embark.

For even as I write this, evening has come to Cairo. The sun hangs low upon the western horizon, casting its red arms across the sands to limn the pyramids, to plate the churning waters of the Nile, to tip in molten gold the thousand minarets of this ancient city until finally they slant, beggar-like, into my window and tug upon my soul. In the distance, the muezzin calls the faithful to prayer, and outside, somewhere, beyond the walls of the Museum, Khaled waits for me. I shall not disappoint him.

For now, this day, I am finally become a man.

And no longer do I dream of pain and death and ignoble endings. No longer do I cry like a child in the night.

Last night I dreamt one last time. And last night my dreams were of war.

And of golden chariots. Of dust in the desert and of the crying of the people. Of soldiers and of blood and of vast and magnificent battlefields.

And of a barque of gold.

And of Isis and Osiris, their arms lifted in prayer.

And then, finally, just before waking, I dreamt of Ra, his hand outstretched, leading the way across the heavens to my immortal glory.

The Frozen Sky

written by

Jeff Carlson

illustrated by

BOGDAN STETSENKO

ABOUT THE AUTHOR

Jeff Carlson was born on the day of the first manned moon landing and narrowly escaped being named Apollo, Armstrong or Rocket. His father worked for the NASA-Ames Research Center at the time, and his maternal grandfather was a science fiction fan whose library included autographed copies of Isaac Asimov's Foundation trilogy. Guess what they talked about?

Since becoming a quarterly winner for this year's Writers of the Future Contest, Jeff has taken his own "giant leap" into the science fiction scene. His first novel, a thriller entitled Plague Year, *was published by Ace in August 2007, with the sequel* War Day *set to follow in 2008. A self-described house dad/writer guy, Jeff is making room for his next solo novel, collaborating with David Brin on another novel, skiing and backpacking while raising two sons with his wife, Diana.*

ABOUT THE ILLUSTRATOR

Bogdan Stetsenko, another talented artist from Kiev, Ukraine, has proven that dedication to a goal can pay off. He has entered the contest seven times since 2002, has been a semifinalist twice, a finalist once and is now a contest winner.

The Frozen Sky

1.

Vonnie ran with her eyes shut, chasing the sound of her own boot steps. This channel in the rock was tight enough to reflect every noise back on itself and she dodged through the open space between, weeping, crashing one shoulder against a slant in the wall. She fell. She glanced back, forgetting the danger in this simple reflex.

The bloody wet glint in her retinas was only a distraction, a useless blur of heads-up data she couldn't read.

Worse, her helmet was still transmitting sporadically, the side-mount and some internals crushed beyond saving. She'd rigged an ELF pulse that obeyed on/off commands, but her sonar and the camera spot were dead to her, flickering at random. And the spotlight was like a torch in this cold.

Vonnie clapped her glove over the gear block on her helmet, trying to muffle the beam. Boot steps were one thing. This entire moon groaned with seismic activity, rattling, cracking—but heat was a giveaway. Heat scarred the ice and rock, and for her to look back was to increase the odds of leaving a trail. Stupid. Stupid.

Even now she didn't want to fight. They were beautiful in their way, the amphibians—quick little starfish rippling with muscle. Rippling with ideas. They'd outmaneuvered her twice and more than anything, what she felt was regret. She could have done better. She should have waited, instead of letting her ego make the decision.

In some ways Alexis Vonderach was still a girl at thirty-six, single, too smart, too good with machines and math. She was successful. She was confident. She fit the ESA psych profile to six decimal points.

Now all that was gone. She was down to nerves and guesswork and whatever momentum she could hold onto.

She lurched forward, groping with one hand along the soft volcanic rock. Her face struck a jagged outcropping in the wall and then her hip, too, safe inside her armor.

Vonnie didn't think they could track the alloys of her suit but they seemed able to smell her footprints, fresh impacts in the ice and lava dust, and there was no question that they were highly attuned to warmth. She'd killed nine at the ravine and covered her escape with an excavation charge, losing herself behind the storm . . . and they'd followed her easily.

Could she use that somehow? Lead them into a trap?

She was no soldier. She had never trained for violence or even imagined it, except maybe at a few faculty budget meetings. An odd flicker of memory. Vonnie held tightly to it, clean and bright. She would've given anything to have that life again, those tiny problems, her tidy desk.

She fell once more, off-balance with her hand against

her head. The suit protected her, though, and she scrabbled over what appeared to be a cave-in.

Maybe here. Burn the rock, leave a false trail, then drop the rest of the broken wall on them. They'd give up. Didn't they have to give up? Nine dead at the ravine, two more in the ice, could they really keep soaking up casualties like that?

Vonnie could only guess at the amphibians' psychology. Even blind, she knew there was light. Alone, she knew someone would find her. Yet she thought the history of this race was without hope. Unrelenting strength, yes, but the idea of hope requires a sense of *future*. The idea of somewhere to go.

They'd never imagined the stars, much less reached up to escape this black, fractured world.

This damned world.

No less than four Earth agencies had landed mecha here to strip its resources, then sent a joint team in the name of science, and Lam and Bauman were both dead before First Contact, crushed in a rock swell. Would it have made any difference?

The question was too big for her. That the amphibians existed at all was a shock. Humankind had long since found Mars and Venus forever barren, not just stillborn but never started, and after more than a century and a half the SETI radioscopes had yet to catch any hint of another thinking race within a hundred and fifty light-years. Some joke. All that time the amphibians were inside the solar system, a neighbor, a counterpart. It should have been the luckiest miracle. It should have been like coming home. But that had been Vonnie's worst mistake, to think of them as similar in any way. They were an intelligence that seemed to lack fear or even hesitation—and that might be exactly why her trap would work.

She decided to risk it. She was exhausted and hurt, and staying in one place would give her time to attempt repairs again, regain the advantage.

She found a small shelf in the crumbling rock face above the slide and settled in to kill more of them.

2.

Jupiter's sixth moon was an ocean, a deep, complete sphere too far from the sun to exist as a liquid. Not at temperatures of -162 Celsius. Human beings first walked the ice in 2094, and flybys and probes had buzzed this distant white orb since 1979. Europa was an interesting place. For one thing, there was a unique oxygen atmosphere created by the slow dissociation of molecules from the surface. It was water ice.

It was a natural fuel depot for fusion ships.

Before the end of the twenty-first century, the investment of fifty mecha and two dozen more in spare parts was well worth an endless supply of deuterium at the edge of human civilization. The diggers and the processing stations were fusion-powered themselves, as were the tankers parked in orbit.

Spacecraft came next, some crewed, some robots too—and eighteen years passed. It might have been longer. Much longer. The mecha were all on the equator, where it was easiest for the tankers to hold position above them without constantly burning fuel, fighting Jupiter's gravity and the tug of other moons.

Eighteen years. But the glacial tides within the ice gave Europa a great many "environments"—grinds, stacks, chasms, melts—and only the smooth, so-called plains were deemed safe by the men and women who guided the mecha by remote telepresence. Looking ahead, they sent rovers in all directions, surveying, sampling.

At the southern pole was a smooth area that covered nearly forty kilometers. Many rovers went there.

3.

Vonnie shivered, an intensely ugly sensation inside her suit. She'd locked the joints and torso, becoming a statue, preventing herself from causing any movement whatsoever, but inside it she was still skin and muscle.

The feel of her body against this shell was repulsive. Again and again she caught herself squirming and tensing, trying to shrink away from it, trying the impossible.

The rut in her thinking wasn't much better. She wished Choh Lam hadn't tried to . . . She wished somehow she'd saved them. Lam grasped so much so fast, he might have already found a way out, a way *up*. She'd cobbled together a ghostling using his mem files but she couldn't give it enough capacity to correct its flaws. She would have to shut down her ears or the override she'd programmed into her heat exchanger, each a different kind of death. Better to forget him. Erase him.

But even at three-quarters logic he was useful. He'd suggested a tranquilizer and Vonnie popped one tab, slowed down enough to feel clear again. Clear and cold.

She shouldn't be cold, sweating inside her hard shell, but the waiting was like its own labyrinth of ice—the waiting and the listening and the deep bruises in her face.

She didn't care how sophisticated the medical systems were supposed to be. On some level her body knew it was hurt, even numbed and shot full of don't-worry.

Her head had a dozen good reasons why she was safe but her body knew the amphibians would come again.

The lonely dark was alive. That truth no longer surprised her and she strained her senses out into the thin, cold spaces reaching away from her, more afraid of missing the amphibians than of drawing in an attack. It was superstitious to imagine they could hear her thoughts, she knew that, but at the ravine they'd run straight to her hiding place despite three decoys.

She had to learn if she was going to live.

This rock shelf seemed defensible when she stumbled over it, nowhere to retreat but only one approach to cover, and there was a spongework of holes overhead where she could dump her waste heat before leaving. Vonnie was on her belly now facing outward, trying to eat and trying to rest, trying to ignore the ugly, anesthetized pressure of the med beetles slithering in and out of her temple, her cheek, her eye socket.

Both eyes were damaged but she'd elected to deal with one at a time in case something went wrong, in case the nanotech needed to scavenge one to fix the other. Lam's idea. He'd also agreed that her helmet would retain integrity if she broke off the gear block completely and stripped it for parts. What else would he have tried?

The plastisteel of her suit should contain all sound

but there was another risk in talking, a risk she ignored just to be with someone even for a moment. Even a ghost.

"You still there?" she whispered.

—*Von, listen, don't close me down again, please.*

"Tell me what Lam would do. Am I safe here? I need to rest. I laid down a false trail like you said."

—*They'll catch us. But listen.*

"Did you check my map? I made it almost three klicks."

—*They will. Eighty-plus percent probability. But I can talk to them, we have enough data now. With temporary control of the suit I could at least establish . . .*

"No."

—*Vonnie, most of their language is shapes, postures, I can't tell you fast enough how to move.*

"No. Self-scan and correct."

—*Von, wait.*

"I said scan for glitches and correct. Off."

Could a ghost be crazy? Her fault. This one was her first and she'd rushed the process, and she had been angry with him. The real him. So she let him remember how he died and it made him erratic. Maybe he'd never doubted himself before.

Bauman would have been a better friend. Bauman was older, calmer, another woman, but she was a geneticist and Lam's biology/ecology skills were too valuable. The choice had been obvious. Vonnie just didn't have the resources to pull them apart, build an overlay with Bauman's personality and Lam's education.

She waited alone. She itched her fingertips inside her rigid glove and did not know it. Too soon she prompted her clock again and was disappointed. Five minutes until her skull was repaired, thirty before she regained her optic nerve . . .

Something was coming.

4.

Europa's great ocean encased a solid rock core, and volcanic activity contributed to the chaos in the ice. Below many of the "stack" and "melt" environments, in fact, subsurface peaks of lava had proved common, long bulges and spindles that could not have existed if this moon had more than a tenth of Earth's gravity. The tides distributed the rock everywhere, and it was a small problem for the mecha. It damaged blades and claws. It jammed in pipes. Even dust would make a site unattractive, and ESA Rover 011 was quick to give up on a wide area of the southern plain when it brought up contaminants in its drill cylinder.

Still, the rover was well engineered. Belatedly, it noticed the consistency of shape among the debris. Then its telemetry jumped as it linked with a tanker overhead, using the ship's larger brain to analyze the smattering of solids.

Finally the rover moved again, sacrificing two forearms and a spine flexor to embrace its prize, insulating the sample against the near-vacuum of the surface.

Impossible as this seemed, given the preposterous cold and the depth from which the sample came, the contaminants were organic life forms, long dead, long preserved: tiny albino bugs with no more nervous system than an earthworm.

5.

Vonnie opened her blind eyes to nothing and her ears were empty, too. But she was sure. Something was coming. Inside the hard shell of her suit, she moved but could not move, a surge of adrenaline that had no release.

Trembling, she waited. Brooding, she cursed herself. But she'd spent a lifetime making order of things and couldn't get her head quiet. She made everything familiar by worrying through it again and again.

The trap. She'd split her next-to-last excavation charge in two, placing one half in the ceiling just beyond her rock shelf, the other below and to her left. The blasts would shove forward and down, but there would be shrapnel. In this gravity there was always blowback, if only from ricochets. Good. The amphibians fought like a handful of rubber balls slammed down against the floor, spreading in an instant, always working to surround her.

Without her eyes that was even more of a problem. Her ELF pulse was far better at sounding out large shapes than at tracking movement, but it was all she had—so she'd smash everything within a hundred meters. Her armor could sustain indirect hits from the porous lava rock. She planned to bait them, bring them close, then roll into the crevice behind her and hit the explosives, clean up any survivors with her laser.

It was a cutting tool, unfortunately, weak at the distance of a meter. Worse, if she overheated the gun she would probably not be able to repair it. Her nanotech was limited to organic internals, and a good part of the toolkits on her chest and left hip had been torn away or lost—

"Stop thinking. Jesus, stop talking," she murmured, the words as quick as her heartbeat. *Just stop it.*

Could they really hear her mind? They definitely had an extra sense, maybe the ability to . . . feel weight, density, that would serve them well in the ice. So they would be able to separate her from the environment.

For once that was what she wanted. She reactivated the suit and rose into a crouch, strobing the fissure below with an ELF pulse. She thought her extra-low-frequency signals were outside the amphibians' range of hearing, but either way she'd committed herself just by standing.

Nothing. There was nothing.

"God—" She choked back the sound and swept the long, bent spaces of the chasm repeatedly now, quickly locating pockets in the ceiling that she could not scour, not from this high angle. It was like turning on a light in what she thought was a closet and finding instead that half the house was gone. And her enemy needed only the thinnest of openings.

Were they already too close? She'd seen it before, a dozen amphibians upside-down on the rock like fat, creeping muscles.

She held up her laser even as she groped with her other hand for a chunk of rock. There was gravel, too, and a good boulder, everything she'd been able to gather. Throw it now? Try to provoke them? Her thumb gritted in the jagged lava as she clenched down on it.

Vonnie was a decent shot with a ball—she grew up with three brothers—but the suit itself was a weapon. The suit had voice programs that made her something like a passenger inside a robot, auto-commands designed for activities like climbing or welding. Humans got tired. The suit did not. Even better, it still had use of the radar targeting that she could not see, and it would limit the velocity of its throws only to avoid damaging her shoulder and back.

She didn't trust it.

She'd had to use that low-level AI as a base imprint for her ghost, another mistake. The programming was rotten with Lam's mem files and twice now the ghost had caused interrupts, trying to clean and reconfigure itself, trying to find control, and yet Vonnie was afraid to purge it. She might lose the suit's amplified speed and strength at the same time.

"You still there?" she hissed.

—*Von, listen, don't close me down again, please.*

The same thing it always said. God. Oh God. No time to argue. "Combat menu," she told it.

—*Online.*

But she hesitated. Right now, the ghost was still somewhat contained. That would change as soon as she gave it access to defense modes, a bad gamble. The extra capacity might be exactly what the ghost needed to self-correct . . . or the stupid damned thing might corrupt the most basic functions of her suit. Was there any other way?

"I need auto-targeting only," she said, "fire by voice command."

—*Von, that drops efficiency to thirty percent.*

"Fire by voice command. Confirm."

—*Listen to me.*

Four slender arms reached out of the ceiling.

6.

It was easy to be friends with Choh Lam. He was freak smart but also patient, hiding himself in a quiet voice, both eager and shy at the same time. He probably didn't realize he had restless eyes because in every other way he moved just like he talked, gently. Vonnie's impression was of a man who'd spent his life holding back. A man who wanted to belong.

He made his break with that kind of thinking before the boards had even agreed how many people to send. Even before the mining groups had reprogrammed their mecha for new, more intensive searches, Lam let all of his intelligence show and posted a sim that guaranteed his place on the mission—for bugs. Just simple, stupid bugs. That was all that had been found and no one believed this ice ball could support much else, and there were fifteen thousand volunteers in the first week. Fifteen thousand, even knowing that the trip out would be two and a half months cramped up inside a hab module; that the food would be slop-in-a-bag; that Jupiter seethed with radiation.

Vonnie still had to smile looking back on it. So much heart and curiosity. So much of the monkey in them still. Fifteen thousand people suddenly didn't care about anything but getting their feet on Europa and grubbing around for exotic life. It was a riddle unlike anything else.

Where did the bugs come from?

These weak little creatures were not burrowers, not with that spherical body shape, not with those dorsal whiskers—and there were variations in the ice. The narrow layer that had the bugs in it was a lot younger than the rest of the sample, and loaded with chlorides and minerals.

Lam's school of thought predicted a world inside the ice, a small, uneasy, vertical world.

They had long known that Europa's great ocean was not wholly solid. The freeze went down as much as ten kilometers, but beneath that was slush and eventually liquid, as hot as boiling where raw magma or gas pushed out of the moon's rocky core.

It had all the building blocks of life—heat, water, organic material from comet and meteor strikes—but this moon was not so gentle a place as Earth. For over a hundred years, a hundred probes had found nothing. No surprise. Lam confined his model to a mere six kilometers, where a fin of subsurface mountains partly diverted the force of the tides, yet even in this safe zone the ice and rock were burned and torn.

Lam was among the first to understand the violence of this environment, and it fascinated him.

Here are the bugs in an open rift, he said. What are they doing? We don't know. Mating? Migrating? Nearby there is a rumble, and a super-heated geyser floods the rift. It collapses, then slowly freezes. But there are more pocket ecologies stacked all through this area, some with thin atmospheres of water vapor from the ice or volcanic gases such as nitrogen and carbon dioxide, poisonous hydrogen chloride, explosive hydrogen sulfide.

Eons ago in some of these holes, in warm water,

single-cell organisms had grown and thrived. Much later there was algae and then vegetation to break down the CO_2, releasing free oxygen into at least some of the pocket ecologies. At least for a time.

Life here flourished because it must, evolving and spreading never more than a few steps ahead of constant upheaval.

7.

Vonnie's head sang with the low buzz of their sonar, too strong to be just one. They were all around. A hint of arms, the clack of a falling pebble—

She stepped back without intending to, thinking only with her nerves, and in response the amphibians' voices rose up like a flood, wild and thick. Her emotions were a different storm but there was one clear idea at the center of it.

She didn't want to die badly. More than that, she didn't want the wrong reasons to be her last.

Then the ghost said:

—*Von, listen, I have six to eight targets but they're all concealed. Nine targets now. If we're going to pick them off before they jump, I need full system access.*

But they hadn't jumped. Not yet. For the first time, the amphibians were being cautious. Curious? Maybe it was an overture. Vonnie moved forward again to the edge of the cliff and made herself small, tucking both arms into her chest.

—*What are you doing?*

The posture was submissive but at the same time she tried to project resolve and strength, keeping her head

BOGDAN STETSENKO

up, keeping it turning from side to side. They understood at least that much of the way she was built. They'd come after her face every time.

—*Von, listen. It's the only chance.*

"No," she whispered, making her decision. "Off."

—*Wait.*

"I said off."

She couldn't hate the stupid thing. She was to blame for everything that was wrong with him, and he was just a ghost anyway, and it had been his idea to try to talk without words. A great idea. It was incredibly dangerous but at the same time it held every bit of hope.

The amphibians sang and sang and sang, measuring her, crowding her. Would they show themselves without attacking?

8.

Christmas Bauman was fifty-two and not so new to success or failure, and that was partly why she won her slot on the expedition, as a balance to Lam and Vonderach. Vonnie had liked her, too. Bauman pretended sarcasm with them but it was only a way of communicating her experience. You could measure her amusement in each fraction of a centimeter that her brows lifted above her muddy green eyes.

She had her own fascination. "What if—" she kept saying. What if those bugs weren't dead at all, but hibernating or otherwise still biologically active? What if their chemistry wasn't too strange to co-opt, and could be used in geriatrics or cryosurgery? Yes, they appeared to have been boiled in magma-heated water and then gradually mashed and distorted by the freezing process—they appeared very dead indeed—but who could say what traits were normal here? It wasn't impossible that the bugs had evolved to spread in this manner, like spores, preserved for ages until the ice opened up again.

Until a genesmith landed on Europa there was no way to know, and Bauman committed to a year's hardship on nothing more than spectral scans and *what if*.

They made a game of it inside the thin, weightless cage of their ship, *what if I trade you my dessert tonight for some of your computer time* and *what if you turn off that friggin' music?* Eleven weeks in a box. There wouldn't have been room for them to start bouncing off the walls and Christmas Bauman emerged naturally as their leader, a little bit of a mom, a little bit of a flirt. She kept the pressure low with her jokes and also made sure they paid attention to each other, because the temptation was to only look ahead. Lam constantly updated his sims as the mecha sent new data, and Vonnie had full responsibility for ships' systems and maintenance, and all of them reviewed and participated in various conferences and boards and debates. Eleven weeks. It could have been long enough to learn to hate each other, or even little enough to still be strangers when they arrived, but Bauman set aside much of her own work to invest in her colleagues instead.

The hieroglyphs changed everything.

It was a Chinese rover this time, running close to the ESA find. Its transmission was both encoded and alter-cast, but the Europeans and the Brazilians each caught enough of the signal to have something to work with. In less than four hours the naked code went system-wide.

Vonnie had learned politics at Stuttgart and, later, consulting for Arianespace. Information was power. There didn't seem to be much sense in withholding the discovery—likely it was just reflex—but the mood back on Earth took a hit. Their radio surged with new worries and protocols, and they were still two and a half weeks from Europa. It could have ruined them. It could have sunk all of their energy into the worst kind of distraction.

Bauman saw them through. "What if he is a dastardly chink spy?" she said, straight-faced, and Vonnie blushed at the slur and Lam laughed out loud.

They were friends enough to understand that they were on their own, no matter what played out back home.

The video was in radar and infrared, the mecha's low-slung perspective trundling forward with gradients of temperature laid over the green imagery. Far left, irregular lumps masked the horizon, warm gas oozing from several vents. The mecha turned closer—and the perspective fell sideways. In front of the camera, six meters of ice bulged like a muscle. Gas spewed upward. Pelting hail. Then it stopped and the mecha extended a wire probe down into the quiet, confirming a glimpse of repetitive shapes in the ice.

In radar the carvings were stark, perfect, inarguable.

"What if we just killed somebody when the air went out?" Vonnie asked, thinking like an engineer, but Bauman said, "No, it's old. And isolated."

109

"She's right," Lam agreed.

They had grouped around the best monitor and Vonnie smiled, glad for their excitement. Then she saw his face and frowned, feeling one step behind.

"Look," he said as he ducked his own eyes in disappointment.

"Very old," Bauman said. "Still . . ."

The hieroglyphs repeated one shape over and over in eight vertical columns of four apiece, a symbol much like an eight-pointed star, with every arm knuckled and bent. From tip to tip each carving was more than a meter wide, and set deep enough into the ice to be nearly half a meter thick through the middle: small domes with tapered limbs.

Vonnie thought it could be a sun calendar. She started to say so, then caught herself. This far out, the sun was barely brighter than any other star, and she'd soaked up enough from Lam to believe that there had never been anything walking around on the surface of this moon.

"Too old," Lam said. "Look at the drift."

The three right-most columns appeared sloppy, hurried, but that was only because the ice had swelled there, distorting the symbols—and in this safe zone, surface tides could be measured in millimeters per century. Vonnie felt a weird shiver down her spine. These symbols might be several times older than the dim, half-forgotten histories recorded in the Bible.

"Cheer up," Bauman said, running her finger across the scroll pad. The first theories from Earth were a mating ground, a food cache, maybe only territorial markings, but consensus was that the site demonstrated at least chimpanzee-equivalent intelligence. "Even if they've all been dead for a thousand years, I guarantee you'll be up for the Nobel and the cover of every magazine you can think of."

"What? He's not *that* smart," Vonnie said, trying for a laugh, but Lam just grimaced and shook his head.

9.

The first one came from behind, undetected, almost certainly airborne. It clamped its eight arms around her helmet and the fissure exploded with bodies.

Vonnie screamed, uselessly. Thrashing was no better. The roping muscles cinched down on her face were lined with cilia—fine, gripping pinchers in the thousands—and the amphibian had landed its body against the rough patch where her gear block had been, chewing there with its beak. The sound was a high squeal, rubbing and scraping.

She flailed at it with both hands. Somehow she managed another sweep of the chasm at the same time.

The echoes of her ELF pulse were close and frantic, overlapping. A swarm. She'd seen it before. The amphibians were spectacular in flight, all arms outstretched like suns. Their hieroglyphs were a literal portrayal of their bodies. To a species that saw in sonar, language consisted of stance and gesture. They always knew each other's mood and seemed to share it, like a school of fish. At a guess there were twenty in the tightly choreographed launch and too many had gotten past her explosives—

"You still there?" she shouted.

—*Von, listen, don't close me down again, please.*

She was already talking over the ghost. "Auto assault, max force! Lam! Combat menu AP, auto assault, do you understand?"

The delay felt like another kind of blindness and separation. She almost froze. She screamed again. She punched at the small monster wrapped around her head but its hard cartilage skin was like pounding on rubber. Only her cutting tool had pierced that hide before, and she was afraid to use the laser against her own face.

Then she jerked sideways, wrenching her spine. At first she thought she'd been hit by a mass of bodies.

—*Auto assault.*

The suit carried her. The suit spasmed and leapt. It put her fist to her temple and drew the laser across the amphibian's arms, a precise stutter of four burns, even as it threw her onto her hip and met the incoming wave with a kick.

Impacts shook Vonnie's foot and shin, and then she was up again. Then three tentacles clunked against her back. Some of the amphibians must have gone overhead when she dropped—they must have completely surrounded her—and the suit spun and surged into the rock, scraping itself clean.

So fast. She lost all sense of up and down. She lost herself. Whatever triumph she'd felt in that first instant gave way to blunt, claustrophobic terror.

The suit did not use its shape like a human would, pinning one monster with its face, and again and again it hurled itself into the rock. It wasn't squeamish, either. It did not flinch at the wretched shrilling of an amphibian

112

caught between its hands, or even turn from the burst of entrails.

In normal gravity, against larger enemies, Vonnie would have been seriously injured. Even here she was shaken so badly she didn't immediately realize it was over.

Or remember when she'd regained her right eye.

Surprise and hope lifted through her in that moment of clarity. "I can— Lam?"

The suit stood at the top of the landslide beneath her small, broken shelf, just short of the explosive charges. Her visor glowed with heat signatures but the only living shapes were fading, retreating deep into the fissure. Eleven more small bodies drifted in the minimal gravity or lay impaled against the rough black lava. The air was fogged with blood.

Mute, she tried to turn away.

Crying out, she knew she was paralyzed. "Lam? Lam, it's over. Off-line. Lam, off-line."

If they attacked again— If the ghost had corrupted all suit functions— Her body choked with that heavy new fear again and she fought without thinking inside her shell.

He spoke in a hush:

—*I have an additional threat.*

"Let me go!"

—*Von, quiet. Something's coming.*

"What?"

—*There were new sonar voices right before the amphibians broke away. Something that scared them off.*

His voice was different, cooler, more confident. Had he finally written out his glitches? With access to so

113

many more systems, he could have duped himself and then cut away the flaws in a microsecond. Vonnie was overdue for a little luck.

"Is it one of our probes?"

—*No. New life forms, also in a pack.*

Of course. Food here was scarce. Any commotion would draw every predator within hearing, and she shouldn't have expected anything else. Still, the disappointment in her felt like a new, raw wound.

—*Do you want to stay and fight? I estimate them at two hundred meters.*

Vonnie cursed bitterly, hating this dark place, hating her own seesaw of emotions. She felt like apologizing even though he was just a goddamn program. She felt grateful.

"Run for it," she said. "All these bodies, that's a big meal. We should be able to get a good head start."

10.

She landed their slowboat on Europa more than a week before the new high-gee launches would arrive, but they were ordered to wait. The two larger ships now en route carried a good many of the experts who'd lost out the first time, and not a small number of bureaucrats—and there was real truth to the idea that this crowd would be better able to process the site.

Still, Lam smoldered. "You see what's happening," he said, his back to the hab module window as if testing himself.

Vonnie couldn't leave the bubble alone and Bauman

made her wipe off her fingerprints every night. The ice was fantastic. "I know it's tough," she said, barely glancing at him.

"You're already talking like them."

"Hey, easy. I'm on your side."

"You think I'm mad because they might grab some of the glory? Because I had to put up with living in a closet with two beautiful women for eleven weeks?"

She turned at *beautiful,* a little wary. So far he'd been scrupulous about keeping his distance.

"Von, you've seen their org chart," he said. "Who do you think's in charge, the people like you and me?" His brown eyes searched her face, then shifted to gaze at the window behind her. "It's being politicized," he said. "The fuel. The water. You have to listen to what they're really saying."

The ice. Everyone was still digging along the equator and even now a CSA robot ship was carefully unfolding in orbit, dropping new mecha. Miners. They had been funded years ago and had been in transit for months, and that kind of inertia was fundamental to nearly every aspect of modern civilization.

The ice. It held barely more than a hundredth of a percent deuterium but that precious gas could be compressed and boxed, and easily lobbed up out of Europa's weak gravity. The tankers filled faster than they could be built. Escaping Jupiter wasn't expensive either, diving close and then slinging away, and the old god was perfectly positioned to feed the inner planets. More and more, surface catapults had been hurling packets equipped with nothing more than a radio beacon into

115

slow, sunward trajectories . . . and if they didn't arrive for years, even if one or two went missing along the way, no problem, they were lined up like endless supply trains and as cheap as dirt.

The ice. Deuterium-deuterium fusion reactors kept people alive on Luna and Mars and on a hundred rocks in the asteroid belt, and everywhere in between—and water/oxygen futures had become more than stiff enough to make tearing up the ice itself worthwhile. The solar system was in bloom. The Chinese had expanded with total commitment and other cultures were growing as fast as they could just to keep from being left behind.

"They've already given up on most of this world," Lam said, still angry over dinner. "It's too easy. They've been ripping it apart for twenty years with every reason to keep at it, right? I even helped them. Look. They're all posting my sim like it's proof, like this safe zone is definitely the only one."

"Okay," Bauman said. "Okay. We all know SecGen Kokubo is going to ride the expedition like a nine-hundred-pound gorilla." The Japanese minister was space born, and represented six thousand colonists who made up a crucial part of the Earth-orbit economy. "What do you want to do about it?"

"We've got a little time," he said, "long enough to post enough info that they can't bury it. You know what I mean—delays for more surveys, delays for safety, maybe send in a few crawlers, five or six months goes by, downplay the whole thing."

"What do you want to do, Lam?"

"I want to go in."

116

11.

All she wanted was *out* but in fifty meters they changed direction seven times through the black ragged rock, dodging through gaps and pockets, jumping one crack and then two loose slumping hills of debris. Vonnie had to grit her teeth. Letting the suit run in this gravity felt too much like fighting—grab, kick, kick again, swimming off the walls and ceilings.

It felt too much like they were going in a circle.

The ghost followed every possible way up but again and again they lost as much elevation as they'd gained, ducking and weaving for open space. They couldn't even maintain a lateral bearing, forced left and then left and then left again.

"Go back! Lam, go back to that last branch!"

—*Radar suggests another upward trend ahead of us.*

"You . . ." She was almost unable to say it. "Aren't you headed right where we came from?"

—*We've paralleled several caverns, yes.*

"Christ." She'd pulled the explosive charges before they left, so it would be easy to blow the channel behind them, shut off any pursuit, but what if they ran into yet another threat? What if this tunnel was ultimately a dead end?

These catacombs had formed millennia ago when liquid water cut through the rock in a mix of geysers, rivers and slow-draining seas. Since then, quakes and fractures had opened new holes and closed others—and the ice was always there, dripping or pushing or smashing its way in.

117

Between radar sims and actual footsteps covered, her maps went eighteen kilometers, although most of that was tangled into a pyramid just four kilometers on a side—and long sections of her trail had gone unrecorded or were literally nonexistent now, destroyed in the rock swell.

It was unlikely she could retrace her steps even if she wanted to, even knowing that something was behind her.

"What was coming, can you tell me?"

—*They were a little bigger than the amphibians. Louder. By my estimate there were only six or seven, but the amphibians retreated as soon as they heard the other sonar.*

Vonnie measured a broad slab of rock as they approached, using her own gut hunch as well as radar analysis. It looked like a good place to drop the roof. All she wanted was *out*. No more data, no more diplomacy, no more trying to vindicate her friends' deaths. No more guilt.

"Is there any way to know if they're ahead of us?"

—*I've continued to see traces of prints and spoor. Look there. And there.*

Across her visor, the ghost highlighted two faint smears of feces close together on a small, level spot on the tunnel floor. Neither was much more than a few frozen molecules. In this place, nothing went to waste or was left behind.

Somehow that made her feel badly again. Somehow...

—*The dung is probably not amphibian. We'd have to stop and test samples. But in retrospect, there's a good probability that the amphibians chased us beyond their own territory and we're already deep into the home of the other life form.*

Vonnie just shook her head. Even with her weapons and size, she hadn't been able to make the amphibians run away. Whatever these new creatures were . . .

Maybe she'd been luckier so far than she thought.

12.

It was the kind of career move you only made once. They would either be heroes or subject to a great many lawsuits, probably jail time in Lam's case. Vonnie suspected he was already thinking of political asylum. The hieroglyphs meant that much to him, more than home, more than family—and for all the right reasons.

He wanted to range as deep as possible. He wanted proof of the diversity of life implied by the carvings, the complex food chain that must support the carvers.

There would be little or no fossil record here, of course. At best the tides would hold a churned-up mishmash of species carried far from their time and habitats, but that was the point. Diaspora. There must be priceless information everywhere across this moon. There must be life in other places. The mining would never stop, he accepted that, but it could be heavily restricted. It could be more careful.

Bauman only argued for a day. She was too much like them or she wouldn't have been there in the first place, and the men on the radio talked like slaps in the face, hard and quick, controlling. She didn't appreciate that. She had Lam concoct a sim that showed the hieroglyphs in danger, which wasn't untruthful. The mecha had resealed the hole but the hieroglyphs were still reacting to near-vacuum, and who could say what data was being lost as the ice slowly boiled away?

They were given permission to enter the trench, only the trench, and Lam laughed and ran for his armor.

"Game over," he said. "Game over. I mean, once we're inside there'll be all kinds of reasons we have to keep poking around, right?"

"Wait," Vonnie said, and hugged them both, Bauman first, blushing a little as she turned to Lam. "You can't feel anything in a scout suit," she explained.

"Yeah." He smiled, looking for her eyes.

They dropped in through a small cut in the roof and instructed the mecha to close it again, Lam and Bauman already bickering contentedly. He wanted radar and x-ray. She insisted on passive microscopy. Vonnie just grinned and flipped through a heads-up of the preliminary soundings taken by wire probe. Their visors were modifying sonar feedback into holo imagery, to avoid burning the ice with light.

It was densely, overwhelmingly textured: an irregular quilt of dewdrops, smooth spots, swells and depressions. Only the hieroglyphs held a pattern.

She seemed to be standing at the end of a tunnel, which made the symbols even more intriguing. Why invest such effort marking the walls of what must be a low-traffic area? Could this be some sort of holy place? Lam would say that was just more anthropomorphism . . . and it wasn't impossible that at one time the tunnel had continued on from here, until the tides collapsed it. But what had the carvers been doing so close to the surface?

"You'll never pack up the whole wall and put it in a museum," Lam said. "We're damaging it just by standing here."

"All the more reason to be careful." Bauman shook her head, the big gear block on one side like a misplaced hat. "We don't know how finely detailed the top layer—"

"Exactly. So we get it all in one burst, full spectrum."

"The heat—"

"Specialist Lam." The other ships were still more than two light-minutes away, which could reduce conversation to a series of interruptions. "We'd like to see the first column again, please stand by for auto control."

"Roger that," Lam answered on the coded frequency, and in a moment his suit carefully adjusted his upper body, aiming the gear block with machine precision. It was a little spooky. The suits weren't supposed to accept remote programs without an okay from whoever was inside, but Vonnie wondered. When they started deeper into the tunnel, would their suits lock up? When they tried to send their data on public channels, would the broadcast come out clean or garbled?

Lam had switched back to suit radio. "There's something embedded in the ice!"

"What?"

"Their computers must've seen it in our telemetry. Pellets. Everywhere. Probably organic. Look."

The tiny spheres were as translucent as the ice itself. Eggs? Food? "What if—" Vonnie tried to get a word in edgewise but Bauman was beside herself, rattling her gloves against her thighs as if to grab and hold the little things.

"We can't pull them, not yet," Bauman said. "We'll have to record and map it first, so I guess your full spectrum burst is the best way to go, Lam, what do you think?"

"I think you're right," he said generously.

"Can we get a wire in, get a sample?"

Vonnie pointed. "What if we pick through the debris against that wall?" The fourth column was the most deteriorated, and among the confusion of arms were several that had crumbled.

"Genius." Bauman clapped her on the back, a dull clank.

Seconds later they had their sample, and Lam and Bauman bent over it together like cavemen protecting a spark, bumping their thick shoulders, both of them chattering into the radio at the same time. They might have stayed all day. They might have stayed until the other ships arrived, happily absorbed in chem tests and new theories.

It was Vonnie who convinced them to move on.

13.

The left knee gave out in midbounce and she pinwheeled sideways, bashing against the rock. In an instant Vonnie hit the opposite side of the gap. But the ghost was quick to compensate. Her right heel and then one hand touched lightly and the ghost had already corrected their spin, regaining speed, clawing forward through the maze.

"Lam?" she said, heart pounding.

—*You're all right. There's no breach.*

Christ. She hadn't even thought of decompressing and tensed at the idea, hurting her neck when the ghost bent to fit a hole. For twenty minutes they'd been fighting through a series of cave-ins and grinds, and now the suit spidered forward with the bad leg trailing awkwardly, protecting it.

"How long for repairs?" she asked.

—*That may not be possible. Every anterior cable in the knee snapped and one medial.*

They were falling apart. The suit had never been designed to take this kind of abuse and Vonnie wasn't doing much better, punch-drunk on stress and stimulants and more than thirty hours on the run, nearly fifty since she'd really slept. She didn't want to make the wrong decision.

"How long, Lam?"

—*Without the toolkit our best option might be to scavenge material from the ankle, weld it solid and restore some function to the knee. I estimate that would take an hour.*

"No."

If they stopped she was afraid she'd close her eyes. It would only be smart to rest but it would be too much like being blind again. "No, keep going," she said.

If his sims were correct, they were still at least two kilometers down—and at some point they'd have to transition from rock to ice. This mountain rose up like a fin, always narrowing, disappearing completely a kilometer and a half from the surface. There would be islands suspended in the ice, broken-off hunks as large as New York and gravel fields like sheets and clouds. The trick would be to find a gas vent that went all the way up. The trick would be to climb through without touching off a rock swell.

Vonnie clenched her teeth, trying to avoid the thought. She knew that too much planning would overwhelm her.

123

They ducked another gap and suddenly the rift widened into a huge volcanic bubble, open on one side. It was half full of ice, but just to look across three hundred meters of open room was disorienting. Vonnie felt the same uncertainty in Lam. The ghost hesitated, scanning up and back.

"What do you think?" she said. "There's definitely some new melt over there. If we dig we might get into a vent, get out of this rock, close the hole behind us."

He lit her visor with radar frames.

—*Look*.

"Oh." Vonnie surprised herself. Her fear twisted in her like a saw but even now, after everything, she also felt a strong, clear surge of excitement.

There were more hieroglyphs across the cavern, a long wall of symbols cut into the rock itself. It was easily twenty times larger than the site they'd found at the surface, and she only wrestled with herself for an instant.

"How fast can you get a recording?" she said.

14.

The pellets in the ice were more than Bauman and Lam had hoped for, and swept away any last hint of doubt. This was a sentient race, or had been long ago—because each little ball looked to be feces mixed with other biologics like saliva or blood, swamped in chemicals. Hormones. Vonnie could only admire the elegance of it. In this resource-limited environment, the carvers had found at least two ways to encode information.

When she started down the tunnel it was with the thrill of history. She would always be first to walk inside this moon and a slavecast kept a swirl of tiny mecha around her feet, sounding the ice, recording everything. Unfortunately she wasn't so graceful. The passage dropped steeply but she tended to crash into the ceiling, misjudging the gravity. Worse, the opening shrank until it wasn't much bigger than her suit, and twice became too narrow for Vonnie to continue on without roughly shouldering through the brittle walls.

Their telemetry betrayed them, as expected. The men on the radio questioned her movement and ordered her back. She kept going. Sonar showed an end to the tunnel after four hundred meters, yet infrared revealed that it was a shade warmer than its surroundings, with a hot pinprick of gas leaking through.

Vonnie preempted any debate. "There's something behind here," she said. "My sonar's going crazy."

"Something alive?" That was Lam.

"I don't know. But this is an airlock. Look at it. So smooth." It was definitely not a formation caused by slow melt or tidal pressures. Amazing. Vonnie would have cringed at the idea of placing such responsibility in anything as flimsy as ice, but there were no metals here. What else could the carvers use? It spoke again of their inventiveness and determination, and she couldn't wait to see more.

It was a test of sorts, a chance to prove herself the way that Lam and Bauman had already done. Every step deeper, every challenge met, showed her worth to the team.

To get through without losing the air, she would need to trap herself between this block and a new seal of her own making—and every surface in the ice showed old

125

scars and stubs. Irregular holes marred the walls where building material must have been dug out.

"I say 'go'," Lam said to the men on the radio. "We're picking up some kind of reading. Noise. Heat. There's no telling what we'll miss if we just sit here."

"I can get us in," Vonnie agreed.

Her friends had less than two hours to live when they joined her near the airlock, grinning like kids. Bauman was last in line, so Vonnie took control of Bauman's suit, dropping frozen blocks into place and soldering the stack together with her laser finger on a minimum setting. "Slow work," she said, apologizing, not wanting to blunt their energy.

Lam only shrugged, running sims on his visor as he waited. "Think what they used," he said. "Body heat? Urine, maybe. There're organic contaminants all through here."

"Some good DNA," Bauman agreed, restless and happy.

Finally they were sealed in, and Vonnie eased through the original lock. Immediately she saw another ice plug further on. That was good engineering, but she was disappointed to realize how many lifetimes it must have been since the carvers had come here or even considered this tunnel important.

Long, long ago, the top of the second lock had slumped open and her suit analyzed the low-pressure atmosphere bleeding over her as nearly one hundred percent nitrogen—a gas so inert, no creature could have evolved to burn it as an energy source. This seemed to be a dead place. Why bother to block it off?

"Nobody home," she said.

"No." Lam was cheerful, even buoyant, bumping her shoulder as he tried to look past.

But maybe the air here was bad *because* this place was unused, she thought. Maybe they controlled oxygen content with floodgates. It could be their most precious resource.

Lam and Bauman were beyond listening, though, lost in the invisible chatter of data. Some of their tiny mecha had run ahead while others lingered to taste the ice, and Lam especially was in his element, pulling files, fitting each little perspective into a working whole.

Vonnie was eager, too, yet meticulously rebuilt the locks behind them. Then she moved in front again, her exhilaration like a shout.

Another eighty meters on, though, the slanting tunnel dropped away completely. A sink. It was encrusted with old melt and across the way was a hollow of uncertain depth, thick with stalactites. There had been a catastrophe here, a belch of heat, probably, but she couldn't feel sad. She walked to the edge. Her sonar raced down the gaping channel like a fantastic halo but did not reach bottom.

Somewhere down there was the dark heart of this world.

"Perfect," Lam said, uploading a sim to her to complete the thought. This shaft was a cross-section through the ice, maybe rich, maybe not. A mecha descending—

"Sure. Give me fifteen minutes." It would be easy to sink a few bolts, play out a molecular wire and send a bot down like a spider. Vonnie rifled through her kit.

"Huh," he said then, and one of the mecha near Vonnie's feet reared back and shot a marker into the ice.

It was dirty ice, like most of the patches that Lam had already targeted, some dark with lava dust, others discolored like milk or glass.

There was a shell. A small spiral shell. It wouldn't have looked unusual on any beach on Earth, but here it was a treasure. Even so, Lam was careful. He merely stuck a radio pin into the wall of the tunnel.

The wall exploded, white ice, black rock. Vonnie was nearly in front of it and that saved her. The blast knocked her out and up, snarled in her wire.

Bauman yelled once, "Lam, get back!"

There was probably no more than a quarter ton of debris stopped up behind the dust pack—a mass of gravel and larger stones that had gradually absorbed just enough warmth to slump forward into a loose, dangerous bulge—and it weighed only a tenth as much as it would have on Earth. But in this gravity, it splashed, and it still had all of its inertia and mass.

It tore the vent. It hit other nodes of rock.

There were three upward shockwaves: the first ricochets, a vicious swell and then a smaller, settling riffle. Vonnie escaped the worst of it, half-conscious and confused, her body slammed into the safe pockets at the top of the vent as her friends disappeared, their sharecasts bursting with alarms and then one massive injury report before cutting off.

But she was still tied to the wire, and it would not break. One end caught in the heaving ice and the swell took her too.

15.

Vonnie lurched sideways across the cavern and pushed against another slab of rock. The torn fragments of the wall had shifted as water and ice intruded, retreated, came again, and some wild feeling in her was able to guess which pieces were only debris and which held hieroglyphs on one side or another.

It made the hair stand up on her arms and neck, uneven and mute. It felt exactly like . . . "Wait."

—*Sonar.*

Somehow she'd sensed it first, even before his machine ears, but there was no time to wonder at the weird creeping changes in herself. "How close are they? We're almost done."

—*At least a thousand meters. It's only echoes. My estimate could be off but I'd say they're still deep in the tunnels. Possibly they don't even know we're here.*

"No. They know."

—*Their voices aren't directed this way.*

"Let's move. Can you pull up that block over there? I think it came out of that corner. If we can scan whatever's left on it we'll have most of this end of the wall."

The suit limped forward.

Vonnie wondered how it would hold up in a fight and knew she didn't want to be out in the open like this. Better to find a hole, place the explosives . . . "It's not amphibians, is it?"

—*No. The others.*

She shoved at the rock, moving feverishly now, but it felt good and right to stay—to have purpose again. She would kill as many as she had to, but she was not just a rat in a trap, running mindlessly. She had worn down to the bedrock of herself and found what she needed, a last reservoir of strength.

Only a few shards left now. Possibly the beginning of an answer. Lam said he'd seen enough of the amphibians' language to try to communicate, but this stretch of carvings was too valuable to abandon. A sample this large would be priceless in translation efforts, and even if she survived they might never find their way back to this cave. And if she died . . . well, if she died, their probes might still find her. Her suit would transmit her files even if she were buried and lost.

Vonnie realized she was crying and wasn't angry. She wasn't ashamed. She had done her best all the way through and maybe that was enough. That was good and right.

She dropped the rock and pushed over a smaller boulder with only a chipped half-moon of a carving on the underside. "Got it?" she asked, feeling close to him again, the real him and the ghost. He was a powerful friend.

—*Three hundred meters, Von. We should go.*

"You got it?" she repeated.

—*Yes. Von, listen. There are more of them this time, at least ten, moving fast now.*

"Help me with this last big one."

The truth was that nobody even really knew which questions to ask. She didn't wonder why there were amphibian hieroglyphs in what was obviously no longer their territory—the catacombs probably changed hands regularly or were deserted and reclaimed—but why she hadn't seen more. These carvings were ancient.

Were the amphibians only coming back now after a long absence? Even then, why hadn't she seen more signs of activity?

Maybe some part of the secret was here, and she was willing to fight for it.

Something else, she realized. The answer might be in their enemies, and Vonnie swung to face the approaching voices with an excavation charge in either hand.

16.

The first little world in the ice would always be her favorite. It was peaceful. The two species of bugs—closely related to each other but wholly unlike the fat-bodied ants brought up by the ESA rover—seemed to feed solely on the gray, sticky algae that grew alongside the wells of the hot springs, where the melt was thick and ever-changing.

At one time this chamber must have been part of a larger area, but ice falls had long since walled it off. Vonnie only stumbled into this open space when she refused to be deterred and started digging. Her mind had felt very, very small in those hours, too small for any thought except to get away from the lethal, creaking weight of the collapsed vent above her.

She wasn't hurt, other than a sprained elbow. She was alone. Communication with the outside had already been staticky, despite the relays she'd left along the tunnel. Maybe those machines were all gone. Maybe she'd fallen further than she thought. Obviously she had to find a way back to the surface. The other ships were still two days out and it might take them another day to gear up and scout for her, even longer to forge their way through the crumbling mass above.

She regretted not having monitors to leave in this place. Bauman especially would have been excited, but nearly all of Vonnie's mecha had been lost in the rock swell. The two she had left she sent exploring and then sat still, grieving, resting—and recording. Her camera lights were dazzling in the wet ice.

The atmosphere here was oxygen-rich, though still nothing that would support a human being, laced with hydrogen chloride. More interesting, the pressure was three times what she'd seen near the surface, due in part to a lower altitude but mostly because this hollow was self-contained.

Neither species had eyes, of course. They used fan antennae and scent instead. They were basically helpless. Droplets fell steadily or in periodic rains, and the chamber floor was pebbled with a thousand specimens. Vonnie collected several. But the mortality rate, while high, didn't seem enough to keep the bugs from outgrowing their food source. This pocket ecology was more than incomplete; it was unworkable; it was temporary.

She was frustrated when she built the ghostling to help her, angry at him, afraid of dying in this impossible place. Bauman would have been a better companion. Vonnie wouldn't have tried so hard to control her and the mess she made of Lam was erratic, missing too much. She'd held back more than half of his mem files, but included the last. She wanted him to know why he died. She wanted him to be cautious, even timid.

She didn't trust the result.

Vonnie dug her way out of the bugs' small world

when her mecha reported a faint current of atmosphere, half a kilometer away. She knew there were more vents nearby.

The tremor was probably another aftershock. The bulk of the fallen vent was pressing out against the surrounding area, and as other networks collapsed they also pushed down or sideways. She felt a long, low creaking sound and suddenly the ice lurched, slamming at her. Then some larger section gave way and Vonnie fell tumbling into the white.

A queer thought struck her as she labored to free herself, sinking ever deeper through the loose hunks and powder, certain after the third hour that she was in her grave.

This was no ocean into which she was descending—it was this moon's sky. Caught here, native species had no concept of anything further up. They would always look for the mountains or the liquid seas below.

She began to dig down instead of sideways, not fighting the avalanche but using it to her advantage, sifting, swimming. Finally she fell into a world of rock, a honeycomb of soft lava worn open at one time by running water. Whether it was an island suspended in the ice or a true mountain she couldn't say yet, but she had at last come down out of the frozen sky.

17.

The cavern seemed to stretch as her fear grew and Vonnie stayed near the wall of hieroglyphs, trying to anchor herself. Deep radar let her track the new creatures while they were still out of sight and there were twelve bodies in the swarm, banging off the walls and ceiling of a gap.

—*Sixty meters. Fifty.*

Vonnie held her explosives. There were too many entrances and she had only four half-sticks. She couldn't throw one until they were almost on her, until there was no chance they'd bounce back out of whichever opening they chose.

—*Forty.*

They would catch her if she ran, she knew that, but the adrenaline was like a hundred blades inside her, it was like them, savage and quick.

—*They're in the second tunnel.*

Suddenly there was less rock in the way and Lam drew each body into clear resolution. They were no longer just overlapping blobs. They were amphibians.

"Christ, you said . . ."

They were bigger, with longer arms and different skin, cousins of the ones she'd fought, but their own breed. There was no question about it. To creatures that saw and spoke in sonar, this breed would stand apart from the others, if for no other reason than the pitch of their voices—and it wasn't this race that had written on this wall. The size of the carvings was wrong. The surface texture.

These hieroglyphs belonged to the smaller species.

War. It explained so much. Even when the environment was calm they had been tearing at each other, fighting for ground and for resources, and that competition had been more than either side was able to withstand.

—*Here they come.*

In an instant her chance to kill them cleanly would be gone, and Vonnie had learned not to hesitate. But she had also remembered who she was and why she'd ever come here.

"Lam, talk to them! You have to try to talk to them!" she yelled, and the suit bent down even as the amphibians swept into the cavern, a crisscrossing wave of bodies high and low. At the same time Lam emitted sonar bursts in exactly the same tone as theirs, greeting them, ducking one shoulder as he drew on everything he'd learned.

It was the right decision. She believed that. This was a new population altogether and there was every reason to hope that they would answer her.

18.

Alone, in silence, she thought about her dead friends too much and kept as busy as possible with maps and data instead. The atmosphere in these big lava tunnels was mostly water vapor, carbon dioxide and the ever-present nitrogen, along with trace poisons. It was also warm, only a few degrees below freezing. Vonnie assumed she must be inside the fin mountain, stoked by thermal heat. Giant lumps of ice grew up from the floor beneath long stalactites, and slow-flowing lakes made waves and swirls against the humps of rock. Beautiful. She tried to let it cheer her as she picked her way through the jumble, following a soft wind. The pressure differential indicated an even higher temperature somewhere ahead, maybe a vent.

135

First Contact was a jolt. She had seen a few pale spores of fungus but only the ice truly grew and thrived here, so when her radar picked out another sun-shape on the wall she assumed it was a carving. Then it moved.

"Hey—" She started closer, stopped. She didn't want to scare the little thing. She was three hundred meters off and there was some chance she was still unobserved.

Maybe that was best. She didn't have the training and the choice she made could affect eight billion lives across the solar system, the human race colliding with another for the first time. It was tremendous beyond imagining. But she didn't waver long. She just didn't have it in her to walk away, not here, not now. More than that, she needed this success to balance everything that had gone wrong.

Besides, what the hell was the starfish breathing?

Vonnie felt a stab of longing and pride at the thought, a bittersweet mix. Lam and Bauman would have given anything to be here, but she would do the job alone.

The creature had disappeared so she paced slowly in that direction, sweeping radar and x-ray up the wall. Nothing. Nothing. Then she found one cold crevice full of bodies, eight of them, and yet she saw no exhalations in infrared.

For that moment she forgot everything else, though she was careful not to get too close or even to let her smile show inside her visor—teeth might be threatening. She knelt to make herself small and drew one finger in the dirt, trying to communicate just the idea of communicating. She must be a complete surprise.

Furless, streamlined, they had almost certainly evolved in water. No skeleton and a lot of muscle. No front or back that she could see, only top and bottom. In fact they had no visible orifices except on their undersides, a few slits that she took to be gills and a single, well-protected beak evidently used both as mouth and anus. Very basic digestion. Two hearts. Brain.

They were perfect, she thought, small enough to subsist, big enough to build. Clever and brave. For creatures this size to cover as much distance as they had was remarkable, and spoke again of strategy and engineering, the incredible success of mastering this environment.

Their lungs were too compact to hold air for long, so they must have evolved some trick of oxygen compression . . . saturating their blood . . . breathing water or good air before leaving one safe place for another . . . homes and farms . . . but where?

That was all the time she had. Their assault was immediate and Vonnie twisted back, stunned. The first body struck her helmet off center, attacking the gear block. Others collided with her arms and chest, trying to bring her down. Vonnie staggered but the suit's musculature kept her upright.

Her retreat was confused. She tripped over a boulder and fell, three bodies still clawing at her. She stood like a drunk, overwhelmed. But most of them had leapt away and Vonnie struck wildly at the one on her face, anything to break free.

They pushed the roof into her. A hundred flecks clattered against her suit and she looked up just as a ragged hunk the size of a car slammed down. The missing ones had gone straight up and scrabbled in the rock, digging and prying, using themselves as pistons to accelerate their weapon.

137

They were ruthless. Impact killed two of their own and hurt three more. It also destroyed her.

Inside her helmet her skull crashed against the buckling armor, where raw circuitry scraped open one cornea. Then she hit the ground. Systems failure was total for 3.3 seconds and Vonnie gasped in the dark, bleeding, twitching.

19.

She saw the new breed react to Lam's greeting as they came across the cavern. There was no mistaking it even in flight, the ripple of motion. Their bodies shared an idea—maybe a command?—and Vonnie realized for the first time that they also used the fine cilia beneath their arms to convey information, lifting one tentacle or more to show dense, wriggling patterns.

Lam was crippled by her shape, of course, and was also canny enough not to try to mimic the hieroglyphs exactly or what they'd seen of the smaller amphibians. The warring breeds might have separate languages, so he was left to improvise and held Vonnie down in an uncomfortable ball, stuttering her fingers alongside her belly. Her visor churned with sun-shapes as he compared these twelve individuals with sims and real data. And there was another ripple among them.

Please, she thought. Please.

But he'd kept the half-sticks against her forearms with a magnetic lock, and now released two with a click.

—*Watch out.*

The split wave of amphibians struck the ceiling and

floor, and did not cling there or bounce away. Instead, the wave collapsed, ricocheting straight into her.

"Please!"

They came with their beaks open, shrieking. They came with their arms thrown wide to grasp and tear.

—*Auto assault.*

She wept for them, monsters all of them, no curiosity, no patience. No promise. The intelligence she knew existed here was stunted and cold, like everything inside this world.

Lam smashed her fist up through the one in front and then turned to swat the next. The rest never reached her. "Do it," she said, and he put both charges into the wall of hieroglyphs and ducked under a wide blast of shrapnel.

Then she turned and ran.

The four survivors kept after her, of course. Vonnie had seen it before, using most of her explosives against the smaller breed, hoping the show of force would be enough, but this clan was no different. Even with two-thirds of the group dead or bleeding out, they were relentless.

She reached a tunnel and jumped straight into the ceiling, crushing the one on her shoulder. Lam pulled at the rock with both hands and nearly cancelled her momentum, ripping debris out over her head. The shower hit the next two and Lam kicked down again, arms out, clubbing the last of them.

Vonnie left the wounded to live or die, knowing it was probably a mistake. Knowing she would always be wrong for trespassing.

For nearly an hour she heard them behind her, crying into the mountain. The echoes faded as she climbed, except once when there were fresh voices. Reinforcements? A new breed altogether? The sonar was too diffuse to be sure and she was glad, dimly, muffled in exhaustion and grief.

She climbed. She climbed without end, and even carried by the suit she passed her limit, tendons straining. Something in her back gave out above the pelvic bone and seemed to grind there—and in her mind it was the same, one hurt that went deeper than the rest. In the monotony of the catacombs, even after she dug her way into a vent, there was no escaping it.

The leaning shaft up through the ice could have been exactly where Lam and Bauman had died, although her radar showed almost no dust or mineral deposits within the melt. Good. Geysers and swells meant instability. This vent looked solid and she thought she could make it even without bolts and wire, although her hands were sore and beaten.

She climbed. She climbed slowly, testing the ice, scanning ahead. At last there was a new sound, the rescue beacon of a probe overhead.

Vonnie tried to laugh and Lam returned the signal the only way he could, a cacophony of ELF and radar pulses.

—*We made it, Von.*

"Yes."

—*Let's wait here. Can you wait? This hand is damaged in four places and the elbow's not much better. I don't want to risk a fall.*

"Yes."

But she still couldn't sleep, hanging there, several hundred meters up and so much more to go. She kept one file open on her visor and let the data burn into her, staring through it even when she lifted her head to watch above.

Lam had put together a rough translation of the hieroglyphs, and with it the beginnings of the truth.

She was wrong. The amphibians' all-or-nothing behavior was not animal stupidity or rage. It was deliberate. It was a survival trait. They had been confronted with aliens throughout their existence, creatures from other catacombs and separate lines of evolution . . . and that they had never seen anything like her before, that she aped their language or wore metal . . . none of this would ever stop them for a moment.

Outsiders were rivals. Outsiders were food. Until they could understand, *if* they could understand, they would always react that way.

The warring breeds she'd fought seemed to be the remnants of an empire that had once reached the top of the frozen sky. At one time there had been a long, calmer period in Europa's lifespan. Maybe someday there would be again. The hieroglyphs were short histories intended to aid the next alliance to rise from the chaos, and she had been nothing but a path of destruction through whatever civilization they had managed to hold onto.

It wasn't what they deserved.

The mecha gathering above her were American but relayed ESA signals. In a heartbeat Lam had the search grid and told her how far she'd strayed from where she went in. Nine kilometers. She was also still two-thirds of a kilometer beneath the surface, so the mecha rigged

141

a molecular wire and dropped other lines around her, life support, suit support, data comm.

Vonnie let go of the ice. She spun slightly as the machines lifted her away, but the surge of voices was more intense. The men and women up top had accessed her records as soon as the data line connected, and at a glance her mem files must be a running nightmare. She still had blood and black rock caught in every joint of her suit, the ruined helmet and battle-worn gloves. She knew what it must look like.

Someone murmured, "Vonderach, my God—"

"We have to help them," she said.

Art and Communication

BY L. RON HUBBARD

With nineteen New York Times *bestsellers and more than 230,000,000 copies of his works in circulation, L. Ron Hubbard is among the most acclaimed and widely read authors of our time. As a leading light of American pulp fiction through the 1930s and '40s, he is further among the most influential authors of the modern age.*

In his article, "Art and Communication," L. Ron Hubbard addresses the subject of creativity as a whole—and when can a work of painting, music or other form be truly considered art. Written in 1977, the article was then reprinted in the March 1981 issue of Professional Photographer *and again in 1997 in Britain's* Darkroom User.

Art and Communication

When a work of painting, music or other form attains two-way communication, it is truly art.

One occasionally hears an artist being criticized on the basis that his work is too "literal" or too "common." But one has rarely if ever heard any definition of "literal" or "common." And there are many artists simply hung up on this, protesting it. Also, some avant-garde schools go completely over the cliff in avoiding anything "literal" or "common"—and indeed go completely out of communication!

The *return* flow from the person viewing a work would be contribution. True art always elicits a contribution from those who view or hear or experience it. By contribution is meant "adding to it."

An illustration is "literal" in that it tells everything there is to know. Let us say the illustration is a picture of a tiger approaching a chained girl. It does not really matter how well the painting is executed, it remains an illustration and it *is* literal. But now let us take a small portion out of the scene and enlarge it. Let us take, say, the head of the tiger with its baleful eye and snarl. Suddenly we no longer have an illustration. It is no longer "literal." And the reason lies in the fact that the viewer can fit this expression into his own concepts, ideas or experience: he can supply the why of the snarl, he can compare the head to someone he knows. In short, he can CONTRIBUTE to the head.

The skill with which the head is executed determines the degree of response.

Because the viewer can contribute to the picture, it is art.

In music, the hearer can contribute his own emotion or motion. And even if the music is only a single drum, if it elicits a contribution of emotion or motion, it is truly art.

That work which delivers everything and gets little or nothing in return is not art. The "common" or overused melody, the expected shape or form gets little or no contribution from the hearer or viewer. That work which is too unclear or too poorly executed may get no contribution.

Incidental to this, one can ask if a photograph can ever be art, a controversy which has been raging for a century or more. One could say that it is only difficult to decide because one has to establish how much the photographer has contributed to the "reality" or "literalness" in front of his camera, how he has interpreted it, but really the point is whether or not that photograph elicits a contribution from its viewer. If it does, it is art.

Innovation plays a large role in all works which may become art. But even this can be overdone. Originality can be overdone to the point where it is no longer within any possible understanding by those viewing or hearing it. One can be so original one goes entirely outside the most distant perimeter of agreement with his viewers or listeners. Sometimes this is done, one suspects, when one has not spent the labor necessary to execute the work. Various excuses are assigned such an action, the most faulty of which is "self-satisfaction" of the artist. While it is quite all right to commune with oneself, one cannot also then claim that it is art if it communicates with no one else and no other's communication is possible.

The third flow, of people talking to one another about a work, can also be considered a communication and, where it occurs, is a valid contribution, as it makes the work known.

Destructive attitudes about a work can be considered as a refusal to contribute. Works that are shocking or bizarre to a point of eliciting protest may bring to themselves notoriety thereby and may shake things up, but when the refusal to contribute is too widespread, such works tend to disqualify as art.

There is also the matter of divided opinion about a work. Some contribute to it, some refuse to contribute to it. In such cases one must examine who is contributing and who is refusing. One can then say that it is a work of art to those who contribute to it and that it is not to those who refuse to contribute to it.

Criticism is some sort of index of degree of contribution. There are, roughly, two types of criticism: one can be called "invalidative criticism," the other "constructive criticism."

Invalidative criticism is all too prevalent in the arts, for there exist such things as "individual taste," contemporary standards and, unfortunately, even envy or jealousy.

Too often, criticism is simply an individual refusal to contribute. One could also state that "those who destructively criticize can't do."

"Constructive criticism" is a term which is often used but seldom defined. But it has use. It could probably be best defined as criticism which "indicates a better way to do," at least in the opinion of the critic. Those who simply find fault and never suggest a practical means of doing it better rather forfeit their right to criticize.

Art is probably the most uncodified and least organized of all fields. It therefore acquires to itself the most "authorities." Usually nothing is required of an "authority" except to say what is right, wrong, good, bad, acceptable or unacceptable. Too often the sole qualification of the authority (as in poor teaching of some subjects) is a memorized list of objects and their creators and dates with some hazy idea of what the work was. An "authority" could considerably improve his status by using rather precise definitions of his terms. The modern trend of seeking the significance in what the artist meant is of course not likely to advance the arts very much.

Viewing and experiencing art on the basis of what one is contributing to it and what others contribute to it is a workable approach. And it would result in improved art and improved appreciation.

Such a viewpoint, interestingly, also includes some things into the field of art not previously so viewed.

The Stone Cipher

written by

Tony Pi

illustrated by

LARS EDWARDS

ABOUT THE AUTHOR

Canadian writer Tony Pi has been fascinated by the printed word ever since early childhood when his grandfather operated a monstrous printing press out of the family home in Taipei, Taiwan. Immigrating to Canada at age eight with his family and not speaking a word of English, he armed himself with dictionaries and thesauri in order to master the language. Today, he holds a PhD in linguistics from McGill University, teaching semantics and researching dialects of Canadian English whenever opportunities arise.

A prior finalist of the Writers of the Future Contest in 2005, Tony began writing superhero fiction on an Internet newsgroup several years ago before trying his hand at science fiction, fantasy and the occasional mystery. He credits authors Silverberg and Zelazny as major influences on his own work, which has appeared in Canada's On Spec magazine and the webzine Abyss & Apex. His particular love of language, puzzles and sculpture collided to produce our winning story. Tony resides in Toronto and has recently finished work on his first novel.

ABOUT THE ILLUSTRATOR

The oldest (and admittedly most hyperactive) of three children, Lars Edwards was an animated shooting star from the get-go. He took private classes from "Mr. Cook," a local artist, where he began drawing comic book characters. But it was one of Mr. Cook's sons, Barry, director of Disney's Mulan, who inspired Lars at age twelve to decide to be a professional animator.

As a high school sophomore, Lars was accepted to Tennessee's Governor School for the Arts, a month-long, University summer arts and cultural immersion program. In his senior year, Lars won the national American Visions award from the Scholastic Arts and Writing Competition and had his work displayed at the renowned Corcoran Gallery in Washington, DC. In 2000, he received a scholarship from the prestigious Rhode Island School of Design to study animation and illustration. Lars has since realized his animation dream; his credits include Time Warp Trio, Squidbillies, 12 Oz Mouse *and Comedy Central's* Freakshow.

The Stone Cipher

14h20 CEST (Central European Summer Time)—Friday, 14 September 2007

Pierre, for seven days straight I've stared at these heads, and I'm still no closer to deciphering their message," said Marie-Claire.

I understood my wife's frustration. Whereas the average length of a syllable in human language was 300 milliseconds, our measurements showed that a statue's mouth took half a day to articulate the same unit, slower than ordinary speech by a factor of 144,000. Patience, then, was essential to our endeavor, though as usual Marie-Claire was swiftly running out of that particular virtue.

My wife first noticed the talking statues three weeks ago when she was still a curator at the Louvre in the Department of Greek, Etruscan and Roman Antiquities. She had been documenting a new acquisition when she noticed that its lips in a photo differed from one taken earlier that day. At first, she shrugged it off as stress, but a stroll through the galleries confirmed that other statues had the same expression. The lips of the *Venus de Milo,* for example, should have been pressed together.

151

Instead, my wife found marble teeth and tongue her sculptor never intended. It was the same the world over: statues' mouths spoke a hidden message. But what? *That* was the mystery of the Stone Cipher.

"We've made *some* progress, *ma chère*." I saved my latest time-lapse clip on my laptop. "There's no local variation. All these heads are in perfect sync." I gestured at the twenty-one heads of the kings of Judah around us in the Gallery of Kings. Their lips were apart, showing teeth. "The clips suggest that the phenomenon is consistent across France."

Marie-Claire frowned. "But we haven't detected a global pattern yet, only local ones. Japan, Egypt, name any place and their statues mouth something different, like they were carved from the blocks of the Tower of Babel. What's God telling us?"

"A chocolate cake recipe?" I suggested.

The two cryptologists working with us laughed, but Marie-Claire was far from amused. My wife was adamant that the carved faces were miracles from God, but I was less convinced of a divine origin. While I was brought up Roman Catholic like so many others, I stopped practicing when my childhood Catholicism seemed irreconcilable with the science I learned to love at university. When Marie-Claire and I started dating, the tension between my agnosticism and her Catholic beliefs had almost ended our relationship. These miracles, as Marie-Claire called them, were bringing that conflict once again to the forefront.

"It was just a joke." I navigated the maze of statuary and gear between me and Marie-Claire. The Gallery of Kings in the National Museum of the Middle Ages had been a tangle of anachronisms to begin with, more so now because of the electronics that my wife and I needed for our project. Here, the rough walls of a third-century Roman bath had been integrated into the architecture of the fifteenth-century Cluny Abbey hotel. The heads of the kings of Judah stood on exhibition, singing their silent mysterious song in unison while staring at their own headless bodies. They had been decapitated during the French Revolution because zealots mistook them for representations of the kings of France. To record the facial movements of the heads from different angles, each king had a webcam of its own. The data cables snaked from the mounted cameras along the floor to link with the cluster of computers, like the serpentine hair of a cyberpunk medusa. Although we had long confirmed their lips moved identically, we left the cameras on out of inertia more than thoroughness.

"I can't work like this anymore," said Marie-Claire. She set her calipers down, took her glasses off and rubbed her eyes. "It feels too virtual with all these web feeds and videoconference calls. Even the radio's getting on my nerves. All this technology is keeping me a world away from where I need to be. I need air."

I made my way to her side. "I thought you felt more inspired with works of art around."

"I do. Just—" She touched the lips of the king's head beside her. "Look at them; they don't belong here. They should be back at Notre-Dame Cathedral, not imprisoned. That's how *I* feel: torn from the place I belong." Hope flickered in Marie-Claire's eyes. "That's it. Take me to Mass."

LARS EDWARDS

I put my hands gently on her shoulders. "The Paris out there is not the Paris we knew a month ago. The city is infested with thousands of religious fanatics, all converging on Notre-Dame. We can't risk them recognizing you and hurting you again."

She sighed. "All I wanted was to tell the world about these miracles. I didn't think I'd cause so much chaos or lose my job."

I drew her in for a hug. "You couldn't have known."

"But it was my decision to announce it to the press." Marie-Claire slipped from my embrace. "Now half of the world wants to burn me at the stake, while the other half treats me like a modern-day Joan of Arc. Why me, Pierre?"

My wife was exaggerating, but not by much. "You gave the world the Stone Cipher." I thought it a kind gesture on her part to call it *le code pierre*. My name, *Pierre*, means *stone*. "They expect a riddler to know the answer to her own riddle. The media loves to put a human face on everything for the public to condemn or adore, and you're their poster girl for talking statues."

After Marie-Claire discovered the talking statues and I confirmed her observations independently, I was excited but wary, cautioning Marie-Claire to keep quiet until we knew more. She, on the other hand, felt it was wrong to hide something so monumental. She did not anticipate that her first interview would trigger acts of vandalism against statues around the world, forcing the closure of many museums and art galleries. While the Louvre remained open, it closed the Sully Wing, moving all its statues there. Because Marie-Claire was at the center of the fiasco, the Louvre administration fired her. Since then, my wife had become more and more withdrawn, and I didn't know how to console her.

"How do I become the prophet people expect?" she asked.

I stroked her golden hair. "By being true to yourself."

She gazed at the cryptologists at their workstations. "If they can't solve it, what chance do I have?"

"Hey." I took her glasses and eased them back onto her nose. "If the stones have a message for us, who better than your linguist husband to help you figure it out?"

"Thank you," said Marie-Claire. "Still, I miss Notre-Dame. Will you help me convince Inspector Sanschagrin to let us attend Mass there Sunday?"

"I'd rather you didn't risk another attack."

"I have to. The current plight of Paris is a crisis of *my* making. *I'm* to blame for the vandalism and the gallery closures. The only way to redeem myself is to solve the mystery of these talking heads. If I stay true to God, He will reveal the truth."

"Like it or not, you're famous now. If you walk into the crowd at Notre-Dame, you'll cause another mob scene. Innocent people will get hurt." A protest formed on her lips, but I raised a finger. "It shouldn't matter where you worship. How about a church farther from the chaos, like Sainte-Marguerite or Saint-Christophe?"

She rubbed her temples. "I suppose you're right."

I sensed that her malaise had deepened to the point where it couldn't simply be cured by another walk in the courtyard. Frankly, I needed a break from this place too. One thing that might cheer up Marie-Claire and give us a new angle on the problem occurred to me.

"In the meantime, how about a visit to the Louvre?" I suggested. "The *Venus de Milo* could be your muse again."

Marie-Claire perked up. "That would be wonderful! But will Zanon let us? I'm *persona non grata* at the Louvre these days."

Zanon was her ex-boss. "Don't worry about Zanon. He'll give in. After all, we have a force of nature on our side." I smiled. "Inspector Sanschagrin."

20h12 CEST—Friday, 14 September 2007

Because I was a linguist and Marie-Claire the first to discover the Stone Cipher, we had been pressed into service by the Central Directorate of General Information. The Directorate was responsible for research and information crucial to the security of France, and Inspector Henri Sanschagrin was our liaison at the Prefecture of Police of Paris. Although Sanschagrin was one of the foremost experts in cryptanalysis in the Sub-Directorate of Analysis, he was better known for his impromptu magic tricks and his unflappable confidence. Nine days ago, when we asked him about using the National Museum of the Middle Ages, we expected our petition to be turned down. But the inspector surprised us, procuring full access to the museum's collection and a team of cryptanalysts and technicians to assist us.

Sanschagrin took no time in setting up the trip to the Louvre, and picked us up at the museum by car that evening. Even though the Louvre was within walking distance, Sanschagrin insisted on driving for reasons of security. Marie-Claire and I hurried into the back of the unmarked Peugeot and greeted Sanschagrin.

"Good evening, Professor Arsenault, Madame," replied the inspector. He smelled of cigars but I had never seen him smoke. "I trust you have everything you need?"

"Yes, Inspector." I tapped my laptop's carrying case. "Thanks for arranging the visit so promptly."

"Think nothing of it," he said, then turned to Marie-Claire. "Your old boss was initially quite resistant to the idea of your visit, Madame, but everyone has their point of leverage. I pointed out to Zanon that the sooner you solved the Cipher, the sooner things will return to normal."

"Will they?" asked Marie-Claire.

"I hope so." Sanschagrin turned the car onto a bridge. "Professor, would a lip reader be useful in your research? I should have assigned you one sooner."

"Thank you, Inspector, but that's not necessary. Visual information is rarely sufficient in distinguishing between similar words," I explained. "For example, the words *du* and *tu* involve the same lip and tongue movements, with the only difference being the vocal cords vibrating for *d* and not for the *t* sound. Lip readers cannot distinguish between those differences, and often rely on their ability to figure out the most likely words by their context in conversation. Without knowing what these sculptures are saying or even their language, it's difficult to figure out the right words."

"It was worth a shot," said Sanschagrin. I caught a glimpse of the Louvre's glass pyramid far to our right, glowing golden in the twilight. The inspector parked underground and waved us through the museum checkpoint. "Doctor Zanon will meet us shortly."

Marie-Claire frowned. "I don't recognize the security personnel."

"Many are from the *gendarmerie*. It was the least we could do to safeguard a national treasure." Sanschagrin sighed. "Alas, there are more monuments in Paris than we have personnel. The city's already lost irreplaceable sculptures. That statue in front of the *Collège de France*? Shattered. The stone soldiers at the Alma Bridge, defaced. The fanatics say the stones are possessed, but it is they who have been seized by demons."

Marie-Claire looked down. "It's all my fault."

"You're right about that, Arsenault, and you deserve to hang for it." The diminutive Vittorio Zanon marched up to Marie-Claire. Last January, both Zanon and Marie-Claire vied to become the Director of Greek, Etruscan and Roman Antiquities, and the competition had been fierce. While Marie-Claire knew much about Greek and Roman art, Zanon was hired because of his expertise in the myths and legends of the Italian peninsula, including the pre-Roman civilization of the Etruscans. "Make this visit quick, Arsenault. I have to catalogue some traveling collections that just came in."

"We won't stay long." Marie-Claire glared at Zanon. "Just take us to *de Milo*."

Zanon snapped his fingers. "Follow, but don't touch a thing." The curator led us through the galleries of the Louvre. "All these closures are your fault, Arsenault. You've single-handedly ruined the museum industry."

I couldn't stand the man when Marie-Claire worked

for him, and now I despised him even more. "That's not fair, Zanon. A museum's supposed to document important events in history. Look at the impact the Stone Cipher has already made. Marie-Claire was only doing her job, and she did it a damn shade better than you ever did!"

Zanon snorted. "She's a glory-hound with dangerous ambitions."

"Stop it, both of you!" shouted Marie-Claire. "Pierre, I can defend myself. Zanon, you're an ass, but there are more important things at stake here than our feud!"

The inspector gently squeezed Zanon's shoulder. "The lady is right, Doctor. I believe that in the heat of the moment, we almost missed an important clue. I assume there were statues on loan to other countries that have just found their way home?" He flashed a golden coin in his left hand and closed his fist. "Do those statues pattern with the place they left"—he opened his left fist to show it empty—"or with the statues here in Paris?" He waved his right hand, producing the vanished coin.

"How will that help?" asked Zanon.

I understood what the inspector meant. "We can determine how the messages are being sent! There are two possibilities. The first, *fire-and-forget:* each statue is programmed once to play the message, like a tape recorder. The second, *broadcast:* each statue could be a radio receiving an active signal. If we're lucky, the other museums might have photographed the statues before they were returned here. If we compare these pieces to the statues in those museums and to the ones in the Louvre, we can determine whether the Stone Cipher is preset or broadcast."

160

"Excellent deduction, Professor," Sanschagrin said. "However, it's simpler than that. We compare the statues to each other."

I slapped my forehead. "Of course. If they are the same, then they've picked up the local cipher. That's why *you're* the inspector."

Sanschagrin smiled. "We will profile the intelligence behind the messages." I caught Marie-Claire frowning at his use of the word *intelligence*. I knew that expression well; my wife always had that look when we argued about the existence of God. "How powerful is it? Why communicate with us in such a strange fashion? Maybe the channel of communication could prove more important. Didn't one of your fellow Canadians once say, *the medium is the message,* Professor?"

"Yes, Marshall McLuhan." I thought back to my undergraduate readings. "He hypothesized that all media are extensions of human beings. For example, a book is an extension of the eye, or a radio, the ear. And since messages are communicated through the new medium, the limitations or advantages of that technology are bound to change our society, often in unanticipated ways. I see where you're going with this. These statues could be considered extensions of the entity or entities in the same way."

"Exactly. The more we learn about the channel, the closer we get to deciphering the message," said Sanschagrin. "Doctor Zanon, could you show us those collections?"

The curator sniffed. "Very well, but be quick about it."

21h39 CEST—Friday, 14 September 2007

It took close to an hour to uncrate the returned statues, mostly ancient Egyptian sculptures, and photograph them digitally. All their mouths were identical in shape, stretched thin and teeth showing. I jotted down the specifics of where each piece originated. "Done. They must have all synced to the local cipher. Now we can double-check them against the ones in the museum."

Zanon sighed. "Come with me."

"Not so fast, Zanon." I tapped my laptop case. "Do you have an Internet connection in your office?"

"Of course. But why?" asked Zanon.

"I need to check the Cipher site." In the short time since the Stone Cipher was introduced, Cipher enthusiasts around the world had risen to the challenge. They had contributed time-lapse movies and live webcam feeds of stone statues all around the globe, from Easter Island to Greece. "With any luck, there will be a live feed from one of the museums on this list, and we can do a real-time comparison. Marie-Claire can take the photos and meet us back in your office."

"She's not leaving my sight," protested Zanon.

"I know my way, Zanon," said Marie-Claire. "Besides, the inspector will make sure I don't do anything rash." Before Sanschagrin could protest, Marie-Claire dragged him towards the Sully Wing, camera in hand. "No time to waste, Inspector." They were gone.

Zanon snapped his fingers again, beckoning me to follow. I trudged along behind him. When we arrived, Zanon unlocked his office door and ushered me into the wood-paneled room. Mythological motifs from Ancient

Greece adorned the walls. Zanon gestured at a sandstone gargoyle on a cluttered worktable. "You can move that. There's an extra cable under the table."

The gargoyle brought back terrible memories of my childhood. I had been a homely child, and the neighborhood kids nicknamed me *Gargouille,* the word for gargoyle in French. It didn't help that my name meant *stone.* When I lifted the distasteful gargoyle to clear a spot for my laptop, walnut-shell fragments fell from its mouth. "You used this as a *nutcracker?*"

The curator blushed. "Done purely in the name of research. I was testing the amount of force the statues applied during speech."

"Sure you were." I booted up my laptop and logged onto the Cipher site. The debates in the forums raged on. Everyone had their own opinion about what the talking statues meant, from skeptics who thought the moving lips were as fake as Bigfoot to religious fanatics who believed the end of the world was nigh. Hundreds of links scrolled up my browser window. Zanon shoulder-surfed while I searched for the locations on my list. I had to be careful which ones I chose; not everyone who contributed to the Cipher project had pure intentions. Any idiot with an image editor could fake a clip.

One of the statues returned came from the Royal Ontario Museum in Toronto, and I found a curator there who was broadcasting a piece from their collection live: the marble bust of Emperor Lucius Verus. Currently, the Emperor's mouth was stretched thinner than the mouths of the Parisian statues. Her website also archived snapshots taken throughout the week.

Zanon recognized the curator's name. "I've met her

at a conference before. She's young, but you can trust her data."

"Thanks." I captured images off the web feed and made measurements of the emperor's mouth using cursor coordinates. "A subtle difference. I suspect they are both pronouncing alveolar consonants like *n, t, d, s, z, r* or *l*. However, I can't distinguish between them without knowing the position of the tongue or the state of the air stream mechanism," I explained.

"The lips match!" Marie-Claire came through the door breathless, waving the camera in her hand. Sanschagrin followed close behind.

I took the camera and scrolled through the head shots my wife took of the Louvre statues. All their mouths were identical to the crated sculptures.

"Judging by the ratio of mouth width to the distance between the lips, I'd say that the head in Toronto is pronouncing *n, t* or *d,* while the statues here are making the *s* or *z* sound. However, it's just a guess," I said.

"I hope you enjoyed your little *tête-à-tête* with *Venus de Milo,* Arsenault, because it's your last," Zanon told Marie-Claire. "If you want to see her again, stand in line with the tourists. That is, if our department ever reopens."

"Shut up, Zanon," shouted Marie-Claire. "Sometimes I wish I could just stitch your big—" She suddenly paused in midsentence, as though a bolt of inspiration struck her. "Big. Mouth. Shut." She grabbed the gargoyle's head off the table and stared at its mouth, her diatribe against Zanon forgotten. "That's it! Their mouths!"

I was puzzled. "What's about them?"

"Most sculptors chisel a closed mouth with lips together. Teeth are hard enough; giving a statue all the parts of a real mouth nigh impossible. In all the video clips I've watched, none of the statues ever closed their lips completely, or it happened so rarely that I don't recall seeing it. But don't you have to put your lips together to make certain sounds?" she asked.

I nodded. "Bilabial consonants are made with both lips making a full seal. In French and English, these are the sounds *p, b* and *m*. Let's see if your observations are right." I picked five time-lapse movie files that I had previously authenticated and tiled them on my laptop display. In the top row were the Lincoln Memorial, a panoramic shot of Mount Rushmore, and a clip of Emperor Lucius Verus from the ROM archive. The bottom row were *Man with the Broken Nose* from the Rodin Museum and our own recording of King David's head from the Cluny Museum. I set each clip to the same Universal Time index five days ago and ran them in parallel. The mouths of the statues slowly moved as the movies played. Natural light and shadow alternated with artificial illumination. In the Mount Rushmore clip, all the Presidents sang in unison. However, their motions differed from the two Parisian sculptures moving their mouths in sync.

"She's right," said Sanschagrin. "Their lips never close."

I nodded, intrigued. "Good job, *ma chère!* There are no bilabials in this particular data set. Coincidence or not?" Where had I come across this same gap before? A piece of trivia came back to me. "Numbers! Bilabial stops rarely appear in low numbers in French and English! If you count up from zero in French, your lips won't make a full seal until *mille.*" Thousand.

"What about the number seven?" asked Marie-Claire.

"*Sept* does have a *p* in spelling, but it's pronounced

165

set. The *p* is silent," I said. "English cardinal numbers do not use the letters *m, b* or *p* until *million, billion* and *septillion.*"

Zanon licked his lips. "So the statues are dictating numbers? Which ones and why?"

"Low numbers, given the lack of bilabials," I said. "Assume that the statues are speaking to us in a language that people in each region would understand. French in France, English in England and so forth. Not exactly fair to the minority languages, but a practical assumption. If these are numbers, we should be able to match the movements of their mouths with ours. We'll pair up. Inspector, if you could work with Zanon on French, Marie-Claire and I can work on English."

Sanschagrin nodded, and Zanon booted up his computer to access the Cipher site.

I pulled up a chair for Marie-Claire. "We'll start with the ROM."

Marie-Claire smiled. "It's been a while since we've been there."

"I know." I stroked her hand. We first met at the University of Toronto while I was finishing my PhD in linguistics, and she was a guest instructor at the Department of Museum Studies next door. Stuck on the same elevator one day, we discovered that we both spoke French. Marie-Claire invited me to an exhibit at the ROM later that week, and our relationship snowballed from there. "Let's start with the clips from September eighth," I suggested, switching to English to get in the proper mindset. I isolated three syllables' worth to start with, and looped the clip.

Marie-Claire began counting up from *one* in English. I correlated her facial movements with the statue's.

"The first syllable is *nine*," I determined. "Wait. Correction: it could be *ninety* or *nineteen*." Marie-Claire pronounced the words for me. "Definitely *nineteen*. Next syllable's *eight*." I added more syllables to the loop. "Make that *eighteen*. *Seventeen*. *Sixteen*."

"Fifteen, fourteen," added Marie-Claire, turning pale. "My god, Pierre."

I nodded slowly. "Inspector—"

"Vingt-deux, vingt-et-un, vingt," reported Sanschagrin. He continued the count until it ended at *seize*, sixteen. He and Zanon came to the same conclusion independently with the French numbers.

Wiping sweat from his brow with a handkerchief, Zanon voiced what all of us feared.

"It's a countdown."

07h50 CEST—Saturday, 15 September 2007

Even though all of us were exhausted, our discovery kept us awake. The mystery was deepening, and still we lacked satisfactory answers. After we drank some wretched coffee in the staff room, Marie-Claire led us back to her muse of perfect marble.

The glow of day came faintly through the windows of the *Venus de Milo* gallery, illuminating the twisting stone torso of the pale Greek goddess. I gazed up at her face. She was pronouncing the French number for fifteen, *quinze*.

"Look at her," said Zanon, eyes red, voice raw. "Acting

coy like she knows what's going on. I wonder if the same thing happened in the past, prompting people to decapitate the statues? Maybe that's what happened to the *Winged Victory of Samothrace*."

"Maybe we have enough pieces of the puzzle now," said Sanschagrin. "Doctor Zanon, did you and Marie-Claire confirm that the same thing was happening elsewhere?" Sanschagrin had paired them up to test the countdown hypothesis. Zanon spoke Italian and Arabic, and Marie-Claire knew enough German to get by. A day earlier and I would have said collaboration between those two was impossible, but in the face of the coming crisis, they had called a temporary truce.

"The statues in Italy are in the middle of saying *dieci,* ten," said Zanon. "The Sphinx at Giza is in the middle of the Arabic number for nine."

"In Germany, they're starting *vierzehn,* fourteen," said Marie-Claire. "Why aren't the numbers counting down in unison?"

"But they are." I had been assigned to work out the timing of the countdown. "Think in terms of syllables. The numbers used in each language have different syllables. In English, the numbers *one* through *six* are single syllables, but the number *seven* has two. If we count the number of syllables left before zero—regardless of the language—there would be sixteen syllables left, including the current one. The statues speak at the rate of one syllable every twelve hours, and my measurements show that each syllable starts at dawn and ends at dusk, or vice versa. Sixteen syllables means eight days from now."

"September twenty-third," said Sanschagrin. "The autumn equinox."

"That's not all," I added, pulling out my Palm Pilot. "The deadlines are staggered, more of a gradient than clean-cut one-hour time zone divisions. Because the statues end their syllables at sunset or sunrise, zero hour changes depending on where you are on the planet. In fact, we can establish two critical zones where the countdown will first reach zero. The Atlantic time zone: New Brunswick, Nova Scotia and Bermuda. The Australian Western time zone: China, Taiwan and the Philippines."

"Why those?" asked Zanon.

"Because the autumnal equinox this year occurs on September twenty-third at 09h51 Universal Time," I said, looking at the notes on my Palm Pilot. "At that moment, the sun will rise in the Atlantic time zone and set in the Australian Western zone on opposite sides of the world. The sun sets in Manila at 17h52 Australian Western Standard Time, one minute after the equinox, or 11h52 Central European Summer Time. Since sunset here on that day is 19h47 CEST, we'd have eight hours before the countdown reaches us."

Zanon whistled. "Bravo. You navigated the time zone calculations with flair."

"They can be confusing, especially with Daylight Saving Time and arbitrary time zone divisions," I said.

"What happens when the count reaches zero?" asked Marie-Claire. "The Rapture? The Apocalypse?"

"Earthquakes?" suggested Sanschagrin. "Meteors?"

"Not a damned thing?" Zanon offered.

The inspector stroked his goatee in thought. "We're

back to the problem of profiling the intelligence behind this. First, we've confirmed that the statues returned from the ROM are following the Paris pattern, suggesting the messages are being broadcast in real-time. Second, it understands number systems in countless languages and is intelligent enough to coordinate a syllabic countdown. Third, it has selected the equinox as zero hour, when night and day are equal. Given these clues, what can we tell about its motives?"

"Only that it's toying with us," said Zanon.

I shook my head. "I don't think so. Let's assume that this intelligence is aware of the principles of communication, which we call in linguistics Grice's Maxims of Conversation. There are four basic principles. First, the Maxim of Quality, dealing with truth: *Do not say what you believe to be false, and do not say that for which you lack adequate evidence.* This intelligence is likely giving us accurate information, and so the countdown must be to *something*.

"Then, the Maxim of Quantity, involving information. *Make your contribution as informative as is required for the current purposes of the exchange, and do not make your contribution more informative than is required.* The countdown might be exactly the amount of information it thinks we need.

"The Maxim of Relation: *Be relevant.* The intelligence intends something with the countdown.

"Finally, the Maxim of Manner requires clarity. *Avoid obscurity of expression, avoid ambiguity, be brief, and be orderly.* The intelligence has thus far kept the message constant: that something will happen around the world at equinox, and that it wants the whole planet to take notice."

"But why not just *say* what's going to happen?" asked Zanon. "Why speak so slowly and inaudibly?"

"God works in mysterious ways," said Marie-Claire, as though that was an answer to anything.

I had a different idea. "Perhaps it's a test. I suspect the intelligence *wants* us to pay attention. If we never noticed the countdown, then it's our own fault. Maybe it wants to know what we'd do if we did notice." I took a deep breath. "Suppose Mother Earth is trying to communicate with us. The Gaea Hypothesis."

"Gaea's the goddess of the earth in Greek mythology, but what's the Gaea Hypothesis?" asked Zanon.

"The Gaea Hypothesis suggests that all life on Earth forms a single living planetary being," I explained. "Perhaps the planet isn't just alive, it's conscious."

"Why communicate through carved stone, then, and not wood? For that matter, why not terracotta or bronze?"

Marie-Claire agreed with Zanon. "I don't buy it. Wood would make more sense."

"It's not just the life forms that make up Gaea. The atmosphere, the oceans and even the soil are part of the self-organizing system that sustains life on Earth," I said. "Some people even think the Earth's crust is part of this cycle."

"Perhaps this entity manipulates stone best because stone is unadulterated. Alloys are mixed, clays are shaped and fired, and wood is dead cells," suggested Sanschagrin. "We may never know."

Zanon looked at the *Venus de Milo* with new reverence. "Spectacular. What if the whole history of human sculpture has been a conversation between the planet and humanity? Think about it: some of the earliest forms of art were anthropomorphic figurines. Each stone statue lends its eyes and ears to Gaea so She could see us and listen to us. Maybe She has just learned enough to speak to us in our own languages!"

"Not a bad guess," I said. "Human children process what they hear, developing increasingly more complex grammars as they mature. It could be the same with a planetary intelligence. Perhaps it took all of human history for Gaea to adapt to our timescale instead of a geological one."

Sanschagrin paced. "It fits. It's logical for a planetary intelligence to set zero hour on the day the sun is directly over the equator."

"Even if you're right—and I don't think you are—we can't tell anyone," said Marie-Claire.

We looked at her in surprise. "But you were so impatient to tell the world about the Stone Cipher in the first place," I said.

"And look at all the misery I've caused already. What I told the world then was simply that statues were speaking. Imagine the chaos if we tell them it's a countdown to an unknown disaster." Marie-Claire closed her eyes. "Worldwide panic. People will try to flee from the unknown, looting and killing others to save themselves. I can't be the harbinger this time."

"But we can't hide something so monumental!" I said. "Consider the consequences of keeping it quiet. What if people found out that we knew but didn't say? Time and again, history has shown us that cover-ups do more harm than good. Right now we still have eight days to prepare. We *have* to release our findings."

"How will it help? How will people protect themselves

against a threat that no one can even name?" Marie-Claire argued.

"I don't know," I admitted. "But forewarned is forearmed. You did the right thing the first time, announcing the Stone Cipher. If you hadn't done it weeks ago, we'd never have collected so much data in such a short time. It was your courage that inspired the world to solve Gaea's puzzle. By revealing the countdown now, other people around the world might discover a way to prevent what's coming, or how to talk to Gaea." I held her hand. "We are not alone."

My wife squeezed my hand but let go. She turned to the inspector. "Please, Henri, I beg you not to report this to your superiors yet. I need time to think this through."

"As do we all," agreed Sanschagrin. "Let's sleep on it and approach the problem anew this evening. Goodbye, Doctor Zanon. I'll be in touch." He shook the curator's hand. "As for you two, I'll drop you off at the safe house and pick you up at six."

15h58 CEST—Saturday, 15 September 2007

I slept like a rock.

When I woke up, Marie-Claire's side of the bed was empty. *"Chère?"*

No answer. I threw on some clothes and wandered into the living room, expecting her to be on the couch reading or standing by the safehouse windows looking into the street below. But Marie-Claire wasn't there, nor was she in the kitchen or bathroom.

I raced to the front door. Her shoes and coat were missing, but she didn't leave any messages.

Where was she? We weren't supposed to leave the apartment for our own safety, but neither were we prisoners. I had argued against a guard outside our door, when the manpower could be used in more effective ways in the city, preferring to call to arrange deliveries and safe transportation. I was beginning to regret my decision now.

I grabbed my cell phone and threw on some shoes. Where could Marie-Claire have gone? Back to the Louvre? No, she could have waited a couple of hours for Sanschagrin. The Gallery of Kings? Nothing there would tell us anything we hadn't learned at the Louvre. Would she have just gone out for a walk?

No. I knew my wife. She wouldn't have gone out alone without good reason, although lately, her judgment seemed clouded by her obsession with the Cipher.

I realized where she must have gone. My heart skipped a beat. I hurried out of the apartment, not bothering to lock the door. I raced down the spiral stairs and burst onto Rue d'Odessa, speed-dialing Sanschagrin on my cell phone.

"Inspector!" I shouted over the phone. "Marie-Claire's gone."

"What? Where?" Sanschagrin asked.

I looked for a taxi stand. "Notre-Dame Cathedral. She's been meaning to go."

"Mon Dieu," breathed Sanschagrin. "We've got to find her before someone realizes who she is. I'm at home; I'll pick you up in fifteen minutes."

"No time. Faster to meet me at Notre-Dame, outside the police headquarters," I told Sanschagrin and hung up. I jumped in a black cab and yelled instructions to the driver.

A few minutes later, the taxi dropped me off outside the Metro Saint-Michel. I had to go on foot from there; the bridges onto Île de La Cité were overflowing with pilgrims and tourists. I pushed through the crowd onto the Saint-Michel Bridge and made it onto the island, heading east along the Seine. The Prefecture of Police headquarters loomed north of me: its imposing presence here was one of the main deterrents of crime on this island in the heart of Paris.

The place du Parvis Notre-Dame, a plaza between the police headquarters and the cathedral, had been packed with pilgrims seeking miracles and epiphanies since the Cipher revelation. After that last attack on Marie-Claire, I was wary of crowds. Individually, the worshippers were harmless, but it took only a few madmen to fire up a mob, and you couldn't predict what mobs would do.

Despite the hundreds of people choking the square, I managed to spot the inimitable inspector waiting in front of the police building. I rushed up to him. "How did you beat me here? Another of your tricks?"

Sanschagrin winked. "A magician never reveals his secrets."

"Did you find her?" I asked.

"Not yet. I could send my men out in force, but that could turn disastrous if the crowd panics. If she's here, she hasn't been spotted yet. Likely she was smart enough to disguise herself. I've alerted a few of my men, and they're searching the square with binoculars from the upper levels of the Prefecture."

"She might be inside," I said.

The inspector nodded. "I'll check around back. Call if you find her."

We squeezed through the surge of people to the front of the cathedral before parting ways. A long line of people waited to enter the southern doors, and I did my slyest to cut in line without upsetting anyone. Though I was watching the stream of worshippers exiting the northern doors for Marie-Claire, I couldn't help glancing up to admire the stone carvings adorning the front of Notre-Dame.

High above the three great doors were the stone replicas of the original twenty-eight kings of Judah, their heads intact in this incarnation. The entrances were surmounted by stone carvings of biblical figures. I was most intrigued by the closed doors in the center: the Portal of Last Judgment, depicting the weighing of souls and the resurrection of the dead. It was a wonder that the carvings escaped vandalism, but how? I looked around: legions of people, young and old, devout and curious, came to worship here. Together they kept the peace. Vandals who sought to destroy the wonders of this place could not freely do so, because of the watchful eyes of a thousand penitents.

This power of the many over the few was the basis of morality and society. Regardless of the specific brand of ethics that each community might espouse, the consensus represented by social norms was backed up by strict laws and punishments.

I thought about the changes in world weather patterns for the past few years. Flooding in Europe, category five hurricanes in the Gulf of Mexico, just to name a few.

Scientists suggested that greenhouse gases and global warming were at fault. Could they be early warning signs from Mother Nature that we humans have ignored?

Maybe the Stone Cipher countdown was indeed Gaea's ultimatum: play nice or suffer the consequences.

I took one last look at the Portal of Last Judgment before the line swept me forward, and wondered if there was still hope left for humankind.

16h37 CEST—Saturday, 15 September 2007

I found Marie-Claire in confession.

The confessionals in Notre-Dame Cathedral were made of glass, allowing others in the church to observe but not hear. My wife sat talking with the priest face to face, another innovation at Notre-Dame that I hadn't associated with Catholicism but was common in the Anglican Church. Marie-Claire hid her golden hair under a dark blue headscarf and her figure under baggy clothes in an attempt to subtly change her looks.

She had been crying.

I had an inkling of what she and the priest were discussing. I felt like a voyeur, watching her make confession through the pane of glass. A confession ought to remain a private matter between a penitent and her confessor. As I was about to move away to give her back her privacy, such as it was, our eyes met.

Marie-Claire said something to the priest, who stood and opened the door. "Please, come in," he said.

"Thank you, Father." I ran my hand over my hair to pat down its wildness. "Marie-Claire, you gave me quite a scare! You should have left a note."

"I apologize, Pierre," she said. "I was so eager to seek guidance, I didn't think to leave a note."

"I thought you didn't want to let the world know, and yet you came here without consulting me or Sanschagrin."

Marie-Claire shook her head. "I trust everything I said to my priest will remain in confidence."

The priest nodded. "You two have a lot to discuss, but this is not the place for it; the crowd will be too curious. I know a place where you two can talk in private. Follow me."

"Merci." We followed the priest past the crush of people to the North Tower and up a stone spiral staircase. We passed the gift shop, arriving at a locked door. The priest took out a key and unlocked it. "The towers have been closed since the Cipher was revealed. Please, take as long as you need."

We thanked the priest and climbed the narrow stairs, Marie-Claire leading the way. We emerged onto the gallery of the North Tower where the gargoyles kept watch. I called Sanschagrin to let him know I found Marie-Claire, while she ventured onto the narrow walkway that led to the South Tower, peering over the balustrade into the sea of people below. She clasped her hands as though in prayer. "This was the only place I could find solace."

"You could have come to me."

"No, I couldn't." Marie-Claire sighed. "You act as though I've gone mad for having faith at all. I accept that not everyone believes in the same God as I do. Couldn't you accept that my view of the world might be just as valid as yours?" She looked down into the crowd. "We all deal with our troubles in our own way. Here, I don't feel out of place. I'm among people who believe as deeply as I do. All I want is for you to respect my beliefs."

I was taken aback. *"Ma chère,* never think that! I know things have been hard of late between us, but I would never scorn you for having such great faith."

"What *do* you believe?" asked Marie-Claire.

A difficult question. "I am a scientist. I believe in observation and data, and what I've learned of the world has led me to believe in something other than the version of God suggested by the Bible. Even with the Stone Cipher enigma, I cannot embrace the rigid interpretation of religion that Roman Catholicism mandates. The Cipher has taught me that there are powers beyond those which we currently have the ability to understand, but the Gaea hypothesis is truer to my conception of the world, just as God is to yours."

"But why?" asked Marie-Claire. "If it's easy to believe in Gaea, then why not God? I think because you rejected God, you turned to science to justify your lack of faith. That's why you've embraced Gaea so readily. Well, I must be true to myself also. I still believe the Cipher of Saint Peter is a sign from God," said Marie-Claire.

It was the first time I heard her call it the Cipher of Saint Peter, *le code Saint-Pierre.* "I thought you named it after me!" I said, flustered.

Marie-Claire blushed. "Well, maybe in part. Anyway, this Gaea of yours doesn't disprove the existence of God. Can you accept that both might exist at the same time?"

"I would be sorry if my beliefs undermined your own,"

179

I said. "Perhaps all religions have something to teach us. I promise to keep an open mind. Come, let us warn people what's coming. Let them decide for themselves how to deal with it. Because I am who I am, I refuse to hide the truth about what we've discovered."

"My Galileo." Marie-Claire brushed strands of hair away from my eyes. "Can we make this work, Pierre? Make *us* work?"

"I think we stand a fair chance." I held her hands in mine. "I can't predict if the equinox will bring blessing or catastrophe, but one thing I do know. I will be with my love and no other."

"And I," said Marie-Claire, and kissed me.

02h30 CEST—Wednesday, 19 September 2007

We made the official announcement three days ago. Although Sanschagrin, Marie-Claire and I all presented our findings, I made sure that the press knew I was the chief investigator: let them paint the target on me this time, not Marie-Claire. I focused on the scientific evidence and made no overt claims that it was a countdown, only that the statues were reciting numbers in a descending order and that the series converged on the Autumnal Equinox.

The world, being the mosaic of cultures that it was, reacted in a thousand different ways. Many remained skeptical, laughing it off as a hoax. Some compared the countdown to Y2K, when computer chips could only handle two-digit years. Experts had warned that computers could not handle the change from 1999 to 2000. Much effort had gone into safeguarding computer systems against the predicted disaster, but when the rollover happened, planes did not crash into the sea and cities did not plunge into darkness. Nothing happened then, the critics argued, and nothing would happen now.

However, not everyone ignored Gaea's Countdown. One benefit to the world's religions was that each experienced a resurgence of worshippers. Record-breaking numbers of Catholics made Confession and sought atonement for their sins, so that they might face Judgment Day with unburdened souls. Even more pilgrims invaded places with religious statuary, all over the world. In Rio de Janeiro, it was the statue of Christ the Redeemer on Corcovado Hill; in Japan, worshippers gathered at sites such as Nihon-ji Temple, worshipping at the feet of the giant Buddha chiseled into the stone cliff.

Adherents of Islam and of Judaism held to the view they espoused previously: that the animation of statues was further reason to denounce graven images. Islam had long been against the representation of humans and creatures in religious art. In countries like Egypt, most of the statuary still intact consisted of ancient Egyptian artifacts and structures like the Great Sphinx, safeguarded against acts of vandalism by the authorities. I had hoped that Gaea's Countdown would not foment further religious strife, but it couldn't be helped. There would always be reasons for clashes between the world's religions, Stone Cipher or not. Increases in vandalism and violence worldwide were other undesirable consequences, but they couldn't be blamed on one religion or another; zealots of all faiths would always sully the name of the more moderate worshippers.

Since the Countdown was worldwide, many believers argued against mass evacuations. Where would people go? One answer: outer space. Countries with space capabilities hurried to prepare shuttle launches.

Some thought alien rock creatures would burst from the Earth's core in a full-scale invasion, or use super science to create stone soldiers imbued with super circuitry.

Vegas took bets on the outcome.

Still others simply went on with their lives.

The last few days flew by. Marie-Claire and I suffered through carefully chosen interviews amid the tightest security measures, and even met briefly with the president of France. We treasured every moment we stole for ourselves, like mornings when light first pierced the windows and we made passionate love.

We continued our research in the Gallery of Kings, now crowded with a dozen new researchers, including earth scientists, astronomers, a biologist and even a psychic. Marie-Claire took the time to get to know them all.

I called a meeting to tell the research team about a joint Japanese-Australian discovery. "There's new evidence on the nature of the Countdown." I turned on a lamp and illuminated a globe, a new addition among our research equipment. "We know that the Countdown reaches zero at 09h51 Universal Time, and based on the statues' mouth movements, deduced two sets of deadlines: one at dawn, the other at dusk. We can divide the world into hemispheres based on those divisions of day and night. Let's call the two lines the Sunrise Arc and the Sunset Arc. Whatever happens on the equinox will begin affecting places immediately west of the Arcs, while places immediately east will be spared for half a day."

Marie-Claire examined the boundaries between light and dark on the globe, spun the Earth from west to east, and nodded.

"We've confirmed that the Sunrise Arc will start in North America. Halifax, Nova Scotia, will be one of the first victims of the Sunrise Arc at 10h02 Universal Time, eleven minutes after true equinox," I said. "However, Louisbourg in the northeastern part of Nova Scotia has its sunrise at 09h47 Universal Time, four minutes *before* equinox. Everything in Louisbourg and east of it in Canada, like Newfoundland, will be spared until the Sunset Arc has swept across half the world."

"But there's something different about the Sunset Arc?" someone asked.

"Yes. If we went by the same logic for the Sunset Arc, Manila in the Philippines would be among the first cities affected, still more or less true. However, our original prediction would place Tokyo, Japan and Adelaide, Australia *east* of the Sunset Arc. Tokyo's sunset is timed at 08h38 Universal Time, and it's comparable in Adelaide. Yet, the statues in those cities pattern with those *west* of the Sunset Arc. They will be affected first by Gaea's Countdown, not last as we had thought."

"So where did we go wrong in our calculations?" asked a geologist.

"The patterns changed somewhere east of Adelaide and west of Melbourne," I showed the team the locations on the globe. "The Australians determined that the Sunset Arc actually corresponds to the end of astronomical twilight instead of sunset. Astronomical twilight ends

183

when the center of the sun is eighteen degrees below the horizon, when the sun's light no longer contributes to the illumination of the sky. Manila will not be affected at 17h52 AWST as we originally calculated, but seventy-one minutes later at the end of astronomical twilight, 19h03. Likewise, the Sunset Arc won't reach Paris at sunset, but at twilight's end, 21h33 CEST."

"Sunrise would be the end of astronomical twilight too, wouldn't it, when it turns to full day? So what's the significance of twilight?" Marie-Claire asked.

"To be honest, I have no clue. However, it should help countries prepare for the Countdown. Maybe the Canadian government should set up shop temporarily in Newfoundland." I grinned.

11h45 CEST—Sunday, 23 September 2007

The equinox was but minutes away, and strangely, the four of us convened again in one place: Sanschagrin, Zanon, Marie-Claire and I. But on this day of judgment—whichever form it would take—we were spending it at the Prefecture of Police headquarters on the advice of Henri Sanschagrin.

Marie-Claire and I had observed the ten o'clock Mass at Notre-Dame from Sanschagrin's office window. The number of worshippers on the island had grown so large that Masses were held both inside the cathedral and outside in the square. The Gregorian chants from the Mass still echoed in my head as we convened in the Media Room.

The police headquarters was quiet compared to my

previous visits. "Some of them have decided to spend today with their families," explained the inspector. "The rest are out on crowd control."

"And you, Zanon? I thought you were heading back to Trento," said Marie-Claire.

Zanon grinned. "You'd like that, wouldn't you? No, the inspector has offered me a seat on the plane." The French government was poised to fly researchers across the Atlantic, hoping they might beat the Sunset Arc to North America and find a way to escape Gaea's Countdown. "Once we know what we're dealing with, I'd like a firsthand look."

I took a seat beside my wife and caressed her hand. Sanschagrin flipped on the banks of TV monitors and set them to world news channels covering the Countdown. In North America, reporters camped out in Halifax, while foreign correspondents filed their stories from Tokyo or Adelaide. A CBC report came out of Citadel Hill in Halifax, while Marie-Claire watched a CNN report filed from Tokyo's Ginza entertainment district. There was a stark contrast between the two: Halifax, still in morning twilight, was deathly quiet, while the bright neon lights in the Ginza district blotted out all indications that evening twilight was coming to an end.

Time ticked on.

We watched with trepidation.

The countdown on the TV screens neared zero. Marie-Claire squeezed my hand.

Three seconds.

Two.

One.

On every screen, all flesh turned to stone.

The cameras still filmed, presumably still in the grasps of petrified cameramen. In Tokyo, the silver-haired CNN reporter became solid rock, as did the pedestrians who were walking behind him. A car plowed into a pedestrian as its driver turned into stone, and the petrified victim shattered into a thousand pieces. Marie-Claire gasped.

In Halifax, the rising sun illuminated the CBC reporter from behind, now a study in marble still bedecked in his suit. Silhouettes of birds still flashed across the brightening sky, flaunting the fact that this curse was for humans alone.

For a long time, none of us could speak.

At last, I broke the silence. "Such . . . *power*."

"The answer was in the medium after all," Sanschagrin said. "Gaea chose stone because that would be our fate. One mystery solved, but chaos will soon descend. God help us all."

"So the world ends in stone. Not fire, not flood," said Zanon, absent-mindedly cracking his knuckles. "Petrifaction is a common motif in world mythology. The gaze of Medusa in Greek myth, Scandinavian trolls turning to stone in sunlight, and animals turning into islands in Malay legend, to name just a few."

"Is this our final judgment, then?" asked Marie-Claire, wiping away a tear.

I comforted her. "It can't be."

"You might be right." Zanon furrowed his brow in thought. "There is a local legend in my region of northern Italy about the Dolomite Mountains. The Dolomites were once partly great coral reefs from an ancient sea, now blanketed by basaltic lava flows. Various tales have been told of those mountains, and one version tells of the King of Dwarves, King Laurino, who lived in the valleys. Laurino fell in love with the Princess Similda, and cultivated a startling red rose for his beloved. He covered the mountain peaks with the roses in her honor, but in spite of his devotion, Similda would not return his love. In anger and desperation, the king cursed his splendid garden so that no one will ever see those roses by day or by night. As he wished, the spell turned the flowers into gray stone, but the King had forgotten one thing."

"The twilight," guessed Marie-Claire.

Zanon nodded. "No longer day though not yet night, the garden of roses lives again in the brief grace of twilight, and the mountains glow red because of their bones of coral."

"An obscure tale," said Sanschagrin. "Are you suggesting that Gaea might let us live again in twilight?"

"I'm not saying anything of the sort. It's a slim hope, but a hope nonetheless," said Zanon.

Sanschagrin looked at his watch. "It's time we headed to the airport, everyone."

"I'm not going," said Marie-Claire.

"*Chère,* we might have a chance to beat this yet," I said.

Marie-Claire shook her head. "No, Pierre. Don't you see? Our place is here. We have to endure Last Judgment to truly understand what it is! You promised me that we would face this together. Will you keep your word?"

My first instinct was to flee Gaea's punishment, but Marie-Claire had a point. How could we establish a dialogue with Gaea if we avoid confrontation? I had said myself that stone was the medium that Gaea manipulated

187

best. What if Her intent was communication, not retribution? If Zanon's legend touched on the truth, then perhaps petrifaction was a temporary condition. My decision came down to two things: how strong was my love for Marie-Claire, and what did I truly believe about Gaea?

I smiled to hide my fear. "You're right, *ma chère*. Gaea could have chosen harsher ways to punish mankind. We will stay."

Marie-Claire kissed me. "Thank you, my love."

"Then I hope I will see both of you again very soon." The inspector came over to shake my hand, and for my wife, he produced a rose from his sleeve. "May God be with you."

19h45 CEST—Sunday, 23 September 2007

Hand in hand, Marie-Claire and I watched the sun set in the west from the top of Montmartre. We had chosen the location because I wanted to see Paris from its highest hill, while Marie-Claire wanted to be near a place of worship. The basilica of *Sacré-Coeur* in its ivory glory seemed like the ideal place to face judgment.

Although astronomical twilight would begin in Halifax and Tokyo at 21h05 our time, a good half-hour before the Sunset Arc swept across Paris, there was no guarantee that news from those parts of the world would reach us. Broadcasts from those places had gone dead in the past few hours, running out of power or suffering other problems incurred by the lack of human control. Perhaps a few webcams or amateur radio broadcasts still operated in those regions, and they might tell us if twilight would indeed revive the petrified people. But neither of us wanted to spend our final hours in front of television sets or computer monitors.

Some other Parisians had the same idea, seeking a last glorious night overlooking the City of Lights. I wondered aloud whether Sanschagrin and Zanon were safe, and Marie-Claire said a prayer for them.

After the sunset, Marie-Claire and I returned to the eastern side of the hill and chose a place on the steps of the basilica. If our last panoramic view before turning to stone was the sunset in the west, should we return to flesh in morning, our first sight would be sunrise in the east.

I sat a step higher than Marie-Claire and kept her warm in my arms. She took off her watch and mine and tossed them aside. "If we kept them, we'll end up petrified with our eyes on the time."

I laughed. "True enough." We watched the sky deepen to blackness studded with the stars, and we talked as we hadn't done in years, of dreams and fears, of faith and love.

Deep into our conversation the change seized us. One moment I was enjoying the heat of Marie-Claire's neck against my cheek, the next we were chiseled out of the same stone. Though we could still see, hear and think, I did not know where my old flesh ended and Marie-Claire's began. I was *Gargouille* and she *de Milo,* twisted together within the same marble. I felt Marie-Claire's mind and knew I could love no other woman.

Another presence touched our minds, seeking to understand us. In turn, She let us glimpse Her.

She was mountains raked by glaciers and streams, forests licked by lightning and rain, oceans roaring with fathomless voices.

She was, and would be.

I knew now that stones could weep.

What would happen at twilight?

Would She deem us unworthy and lock us in stone, fossils to educate Her future children?

Give us only the twilight to live, granting our species flesh for scant hours each day?

Return our lives to us, now that we knew the edge of Her guillotine?

Neither Marie-Claire nor I could say which fate would befall humanity.

Only twilight would bring the answer.

Obsidian Shards

written by

Aliette de Bodard

illustrated by

MARCUS COLLINS

ABOUT THE AUTHOR

Novelist Orson Scott Card has played an influential, albeit indirect, role in the career of French writer Aliette de Bodard. She started writing at sixteen after she read a writing how-to book by Orson in her local library. In 2004, Aliette began entering the Writers of the Future Contest and has since submitted stories to the Contest every quarter. By the time she attended a literary boot camp run by Orson in 2006, Aliette was on her way to literary success. Her stories have just started appearing or are scheduled to appear in various publications including Britain's Interzone *and Australia's* Andromeda Spaceways Inflight Magazine.

When she's not busy writing, Aliette holds a day job as a computer vision engineer. She's a huge reader in all genres and credits writers like Le Guin, McKillip and Zelazny as big influences. She also extends thanks to numerous English poets old and new for giving her a love of the English language. When she's not writing, reading, or working, Aliette loves to travel—visiting old monuments and discovering different cultures.

ABOUT THE ILLUSTRATOR

As a young boy, Marcus Alexander Collins always was interested in the visual arts around him. He spent much of his childhood in Miami, Florida attending art workshops and drawing. In his early teens, he auditioned and was later accepted into a magnet art program for middle schoolers which introduced Marcus to various artistic techniques and use of materials. He repeated the process for high school and was accepted into Design and Architecture Senior High (DASH)—devoted entirely to the visual arts.

At DASH, Marcus majored in industrial design, which emphasized the fundamentals of perspective and encouraged strong drawing technique. For the summer of his junior year, Marcus was selected to attend a two-week workshop at Art Center College of Design in Pasadena, California. Inspired by the workshop and the high level of the work he saw, Marcus made Art Center his number one choice after high school. This year will be his third year as a full-time student at Art Center, where he majors in product design with a strong focus in entertainment design.

Obsidian Shards

The obsidian shard, half the size of my palm, lay in my hand: a sharp, deadly thing still stained with blood. Its black surface shimmered with green reflections, and it quivered with the aura I associated with the underworld: blood and pain and death. Odd, to say the least. One did not find such objects in a dead warrior's house.

I raised my eyes to look at Magistrate Macihuin, who stood in the courtyard, a few steps away from me, watching me intently.

"Where did you find it?" I asked.

He shrugged. "It was embedded in his heart, and quite deeply—the guards and I had some trouble extracting it."

"How did you think of opening the chest?" I asked.

Macihuin's face was grim. "From looking at the corpse, I would have said his heart had failed him. But the neighbours heard him scream. And once we undressed him, there was a small splotch of blood over the heart—not large enough to be an entry wound. Just . . . a mark. What do you make of it, Acatl?"

I was a priest for the Dead: I assisted in preparing the corpses, in saying the proper prayers and making the proper sacrifices. And if the underworld was involved

193

directly in a death, as seemed to be the case here, I advised magistrates such as Macihuin.

"There's magic involved, to put the shard straight into the heart with so little damage to the skin." I closed my hand around the shard. I had handled obsidian blades before. This felt wrong—too smooth, too charged with latent power. I had felt this once before, but . . . "There is underworld magic in this, but I don't know what kind exactly. Not yet," I said.

"Do you want to see the body?" Macihuin asked.

We moved from the courtyard to the inside of the house, where two guards watched over the victim's body.

There was not much to see. It lay on the reed mat in the bedroom, its face bearing the blank expression of corpses. Behind it, the rich fresco on the adobe wall depicted Tezcatlipoca, God of War and Fate, and His eternal enemy Quetzalcoatl, God of Creation and Knowledge. Tezcatlipoca's clawed hands carried the obsidian mirror that held His power, and His face was creased in savage laughter, as if the death amused Him. Quetzalcoatl stood next to Him, holding a skull in His hand. His eyes were sad.

Macihuin's guards had opened up the chest to remove the shard: jagged cuts marked the edge of the wound, and the strong smell reminded me of the altar room of a great temple, encrusted with the blood of hundreds of sacrifices.

The heart had been cut in two, but everything else seemed normal. I had seen enough open chests to learn something of human bodies.

Macihuin said, "His name was Huitxic. He was a warrior and a respected member of his clan. Beyond that, I know nothing of why he might have such a shard in his heart. I was hoping you'd tell me."

I could sense his impatience, his worry. For him, this murder involving magical obsidian was unfamiliar territory, the intrusion of something dangerous into his life. For me . . . I did not know the dead man. However, the shard was all too familiar: seven years ago, I had found a similar one in my student Payaxin's chest.

"It's from the Wind of Knives." I felt a chill in my heart as I told him this. "The guardian who sees that the boundary between the underworld and the world of the living is maintained."

"The Wind of Knives? And why should He come here and kill Huitxic?" Macihuin's face had hardened, but I could hear the fear in his voice. He had probably hoped I would deny the underworld's involvement in this death, that I would say it was a purely mundane murder. No such luck.

"Huitxic must have transgressed," I said. "He must somehow have blurred the line between the underworld and the mortal world."

Macihuin's gaze would not meet mine. He had sounded far too worried, even for such an unusual death. "What are you not telling me?" I asked, softly.

At length he said, "He's not the first man to die like that. The first were dismissed as heart attacks. This one would have been, too, if the neighbours had not heard the screams."

I did not like this. It was one thing for the Wind to

kill a man, but several of them? "How many have there been?"

"Two before this one. They all had the same mark, but I did not make the connection until this death, and they were buried normally. They were warriors all," Macihuin said. "Pochta had just taken his first prisoner, and shaved his childhood hair. But Itlani, the first one, was a *tequiua*."

A *tequiua*. One entitled to tribute. An important man, then. I shook my head in disgust. "Three deaths."

"Yes, and not peasants' deaths either. I need explanations, Acatl. And fast. If they have indeed transgressed, I need to know how."

"We all need to know," I said, softly. "If those dead men have summoned anything from the underworld, it is a danger to us all." I knew what kind of monsters peopled each level of the underworld: beasts of shadows feeding on human flesh, giant birds that ate human eyes, monsters standing on two deformed legs, with claws instead of hands. The thought of their walking among us was not a pleasant one.

The Wind of Knives would kill the human transgressors, but His role ended there. It was priests and especially Guardians who kept the balance of the world, by preventing monsters from coming among us.

I sighed. I stared at the obsidian shard I still held in my hand. The Wind of Knives. After my student Payaxin had died, something had withered in me. I could no longer trust the Wind of Knives, not when He killed so casually.

Still . . . Still, I was a priest for the Dead, and responsibilities could not be evaded so casually.

MARCUS COLLINS

"I will summon the Wind of Knives," I said. "And see what He has to tell us."

"Good," Macihuin said. "I will look further into the registers, and find out what I can about those men." He moved away from me, and then seemed to change his mind. "Oh, I forgot." He gestured, and one of the guards handed him something. "This was around his neck."

It was a small jade pendant with two glyphs engraved on it. "Four Wind," I said aloud. "His birth date?"

Macihuin shook his head. "The register says he was born on the day One Rabbit."

"Odd," I said.

We finally parted ways at the entrance of the house; Macihuin walked back to his tribunal, and I went back to my temple. As I walked through streets clogged with people, from warriors in feather uniforms to humble peasants wearing only loincloths, I dwelt on the summoning I would have to perform.

I did not look forward to it.

Priests for the Dead lived alone. There were plenty of temples like mine within the city of Colhuacan, hidden at the end of small alleyways, their facades unadorned. Inside, a single priest would wait for the bereaved. Sometimes a student waited as well, learning the craft of his master. I had taken on no one since Payaxin's death.

In my temple, I laid the shard on a low table. The midmorning sun created further reflections on the obsidian, images with glimpses of deaths: warriors dying ignominiously of old age or sickness, far from the glorious battlefields, women clutching their chests as they fell, their faces contorted in pain.

The underworld. The Wind of Knives.

Four Wind. If it was not the dead man's birth date . . . I knew only one other thing it could mean. Four Wind was the day on which the Second Age of the World had come to an end.

There had been Four Ages before our own, each named after the day that had seen it end. Each Age had been created by a god, who then became the sun in the sky, the giver of warmth and life. Different people had worshipped each Sun—until the gods grew tired and ended each Age in a cataclysm.

This Age was Four Movement, the Fifth Age, and it was said that Tezcatlipoca, God of the Smoking Mirror, would end it in an earthquake, tumbling the Fifth Sun from the sky, and rising himself as Sun of the Sixth Age.

But why would a dead man wear this around his neck?

The Wind of Knives would perhaps know, if I dared to ask Him.

I could wait to summon Him, always running from that moment when I would speak the words—knowing that if I did anything wrong the Wind would kill me as He had killed Payaxin.

No, better to do it now, and have it behind me.

I went out again, to the marketplace. It took me some time to wend my way through the various stalls, every one of them displaying more outlandish things than the others: feather cloaks, yellow makeup for women's faces, embroidered tunics with gold and silver threads . . .

I reached the district of bird-sellers. Raucous cries echoed around me as I went from stall to stall. I finally found what I wanted: a small grayish owl in a wicker cage, dwarfed by the other, more colorful birds the seller kept for their feathers. I bartered a copper bowl for the owl. It kept hooting on the way back—clearly it did not care much for daylight.

I had not summoned anything from the underworld since Payaxin's death, and especially not the Wind of Knives. I had resumed my life without Him.

I knelt behind the small altar, and opened the wickerwork chest that held my own possessions. Inside was a jade plate, much bigger than the pendant on Huitxic's corpse: it depicted the voyage of the soul through the nine levels of the underworld, from the crossing of the River of Souls to the Throne of Mictlantecuhtli, the God of the Dead. I also took out a small bone carving of a spider.

On the altar I laid both these things, the shard of obsidian, and the wicker cage with the owl. And something else, something I had kept all those years: another obsidian shard, the one I had found in Payaxin's heart.

The owl struggled as I opened its chest with the obsidian knife, but I had had years of practice. Blood spurted out, staining my hands and my tunic; I retrieved the heart on the tip of my blade, and laid it on the altar. Then I traced a square with the blood, and drew diagonal lines across it. I ended my drawing in the center of the square, laying the knife point near the middle of the jade carving, on the fourth level of the underworld.

My hands shook as I recited the words to complete the summoning.

> Jade for safekeeping
> Owl and spider to honour
>   the God of the Dead
> I summon you
> From the Fourth Level of the
>   underworld I call you.
> Come.

At first nothing happened and I thought I had failed, but then darkness flowed, catching me in its grasp. The hollow in my stomach was an all-too-familiar feeling, dredging up old memories, old fears.

A wind rose, whispering in my ears words of mourning.

The Wind of Knives coalesced into existence behind the altar. I saw nothing but a blurred, shining impression of shadows, planes of obsidian shards making the vague humanoid shape, a monstrous head and eyes that glittered. And I felt His presence in my mind, battering at my own barriers, trying to get in. But I would not yield.

"You summon me," the Wind of Knives said. His voice was the lament of dead souls.

"My Lord. I need answers."

"You are brave." He sounded amused. "I answer to no one."

As I well knew. He did not answer, even to pity.

"But you may ask, all the same."

I raised my trembling hand, pointed it at the two

obsidian shards lying side by side on the altar. "One of those was found in a dead man's body this morning. I want to know why you killed him."

One hand glided towards the altar. The fingers were blades of obsidian, each catching the sun's rays and making the light cold and lifeless. They closed around Huitxic's shard, lifted it to the light.

"That is not mine," the Wind of Knives said.

It had to be His. "I don't—"

"You don't believe me? That is a dangerous path for a priest of the Dead."

I shook my head. "I—"

He extended His hands towards me. Each held a shard of obsidian. The left-most one, the one Macihuin had given me, glinted green even in that cold light. The right-most one, which I had salvaged from Payaxin's body, did not. "This is mine," the Wind of Knives said, lifting His right hand.

"You left it in Payaxin's body."

"Your student had transgressed," the Wind of Knives said. "You know the law."

"Yes," I said, bitterly. "I know the law. He meant only to summon a ghost, to comfort a widow."

"Then he should have paid more attention to his ritual. He should not have summoned me," the Wind of Knives said.

I could have argued for hours over Payaxin's death, and still I would have gained nothing. So I held back. "Then whose is it?" I asked.

"Any priest can have access to magical obsidian." He shrugged. "It is none of my concern."

But His voice did not resound as before. If He had been

human I would have said He was lying. I knew better, of course, than to accuse Him, even though Payaxin's death still filled me, still clamoured to be accounted for.

"Is that all? Didn't you know the dead man?" I struggled to remember his name. "Huitxic. Does he mean nothing to you? Pochta? Itlani? Had they transgressed?" All He cared about were rules.

"I did not kill him," the Wind of Knives said. And He did sound sincere, gods take me. "Nor those other men."

"And the pendant? The pendant with the Second Age of the world?" I asked, but He was shaking His head in a blur of obsidian planes.

"I have given you enough."

"I need to know whether they have transgressed," I said. "What they have summoned."

"They summoned nothing from the underworld," the Wind of Knives said, fading already. "And I end all transgressions."

And then He was gone. I remained alone, shaking with the memory of that presence.

I slowly put away Payaxin's shard, and cleaned the altar, wondering what the Wind had not told me.

The deaths definitely are connected," Macihuin said to me that afternoon, as we walked on the canal banks. He sounded worried. "I went to the temple, and the registers. The dead men are noted as members of a religious sect."

"What kind of sect?"

"The Brotherhood of the Four Ages," Macihuin said.

Four Ages. The pendant made sense. I told Macihuin that, and he nodded.

203

"Yes, there are four members noted in the registers. I found where the last man lives."

"I suggest you keep a watch on him," I said.

"Possibly." Macihuin scratched his face. "And on your side?"

"They didn't transgress. At least according to the Wind of Knives. And He didn't kill them either."

Macihuin's gaze moved away from me. "So we do not have monsters abroad?"

"No," I said. It was a relief, but still . . . if the Wind of Knives had not killed them, someone else had. And I didn't relish the thought. A sect. Well, there was someone I could ask about sects. Again, not a pleasant thought. "I know a woman," I said cautiously. "She could tell us more about those men."

"Who—?"

"She's the Guardian of Colhuacan," I said, darkly.

Macihuin grimaced. "I had no idea you knew her."

I shrugged. "I met her a long time ago. I don't know whether she will remember me. But part of her role is watching over the religious sects—in case one of them upsets the balance of the world and she has to step in and restore order."

Macihuin pondered this for a moment before saying, "But she is only accountable to the other Guardians in the Empire. If there has been no transgression, she may not want to waste time with a murder investigation."

"No," I said. "She may not. But it is worth a try."

I left Macihuin to his own devices. He was going to interview the last survivor, and I was going to find out all I could about this sect, and why its members had died.

Unfortunately, that might involve going straight to the person who was killing them. For Ceyaxochitl was known over Colhuacan for another thing than her role as Guardian: many years ago, she had dispatched the members of a harmless sect, coldly going after them and opening their chests with obsidian blades.

She had said they were a possible danger to the Empire, and the matter had been hushed.

She had called it justice.

I called it murder.

Ceyaxochitl lived in the district of Teopan—the Place of the Gods. Her house stood only a few paces from the Great Temple. Every day she must have seen the great pyramid rising to the heavens with the shrine to the Sun at the summit, heard the cries of sacrifices as their blood flowed on the altar. But I doubted she had ever worshipped the gods in their heavens. A Guardian acknowledged the gods' existence, but served none of them.

The gods do not maintain order. To us humans falls the task of averting the end of the world. By our constant offerings of blood, we maintain the sun in the sky, and by their constant watch over the world the Guardians know when the gods falter.

Ceyaxochitl's slaves were courteous but cold; I could sense I was not welcome. I sat down in the courtyard, under a pine tree, and calmly waited.

At length a slave took me to the audience chamber. The walls of the room bore frescoes depicting Tonatiuh, the Fifth Sun, rising from the flames of His pyre into the sky, the world blossoming under His warmth. Tezcatlipoca watched from behind, His hands already reaching out as if to end the Age before it had begun.

Ceyaxochitl was older than I remembered: time had sprinkled white into her black hair, and some wrinkles had crept onto her face. But she sat very straight on her dais, and her eyes saw everything.

Behind her was a low table, on which lay the materials for some ritual unknown to me: three obsidian knives, and the fleshy leaves of a maguey cactus.

"Acatl," she said. "What a surprise."

She did not sound surprised. I waited until I was seated next to her before speaking. "You know why I came here."

Her eyebrow rose. "How could I know?"

"I need information about a sect," I said.

"I give nothing without a good reason," Ceyaxochitl said.

"I will give you a reason. Three men have died. Huitxic, Itlani, Pochta. Do the names mean anything to you?"

"Calm yourself," Ceyaxochitl said. "Yes, I know those names. What does it change?"

"They died with obsidian shards in their hearts."

Ceyaxochitl sighed. "I know nothing of it." But her voice quavered perhaps more than it ought to have.

"You do."

"Are you accusing me?" she asked, her hands tightening on the cloth of her skirt.

"It would not be the first time you killed the members of a sect without reason."

Her eyes flared with anger so cold I regretted having

taunted her. "It was many years ago. And they would have been a danger to us, in time."

"So you said. And the city believed you."

"Why not?" she asked, scathing. "I am not the only one to have dead bodies on her conscience. Your student—"

"You will not speak of Payaxin here."

"You think you can control me, Acatl? In my own house? Your student couldn't even close his circle of protection. You should have taught him better."

"You—" I said, fighting an urge to strike at her. I remembered finding Payaxin's body, thrown backwards with such force his neck had broken. He had died instantly, of course: the obsidian shard embedded in his heart had seen to that. I had knelt, collected the scattered materials for the ritual he would never complete, said the prayers for his soul. I had not wept. Tears would have been useless. But I had not forgiven the Wind of Knives.

Ceyaxochitl's eyes focused on me, and they sparkled with something like amusement.

"You will not use that against me," I said, softly.

"Why not?" she said, and paused. "But you are right. Let us put petty quarrels behind us. I did know those men, but I did not kill them."

Liar. Her hands still trembled.

"Then who were they?" I asked.

"The Brotherhood of the Four Ages? Fools, like so many over Colhuacan and the rest of the Empire. Fools who think they can stop the sun in the sky, or summon monsters from the underworld to cause that final earthquake to sweep us away. Sometimes they try to call on Tezcatlipoca Himself, as if it were easy to summon the God of the Smoking Mirror. Fools who think Tezcatlipoca will reward them for their acts when He rules over the Sixth Age as the new Sun."

"Then they were a danger," I said, quietly.

"They? They had no idea what they were dealing with. Between them, they didn't have enough magical talent to fill a copper bowl. They couldn't have summoned a minor monster without making a mess of the ritual."

"Tell me why they died, then."

"I have no idea," Ceyaxochitl said, more calmly. "But this is the truth, Acatl. They could not have summoned anything."

That last sounded sincere, but it did not exonerate her.

"I see," I lied. "They had jade emblems?"

Ceyaxochitl shrugged. "The past Ages of the World. Four pendants, one for each of them. Itlani was their leader: he bore the sign for Four Jaguar, for that is the age in which Tezcatlipoca first reigned."

"He was also the first to die."

She did not answer. She clearly did not want to give me more. I rose, slowly, shaking the stiffness from my legs and back. "Thank you."

Ceyaxochitl did not rise at once, which allowed me to take a good look at the three knives spread out on the table by her side. They had a good edge, and all shone with a peculiar color. Not green like the shard I had, but an aquamarine hue that was similar.

I laid one hand on the left-most blade, before she could stop me, and felt the power pulse deep within. The same power as the shard that had killed Huitxic.

Liar.

"You have overstayed your welcome," Ceyaxochitl said, coldly.

I withdrew my hand from the knife.

"What are these knives?" I asked.

"God-touched." Ceyaxochitl would not meet my eyes. "That's all you need to know, Acatl. Now get out of my house."

I left. There would have been no point in talking further with her.

By the time I came back to my temple, I was exhausted. I sent a message to Macihuin, and then spent the rest of the evening making my own offerings of blood to the gods. I could not keep my thoughts from returning to Ceyaxochitl. Three dead warriors: Itlani, Pochta and then Huitxic, with that obsidian shard in his heart. Obsidian that did not belong to the Wind of Knives, but throbbed like Ceyaxochitl's knives. Three members of a sect worshipping Tezcatlipoca and hoping He would end the world. And the fourth still alive, watched over by Macihuin.

They had been incompetent. I did not think Ceyaxochitl was lying on that point. But it changed nothing. As Guardian, she still might have taken it upon herself to remove them.

My sleep was dark and dreamless, and I woke up to an angry cry.

"Acatl!"

Macihuin's face hovered over me. In the blink of an eye, I was awake and sitting upright on my reed mat.

"What is it?" I asked. Outside, it was still night; I could hear owls hooting to one another. The air smelled of steam baths and cooked maize.

"He's dead," Macihuin said.

Nayatlan, the last member of the sect, had found the same ending as his brethren; he lay on his back on his reed mat, in the bedroom. He had the same mark as Huitxic on his torso.

I opened up the chest in three swift cuts, and retrieved the obsidian shard in the heart: a shard similar to the one that had killed Huitxic.

Macihuin stood to the side of the mat, his face dark. I held out the bloody shard to him, and he nodded. From the next room came weeping sounds: Nayatlan's wife.

"Four Rain," I said, lifting the jade pendant. The Third Age, which had ended when the gods sent down fire that consumed the earth.

"As if we didn't know." Macihuin sighed, and knelt to look at the body. "It was foreseeable, but still . . ."

"You had a watch on him."

"From the outside of his house. Did you think I could place guards within the house of a respected warrior without raising an outcry?"

"No," I said, shaking my head. "But this is serious." Macihuin did not speak.

"Did you get a chance to interview him?"

"I did," Macihuin said. "Not a very productive talk: he denied everything."

I laughed, without joy. "Of course. So did Ceyaxochitl."

"The Guardian? I had your message, but . . ."

"She's involved," I said.

"That's a serious accusation, Acatl. Do you have anything to support it?"

"No. But I hope to find something here."

We searched every corner of the house; the dead man's widow helped us by showing us the chests where her husband had kept his most precious possessions. We found nothing.

The last wickerwork chest we examined, though, was not as deep as it ought to have been. I raised my eyes to Macihuin, who was kneeling by my side, his hands full of clothes; together we tipped the chest's contents onto the ground.

It turned out to possess a false bottom, full of sketches and papers. Nayatlan's widow swore in a voice still shaking with grief that she had never seen them. The glyphs on them were so faded they were almost illegible.

"I need some time to study these," I said.

Macihuin was silent for a while. "I may have to refer this to the palace courts," he said at last. "This is going beyond me."

"Don't. I need you."

"Why?"

"They're all dead," I said. "She's done her work. The longer we wait, the more proof disappears."

"And what do you think I should do?"

My eyes rested on the first of the papers: it showed Tezcatlipoca, God of the Smoking Mirror, presiding over the first race of men in the age Four Jaguar. "Have Ceyaxochitl's house watched, as best as you can."

We did have a brief talk with Nayatlan's widow, but she did not even know her husband had been part of the sect. It was going nowhere.

I studied the manuscripts as best as I could, between the wake and the sacrifices for a dead man—for I still had my own work. The spells written in the manuscripts were old ones, so powerful they would have been beyond the grasp of an untrained sect.

One of the spells was annotated as if in preparation, but half the glyphs were missing, which made it hard to decipher. A summoning, probably of some monster. Thank the gods they had not succeeded. I almost was grateful to Ceyaxochitl, until I remembered her arrogance. She had killed innocents.

The rest of it was dull: all of it was praise to Tezcatlipoca, to His magic that could bring both life and death. *God of the Smoking Mirror,* the faded hymns said, *you who hold the destiny of the world in your hands, you who will rule over the Empire.* There, too, Nayatlan had written things, and I could piece together enough. He had had a son, I understood, who had drowned in the marshes while still very young. The fool had hoped Tezcatlipoca would bring him back in the Sixth Age.

Fool. But still not enough to justify his death.

I got messages from Macihuin, all attesting to the same lack of progress: Ceyaxochitl did not go out of her house on the following day; nor on the next one. He had had the houses of the other three dead men searched, to no avail.

Macihuin himself finally came to tell me the investigation was being withdrawn from him. The last victim had been not only a warrior, but a member of the Eagle Regiment, and his exalted status demanded more than a minor magistrate. Macihuin had to withdraw his guards while a more competent magistrate was found.

I took the watch myself on the second night. Nothing happened. I sat all night on a neighbour's roof, watching the inner patios of Ceyaxochitl's house, and my clothes were wet by the time I finally came back to my temple.

I had laid on the altar the three shards of obsidian: the two that came from the murders, and the last for Payaxin. Each time I came back to my temple I was reminded innocents had died.

On the second night of my watch, I saw Ceyaxochitl going into her courtyard with an owl cage. I saw her lay down the jade, the spider carving and the obsidian blade. I saw her kill the bird and trace the square in blood.

I saw her summon the Wind of Knives. He came to her call, and moved to stand near her, the hundreds of obsidian knives glinting under the light of the moon. She whispered something to Him.

No. I rose from my precarious hiding place, and almost fell from the roof. But still I could not hear the words any of them spoke. Ceyaxochitl dismissed the Wind of Knives, and He faded away from the courtyard, taking with Him the coldness and the sense of despair.

Not possible. The Wind had not sounded so much of a liar.

Had He? What did I know of underworld creatures, after all? I only knew how to read men. Supernatural creatures remained beyond me to encompass.

I came back to my temple at dawn, shaking from the cold, and sent a messenger to Macihuin, begging him to come. I waited and waited, but there was no answer. At last, a bedraggled boy brought me a crumpled piece of paper from Macihuin. *I cannot help you, not now. Tonight, when I have finished my work.*

Something was afoot. Why had Ceyaxochitl summoned the Wind of Knives once more? Did she think to kill more men, more foolish sects who spoke of things they would never dare accomplish? Did she . . .

My heart missed a beat. Did she think to kill both Macihuin and I?

I sent my answer, telling to Macihuin to take care, and I waited.

On the altar, the shards of obsidian glinted with sunlight: two of them green, the last without any color at all.

The sun seemed to take an eternity to move; I watched the shadows of the obsidian shards expand and then shrink again. The light turned from golden to white to golden again.

The shards . . .

I picked the two which shone with green reflections, one in each hand, and looked at them carefully. They did not look like the one in Payaxin's body; in fact . . . I put both of them in my right hand. They fitted together along part of their length, to form a narrow piece almost twice as long. Pieces of the same shattered blade?

It did not look like a blade, no matter which way I turned the assembled pieces. Still, there was something odd about them . . .

The sun was still high in the sky. I wrapped the three shards in a cotton cloth, and went into the district of artisans.

I had trouble finding a knifemaker who would receive me; they had work to do, more important work than accommodating a priest for the Dead.

At length a very old man shuffled out of a workshop. "You need a knifemaker? I have time."

He must have seen my grimace in spite of his rheumy eyes. "I am not so old, boy."

I sighed and handed him the cloth. "Can you tell me where those knife shards came from?"

He laughed as he moved back into the shadows of his house. I followed him.

"From which quarry, you mean? That's hard. Perhaps, if the pieces are big enough . . ." He unwrapped the cloth, bent over them.

His finished knives lay on a low table, each of them a testimony to his skill, the blades sharp, the handles carefully crafted. Obsidian flakes lay everywhere.

At length the old man raised his eyes. "Those are not knife shards."

My heart went cold. "What do you mean?"

He moved, picked one of his own knives, and showed me the edge of the blade. "A knife blade is . . . peculiar. We make it by shaving off flakes from the rock, and it shows: you can still see the places where we removed the slivers." His hand hovered over Payaxin's shard. "This is a knife shard. This was made to cut. You can see the indentations on the edge."

"And those?" I asked.

"Those were polished," he said.

"But they're sharp."

He shook his head. "They're sharp because they were broken. Broken obsidian always cuts."

I asked my next question carefully, unsure of where his answer would take me. "Then where do those come from?"

"I only make knives. But . . ." He laid his knife back on the table, and looked me in the eye. "It's a mirror, an obsidian one such as a woman would have in her house."

A mirror.

I thanked him, picked up the shards and went home. All the while my mind was running on unfamiliar paths, desperately trying to fit the pieces together. Tezcatlipoca, God of the Smoking Mirror. The mirror of obsidian that gave life and death.

Shards of a mirror that throbbed with power under my hand, speaking of death. Not the underworld. Never the underworld. Deaths, because Tezcatlipoca was also the God of War and Fate.

Despite everything that Ceyaxochitl had told me, despite everything Macihuin and I had found out, the sect had indeed summoned something. But not something from the underworld. The Wind would have killed them then. No, they had set their sights higher.

They had summoned Tezcatlipoca Himself, so He could end this Fifth Age. And Tezcatlipoca, who was god of destruction as well as of rebirth, had killed them one by one.

Only one person in Colhuacan had the knowledge and power to fight Him; only one person stood between the god and the end of this Age.

Ceyaxochitl.

I had been wrong. She had not summoned the Wind of Knives to kill the sect. She had summoned it to protect her. But the Wind could do nothing against a god.

There was no time. I sent Macihuin yet another message, knowing inwardly that I was alone, that he would not find me before it was too late.

Within my temple, I girded myself for battle. I had only pathetic things: I, who had not been even able to protect Payaxin from the underworld. Three obsidian knives went into my belt, and around my neck I hung a jade pendant in the shape of a serpent—Quetzalcoatl, the Plumed Serpent God: Tezcatlipoca's eternal enemy.

And then I ran back to Ceyaxochitl's house.

Everything was silent when I arrived; the air itself seemed to have turned to tar. I struggled to reach the front door.

Inside, magic filled the courtyard, throbbed to the rhythm of my heart. Magic such as I would never wield. Still I pressed on, although the air burnt my lungs, and raw power quivered on my skin. I was too late.

Ceyaxochitl lay on her back on the dais of the audience room, blood staining her blouse. Around her lay the remnants of her ritual: the owl with its throat slit, the spider carving on the low table, the jade plate. But the pattern was incomplete: a square filled the plate, and around the fourth corner of the drawing the blood of the owl pooled on the table, slowly dripping to the floor. Ceyaxochitl had not traced the diagonals. She had had no time to complete her summoning.

And darkness stood over her: the god Tezcatlipoca in all His twisted glory.

"Stop," I said. I wanted to scream it, but my tongue stuck to my teeth. "Stop," I repeated, lifting one of the obsidian knives.

217

ALIETTE DE BODARD

The god laughed. It wasn't the laughter of an immortal, but that of a madman. He turned to me in a fluid, inhuman movement, and I saw the flash of jade where His throat should have been, submerged in the darkness. I did not need to be closer to see the pattern. Four Jaguar.

What had those fools done?

"Priest," the god said. "You have no place here." He moved towards me, His power overwhelming me. I fought to raise my hand, and threw the knife at Him. It fell to the ground paces away from Him. He did not slow down.

"I stand against you," I said, moving towards the low table and Ceyaxochitl's body. "You are Itlani," I said. "The first member of the sect to die."

"No longer," the god said. "Itlani is but my vessel. I have returned, priest." I flung my second knife at Him, but He batted it aside. And then He reached out with hands like claws, and, grabbing me by the shoulders, hoisted me in the air.

I could not breathe. I could not focus on anything. Everything was folding back on itself, everything blurred. The hands holding me were blades of obsidian, green and throbbing with magic. The god's broken mirror. The shards that killed.

He flung me against a wall, contemptuously. I slid down, landed hard. Pain flared up in my back. Blood ran on my shoulders where the god had held me, on my arms and legs, which had been grazed by the rough surface of the walls. My ribs ached.

"It is over, priest," Tezcatlipoca said, once more coming to lift me. I rolled aside, gritting my teeth not to cry at

218

the pain. His hands found only air. "Why prolong your agony? I kill swiftly."

As He had killed Ceyaxochitl. I rolled aside once more, but I was weakening, fast. I had only one knife left in my belt. Think. I had to . . . think.

The mirror that gave life and death. The sect had summoned Tezcatlipoca and made a mess of the ritual. They had broken the mirror, and the shards became embedded into Itlani's body. The shards that later enabled him to rise as this twisted shadow. They gave life, and they took life.

The god was not wholly here, not yet. He inhabited Itlani's body. And that human body, neither dead nor alive, belonged both to the mortal world and to the underworld. The body transgressed.

I crawled towards Ceyaxochitl's low table, as fast as I could. My body screamed its agony, but I paid it no heed.

My hand closed around Ceyaxochitl's obsidian knife, dipped it into the blood of the owl. I swiftly completed the pattern, tracing the square's diagonals so that they met over the fourth level of the underworld.

The god lunged for me, and I threw myself aside. Tezcatlipoca's hand stabbed through the place where I had been, and grazed the skin of my arm. I did not care. I needed to speak the words.

"Jade for safekeeping . . ." My voice caught on the last word. It was hard to speak.

The god moved towards me. I left the table's side, but everything was blurred again. I raised shaking hands, but could not maintain them in the air. I was . . . I had to . . .

The words of summoning had been ingrained in me, too deeply to be forgotten. I spoke them, quickly, as the world turned and turned and shrank to darkness around me. "Owl and spider to honour the God of the Dead . . . I summon you . . . From the Fourth Level of the underworld I call you . . . Come."

I closed my eyes, knowing I had done all I could. The god was close to me; I could feel His power, straining to fill me. But I was too weary to get up.

A wind rose, whispering words of mourning in my ear. The air became cold, as cold as morning frost, and my stomach filled with that familiar hollow. I almost welcomed it.

Acatl, a voice said in my mind, a voice like the lament of dead souls. *I am here.*

When I managed to open my eyes again, the Wind of Knives was fighting Tezcatlipoca. They flowed over the furniture in the room, one darkness lunging at another. Obsidian clashed against obsidian with a sickening sound.

I crawled back to Ceyaxochitl. I passed over my own trail of blood, ignoring the pain in my body.

Ceyaxochitl still lay where she had fallen. I laid a shaking hand on her chest, felt the faint heartbeat. Her eyes stared vacantly at the ceiling. Her mouth moved, slowly. "Acatl . . ."

"Spare yourself," I whispered, not feeling stronger than she was.

"It's . . . not . . . enough."

The Wind of Knives and Tezcatlipoca were still tearing at one another. The god's body had transgressed, but He remained a god. The Wind of Knives did not kill gods, and in my mind I could feel Him weakening. Not enough. Curse it, not enough. What would be enough?

Ceyaxochitl's eyes did not look at me. "It's . . . us . . . Acatl. . . . We . . . maintain . . ."

Us. Human blood. Well, there was enough of it around, I thought hysterically.

I called in my mind to the Wind of Knives, as He had done when He had arrived. *You need more,* I said.

He continued His dance with Tezcatlipoca, stabbing futilely at the darkness. *And you would give it, Acatl?*

Yes.

I need more than blood, the Wind said, barely stepping aside to avoid one of Tezcatlipoca's claw swipes. *I need us to work together. I need your trust.*

You have it.

No. Those are words, Acatl. Do you trust me?

I . . . Payaxin's dead body filled my mind. *You kill for nothing.*

I am necessary. Would you rather have gods and monsters walking the world?

No, I cried in my mind. *You are . . .*

I do what I was made for, the Wind said.

He had killed Payaxin. He had . . .

No. Blame was shared, equally. If I had taught my student better, he would not have rushed into such a foolhardy enterprise. He would have known better. I, too, bore the guilt of Payaxin's death, and it had been gnawing at me all those years, when I had cut myself away from the underworld. I could not go on like that. I could not be ruled by guilt and hatred.

The Wind of Knives was still moving, but His gestures were more sluggish. *Acatl!*

I closed my eyes. *I trust you,* I said, and opened myself to Him.

It was as if I were moving through a rush of water; every thought alien to me, every image His mind held too horrible to focus on. Skulls and stains of blood flashed before my eyes, but I held on.

And He showed me, without words, what I needed to know. Human blood. Human blood would dissolve the shards, if it went to the heart, driven by a human hand.

I rose, slowly. My hand went to my belt, retrieved the last of the obsidian knives I had brought here. Clumsily, I plunged the blade into the wound on my left shoulder, biting my lip not to cry out at the pain. Then, step by step, I moved towards the battling shadows.

"You are a fool, priest," Tezcatlipoca said, and His voice rumbled, like the earthquake that would end the world. "A fool."

I came, with the blood-stained obsidian knife. I came, and the Wind of Knives redoubled His attacks, until He had Tezcatlipoca pinned against a wall.

And in that moment I plunged my knife into the shadow god's chest, all the way to the heart. I felt obsidian give way, dissolve under the thrust of the blade. I felt the Wind of Knives seize hold of my mind and push, push deep into the twisted mind of Tezcatlipoca's incarnation. And everything gave way under our attack.

The god screamed. I had never heard such anguish contained in a voice. "I would have reigned," He was screaming, even as the shards fell from His hands, from His whole body. Blood welled up from inside His chest, filled Him, until the darkness before me was tinged scarlet. "I would have . . ."

And the last shard dropped away, and Itlani's dead body fell at my feet, a grimace of fear on its features.

It was all I could do to remain standing. Shivering, I kept staring at the corpse, wondering if it was truly over, if the nightmare had ended.

A hand was laid on my shoulder, and gently turned me round. I found myself staring at planes of obsidian. "Acatl," the Wind of Knives said. "It is ended."

"Will He come back?" I asked, slowly.

"Perhaps." The Wind's voice was toneless. Coldness travelled from my shoulder into my heart, until I felt nothing, nothing at all. "Not so easily."

"And Ceyaxochitl?"

His face turned towards the unconscious body of the Guardian. "She may survive."

I wanted to rest, to lie down. I wanted the underworld to go away so that the coldness would abate. "It is ended," I whispered.

The Wind nodded. "You have no more need of me."

I stared, not sure I had heard Him correctly. I had never heard Him speak such words. He seemed to be waiting for some answer from me. "No," I said, at last, not completely trusting my voice. "I have no more need of you."

He had started to fade on the last word; obsidian planes blurred into nothingness.

By the time Macihuin and his men reached the house, and summoned a physician to take Ceyaxochitl away, He had disappeared.

But I still could hear His last words to me. "Until next time, Acatl."

I stood over Itlani's body, shaking and weak from loss of blood.

"Acatl," Macihuin said. "You have some explanations to give."

"Yes," I said. I let the physician bind my wounds, and fuss over them. I let Macihuin ask me questions which I was too weak to answer.

Evening was falling; darkness filled the house, but it was a darkness that the sun would dispel, come time. The Fifth Age would continue.

Until next time, Acatl.

In the end, there were enough things to sort out, and I could tell Macihuin would be very busy in the hours to come. They left me alone, sitting on the dais with the remnants of my summoning, with the memory of the Wind's voice in my mind.

Payaxin was dead. We both had a share of guilt in that, and perhaps not even one. After all, he had been his own man, and had made his own choices. I could no longer go on, cutting myself off from the underworld and hating the Wind. As He had said, He was necessary.

I said, quietly, to the silent night, "Until next time."

Ripping Carovella

written by

Kim Zimring

illustrated by

ARTEM MIROLEVICH

ABOUT THE AUTHOR

Kim Zimring literally feasted on science fiction as a young child growing up in Charleston, South Carolina. She'd swallow pages from issues of various Asimov and assorted magazines scattered about her father's large SF library. By college, she could go to a local bookstore and find that she had read everything SF on their shelves. She also tried her hand at writing science fiction, but it just didn't "click" right away. Back to the bookshelves she went. After college, Kim started hearing her literary clock ticking, and she listened.

Kim holds a PhD in immunology and practices internal medicine as a hospitalist in Atlanta. She lives with her husband, Jim (also an MD).

ABOUT THE ILLUSTRATOR

Artist Artem Mirolevich's world is filled with heroes and villains, the ordinary and the mythic: dwellers of Babylon, lost soldiers of Alexander, Einstein, samurai warriors, urban legends, time travelers and scientists of subterranean worlds. Artem's multidimensional view comes from his own experiences. Born in Minsk, Russia, his family settled in Buffalo, New York when he was seventeen. New York City beckoned next, where he became a scholarship student at the School of Visual Arts. During a semester's study in Amsterdam, his sense of architecture and culture blossomed as he found himself creating images of a post-apocalyptic city submerged under water. Next were extended journeys through the Middle East and Europe, which further broadened and shaped his perceptions and world vision.

For Artem, each picture tells a story. The movement of the story is carried throughout the piece by the movement of the characters and the fluidity of watercolor, his favorite medium. Artem resides in Brooklyn, New York, its own microcosm of world traditions and culture.

226

Ripping Carovella

The painting of my mother's death is famous. The original hangs in the National Gallery in Washington, DC, which quietly acquired it after the controversy had died down. It would have been a terrible disappointment to her. She always preferred the Io Institute—so much more avant-garde.

The reproduction over my client's desk is not only in terrible taste, all things considered, but it also fails to grasp the point. The brilliance of it, artists have agreed, lies not just in the concept of peri-mortem portraiture, but in the materials from which she had it made. Still, it affects me to see it: my mother, seated, her brown hair long, her back to the viewer as she reads to me, age eight. The scene is so warm and finely detailed that it takes a long time before you see the gun.

"Do we have to do this here?" my client was saying, as he walked around the desk.

I dragged my eyes away from the picture and looked at him. He was staring at the violinist in the corner, who was clutching his instrument case and looking scared. What he meant was: why do I have to see this? Why don't you do it elsewhere, out of sight, and then bring me what I want?

227

"It's not a kidney, sir," I told the client. "You can't put the cells on ice and then transport them across town. Neurons can't tolerate being outside the body for more than a few minutes at the most."

He nodded as if he understood. I had no idea why he wanted to be a consummate violinist, if he really did. Most of these rich guys were just in it for the bragging rights—yeah, I got *art,* I got *music* in my soul.

I put my kit on the desk, opened it up and spread it out.

"You're a ripper," the violinist said. It came out on a single breath, as if that were all that he could force past tightened vocal cords.

I almost didn't reply, as the question seemed rhetorical. "I prefer the term *talent scout,*" I said finally, with a nod. Ripper is a scare sheet phrase and besides, the physical extraction of the neurons is actually the easiest part of what I do.

The violinist said nothing to that, though his eyes strayed to the door. I shook my head, almost imperceptibly, but he got it for the moment. I hadn't tied him yet, hadn't had to, and I didn't think he'd get away.

I pulled out the cap with the electrodes still retracted and the violinist began to shake. This was the part I hated—the anxiety, the fear.

"It's not going to hurt," I said, scooting a chair over and propelling him into it with a firm hand. "I promise you that." It settled him, and he felt safe enough to get mad.

"What makes you think you can just—" he said, sputtering a little as he tried to get it out. "You can't do this to me. It's not right." His hands were shaking on the armrests and his pale brown skin flushed red.

He peered around me and focused on the client. He raised his voice and it almost didn't waver. "You want to play the violin, take a freaking lesson. You ever hear of practice, you—" I stepped back to get my kit and he launched himself out of the chair in midsentence, bolting upwards as I turned.

Nice. He hadn't telegraphed it much, though I'd caught the telltale motion forward of his chest from the corner of my eye. That's the spot to watch. Arms and legs, peripherals, can feint you out but the sternum doesn't lie.

He swung as I reached for him, but I slid sideways just a hair and it slipped past harmlessly. He had a reasonable upper body—all that bow work?—but he couldn't throw a punch worth crap. I twisted in behind him, wrapped my left arm around his neck and took him down. The client looked impressed, which I ignored.

Back in the chair he started trying to talk me out of it. "I know this isn't going to kill me. I'll call the police as soon as you let me go."

He'd seen both our faces. If it was likely that the police would get involved, do you think I'd have let that happen?

My lack of concern seemed to worry him. He stopped making threats and started thinking about it.

"Oh God, you're just going to kill me afterwards, aren't you? Taking my talent's not enough—you're one of those ones who rip people off, then dump them in a back way to die, or slit their throats to make sure of it, aren't you?"

"No," I said, strapping his arms to the chair with the

restraints and feeling a touch offended. "I don't do that." I retrieved the portable monitor and set it up next to the chair. "You'll be generously compensated. You won't go to the police."

"I don't want the money. I just want to play. Need to." He caught my eye, looked so earnest it almost broke my heart.

I pulled out the electric razor. Artists and addicts, I reminded myself; they were all the same.

"Shhh," I said, putting a hand on the back of his neck, starting there with the razor. His muscles tensed and shivered as I worked. "You can make that decision in the morning."

By tomorrow he'd have realized that he'd lost not only his talent but the way he made his living. He'd take the client's money and keep his mouth shut. If not . . . well, they have other methods of persuasion. They don't involve me; they know I don't approve.

I finished shaving his head efficiently and ignored my client's protest about the mess of clippings on the floor. I used a thin foam and a safety razor for the final pass as always—careful attention to the field of operation decreases infections and other complications.

I finished, wiped the violinist's skull, and stepped back to take a look. He looked younger, more forlorn without his hair, like a new recruit. I pulled on sterile gloves and smoothed an antibiotic cream across his scalp, followed by a numbing one. When I backed off to get the electrode cap, he found his voice again.

"How can you do this to me? You're not a bad guy, I can tell." He was sweating thickly now; when I leaned over him and tightened down the metal cap, I caught a heavy scent of musk and fear.

"Thanks," I said, dryly, but appreciating it nonetheless.

I hooked the headpiece to the monitor and booted up the program, then moved back and leaned in close. His face was white and set and I placed one hand along his chin and the other on his shoulder, holding him securely against the high-backed chair.

This was the part where it was important that he didn't move. Drills whirred inside the headpiece.

"Okay, you're going to feel some pressure now," I warned him. His eyes teared up; it was a private moment, and I was glad my body blocked that from the client's view.

The violinist squeezed his eyelids shut and he shuddered slightly; that was the electrodes, going through the bone. No pain, just like I'd promised him, but his breath still came fast against my face.

I undid the restraints once the electrodes were locked in place and handed him his violin. He looked confused.

"You have to play it," I said, patiently, pulling the monitor over but giving him a little space. "So I can find the right neurons, the ones you use to do it."

He considered escape again—I could see it in his eyes—but you can't get far with electrodes deep inside your brain. He settled the violin on his shoulder instead and played something I didn't recognize. Badly.

It was a typical ploy. I study all my artists' work, so I know what I need to look for to capture the essence of their skill. This wasn't even close.

I let him finish, taking some background readings. "Nice. Now play Bach's *Chaccone* from the Sonata for

Violin Solo in D Minor." That was the recording that won him critical acclaim, the one he'd used a pseudonym for, as if that would keep him safe.

His eyes slid to the old-fashioned gun in my shoulder holster. He started to play the solo, a little shakily, and I marked off the necessary cells as he moved into the piece: a chain of interlocking neurons from the temporal region, then another cluster from the motor cortex, and, interestingly enough, a bright spot of two or three down inside the amygdala.

It was a nearly five-minute solo, and it got better with every moment, as the violinist sank deeper in the sound. This was the one that should have been recorded, the last time he'd ever play.

He finished, and I ripped his neurons out.

He sobbed once, heavily. I squeezed his shoulder, removed the headpiece, gave him water and Tylenol, nothing narcotic or too dangerous.

I moved on to the client's side of things, after coating the cells to prevent infection or rejection. Insertion is easier than removal and a few minutes later the client was sitting up, done with probes and headpieces himself, and transferring my fee.

I bundled up the ex-violinist and took him from the office. He leaned on me, heavily, as we went down the corridor. The strains of music followed us, first hesitant, then quickly more and more assured.

By the time we hit the slideway, my client's talent was mature.

Vampire. Demon. Monster." Carovella, my love, was looking particularly wrecked this morning. The *Chaccone* was playing on the bedside speaker, so I knew what this was about.

"Good morning, dear," I said, bringing her a cup of sava and admiring the way she looked with her short dark hair all mussed from sleep. We hadn't talked last night; I'd gotten home late after dropping off the former violinist and Carovella's medication means she's fast asleep by ten.

"I hope your client rots in hell." Carovella tried to take the mug with her right hand, the one the stroke affected. She didn't have her assists on yet, so I held it back until she sighed and reached out with her left. It's worst in the mornings, when her dreams make her forget that she needs help to walk and tie her shoes.

You'd think she'd hate me, considering what I do, considering that Carovella's troubles stem from being ripped.

And sometimes, honestly, she does.

In my defense, I wasn't the one who'd scouted her out. It was Jacko, a ripper in the truest sense, who'd done it for some writer who'd liked Carovella's way with words. Jacko's work was sloppy, inexcusable, criminal, if you understand me, and she'd stroked out at the end.

I watched her drink the coffee, each sip slow, the way she'd been retaught to swallow. She watched me right back over the rim, with the covers still pulled up over her lap. I sat down facing her, running my arm down along her hip and in across her thigh.

I felt something. There was a bump, a flat surface hidden underneath the blanket on her lap. My face felt hot—I knew what it must be—and my mouth went dry.

"Christ, how can you, Carovella—" I grabbed the

233

sheet and pulled it down, exposing the pen and journal on her lap.

I felt sick. I would've rather come home and found her with a lover in our bed.

"It might be dangerous," she said, leaning forward into me, aggressively. Her right side was twitching, the way it does when she gets too excited. "But that doesn't make it wrong. There's no reason I shouldn't write if I still can."

I picked up the journal and twisted the cover, wanting to throw it straight across the room. She was reckless, irresponsible . . . "Isn't one ripping enough? An arm and a leg not enough to keep you out of this?"

There's a point in arguments where you start saying things you'll regret for months. You know this, but it never changes what you say.

I kept on going. "I wish Jacko'd got it right. I wish he'd gotten all of them." I managed to bite back the final bit, but she could read it in my face. I would have done it better—no stroke, but no art-addicted neurons left to make her write and put herself in danger. "You know I can't protect you—you think we've got the money to keep the other rippers out? If you've got any talent left at all, then this is suicide."

She practically spat, my fighting Carovella. "It's all about your mother, isn't it? This art is death, art is suicide thing. It all comes back to how she killed herself."

I was almost glad when she segued into my mother. That's a bad topic for me, practically unmentionable, so if she went there we were even. "How Freudian of you," I said, sitting back and collecting myself as best I could. "He killed himself too, you know."

"God, Rex, you're completely crazy on this subject."

Carovella's left hand was balled into a fist, like she wanted to take a swing at me. The right one just lay there on the bed. "I can't believe I'm with one of the few people in the entire city who could find my neurons and rip them back, and he won't do it because he thinks they're *bad* for me."

"It's a freaking cancer," I said. I meant it. "You, my mother, everyone—you're safer without those screwed-up cells. It's not all of your brain—it's just those one or three or ten neurons, wanting all your time, your attention, all your life. They bring you down and get you killed." Hemingway. Van Gogh.

Carovella tensed, then sighed, and the anger seemed to leave her in a rush. "What your mother did was wrong."

"It was sick." There's a difference.

Carovella looked at me so sympathetically I nearly couldn't stand it. Rothko. Cobain. Woolf.

"Your mother killed herself for her art, because she thought it would make a masterpiece." Carovella tilted her head to the side, considering. "And it did."

"Thank you for that honest appraisal. It means a lot to me." I knew I was hiding behind sarcasm here, but this was getting much too raw.

She continued, reaching for my hand. I moved a little further back. "The thing is, your mother shouldn't have involved you, even if it was for *art*. That was gruesome and wrong. I can't even picture it."

I can picture it so clearly, can't stop picturing it some days: my mother seated, holding a nursery book, me standing facing her as she reads aloud. But first: *Hold this, Rex. Yes, it's just like your toys, except a little heavier. Now point it right here, at me, up above the book.*

"Do you know how she arranged it?" I'd always dreaded asking what Carovella's heard. Might as well do it while I'm already upset.

Carovella nodded. "I've read about it. She had the canvas blocked and ready. She had the photo. But how did she get the painting made, after she was dead?"

Nice psych technique, Carovella. Get the guy to talk, to open up and *share*. If she knew that much, she knew everything. There's at least one biography that gets into all the details, or so I've been told.

I looked down and opened up her journal instead of answering. She tried to grab it back from me and I scooted out of reach, taunting her, maybe moving toward a smile. I opened to the first page, she made another desperate grab—

My stomach dropped. I thought I would throw up.

"Oh God, Rex, don't take it that way. I needed to write about it, can't you see . . ."

Roses are red, violets are blue, I read on the first line. That's the beginning of the rhyme my mother's reading to me, in the painting. How could she write about my life without even asking me?

Her eyes looked huge, sincere; her pulse was throbbing in her neck. "It's part of my life too, now that I'm with you. I need to write about it but I don't mean to hurt you."

I felt numb. I flipped the exercise book back on the bed, stood up and grabbed my jacket. "Don't sweat it, Carovella. I make a great muse." Experienced, in fact.

"Come back, please, Rex. Sit down."

I put her med-assists up on the bed, where she could reach them. A helping hand or a reminder? A very expensive girl, my Carovella.

"I've got to go. I should get another case today." I'd planned on getting some rest after last night but now I needed to get out.

It isn't her fault, I reminded myself as I walked out the door; she's still got some of those twisted cells inside her.

Carovella's wrong. It *is* a cancer, and it always kills.

I cooled down as I headed down the corridor, trailing one hand along the warm and bumpy wall. The hallways aren't as narrow here as the place they sent me after my mother killed herself, but they're also nothing like the open, airy spaces at the top of the city where my clients live.

Hardly the popular image of the successful ripper, I know, but the protection afforded by wealthy clients only goes so far; live too large and they'll find a way to bring you down. It's always a fine line when you practice a trade the elite desire, but can't afford to admit that they support.

The lights grew brighter as I moved toward the city center and the air grew cooler too. I don't know how people live in the outer shell; last time I was out there it was so hot that I could barely breathe. Better than being outside the dome, I suppose, but then, isn't that just another way that they make the system work? Keep your nose to the grindstone—there's always a little farther you can fall.

I took the ladder system up rather than waiting for a lift. Almost everyone avoids the back ways, considering them too dangerous, but that's one advantage of working in the hunting class—experience has taught me that any place truly deserted is generally safe. Why would muggers wait in a place that no one ever goes?

I emerged on the ninety-eighth level, just across from the place that I'd been heading for. It was called the Grounds, a coffee reference I guessed, not that the writers who hung around here could afford a drink like that. They'd probably be disappointed anyway—a client served me an espresso once and it wasn't nearly as potent, caffeine notwithstanding, as the things the creative types prefer to drink.

I touched the door and it swiveled open, revealing a small bar and a scattered assortment of scruffy types, most of whom looked like they wanted to sink into the floor at the sight of me. Despite the early hour there were plenty of people here, probably the night shift getting off. The types who came here certainly weren't making a living from their writing, anyway—the successful ones have long since learned to keep themselves safely locked away.

It didn't matter; I wasn't here scouting for a job, despite what I'd told Carovella. It was information that I needed: specifically, whether she had already published what she'd written. That was something I could discover from the types that frequented this place.

I stepped up to the counter and before the server could run away I pointed to a bottled soda-type thing on the display behind her. Bottled was definitely better in a place like this, given my profession. I wouldn't drink anything that they might have a chance to spit in before they served it.

I took the drink and paid for it, then turned my back to the counter and leaned against it as I surveyed the room.

I needed someone I could lean on, someone who would know the latest underground publications, someone who wouldn't be too afraid to talk to me.

In short, I'd decided on the way over here, I needed a poser. I scanned the room, letting my eyes pass over a couple of wild-skinned spilsters, a pack of dog-tired-looking ordinary types, and a few others here and there.

My gaze snapped back—there was one, in the corner. He'd shaved off an odd few areas of his head in imitation of the bare patches that sometimes plague people who've been ripped—the electrodes are small, but the hair doesn't always grow back where they've been inserted.

I watched him for a moment more, trying to be sure he was a fake. He hefted his glass with a steady right hand and that decided it. It was a rare ripper who could take from the left prefrontal and not leave a tremor on the right. If this guy'd had enough talent to merit a high-caliber ripper, then I would've recognized him.

I walked across the room and slid into the chair opposite him. He recoiled, but it felt like it was just for show; underneath it he exuded satisfaction. I understood the mindset even if it pissed me off, given Carovella's state—it must be galling, to think that you've got talent, and find that nobody even cares enough to rip you. Rippers are the ultimate critics nowadays, they say—if we don't think you're worth stealing from, then you just haven't got it.

"Ripper," he said.

"Rex," I corrected.

I watched him check his finger pad, and saw his eyes widen as he confirmed who I was.

239

He preened, visibly. I knew he'd spend the rest of the week, maybe the rest of the month, bringing up the fact that Rex Etiam was hot on his heels, tracking him down in all his haunts.

As if rippers chatted up their marks in cafés before they did the deed.

"I need some information," I said. I held up a hand to stop his protestations—*I'll never talk, you'll never take me alive,* blah, blah, blah, whatever his variation on that theme might be. "I need to know if you've seen this in any of the recent zines." I pushed a scrap of paper across the table, one on which I'd written Carovella's Roses opening.

The poser looked at it, longer than he needed to, and my heart sank. He'd recognized it, obviously, and now he was trying to decide what to do.

He looked up, warily. "Why should I tell you?"

I considered what I was originally going to say—I'd out him as a fraud, I'd tell everyone he'd never been ripped, would never be ripped, because he didn't have enough talent to make it worth anyone's while. Instead, I opened my mouth and the truth came out.

"Dang," he said. "Your girlfriend? Is she, well, naïve or something? 'Cause I saw this in Falcrow's zine and everybody who's connected knows he's just trolling for new talent. He ripped his way into everything he's got, I've heard."

Falcrow? I heard the poser say something else, something worried, and I wondered how bad I looked. Falcrow was the one who had gotten to Carovella the first time, back when she really *was* naïve. Why would

240

she do this? Why would she put herself out there for the same damn guy to rip her open again?

I fought an urge to bang my head against the table. This was suicide, pure and simple. I'd been right; there were still enough of those twisted, wretched writing-loving cells inside her head to make her do something as dangerous as this, just for the sake of being published.

"I have to go," I said. I stood up and signed to the server that I'd be picking up the poser's tab. I owed him more than that, I thought, but at least it was something.

I don't even remember the trip across the city to the ripper bar; I just remember all the calls, unanswered, that I made to Carovella. Did they already have her?

I stepped into Pull's and went right to the long silver bar that lined the whole right wall. Skim was there, thank God—if there was a rip going on anywhere in the city today, he would know about it.

He slid a glass of something oily and strong-looking my way, which I think was his way of confirming that I had trouble. I ignored it; I had no intention of drowning my sorrows instead of doing something about this.

Unless, maybe, that's just what I should do? What if this rip went okay, what if whoever did it got rid of the rest of those neurons, and then Carovella would be safe, with all of this behind her? Of course, a second rip was so much more difficult than the first; it would take a skillful ripper to get it right without killing her in the process.

"Jacko," Skim said, before I could even ask the question. "Falcrow always uses him."

This time I did bang my head into the counter. It's an old, bad habit, head-banging, and I thought that I was over it. Apparently stress could bring it back. Jacko, that dimwit. She'd never make it out of this alive, if I didn't get there first. I felt my gut knot up.

"Where would he have taken her? To Falcrow's place? Do you know where that is?" I had a hundred more questions ready to run out between my lips, but I bit them back.

Skim shook his head, slowly, not like he didn't know the answer, but like he wasn't sure if he wanted to tell it.

"It's Carovella, Skim," I said, feeling a begging urge creep into my voice. "You remember her? You liked her, when you met." Not that I would ever have brought her to a place like this, if I'd known she still had some talent left. . . .

Skim smiled. "Yup." He twisted his neck back and forth, like he was getting a crick in it, but he didn't say anything else.

I didn't understand. They'd hit it off when they met—Carovella had been fascinated by Skim's stories of ripper life, the ones that I would never tell her—and I was sure that Skim would want to help her out. "Whose side are you on anyway?"

Skim gave me a funny look. "Yours, I guess."

"Then tell me where they've taken her." Skim knew, he had to. He knew every rip that went down anywhere.

Skim sighed. "Your life is messed up, I gotta tell you that, Rex. You do know that, don't you?" He grabbed an address slip from under the bar and padded the information out.

I didn't know what he meant, other than the obvious, but I took the address gratefully. "Thanks. I owe you."

Skim waved me off, and disappeared before I could even take in the address. Not that I would have had any time for words when I saw where they'd taken her. . . .

My sides felt like they were on fire by the time I made it there, thirty stories down. My mother's old studio.

They'd turned it into a pretentious gallery, up front, with a little museum in the back for the gawkers who wanted to see where her most famous painting had been made. I disarmed the front lock and slipped within, grateful both for the skills I'd had to develop, as well as the dark within the room.

Once inside, I could hear voices coming from the back. Someone was yelling, a male voice that I didn't recognize—Falcrow maybe. I used the noise to cover me as I reached the door that led into the back.

I kicked the door open. I had a clear shot at the person with the gun.

I didn't take it. Carovella?

"Rex. What are you doing here?" Carovella's grip on the gun was two-handed, but shaky as might be expected. It was pointed at a seated Falcrow, whose mouth was still open as if waiting for the squealing to return.

"Carovella. Dear." I entered the room, feeling my face twist in confusion. "Just one question. Am I rescuing you or am I in the way?"

She shrugged, then gave me a sweet smile. "In the way, pretty much, Rex."

243

She motioned Jacko over and I gave up my gun resignedly. What was I going to do, shoot her? He pointed to a chair and I swept off the pile of ancient sketch books and took a seat. Carovella, never passive. Carovella, with a mind of her own.

Jacko ignored me once I was sitting down and went back to opening up his kit. His monitor was old and the headpieces looked outdated. I focused on Carovella instead, who was watching Falcrow, who was pulling at his restraints.

"Carovella, what are you planning?" That you couldn't tell me about this morning, I meant.

"They're my neurons, Rex," she said, a touch defensively. "Why shouldn't I take them back?"

Oh, oh. It was all coming clear now. She'd set Falcrow up—she must have known Falcrow could never resist the inside scoop on my mother's story—sell a million, wouldn't it, if you told it right? "How much did she offer you, Jacko?" I asked. I didn't need to ask how she'd found Jacko, thank you very much, Skim.

Jacko grinned. "Twice what Falcrow did the first time. And I know you're good for it." He wiped off the headpiece with a towel I hoped was sterile and advanced on Falcrow.

It was Carovella's decision. Who was I to stop a ripping?

Still . . . still . . . it wasn't good for her. It wasn't right.

I couldn't let her do this. I couldn't let her put that cancer back inside her brain.

"Stop, Jacko." I thumbed my handheld, froze all of my accounts.

I looked Carovella in the eye, which was the second

244

hardest thing I'd ever had to do in this studio. "I can't let you do this. I won't pay for you to put those monsters back inside your head. You're better off the way you are right now."

Carovella froze, looked betrayed. "Better off?" she mouthed.

She recovered quickly, then, and snorted. "On the one hand, Rex," she said, still holding the gun on Falcrow. "It means the world that you love me just the way I am." She motioned Jacko to keep going. "On the other hand, on this one subject you're a bastard, and, frankly, a complete loon."

"This won't fix the stroke, you know," I said. "Is that what this is about?" Jacko had severed her internal capsule when he yanked out his electrodes. That was white matter, not gray, a bundle of axons weaving their way from the motor cortex to the spine. Cutting that was like severing a power cord—all the neuronal bodies in the world at the top wouldn't make it right.

"I know it won't," she said. "I talked to the surgeons about it too. I just want my own brain cells back—that's not even theft, Rex. It's recovery of stolen property."

"I mean it, Jacko," I said. I held the screen out so that he could see it. "She can't pay you now and I'll never release the funds for this. Don't do it."

Jacko looked inquiringly at Carovella and moved closer to put the headpiece down. Good boy. He'd always follow the money.

Carovella didn't let it go. "I'm your sole inheritor. If something happens to you, I'll get everything. I can pay for anything I want."

I nodded, feeling sick. This was what it came to, what

245

it always came down to. Mother cells, that's what the neurologists called them—that was their name for these type of cells, the ones that were at the center of this *art*. My whole life had just been one big circle, leading back around to this wretched place.

"You want me to, uh . . ." Jacko kindly offered. He unholstered his own gun and came over and held it against my head.

Carovella stepped over and stood next to him. She was nearly as tall as he was, but dark where he was light. They looked like they'd make a good couple, if he didn't mind the droop that pulled her right side down.

"Rex," she said. There was a year's worth of argument in that one word.

"Carovella," I said right back. There was no calling my bluff; it wasn't one. If she'd rather have me dead than let those cells go, then I'd rather die.

"Fine." She looked terminally pissed, but she let the gun fall to her side. "Forget it, Jacko. We won't do the transfer."

I had my mouth open to speak. I couldn't believe it. She'd let her talent go, for my sake, even if she thought that I was wrong? She wouldn't just kill me to get what she wanted? I couldn't believe it, couldn't even process all the implications, before the realization . . .

Carovella, give me the gun, was on the tip of my tongue when Jacko moved, and twisted it out of her hand, so easily.

"Look, I'm gonna get my fee and rip someone tonight," Jacko said, backing off carefully and keeping the gun on me as he ushered Carovella into a chair across the room. "This is ridiculous. I didn't run all over town to watch you fight with your girlfriend, Rex."

"Looks like we're on, Falcrow." Jacko nodded at Falcrow, then waited as the writer pulled himself together.

I hoped Falcrow would argue about the fee, or Jacko's lack of ethics, or something insanely stupid like that, but he had the sense to smile and nod encouragingly.

"Absolutely, Jacko," Falcrow said. "Same contract as the first time, same fee, as soon as the neurons are delivered." He grinned as Jacko untied him, which I thought was poor sportsmanship.

"Don't you have any sense of collegial behavior?" I asked Jacko. I thought the answer was *no,* but it was worth a shot. "No professional courtesy?"

To his credit Jacko looked abashed. "I'm not ripping you, Rex, so don't get that way on me. And it's not like she hasn't been ripped once already, and that doesn't seem to bother you too much." He advanced on Carovella with the razor.

I didn't answer. I didn't trust myself to speak. I watched him with the razor; he shaved her head with a proficiency nearly equal to my own. He kept talking to me, as if we were having a conversation, as if I wasn't contemplating what he'd look like with his head blown off. "Plus, what are you doing dating a talent, Rex? Isn't that, like, a conflict of interest or something?"

He put the headpiece on her and then I couldn't look any higher than her hands, which were trembling, and as white as if the temperature in that one spot were nearing zero. I heard the drills, and maybe the scrape of the electrodes, and wished that I were deaf.

"What am I looking for in particular, writer-man?" Jacko asked, when he was in.

Falcrow sauntered over. He had recovered his equilibrium quickly, and now seemed to swell at the sight of my invaded Carovella. He picked a sketchbook and a pencil off the floor and handed it to her. "Start writing. The new stuff, about that crazy woman painter who killed herself."

Carovella flipped the sketchbook open, thumbing past pages of nudes and still lifes until she reached a blank sheet. She glanced up at me, an apologetic look; her gaze slid past Jacko's gun, then she started to write out the lines I knew so well. I could read it even from across the room, and upside down. I wondered, for the first time, where in Carovella's mind the story ended.

Falcrow wandered around the room, as Carovella scribbled and Jacko's screen lit up with mothers. He marked them carefully, and I started to hope that this wouldn't go too badly. Falcrow wasn't even watching. Probably wanted to pretend it didn't exist before it hit his mind. He reached the far end of the room, and pulled down the sheet that was tacked to the white plaster.

Ugh. I'd forgotten about that. The full-sized sketch for my mother's painting was there, drawn onto the wall; myself and her and the book, the studio's white walls, the plants she'd had back then, thick and green and hanging close, and the gun, dark and bigger than my hand. Even the writing on the right-hand leaf of her book was penciled in. He leaned in, reading it.

"Roses are red, violets are blue, horses that lose are made into glue." He laughed. "Harsh. A life lesson for the young 'un."

248

That, or an apology. I'd never known which, and I wasn't going to discuss either interpretation with this creep.

"This is a sketch of the painting?" Falcrow continued. He ran an admiring hand down the lower part of the drawing. "Is this the actual studio, the place where she died?" He turned to Carovella, his hand propped on the old image of my face. "So what happened to the kid?"

"That's why I'm here, for research," Carovella said quickly, before I could think to answer. The stroke had given her a poker face, when she cared to use it, and she carried the lie off beautifully. "I needed to study the background, here in the place it happened."

Covering for me. Stroked out once, and getting ripped again, and worried for me—trying to hide the fact that I had something Falcrow would want to rip. The original vision of the death, the central source, as he might say—let that fact out and it would boost the sales, not to mention what it could add to the work itself.

"I've got 'em," Jacko said. He ripped and Carovella gave a little cry. I thought that I would die. He put the recipient headpiece on Falcrow—not so much different from the donor's, except maybe a little cleaner—and he prepared the cells and dropped them in. So fast, it seemed, almost between one heartbeat and the next. Maybe it was over?

"It's not enough. It's almost right, but not everything is there." Falcrow's eyes were turned upward, as if he were reading off the ceiling. I wondered if he could see Carovella's soul up there. "Look some more. You've missed some, just like last time. I haven't got the death scene yet."

Jacko poked some more as Carovella wrote. Her face was pale and her body quivered, but she hadn't stroked again. Yet.

I could see the pattern forming on the monitor as she scrawled; a subtle one, with unexpected spikes in the temporal lobe and a beat or two along the hippocampus. Jacko's shoulders hunched with stress; he didn't see it. He never would. He'd rip her whole brain out, stroke her into brain death and still miss the vital spark.

I studied it further and realized there was no way to rip the rest out safely at this point. It was too diffuse, probably because of that first stroke. Mothers rebound strangely, I'd always found, if they're missed on that first rip, and they twist and twine around the parts that you can't live without.

I coughed, caught Jacko's attention, and waited until he had the gun trained on me.

"Here, let me do it," I said. I smoothed my face into sincerity. This was it, this time, the cycle coming round again. "I can pull out what you need, Jacko. I know her better than anyone, after all."

I saw the shock on Carovella's face, betrayed again it said. Jacko looked interested, and possibly a touch relieved. He held his ground with the gun still, though, feeling out the edges of his trust.

"Look." I pointed to the monitor, to the flash of color lizard-brain deep where rage and fear are felt. "Carovella thinks I'm going to help you and she's damn mad about it. But I don't care—I just want this over with."

I caught her eye and channeled every bit of hate of art that I've ever felt. "I've always wanted the last of those cells out of her head, she knows that."

Jacko watched the screen, and had skill enough to recognize that Carovella believed me. I rose carefully, and came over with a smile. He held the gun in his right hand, then changed it to his left as we considered the pattern on the monitor.

I helped him reposition the electrodes. I listened to Carovella curse my name. I made her write again, and I showed him how to read the screen to find his cells. The hunt absorbed him then, and when he was thinking only about those mothers, I lifted my left hand and put it next to his.

I adjusted the monitor so he turned his face from Carovella. I pointed to a deep bright flash in the lower prefrontal cortex. He squinted, grinned in triumph at the catch, and was just turning the smile on me when I took the gun and shot him through the head.

Jacko's body held a moment or two more, steadied by the monitor, then crumpled to the floor.

"Well," said Carovella, moving her feet a little closer in. "You seem to do that a lot in here, don't you?"

Falcrow was a beat or two behind then he let out a smothered squeak and bent down, feeling for Jacko's pulse. Nothing, I could tell from here, and I couldn't bring myself to mourn. Falcrow looked up and his eyes widened in recognition, as his new neurons kicked in. "You're the kid. The one who shot his mother, in the painting."

The one who's going to shoot you now, too, I didn't say. Carovella saw it though.

"No. No way, Rex. You can't."

"I have to, Carovella." Didn't she get it? We had the upper hand tonight, but that would change as soon

251

as Falcrow got inside his own front door. He could commission any number of rippers to take her out then, and me with her.

I grabbed Falcrow by the collar before he could move away. Solve the problem now, or count the days that Carovella had left, I figured. "There's not another option. There's just not. I have to kill him."

"Whu . . . why . . . I wouldn't . . ." Falcrow was saying, which I ignored.

Carovella's hand went to her head, and she rubbed her right eye hard. I bet she had a migraine, but she didn't back off on the fight. "Don't you get it? He's got part of my brain in there—you put a bullet in him and you might as well be killing me."

Falcrow brightened. I supposed he liked any comment along the lines of "don't kill him."

I kept the gun on him and went over to take the headpiece off Carovella. That was one thing we could agree on, at any rate, I figured.

But no. She waved me off with an angry flick of the wrist. "Then finish what Jacko started," she said. "Find the rest of the story, and give it to him."

Falcrow looked interested, and eager. It was all I could do not to backhand him, hard, so I settled for dumping him into a handy chair. There's part of Carovella in him, I told myself again. This time I started to get that it was true.

"I can't rip you," I said, "not and leave you functioning afterwards. How do you feel about respirators, Carovella?"

"I trust you," she said.

I opened my mouth. I was about to get into it again, how it wasn't a matter of trust, or even of ability—it just wasn't possible without taking too much out—when I got it. She was okay with that. Wanted this book written enough to do that, and then go.

Suicidal mother cells. It always came back to them.

"We're not going to do that," I said. I suppressed a sigh. I had a solution, and I was going to have to take it, and damn the consequences.

Falcrow just needed the final scene—he had the rest already. I decided to start him off with a bonus.

I unlocked the large back storage closet. My mother's coffin-shaped device was still inside; it looked clean and I wondered if the agent's renter had been experimenting with it. A moment or two of drag-n-dump, with Falcrow's unwilling help, and I had Jacko stuffed inside. The lid shut tightly, the topmost button clicked down and the burners flamed, turning all the evidence into a fine cremation ash.

The printing portion at the front was my mother's own creation. It was designed to take the ashes, dye them with ink as needed, then spray them on a canvas using a photo as a guide. Just like a color printer, on a larger scale. Pity—it didn't seem to be back in working order yet. We could have commemorated Jacko's death with a fine posthumous portrait.

"This is sick," Falcrow said. He'd gone pale, which cheered me up no end.

"Art," I told him gravely, "is all about the raw materials."

Carovella was glaring at me when we emerged. I couldn't stand it any longer; I went over and got that thing off her head, over her protestations. I handed her the gun instead, figuring she wouldn't keep still unless she was in charge of something.

"Are you sure, Rex?" she said, quietly, when I'd gotten the headpiece off. Her way of saying yes, I realized—letting me detach it, not insisting on her way of getting ripped to pieces. Falcrow wouldn't quit until he had enough to write the book. I couldn't get it safely out of Carovella, but I could get it from myself.

I shaved my head by way of answer, using Jacko's mirror. Falcrow and Carovella both looked on, neither saying anything. I didn't bother with the numbing cream, just sat down and put the headpiece on, adjusted the monitor and set the drills.

I hadn't lied, I was pleased to note. It didn't hurt, although the smell of drilled bone was nauseating from below. I slipped the electrodes in and concentrated on the occipital cortex, the seat of vision, looking for the memory of that old horrendous day.

I closed my eyes and pictured it. So easy, here in the old studio, within these same close walls. I remembered my mother making the sketch, standing on a chair to do the high bits. I remembered her letting me choose the colors. A moment more, and I was back there, on that day.

"Rex, stand over here, just in front of me." My mother sat down, book in hand, and smoothed her dark blue dress into a graceful fold. Her brown hair she swept behind her, loose, so it cascaded down her back.

"What does it say?" I remembered asking, trying to peer over the top of the thick book she held. I waited for her to read the lines to me, not shutting down the memory like I always had before. *Roses are red . . .*

ARTEM MIROLEVICH

It didn't come. I'd seen the words, but she hadn't read it to me.

I heard, instead, my mother tell me she was sorry, that she couldn't see another way. That the portrait would be better for me than she could ever be.

I remembered that she handed me the gun. I remembered that she told me to aim it, just above the book. I remembered that I didn't understand, I remembered that she said she loved me, and I remembered that I fired it right between her eyes.

She died; the camera flashed.

I checked the monitor. The cells that held that memory were bright and red and pulsing, a thick and tangled cluster in the middle of the vision center of my brain.

I set my spine and ripped it out.

Something went wrong with my eyesight after that. Not easy, to rip yourself and keep everything intact. Carovella helped me get the neurons into Falcrow, then sent him packing with a look.

Falcrow'd been delighted. He smelled the advance already. I didn't care, really, as long as the book got written and we were left alone.

Finally, Carovella took me home.

Some neurons are more important than others—the Ayn Rand philosophy of brain, I'd always thought. I know now it isn't true, despite everything I've lost. I'm still me, for better or for worse.

I can still see clearly from the corners of my eyes. The center of my vision is permanently dead, stroked out in that final rip. Stand to my left or right and I can see you plain as day, but move in front of me and it's as if you disappear. I can't rip anymore, needless to say, and it's not just from the changes in my sight. Turns out ripping is a talent—identifying just the right cells and no more—and it was all twisted up with that old memory.

I'm not sorry that it's gone.

Carovella bought Falcrow's book when it came out. I thought we should get one for free, all things considered, though money's not quite as tight as I expected. We get by, with this and that, and we don't have to argue about where it's coming from.

I held the book up for Carovella, as we stood together in the bedroom. I was better than the med-assists, and a lot cheaper too.

She told me the front page had Falcrow's name, set in large bold type above a subtitle that read "The True Story of a Suicide for Art." The back jacket, she said, read "Finally—a Worthy Successor to Capote's *In Cold Blood*."

I bit my lip. "Truman Capote drank himself to death," I said.

Carovella swatted at me. Old arguments never die, but sometimes they simmer into warmth.

"Are you angry?" I asked, feeling her flipping through the pages. "About the talent that you lost?"

She stopped. I thought she read a passage to herself, and then she brushed my face with a light kiss of fingertips. "They're not dead, Rex, those mother cells I had."

She flipped back to the beginning, and pulled me down beside her on the bed. "It's more like, I think, that they've found a home away from home."

I settled in beside her, and pulled the comforter up
to keep her warm. Then she read to me.

And much later, when we came upon the ending, it
was far better than I'd ever thought that it could be.

If Only I Had the Time

BY KEVIN J. ANDERSON

Kevin J. Anderson has more than twenty million books in print in thirty languages, including Dune novels written with Brian Herbert, Star Wars and X-Files novels, and a collaboration with Dean Koontz. He just finished the sixth book in his epic space opera, The Saga of Seven Suns. He and his wife Rebecca Moesta have written numerous bestselling and award-winning young adult novels.

An avid hiker, Anderson dictates his fiction into a microcassette recorder. Research has taken him to the deserts of Morocco, the cloud forests of Ecuador, Inca ruins in the Andes, Maya temples in the Yucatán, the NORAD complex, NASA's Vehicle Assembly building, a Minuteman III missile silo, the aircraft carrier Nimitz, the Pacific Stock Exchange, a plutonium plant at Los Alamos, and FBI Headquarters in Washington, DC. He also, occasionally, stays home and works on his manuscripts.

If Only I Had the Time

During the 2005 Winter Olympics, the world watched great athletes from all nations perform seemingly impossible feats with breathtaking skill. When those well-toned men and women received their medals, we admired them for their almost superhuman abilities. Most of us didn't kid ourselves (as we were sitting on the couch munching potato chips) that we could be just as talented, just as fast, just as strong . . . if only we had the time.

For some reason, though, a lot of people seem to believe such an absurd thing about *writing books*. I've had many people tell me that writing is easy, that they themselves could do it, if they merely sat down and put their minds to it. Here's how the conversation often goes:

A person at one of my book signings or appearances: "I've always wanted to be a writer. I could write a novel."

Me: "Oh? Why haven't you?"

Person: "I just don't have the time."

Me: "Hmm. You know, nobody gives me the time, either. I have to make the time, set priorities, discipline myself to get my writing done each day, no matter how tired I am. I worked a full-time regular job while I wrote my first novels, scraping out an hour here or there in evenings and weekends. That's how I've become a successful author."

Person: "Yeah, right. I think you're just lucky."

Olympic athletes usually start their training as kids, practicing, competing, clawing their way up year after year. Some of them get up before dawn just to grab enough hours of training during the day. They strive to improve their performance, stretch their abilities, beat their personal bests and then beat them again. They practice until they're ready to drop, and then they keep at it. Many are injured along the way. The vast majority of those who try out don't make the Olympic team. They may win semifinals and regional competitions, but only the best of the best become part of the team—and only the very best of those will win a medal.

I've received dozens of letters posing the same question: "I want to write a bestselling novel. But it seems to take so long, and it's an awful lot of work. Can you tell me what the shortcut is?"

Without doing a full count and comparison, I wouldn't be surprised if there are about as many *New York Times* bestselling authors as there are members of the various US Olympic teams. The competition among bestsellers is just as tough, and your chances of success are just as slim.

But does anyone really say, "I want to win a gold medal in figure skating, but I don't have the time for all that practice and training. In fact, I don't even own ice skates. Can you tell me the shortcut to winning a medal?"

To make a short answer long, I've wanted to be a writer since I was five years old. I sat in my dad's study and plunked out my first "novel" on a manual typewriter when I was eight. By the age of ten, I had saved up enough money to buy either a bicycle (like a normal kid), or my own typewriter. I chose the typewriter. I got my first rejection slip by the time I was thirteen, had my first story published when I was sixteen (after I had gathered eighty rejection slips), and sold my first novel by the time I was twenty-five.

I have a trophy in my office proclaiming me to be "The Writer with No Future" because I could produce more rejection slips by weight than any other writer at an entire conference. My files now bulge with more than eight hundred rejections. On the other hand, I also have ninety-four books published, forty-one of which have been national or international bestsellers, and my work has been translated into thirty languages. I've written almost ten million words, so far.

No, I don't know any shortcuts. Sorry.

Where does this notion come from that just *anybody* can write a novel, if they could only get around to it? I never hear the claim that just anybody can be an Olympic athlete, or a brain surgeon, or a space shuttle commander. Even if we did "have the time" to raise capital and invest wisely, few people could manage to be as rich as Donald Trump.

But somehow, publishing a novel apparently involves nothing more than unskilled labor, stringing a lot of sentences together until you fill enough pages with words.

Every author has heard this one from a friend or a fan: "I've got a great idea for a novel. I'll tell you the idea, you write the book and then we can split the money." (As if the *idea* is the hard part!) In all honesty, I'm not short on ideas. In fact, I'll never have time to flesh out all the novel possibilities that occur to me on a regular basis, so this proposition never ceases to amaze me.

I've often wished I had the nerve to reply: "I'm pretty busy right now, but why don't we try it the other way around first? I'll tell *you* an idea off the top of my head, then you can do all the research, the plotting and character development. You can write a hundred thousand words or so, then edit the manuscript (I usually do at least five to ten drafts), sell it to the publisher, work with the editor for any revisions, deal with the copy editor, proofread the galleys, then do book signings and promotion after it's published. After all that, we'll split the money. Sound fair?"

Now, I'm not comparing myself to an Olympic gold medalist. I can't even stay up on ice skates. I don't change the oil in my car (though I could probably figure it out, "if only I had the time") or balance the monthly checkbook. But I do have a pretty good idea how to write a novel. I've been practicing and training for most of my life.

Maybe as a public service I'll write a self-help book of shortcuts for these would-be authors who live all around us. I could call it, *How to Become a Bestselling Author in Twenty Years or Less*. Now, if only I could find the time to write it. . . .

Our Last Words

written by

Damon Kaswell

illustrated by

AMELIA MAMMOLITI

ABOUT THE AUTHOR

The son of a painter and a musician, winning writer Damon Kaswell always has had an interest in the creative arts. As an avid reader of science fiction and fantasy, Damon enjoys immersing himself in the worlds of such luminaries as LeGuin, Saberhagen and Zelazny. Three years ago, at the encouragement of friends and family, he began writing his own stories. He is now a member of the Wordos, one of the Northwest's premier writers' groups, whose members actively participate in the Writers of the Future Contest.

Damon's wide range of other interests informs and inspires his writing. He's a voracious newshound and amateur science buff. He dances the Argentine tango, tinkers with computers, plays role-playing games, collects animation videos and studies martial arts. He also contributes software to the Open Source community when he sees a need. Damon relates that everything interests him and everything is a story. Of his winning entry, he says "I was reading something in a scientific journal about how we perceive time, and it all came together." Damon lives in Eugene, Oregon, with his wife and their newborn daughter.

ABOUT THE ILLUSTRATOR

The list of creative filmmakers, game producers, and concept artists who have inspired illustrator Amelia Mammoliti's work may seem endless, but she points to one person as her primary influence: Phantom of the Opera *author Gaston Leroux. "He's had a very interesting influence on the meanings of my illustrations," she says. And though she has many interests, she admits her only real hobby is illustration.*

Sacramento-born and raised in Southern California's Simi Valley, Amelia's been drawing since her teens. It was her father who first told her of the Illustrators of the Future Contest when she was just 16. Amelia remembered that advice years later when she entered art school, taking the chance to land in these pages. To get inspired, Amelia spends a lot of time with her head in the clouds creating scenarios or images to work with, then simply gets to work drawing them. She lives with her husband in California.

Our Last Words

1:1

I volunteer to go, because I have no connections. I've lost my wife, Amanda; my parents; even my small son, Daniel. Gone in the war. I've lost God, or at least misplaced Him.

The volunteers are psychologically profiled, analyzed and eventually narrowed down. There are ten, then five, then one. My commanding officer calls me into his office. "Are you sure, Bill?" he asks.

"I'm sure."

The US Army flies me out to the facility that night. It's just a small, stubby building surrounded by trees, and beyond that, a vast open field with the Chamber in the middle.

The Chamber is my new home.

I step out of the copter and off the landing pad. "You must be Corporal Glassbury," says a soft-looking man in glasses and a lab coat. He sticks out a hand, which I accept. "I'm Doctor Efrem Castellano, head of Project Slowdown. I'm sorry for your losses, sir, but rest assured, you'll be doing a service to your country."

What's left of it, I think.

"Let's get you ready."

Inside the stubby building, I'm taken to surgery and then to orientation. Surgery is simple; small but important adjustments to my Embed, the organic computer in my brain.

Don't worry, they tell me. You can still listen to music. You can still use the Army's neural network. You can still get online. These changes are only for the Chamber.

They tell me I'm still connected, which makes me want to laugh.

Orientation doesn't make a lot of sense to me. Project Slowdown, explains Efrem, is how we'll know whether we win the war. Whether we win *all* wars. We'll be able to check as far forward as we need to. The military applications are endless.

But I can see in his eyes, when he says, "Imagine being able to see the ends of a civilization," that military applications don't matter to him. They're a means to an end.

As a soldier, I can respect that.

They train me on the controls, which are simple enough. Set Rate. Set Duration. Through my Embed, they'll be able to talk to me, even as I sail into their future. I don't understand how that will work, but I don't need to.

They let me sleep for the night, which isn't necessary, and then bring me out to the Chamber in the morning, in an Army jeep. It's cold and windy out. I can feel my face go numb as we cross the open field. I relish the sensation.

The Chamber is huge, much bigger than it looked from the helicopter. Efrem grows excited as we get closer, and tells me about its features.

"The front area, that's the observation room, and you'll recognize the controls from orientation," says Efrem, pointing at a large, see-through room. "Behind that, you can see the maintenance systems. Food, recreation, exercise, air circulation, all your needs accounted for." I think it looks like a warehouse behind and a greenhouse in front.

There's a large pavilion set up outside the Chamber now, with Efrem's communication equipment. But none of it's directly connected to the Chamber, which stands alone.

They put me inside the observation room, position my chair at the controls, then stand outside. They salute me through the Plexiglas walls, and take photographs. I salute back, and smile. My smile feels ghoulish. I just want to go.

When it's almost time, Efrem goes to his equipment and taps a microphone. I hear it in my head. "Bill, this is Efrem. Tell me if the link is working."

"I can hear you fine, Doctor." I give the thumbs-up.

"We're sealing the Twist field on three . . . two . . . one . . . mark." His finger descends onto the button that will sever me from time.

The Twist. They told me it's a way of moving things out of time phase, whatever that means—not a dance from more than a century ago.

It's a one-way trip. I'm sacrificing myself for my country. They told me that a human being must go, because the Embed is the only thing that can communicate off-phase.

They hope to have the technology to bring me back into phase one day soon. I may not use all the food,

269

the games, the books inside the Chamber. But there is a year's worth, just in case.

The Twist—and it really does feel like something's twisting around and inside me—descends on the Chamber. Time outside seems to slow down for a moment, then speed up again. Efrem waves to me, and I wave back. And then he does something unnerving, even though I know it's coming: he tosses a baseball into the Chamber. It passes through the glass, the controls, and through me without any sensation of touch.

It's done, then. I'm unanchored in time.

"Bill," says Efrem through my Embed, "can you still hear me?"

"Yes, Doctor."

I can see—but not hear—applause outside the Chamber. My comrades in arms cheering the success. "Godspeed, Bill," says Efrem.

I laugh. "I thought we wanted slow, not fast."

Efrem laughs too.

1:2

My first job is to test the mechanism that will allow me to tell the military its future. I set the Rate to double and the Duration to fifteen minutes local time. That's time inside the Chamber.

Outside, everyone starts moving quickly. Walks become runs, and conversations move at chipmunk speed. I see Efrem's lips move before I hear his words in my head: "Time to start the first test, Bill."

"I'm way ahead of you," I say, savoring the pun. "This is really strange."

270

Efrem laughs. "I'll bet. It's strange from this side, too. It's like watching a video in slow motion."

I sign off for the moment, and just watch them scurry around. For the first time, it occurs to me on a gut level that I'm seeing the future, even if it's just the immediate future.

Fifteen minutes after it started, I'm back down to 1:1. Everyone outside is moving normally again. But the words are out of sync. I see Efrem hold up a sign that says "Our time—14:30. Your time—14:15." I nod. He says something, but I suppose I won't actually hear it for fifteen more minutes—

Thinking of these things is already beginning to give me a headache.

"Bill," says Efrem in my head. "Have you arrived at the preset?"

"Yeah. You're holding up a sign that's giving me the time difference."

"I'll do that in fifteen minutes, but I think we can call it a success. Let's go to Checkpoint 1, shall we?"

The first Checkpoint is one week from today. There will be television screens set up facing the Chamber. The plan is to report news back to the present, so the army will know what to expect. It's time to go.

1:10

With ten seconds passing outside for every one in the Chamber, people move around almost too fast to see. Winds, which were mild before, look like monstrous storms to me, whipping trees and plants into a frenzy. Efrem is still for the longest time, apparently talking to

271

me, though I won't hear him for hours, and his face is a blur.

Out of curiosity, I look up. The clouds race across the sky, and I can even see the sun moving perceptibly.

Still, it would take almost a day for me to reach next week at this speed, so I go higher.

1:100

I wish you could see this," I say aloud, almost involuntarily.

"I'll put on some time-lapse videos," Efrem says, laughing.

"They won't really show you what this looks like."

The clouds whip across the sky like driven beasts, and the sun follows rapidly. Shortly, it's nighttime. The moon comes up, and I watch her path from one horizon to the next. It doesn't take long.

"How's the blue shift?" Efrem asks.

"There isn't any. I think the filters are catching it."

I hear some faint echoes of applause in my head. That would be Efrem's scientific team. "I'm holding that sign up now, by the way."

"Yeah, I figured as much. I'm going to take it to a thousand now."

1:1,000

A day goes by in less than a minute and a half. I watch the sunlight flick on, and then off again. It gives me a sudden sense of vertigo. The Earth feels wobbly at this speed, even though I know I can't really feel it at all anymore.

I sit down so I won't get dizzy, and watch the sky spin. Before I know it, it's been a week, and I'm back down to 1:1.

At the same time Efrem speaks again in my head. "We're having some trouble syncing up with you on this end. How far ahead are you?"

I check the Chamber's chronometer. "One week, fifteen minutes and twenty seconds since you closed the Chamber."

Efrem mumbles something to an assistant, then returns his attention to me. "Fantastic. We were only twelve minutes off, and I think we've got it now. Take a look outside, Bill. What do you see?"

Outside, I see Efrem standing next to one of the televisions. He has a full military guard around him.

Future-Efrem glances at the television screen, which is tuned to CNN, and back at me.

"The headline reads, 'More Trouble in Israel.' The closed caption says, 'The acting Israeli prime minister threatened nuclear strikes today.' And you look really worried, Efrem."

"Oh my God," he whispers in my head. I read the rest of the newscast, watching the anchorman try—and fail—to pretend everything's fine. I wonder, for the first time, if it's possible to actually change history, but I know from orientation that it isn't. What the military is hoping to achieve is more along the lines of self-fulfilling prophecy.

This isn't the prophecy they wanted.

I study future-Efrem, as well. He looks like he hasn't slept in days.

I almost wish I felt something about it. I'll do my

273

duty, but I refuse to care about the war anymore. It's no longer my concern. It's no longer real.

I leave it at 1:1 for a while, and go back into the living quarters behind the glass front of the Chamber. I eat, I watch a little bit of a movie and I take a nap. For some reason, I'm feeling worn out by all this.

"Sleep well," Efrem says in my head. I wish him a good night, too, but I know he won't have one. Won't have any for at least a week.

1:10,000

When I wake up, I'm feeling a little better. I go back to the controls, and key in another week and an even higher rate. It only takes about a minute for the time to pass.

"Efrem, are you there? There's no one outside the Chamber. No messages. Nothing. Even the television screens are down. Wait . . . It looks like there's another pavilion far off, and I think I can see some people talking."

Efrem is quiet for a moment, and I start to think he's sleeping. Then: "Bill, go ahead another two weeks, would you?"

I have no problem with that at all. In fact, although I'll never tell him, I'm planning on eventually going much farther than that.

1:100,000

It takes a little over five seconds. The sky goes a uniform shade of gray blue, and the earth jumps around a little bit, as if it's boiling, then stops. Everything's normal.

274

No, not everything. Efrem is standing in front of the Chamber again, but he's alone. He holds up a newspaper—the last newspaper, probably. Now I know why he looked so tired and sleepless before: he already knew what I'm about to tell him.

"Nuclear war, Efrem."

Future-Efrem outside nods, while I hear choked sobs coming from present-Efrem. Outside, he looks like he's done all his crying.

"I'll do everything I can to stop it, I swear."

Could he end the war? End the aggression? Force the US to admit defeat? I know it's beaten. It beat itself.

But I don't think Efrem will convince the government to end things. Even now, when they know where it will lead.

"Never mind, Efrem. I've lied. The headline is "'The War is Over. The United Arab Bloc Admits Defeat.'"

Efrem says nothing to this.

I go forward a few more times, in unplanned fits and starts. It isn't very long before I see the mushroom clouds.

It changes nothing. My family is still dead. I stop speaking to Efrem at all for a week, and just let time run normally.

Movies. Food. Staring at the blasted landscape outside that can't touch me. I can see shreds of the pavilion, shreds of computer systems that can no longer be used to reach me. They don't make me sad.

For some reason, I keep exercising, and I shave. Military habit, I guess. But I ignore the insistent buzzing in my head that tells me somewhere in the present, Efrem and my commanding officer are trying to talk to me.

And then, for no reason I can name, I decide to let them. "Bill here."

"Corporal Glassbury, explain yourself! You've been off-line for a week with no explanation."

"Sir, sorry sir. But if you'd seen what I've seen, you might take a moment to contemplate it."

"My God, it's true, then?"

"Yes, sir." I close my eyes, picture the mushroom clouds. Picture Amanda, holding our baby boy. "I suppose you will have a moment to contemplate it, sir."

He's quiet for a long time, then: "What will you do, Bill?"

"I think humanity's done, sir." I disconnect him again. They have no more need for me. I'm a time capsule from a dead people.

For the first time in a week, I sit down at the controls. And I enter a Rate. I don't enter a Duration.

1:100,000,000

A few years a second. I watch the landscape buck and jump. Seasons pass almost as they arrive, only winter seems to take a long time. Nuclear winter. I watch the gray globe that is now the sky, and if I'm careful, I can make out a slightly brighter band of light, moving constantly, that indicates where the sun is. I leave it running this way for a while as I take a nap.

When I wake up, I go back to 1:1, to look at the world of a hundred thousand years from now.

I turn my Embed back on, and this is what I say: "Life has come back to the Earth. It looks like some kind of jungle. I can't say what the plants are, though. A lot of it's unfamiliar."

AMELIA MAMMOLITI

Everything is quiet for a moment, then Efrem comes back. He sounds like he's done crying. "Is it beautiful?"

"Yes. It's really overgrown, though. I think the ground shifted a little. The Chamber is maybe half buried."

"Any human life, Bill?"

"No."

"The missiles are really coming, Bill?"

I chew my lip for a moment. "Yes, Efrem."

I hear him talking to other people. The chain of command hasn't broken down quite yet in his *when*. There are sobs, accusations. Then he comes back to the microphone. "My wife told me to tell you something: We were here."

"We were here."

"You'll remember us, right?"

Amanda, my wife. Daniel, my son. My parents. Much of Los Angeles. "Yes, I'll remember, Efrem."

"Goodbye."

Efrem cuts out, and it feels final. For some reason, I'm crying. I feel, for just a moment, a connection. It's small, but it's there.

Resting

I pace, and listen to music. Read, and watch videos. There are so many things to do. I can never leave, but at least I'm not bored. I am endlessly bored.

Sometimes, I try to contact Efrem, but he never responds. He is . . . was . . . probably spending time with his family. He will return one last time, to show me one last headline. I will never hear him speak again. I do not miss his voice.

I miss his voice.

I spend many hours watching the world of the future. Plants grow up and around—and through—the Chamber. I am Twisted, just far enough to the side of time that I and my Chamber aren't really there at all. The ones sprouting through the floor are barely visible to me, just the ghosts of plants, but they're there if I look very closely.

I stop shaving. I stop bathing. How my CO would be ashamed of how I look now! My hair is getting long by military standards, my beard thick and full. Amanda wanted to see what I would look like with a beard, so sometimes I tell her, "Look at me now, Amanda. I have a face full of hair. Wouldn't Daniel love to tug on his daddy's beard, tangle it in his tiny fingers and laugh?"

I weep for hours.

When I'm not out of my head, I watch the world outside the Chamber, and try to recognize the ancestry of the plants and animals.

At one point, something fast and light goes through the air, and I think, that was an airplane. That was an airplane, and it means there are people alive. Some kind of people. Civilization has found a way.

I watch it until it passes beyond the horizon, and I wonder what civilization looks like now.

I haven't touched the controls in months. I could go forward, just a little bit, and maybe see this civilization up close.

It occurs to me that several civilizations could have risen and failed around me as I blasted my way into the future. How did I look to them? Was I a strange artifact of long-forgotten technology, a figure frozen in time, visible but untouchable? I laugh when I think of

279

laboratories—or religions—built around me, then gone again before they ever registered in my sight. I imagine scientists of a strange future trying to break through the Twist, haul me out of my slowed state, and ask me about my era in broken English.

They obviously failed, if they ever existed.

I sit down at the controls, and make small, quick jumps into the future. A couple hundred years, and my imagination is proven right; a city has formed around me. I am inside a laboratory of some kind, built large enough to house my entire Chamber.

There are a few people outside, probably scientists. Incongruously, there is a child sitting with a woman who might be her mother at some kind of . . . computer? Engine? I don't know what I'm seeing.

I stand up, and they jerk back from me in shock. One of the adults faints dead away. The others, three males and two females, stare and point, and maybe they're yelling, although I can't hear it. I want to stare and point, too. They look like every race of people I can remember, blended together. Beautiful, with dust-colored skin.

I go back into the recesses of the Chamber, where my supplies are. I bring out paper and a pencil, and write "Do you speak English?" on a page. I hold this out to the glass wall of the Chamber.

They stare at it uncomprehendingly, then one of the females takes out a contraption that looks a little like a camera, and there's a flash.

I smile. The child smiles back. Then I sit down at the controls and push another fifty years through in a couple of seconds.

The laboratory has changed a lot, and there's a crowd

looking expectantly at me. One person holds up an enlarged photograph of myself, holding a sign that reads, "Do you speak English?" in a scrawl I recognize as my own.

"Clever," I say out loud, my voice unfamiliar in my ears. They've figured out what my controls mean; of course, they can walk right into the Chamber and study them, if they want to. They knew when I'd go from frozen statue to active man again.

The one with the photo holds up a different sign now. It says, "Yes, we speak English."

I work with their scientists, who try to learn from me about the Twist, and how to break through it. I learn this city is called Gaila, in a country called Emboshe. I think my pronunciation is lousy, because I can't hear their voices, but I get the gist of it.

They don't speak English, as it turns out, but they're good at learning new languages, and figured out what I was asking by comparing it to archaeological findings.

Archeology on the American continent for findings from American and post-American civilizations intrigues me. The things they get right, and the things they get wrong. One thing they learn from me: through drawings, descriptions and pantomime, I teach them the game of baseball.

Eventually, I'm visited by a woman alone. She looks, if I'm any judge of age for these lovely creatures, about thirty years old. She tells me she's actually sixty-four, and has devoted her life to the study of me and my situation, since seeing me move the first time.

I recognize in her face the child who looked at me the previous time I went to 1:1.

I write, "It's been a month to me."

"That's sad," she writes on her own pad of paper. "Everyone you know dies."

"I won't ever really know anyone again."

She is inside the Chamber with me. There is a chair and a platform set up that my visitors can use to sit beside me, where we can compare notes more easily. She looks, like the plants before, ghostly and translucent. Not really there.

Nevertheless, she puts a hand on my cheek, and I imagine I can feel it. Then she writes, "Why not?"

So I tell her about Amanda and Daniel, my wife and son. I tell her I'm beginning to forget their faces, and it's better that way.

I ask her—her name is Keeru—why she's crying, and realize I'm crying too.

She visits me every day, without fail. She teaches me her language as well as she can, and I learn for certain that Keeru's people are descendants of my people.

Then she misses a visit, and I'm antsy all day. Lately, whenever I close my eyes I see Keeru's face.

She's back the next morning, and she's been crying. "What's wrong?" I write.

She writes, "You are running out of food. We are trying to get you more."

It's impossible, I think. There's a year's worth. And then I wonder, how long have I been in here?

I start rationing food and water. I even ration air, keeping myself as inactive as possible. Outside, Keeru and the other scientists keep trying.

I don't say so, but I know they're failing.

"I'll go forward again when I have to," I tell Keeru

one night. She is staying late with me. She stays late most nights.

"I know," she writes. "You have to live."

I nod, but it's more than that. I don't want her to watch me die.

Keeru pretends to hold my hand. It's all we can do.

At the end, I don't want to leave. I fall in love easily now, with anyone and everyone. Children, men, women, it doesn't matter. I love them all. I tell Keeru I love her the day I run out of food. It's my last day here, in Emboshe.

She reads that in my eyes, maybe, this lovely not-quite-human woman. And I understand that she's been in love with the idea of me since she looked up and saw me move the first time.

I tell her and the other scientists that I will do everything I can to help them. I will leave all the books in the Chamber open, to minimize the difficulty reading any pages. I will transcribe what little I know about the Twist. And then I will move on.

They promise they will break through, get me out of my Chamber. It may take years, centuries, but they'll do it. They have a whole society to show me. A whole new world.

When my brain is exhausted, and I can't help them anymore, I say goodbye. Keeru holds my hand.

I never tell them that I don't believe they'll free me.

1:100,000,000

She disappears. After an eye-blink, the building surrounding me disappears. A hundred years whisk by me in less than thirty seconds, and I watch their

283

civilization rise and rise around me, the ground boiling with both tectonic activity and a frenzy of construction. God only knows what Keeru's descendants think of me.

But I have all too brief a time to witness it, because it collapses around me. I cry out as I witness the end of a civilization I barely knew. They never broke through the Twist, and they never rescued me.

The city decays, disappears, eaten by the ravenous jungle under the eerie gray of a million days blended into one, and I finally understand: I will be silent witness to the death of the Earth.

I decide it's not coming fast enough.

1:1 Billion

The land churns as a hundred years pass in less than four seconds. The sky is more uniform now, and I can barely even make out the life cycles of trees ripping up through the rapidly disappearing concrete, growing huge and then fading away.

Still not fast enough.

1:100 Billion

I grip the seat, feeling a sense of vertigo. The ground drops away below me, a burning, boiling, churning mass of green and gray that no longer has any recognizable features. The sky is getting brighter, and visibly redder. I find myself wondering if the Chamber's filters are having trouble at this rate.

No, I decide. It's not the filters. The sky really is getting a little redder. Pollution? Some new microorganism?

It couldn't be, I decide after a bit of math. Ten thousand years are going by in a couple seconds. I stare at the tint in the gray light with wonder as I realize I'm seeing the reddening light of the sun itself. It's not very much yet, but it's the light that signals the eventual death of Earth. I wonder what civilizations, if any, are bearing witness to it. Do they even know?

I decide a couple of hundred thousand years is long enough to spend watching this. It needs to happen faster. And this time, I decide it will be much faster.

1:100 Trillion

There's a brief flare, there and then gone, and the world goes black. I suppress the urge to turn on my Embed and tell Efrem that the sun has burned out in an instant. It's so strange—I can still feel gravity, as if the Earth is still there, but it's gone. Long gone, from what I can see. Maybe, in some small but significant way, the Chamber is still there, in that moment when they closed the door and turned on the Twist.

I look out at the endless night, then turn off all the lights inside the Chamber.

The stars are so bright, but they're winking out in nova flares very quickly. They're moving, too. And that movement, finally, seems to be a little too much for the filters, because they're all turning blue. I can see the Milky Way moving.

Humanity is done, then. If any of them survived, I think, then they're no longer recognizably human. They've moved out into the stars. And now, at a rate of almost 200 million years a minute, I know that if

285

they do exist, their civilizations are rising and falling too quickly to be counted.

I turn on my Embed anyways, a radio connection to nothing. "Efrem, anyone, everyone, this is so beautiful."

Faster.

1:10 Quadrillion

I'm watching Andromeda crash into the Milky Way galaxy. It looks like a great, spinning disk of light. Oh God, Efrem, it's *eating* our galaxy. The lights are . . . they're connecting, they're merging into one, it's all pulling together.

I know Efrem isn't there to hear this, but it comforts me to say it out loud.

Faster.

1:1 Quintillion

I can't see stars anymore. Rather, I'm seeing superclusters. Star clumps. I don't know what part of the life cycle of the universe I'm seeing. I don't know how many years are going past in a second. The sky is dancing, and it's a death dance.

Then the superclusters start gathering. I think the scientists of Earth would call it the Big Crunch. The long-abandoned force of gravity is gathering everything together. I can see it all flowing into one great galaxy. The last one. I'm pulled along with it.

Faster.

1:10 Quintillion

I fall into the light, it's everywhere, writhing and smashing violently into itself. I pass through a hundred suns, a thousand, in a heartbeat. The filters work overtime, but I'm still blinded. Somehow, it's not a real blinding, though. As the lights begin fading around me, collapsing in the long decay of the last galaxy, I find I can see again.

The clusters of light flicker red, white, disappear, replaced and consumed by other clusters. If there is life here, it's heartier than anything terrestrial. "Efrem. The universe is fading."

For the first time, I become aware that I am not alone. I stare out of the Chamber, through my Twist, into someone else's. There are a dozen . . . No, a hundred . . . No, uncountable. There are an uncountable number of other Chambers, and we've been drawn together by the death-gravity of our universe. Their inhabitants are of all descriptions, all sizes, clustered together. Some are hideous, some are beautiful, some are both.

I put my hand against the glass. Another Chamber drifts close, touches mine and our Twists wrench through one another, merging.

It is a long, gray being, with many limbs and many eyes. I love it, instantly, because it moves at my rate, it moves and it looks at me. Its Chamber is not, in the end, so different from mine. It is not so different from me. It raises a limb, touches the glass and I feel a connection.

Finally, I feel a connection. My vision blurs, and somehow I know, I *know* the being in the other Chamber understands, because it feels the same way.

287

Another, and another, and another touch, and we all merge. The last flight of conscious beings through space and time. I scarcely consider myself human anymore, as a million minds touch mine and merge. We aren't lonely anymore, for this brief time of connection.

They see my life, my losses and their stories are largely the same. We are all more similar than different.

And now we know what's coming, what must happen. We tell each other not to worry, not to fear, but we do anyway, because this all too brief connection is about to break, torn apart by the forces gathering around us.

At long last, the universe is in its death throes. And we all have a single thought, before our Chambers split apart and our connections are severed.

Faster.

Unknowable

These are my last words: "The universe has died, Efrem."

The last event horizon pulls me in. The last black hole, containing all the cold, dead mass of Creation. I pray to a hundred million gods, but I already know it's pointless. I'm looking, I'm falling, I'm . . .

What is speaking in my mind? I can hear thoughts that take a billion years to think. . . . The universe is thinking, it's wondering what it will do next. I'm inside its mind.

It decides, as it always has. As it always will.

The singularity draws me in, breaks my Chamber, frees me. I die. I know I am dead, because there is light everywhere.

Faster.

288

1:1

I am born. I pass through childhood and youth. This happens on Earth; this happens in worlds entirely unlike Earth.

I meet her, and fall in love. Amanda, Keeru, a thousand others. I meet him, and fall in love. Daniel, Efrem, a thousand others.

I am connected.

Saturn in G Minor

written by

Stephen Kotowych

illustrated by

RANDALL ENSLEY

ABOUT THE AUTHOR

Science fiction has loomed large in Stephen Kotowych's life ever since a story he wrote appeared in his grade school's bulletin, and he was forever hooked on seeing his words in print. The genre influenced his choice of university courses—Byzantine history and ecology—and its questions of technology, society and human nature underscored his master's degree in the history of science and technology. He became serious about writing speculative fiction in 2003 after meeting Robert J. Sawyer, who invited him to join the Fledglings, a Toronto-area writers' group. The group's help and encouragement were instrumental in helping Stephen develop his craft, and his deepest thanks go out to them.

Stephen lives in Toronto, and, in his non-writing moments, he plays guitar and keeps tropical fish. He also has something of a green thumb, tending a large balcony garden in the summer.

Saturn in G Minor

Come if you must, but you only, the e-mail read. *You must leave on the first freighter departing after your arrival. No extended stay. No exception.*

That four-year-old e-mail was the only contact Jacinto Corone had ever had with Paulo, the famed composer. Paulo lived alone on a tiny space station at Saturn's rings and, as far as Jacinto could tell, that e-mail was the only contact Paulo had with anyone, save the freighter captains, in nearly thirty years.

You must leave on the first freighter departing after your arrival.

Sixteen days. One orbit of Titan around Saturn. That's how long the supply freighter would take dropping off the new science team and resupplying the research station at Titan before starting a four-year trip back to its berth at Mars.

BANG. The deck plates rattled as a large ice meteoroid struck Jacinto's shuttle. Containers of supplies surrounding him—enough to support Paulo and his small space station for another four years—shook and shifted under their cargo mesh.

He was holding his breath, Jacinto realized, and let it

escape as a slow hiss through his teeth. More impacts followed as smaller chunks buffeted the hull.

Crewmen on the freighter who'd helped him get strapped in, told Jacinto to expect a bumpy ride. The shuttle's course took it close enough to the plane of Saturn's rings that hitting stray ice was to be expected. "Don't worry," a crewman had laughed as the hatch was closing. "There probably won't be a hull breach."

The containers settled as the large impacts stopped. Swishing sounds of dust and the plink-pop of micrometeoroids against the hull again filled Jacinto's ears. It was a comforting sound, like soft rain on a tin roof. How long had it been since he'd heard rain? Almost six years, he thought; the last time he'd been on Earth. He loosened his white-knuckled grip on the chair arms.

Six years of travel for sixteen days on Paulo's station. A long way to come for so short a visit. And when the cargo sled left the station to auto-rendezvous with the freighter, Jacinto had to be on it. Another four years would pass before the next freighter relieved the crew at the Titan research station and dropped off new supplies to Paulo. *No extended stays.*

What would it be like to meet him? Jacinto wondered. There was so much to talk about, so much to ask him. Where to begin? He had his list of interview questions for his research—he could start there. Other questions could wait. He read the e-mail again; he'd lost count of how many times he had read it before.

Everything else he knew of Paulo had been learned in the course of his doctoral research. He'd read every book, every article, seen the old documentary streams and the rare interviews Paulo had given about his rise from academic obscurity to international celebrity. And there was what his mother had told him, of course. She'd been one of Paulo's graduate students at Concordia before he hit it big.

Getting e-mail from the orbit of Saturn had impressed Jacinto, almost as much as that it was from Paulo. He'd never been off-planet before, so to think of the signal coming millions of miles by laser pulse was almost too much for him to imagine. Now he'd come all that way, hadn't he? It hardly seemed real.

The auto-guidance computer slowed the cargo shuttle on approach to the station, matching its axial rotation. Jacinto felt the soft kiss as shuttle and station met. He waited until the air lock pressurized, and as the small light beside the door turned green he reached for the handle. Before he could grab it, the door swung open and there on the other side was Paulo.

He was no longer the suave, vigorous man from the documentary streams and old photos. Gone was the lush, jet-black hair, replaced by a thin white fringe around his otherwise bald, spotted head. A bushy salt-and-pepper beard obscured his strong jaw line. His frame, once broad and muscular, had withered. Paulo's shirt, decades out of fashion, might once have fit, but was now too big; his spindly, liver-spotted arms were lost in the billowy sleeves.

His eyes, though, remained bright. People who'd met Paulo before he left Earth, especially women, always mentioned his piercing gaze.

"You're Corone?" Paulo asked, his Montreal accent still noticeable.

"Jacinto Corone." He smiled and extended his hand. "It's a real pleasure to meet you."

Paulo took Jacinto's hand in a weak grip and gave it a few slight pumps.

"This way," Paulo said, and he inched down the corridor and around a corner. Even his steps were frail. Jacinto followed, not sure what to make of the welcome.

The corridor was white and empty except for a hatch that didn't match the station design. Paulo had retrofit the station with an escape pod. Jacinto laughed to himself. What point was there in having an escape pod installed when no one would be around to rescue you in an emergency?

Paulo showed him to quarters that were clean and prepared for a guest, but were as far from Paulo's room as could be found on such a small station. Except for areas frequented by Paulo (which were clean and impeccably organized), most other sections of the station were run down.

Conversation over a dinner of freeze-dried food and hydroponic vegetables was stilted at best, with Jacinto doing most of the talking. He was painfully aware at times how fawning he sounded, and would retreat into silence.

For his part, Paulo was quiet. He kept his eyes downcast or closed altogether. Wincing sometimes as if in pain, he would hum softly, without noticing, Jacinto thought.

It was slightly more than an hour's delay for transmissions by laser pulse, but Paulo had little knowledge of current events on Earth or Mars, and no interest in being brought up to speed. He didn't want to talk politics, pop culture or even music.

"I don't know his work," Paulo said when asked his thoughts on the latest piece by Gibson-Fraser. Jacinto didn't think it right to tell him it was a two-woman composing team.

"Music today is just a derivative form of the work I was doing thirty years ago," he said. "It doesn't interest me or bear talking about."

Jacinto would have liked to debate the point—Paulo had single-handedly brought electroacoustic composition into vogue all those years ago but there had been a lot of innovative work done since—but he decided not to press the issue until he knew the man better. An argument wouldn't do on the first day they met.

When asked questions, Paulo would answer succinctly and then fall silent. Jacinto had expected he would welcome the opportunity to talk, the opportunity for human contact. But perhaps, he now thought, conversation was like a muscle that needed exercise to remain vital. Paulo's conversation was as withered by isolation in space as his body had been.

Paulo grimaced, as if in pain. "I'm going to bed. My head . . ." He rubbed at his temple. "You have questions for me, an interview for your research? Give them to me tomorrow; I'll look them over. We'll talk in a few days. I have a schedule of work. It won't change just because you're here. I don't sleep much, and I'm up at 0400. I'll be in the main control room working tomorrow. When you're awake we'll unload the shuttle."

With that, Paulo stood and left the mess.

Jacinto spent the next hour exploring the small station. It was the original Titan research facility, *Gurnett Station,* built for a crew of sixteen, and bought by Paulo when the new station came online. Many sections of the sixty-year-old station were on low-power standby or sealed off. The hydroponics garden was suffering neglect. Jacinto thought its yield could dramatically increase if Paulo put in even a little effort. Like much else there, it seemed forgotten by the station's only resident.

A great deal of work had been done modifying the other sections of the station, though, with the addition of an escape pod being the least of it.

Jacinto yawned as he passed another case of freeze-dried food through the airlock. He'd thought it best to impress Paulo and get a 0400 start, too. Three hours slugging cases of supplies had him questioning his decision.

Paulo, conversely, was a morning person. He was no more talkative than the night before, but he had energy to burn.

Despite Jacinto's efforts at small talk Paulo kept silent, save the occasional instruction on which case he wanted next. Even questions about Paulo's career and compositions went tersely answered.

The tedium was numbing.

Most of the composers Jacinto had interviewed for his dissertation had been only too happy to talk about themselves. Paulo's laconic nature didn't bode well for his usefulness as an interviewee, all the worse given Paulo and his compositions were the focus of Jacinto's research.

Jacinto bent down to lift one of the cases and let

out a grunt when he couldn't get it more than a few centimeters off the shuttle floor before dropping it.

He stood and stretched his back. "What's in this one—rocks?"

From the far side of the airlock Paulo peered over at the case. "Yes, actually."

Jacinto turned, incredulous. "What do you need rocks for?"

Paulo smiled for the first time since Jacinto arrived. "Come. I'll show you."

I call the system the plectrum!" said Paulo, as he and Jacinto dumped the last of five containers of pebbles into the hopper.

"I've spent almost my whole fortune to build the plectrum and keep this station running," said Paulo. "These pebbles are regolith from asteroid mining."

That made sense, Jacinto thought. His hands were coal black from the dust and felt like they were coated in toner.

"They're such small sizes—only a centimeter to ten centimeters across—there's not much use for them industrially, so I get them cheap from the mining companies. This is the last batch; the system's ready for the performance. The key is the size of the objects striking the rings."

Jacinto didn't understand, but this at least was a sign of life from the man. He didn't interrupt.

"I hear music, you see," said Paulo as he closed the hopper, snapped tight its pressure fitting, and mag-sealed the housing. "Airtight now," he said, smiling. He strode down the corridor toward the control room and Jacinto followed.

"All my life I've heard music, constantly, the way Beethoven did. In some ways, I've felt a fraud as a composer. I transcribe what I hear in my head. Where does it come from?" He shrugged and keyed in the door code. The control room doors hissed open.

"I would compose, arrange, but I could never get the music to sound as it does in my head. Oh, it would be the right notes but the *sound* of them was wrong, the essence. That's what drew me to electroacoustics," Paulo said, climbing into the console chair.

"It was a very old style of composition when you came to it," said Jacinto. There'd always been a small, dedicated core of electroacoustic composers since the genre's birth in the mid-twentieth century. Once, it was even considered avant-garde—art music for a post-modern age. But it fell out of fashion, the post-modern was surpassed, and it was kept alive in university music departments. Concordia University, where Paulo had taught and where Jacinto was doing his doctorate, had one of the world's oldest programs, dating back almost one hundred and fifty years to the 1980s.

"You didn't feel it might limit you?"

"Hmmm . . . It did at first," said Paulo. "For years I worked in the genre. My inspiration was one of the earliest examples in the genre—the prepared piano. I turned the exotic into instruments to get the sounds I needed. Remember the concerto using the Golden Gate Bridge?"

Jacinto nodded. Paulo had used the girders and tension

wires as his instrument, the sound resonating across San Francisco Bay. The city still had it performed every summer.

"That was just one example. My works were always well received but they weren't what I was after."

Jacinto grinned. Now he was getting somewhere! To think of Paulo describing his works as "well received." Paulo had arrived at one of those rare moments when artist and audience are in perfect confluence, when his work had redefined the basis of modern popular music for decades. Besides spawning legions of imitators, his music had made him one of the richest men on Earth, and the richest on Mars once he'd moved there. But his compositions hadn't been what he wanted? That would be news to everyone. Jacinto wished he had his recorder with him.

"Then I happened upon the records of the Cassini probe from the early twenty-first century. Completely by accident, you understand. And that's when everything changed."

Paulo stood up and walked to the back of the room where five large objects lay under heavy plastic sheets. He pulled them off to reveal banks of keyboards, twenty in all, set in tiers along the wall.

"What the Cassini probe discovered was that as a meteoroid strikes the icy chunks making up Saturn's rings, it generates a pulse of energy and emits radio waves. Reduce the frequency by a factor of five and you bring those radio waves into the range of human hearing—tones. We have our instrument! But it's limited in range, random in its execution.

"So, we take charge of the meteoroids," said Paulo.

He moved back to the console chair and turned on the computer's 3D display. "We use pebbles of different sizes, fire them at different speeds, they strike with more or less energy, generating different radio frequencies and suddenly the rings become *strings*! Pluck and strike them as you would the harpsichord, the piano or the harp. The rings bow to our command, and the music we play—the music of the spheres!—is what we compose. All we need is an interface of some kind, a controller like these keyboards. We program them to regulate the cues for the firing sequence and all of Saturn becomes our hammered dulcimer."

"You're going to play music on Saturn's rings?"

"Yes," said Paulo. "An entire symphony. And you will help me finish it."

Why won't you let me work on the last movement?" Jacinto asked over a dinner of rehydrated chicken.

He and Paulo had been working furiously for days inputting the final sequencing for the *Saturn Symphony,* as he'd begun to call it. Paulo would input the notes using the keyboards—each key set to trigger the release of certain sized pellets from the sorted hopper bins of the plectrum—and Jacinto would add in, by hand, dynamics where Paulo had indicated. The composer had it all planned out and just needed Jacinto to do the tedious grunt work, as it turned out.

Rinforzando, fortissimo, diminuendo, mezzo piano—all entered as long, increasing strings of digits into the command protocols for the firing sequence. But Jacinto had four days left on the station and had yet to see the sequencing for the finale.

301

"That section is mine," Paulo said before taking another bite. Back to his prickly self, Jacinto noted. That was the pattern—tolerable in the mornings, difficult at night, once the headaches set in.

"If I could just get a look at it, for my research—"

"The final movement is off limits to you, and your research, until it's finished," Paulo said, pointing his plastic fork at Jacinto with every emphasis. "It will all be done in a few days; I'll answer questions for your research, and then I will perform the symphony at last . . ." Paulo had a longing look in his eye, one of anticipated relief.

"Will you be returning on the freighter?" Jacinto sounded more hopeful than he'd intended.

"Why did you come here?" Paulo asked. He winced, as if something pained him, and rubbed at his eyes.

"I came to meet you. For my research," Jacinto said.

"You're a young man. You've wasted a lot of time coming all this way, only to have to go back. Don't waste your time traveling. No one finds what they seek in traveling."

"But I've found you."

"All you've found of me is a cross-section, a fragment. You'll take what you want to, never knowing the whole. You've wasted all this time, and you'll have nothing to show for it."

"Did you waste your time? What have you got to show for all these years out here?" It was angrier than Jacinto meant it to sound, but not angrier than he felt.

"Ah, but you see I belong here—you don't. I've arrived where I'm going."

"You know, my mother's told me a lot about you,"

Jacinto said with an edge to his voice that surprised even him.

Paulo looked up. "Your mother?"

"Cassandra Corone. She was one of your grad students at Concordia."

"I know who she is," Paulo snapped. "Why do you think I agreed to your visit? What did she tell you about me?"

"Stories about being your student, seeing you in concert, watching you become famous."

Paulo considered this a moment. "You look a lot like her."

"That's what everyone says." Jacinto gave a cold smile. "She says I have my father's eyes, though."

Paulo chewed his last bit of chicken without looking up from the table. When he was finished, he stood and left without cleaning up his mess from the table.

Paulo spent the day after their fight in his room. It must have been a terrible migraine, Jacinto decided. He could hear Paulo whimpering and crying through the door when he went to check on him that morning. Did the music cause his headaches? He wondered.

Settling into the console chair, Jacinto turned on the computer's 3D display. He began tabbing through the program files for the firing sequence, looking for anything that might be the final movement.

Paulo seemed determined to thwart his research. With only three days left before he had to depart, Jacinto had yet to see any results from the final section, and had no interview with the focus of his research . . .

Empty-handed—isn't that what Paulo had said? He'd be damned if he was going to let Paulo be right.

There! That menu was what he was looking for. It was the only one listing a final movement. *"Dénouement,"* Paulo had named it.

He reached out and pushed the floating command icon to begin playback. Leaning back in the chair, Jacinto folded his arms, immensely satisfied. He'd pulled one over on the old man.

As soon as the playback engaged, he could hear and feel the change in the station. It was a power down, station wide.

Sudden queasiness filled Jacinto's stomach as the station section he was in slowed its spinning. He wished he could blame his nausea on the gravity loss.

The whole of the small space station shuddered as the spinning sections ground to a halt. He remembered what Paulo had said to him about the power drain when the sequence was performed. Gravity was a luxury that could be sacrificed.

Jacinto raced through menus on the holographic display, 3D command icons spinning in the air around him, trying to find some way to abort the sequence. He couldn't find a straightforward cancel command, and worried about selecting something that would do more damage.

"Putin!" Paulo cursed. "What have you done?" He had appeared at the compartment door, floating in zero-g. Pushing hard off the doorframe, Paulo rocketed across the room. "Out! Get out!" He shoved Jacinto from the console chair, pulled himself down and strapped in.

Paulo punched keys and scanned the read-outs. "The sequencing is cueing to start!"

"I—I didn't mean to! I was just . . . I wanted to finish

some of the programming you asked me to do." Jacinto's denial sounded weak even to him.

"Don't lie to me! You accessed the sequencing for the final movement. I told you it was off limits to your damned research."

"Why the hell wouldn't you show me?" Jacinto banged his fist against the console. He started to drift in the zero-g and grabbed hold of the chair to stop, raging at himself.

"I never should have agreed to let you come," Paulo said.

"Can't you just shut it down?" Jacinto asked. He struggled to position himself in zero-g, Paulo's chair his only anchor. "Shut off the power. Will that reset the sequence?"

"And what then?" Paulo turned, a wild look in his eye. "This station is almost as old as I am. What if the power won't come back on? Then we *both* die . . ." Paulo turned back to the console.

Why had he said "both" that way? Jacinto's queasiness grew stronger.

"What about overriding the controls for the rotating sections?" Jacinto asked. "Won't setting them in motion again cause a power drain and cancel the firing sequence?"

"That's not the way it works!" Paulo began rubbing at his temples.

"Stop yelling at me!" Jacinto shook Paulo's chair with both hands. "I'm trying to help!"

"By trying to destroy the station?" Paulo shot back. "It's going to take all available power to operate the plectrum and keep the station's attitude constant at the same time. If those sections start rotation, not only will the plectrum's firing sequence not run properly and the whole performance fail, but the station will spin out of control and smash into the rings. Or it may simply tear the station apart first—do you wish to choose?"

A klaxon sounded and four 2D video streams popped up from the display, each showing different angles of the station's exterior.

Taken from the station's own system of microsatellites, two videos showed the station in relief against the backdrop of Saturn. The field of view was too small to show the whole planet, but the swirling gas clouds and the vast cream yellow face of Saturn were still breathtaking. The other video streams showed the bottom of the station, now only several hundred meters above the plane of Saturn's rings, and the hatch doors of the plectrum system opening.

Another klaxon sounded and Paulo spun his chair around. There, along the back wall of the control room, the bank of keyboards powered up. Keys on the first synthesizer began to move in their pre-programmed dance, one at first, then two, then whole chords. Then another of the synthesizers, then another, until keys on all twenty writhed and moved as if commanded by an orchestra of spectral players.

From unseen speakers came the first notes of the symphony from Saturn's rings.

"Merde," said Paulo.

Though he'd helped program in the sequences for many sections of the symphony, as the music came through the speakers for the first time, Jacinto knew he hadn't expected this.

He'd played through sections on piano, trying to work out the dynamics from the notation Paulo had given him. The timing was strange, though, and Jacinto couldn't grasp the whole. He thought he had, intellectually, some idea what to expect when he heard the piece performed, but now . . .

Each note was a distinct tone and not the eerie, theremin-like noise of other space phenomena Jacinto had heard recorded. As clear as notes played on piano, but the *sound*! The sound was unique, unlike any sound—real, synthesized, or manipulated—that Jacinto had ever heard.

And the limitations of using the plectrum to play the rings gave unique structural qualities to the piece. No bent notes were possible, no vibrato or glissando, no sustains longer than two or three seconds, and even with all the careful programming an element of uncertainty pervaded the piece. There was no way to know the composition and layout of the rings below or how they would react to the strikes from the plectrum.

The piece was characterized, instead, by playfulness as Paulo fooled and tricked the ear of the listener.

Careful overlapping of note voicings mimicked some of the impossible elements of technique—doubling and tripling notes gave artificial sustain, produced delay and echo effects.

As he listened, Jacinto realized the whole was made up of four different satellite streams. Radio and plasma wave detectors on each of the station's four microsatellites detected the same frequencies at slightly different intervals based on distance from the source. The result was four threads of music, binding together to make the whole. Paulo had incorporated the slight delay and variations into the composition. The symphony shimmered with texture and life.

Paulo had married the most innovative elements of his atonal, avant-garde composition with the forms and patterns of the classical. This would do it, Jacinto realized. This would redefine music again, the way Paulo had decades ago.

Jacinto turned to congratulate him on a masterwork but the console chair was empty. He looked behind him to see Paulo disappearing out the control room door. Where was he going?

Turning back, on the 2D Jacinto saw the streams of pellets from the plectrum falling like glittering rain from the station. But there was something else. He looked closer. The station itself was moving farther and farther from the rings. It was picking up speed.

He pushed off the console chair and sailed to the open door. Kicking hard off the doorframe, Jacinto launched himself down the corridor. He saw Paulo round the corner at the near junction, turning down the empty white corridor.

He wouldn't . . .

Jacinto pumped his arms and legs as if swimming, but it didn't help and he cursed zero-g again. He had to catch Paulo.

His arms flailed for a hold, something to slow him as he approached the junction. Fingernails skipped and skittered along the plastic and metal walls of the corridor. Sailing past the open doorway, he saw Paulo punching in a code at the escape pod door.

"No!" Jacinto yelled. His fingers ached as he strained for purchase on the wall. Fingertips found a thin edge of the doorframe. It was enough. His body swung around, slamming flat against the bulkhead. He pulled himself around the doorframe as Paulo slipped through the escape pod hatch.

Jacinto kicked off one last time as the hatch door slid shut, his arms outstretched. "Don't leave me! Don't leave me here, you son of a bitch!"

He pounded on the solid metal door, screaming, but no answer came. His throat raw and with tears in his eyes, Jacinto pushed himself back down the corridor.

Jacinto rushed to the control room. He had to stop the escape pod from leaving. Instead, he found Paulo's face on the 2D.

"You bastard!" Jacinto yelled as he pulled himself into the seat. "You're not leaving me here to die." He scrolled through menus, looking for an override.

"Damn fool," Paulo said. "You're not going to die. There's no stopping the sequence once it's started, and it's almost time for the final movement. So listen to me!"

Jacinto looked at the 2D, tears in his eyes.

"Everything is working just as it should," Paulo said.

"The station is moving!" Jacinto checked the other 2Ds, and the station was moving faster than before.

"Of course it is!" Paulo barked. "It's taking all the station's power to run the plectrum and the stabilizing thrusters to keep the station's attitude constant. *Altitude* is another matter. I built it into my composition. That's why the number sets you entered kept getting bigger—longer intervals between striking notes. It's for the station's . . . for *your* safety. You can't be too near during the final crescendo."

"Why not?"

"On cue, this escape pod will launch into the rings and play the final movement of my symphony." Paulo moved away from the camera lens and Jacinto saw the interior of the escape pod behind him. Dozens of gray bundles lined the walls, connected by coils of yellow wire. "When this pod explodes it will set a chain reaction of collisions in motion—generating more notes than I could ever play in a lifetime of playing music. A last great sustained cacophony to conclude my masterpiece."

Jacinto's mouth worked, but no sound came out.

"This is the way I want it, Jacinto," said Paulo. "I've suffered too long with this music, with the headaches it brings me, the sleeplessness, the agony. There's no stopping it short of this." Paulo reached out toward the camera to kill the feed.

"Wait!" Jacinto yelled, and Paulo hesitated. "But maestro—you won't be able to hear the final composition if you die!"

"Ah, I've already heard it," Paulo said, wincing again. "I've heard it a thousand million times through every moment of my life. Waking or sleeping, it never left me. It's been my lover and my demon—caressing and tormenting me all this time. My other works have been pale imitations of this piece, simple warm-ups. A composer gives part of himself away every time he writes a piece. He writes himself into the music in ways he doesn't even realize—the music demands it. This piece—well, it demands more. I must die; it must live."

"No! Please, no—"

"Goodbye, Jacinto," said Paulo, reaching toward the camera. "You'll find what you need in my cabin. Tell your mother . . . Tell her I'm sorry. For everything." The image on the 2D died.

Jacinto felt the station rock as the pod blasted away. He screamed in impotent rage.

The tiny cargo shuttle seemed cavernous now; it was as empty as Jacinto felt. It was only a few hours before the rendezvous with the freighter, not that Jacinto relished the idea of company.

On a handheld, he scrolled through the answers Paulo had left to his research questions. Paulo had never intended to sit down for an interview, instead writing paragraph after paragraph of response for Jacinto to sort through later. It would make a groundbreaking thesis, but the thought brought Jacinto no joy.

He'd gathered up Paulo's few possessions and fit them all in two small cargo shells for the journey home. Paulo had left a will, too, though Jacinto hadn't the heart to read it.

A recording of the symphony played over the shuttle speaker system. It was so loud the speakers crackled with distortion; the volume was almost painful. The station's computer had recorded the whole piece as it played out, so that was preserved at least. It was the first and last performance of the *Saturn Symphony,* Jacinto thought. No one could imitate Paulo this time. There would be no derivatives.

On the four-year voyage home, Jacinto knew he would listen to the *Saturn Symphony* as many countless times as he'd read that brief e-mail on the journey out. And he would cry each time, as he did now.

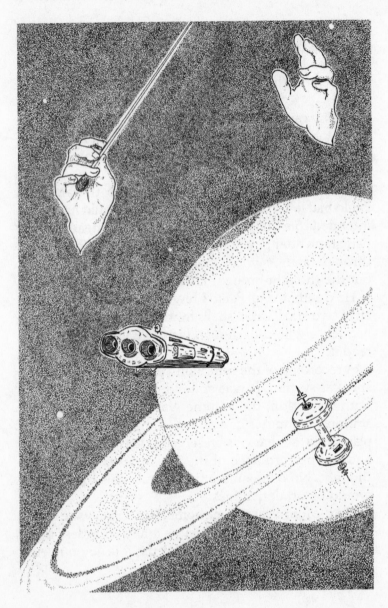

RANDALL ENSLEY

He had the shuttle's 2D on, the exterior camera trained behind him. The station was long since out of view. Momentum from the plectrum would carry it far into space.

Instead, Saturn filled the screen. He couldn't see the whole planet, perhaps just a quarter. But the width of its rings was clear enough. A dark bruise marked the A ring, where Paulo had struck his final chord. Matter spilled out into the Cassini Gap and toward the B ring like salt spilled against the blackness of space.

Saturn's rings turned slowly, like an old gramophone record, playing their endless symphony.

By the Waters of the Ganga

written by

Stephen Gaskell

illustrated by

ARTEM MIROLEVICH

ABOUT THE AUTHOR

Stephen Gaskell was born in Brighton, UK, the same year the Viking 2 spacecraft landed on Mars. Embracing his inner geek early, Stephen became fascinated with science while pondering whether invisible men, time machines and other esoterica of his favorite SF authors (Banks, Clarke, Asimov, Wyndham) would ever become reality. After graduating in physics from Oxford University and working as a software engineer, he decided that while the foci of his fancy might exist eventually, they probably wouldn't appear in his lifetime, and they certainly wouldn't result from his labors. To soften the blow, Stephen began writing.

In addition to his literary efforts, Stephen is nonetheless pursuing at least some of his SF dreams with master's studies in evolutionary and adaptive systems (biologically inspired "AI"). Stephen imagines that one day an SF writer will win the Nobel Prize in literature. This is his first published story.

By the Waters of the Ganga

They shall guard thee, they shall protect thee.
Reverence be to them.
Hail be to them!

—*The Artharvaveda*
(Book VIII, Hymn I, Verse 14)

Revelation is coming! I feel it in my brittle bones which poke through loose flesh into the thin mattress beneath. I feel it in my sagging muscles as I raise my head and Ramanuja—as sprightly as the day we met—guides a little water to my parched lips. I feel it in my spent heart and my pained lungs. I feel it in my rheumy eyes that catch the dawn light from the room's single, bare window, and in failing ears that still hear the traditional chant, *Ram Nam Sata Hai,* as the dead are laid on pyres on the bank of the *Ganga* outside. But most of all, I feel it inside, in my *Atman,* my soul, where the history of my life as man—and alien—mingles with *Brahman,* the universal spirit.

How I came to this land I know not. All I know is that one day I awoke and I was here, dispossessed of

my body, my kind, my world; everything save for my
memories.

Get up!" The words—whose meaning I understood clearly
even though they were the first I'd ever heard—were
followed by a sharp stab of pain from somewhere below.
The smell of cow dung, urine, rotting vegetables and
exhaust hung all around.

"Get up!" Another stab of pain. "Dirty beggar! Find
another place to lie!"

I opened my eyes (for somehow I knew I had eyes
and they were more useful than the light-sensitive cells
of my past form) and gasped at the richness of color and
detail in the visual field, a world away from the vague
impressions of light and shadow of before.

"Dirty, miserable beggar. Seeking alms on the temple
steps! You will be reborn as a dung beetle!" The stabbing
pain was replaced by a more diffuse pain and I saw the
words were coming from an ancient, living thing who
thrashed a slender, dead object against . . . me!

An old woman is beating me with her walking stick, I
thought, and marveled at the strangely familiar concepts
blossoming in my head.

She continued cursing and prodding and hitting me
while I examined my new body. No longer did I have a
flotilla of tentacles; instead two sturdy limbs, two less
sturdy but more deft ones, and one bulbous node which
seemed to hold the seat of my being. I knew the names:
legs, arms and head! Moving these appendages, I found
they offered no locomotive force, and in general—my
sore and red midriff a noticeable exception—they were

dead to the lively world of motion and color all around. I brought my hands up to my face and discovered the channels by which this body was made aware of the world: eyes, ears and a crooked nose. My face was thin and bearded. The gaping wound across my face leading to my innards was my mouth, and touching my tongue with my calloused, grubby fingers I found the fourth sense, taste, reflexively spitting as I did so.

"He spits on sacred ground!" The old woman appealed to a couple of passers-by in the alleyway adjoining the temple. They rolled their eyes and didn't break step. "Nobody gives a damn anymore!" she wailed, beating me with less enthusiasm now.

Whereas I was bare, save for a ragged white loincloth, the woman was clothed in a colorful *sari*—a riot of cherry red and fierce orange—with a plain towel draped over her shoulder.

At that moment there was creaking noise from behind, and turning my head (I'd noticed my vision was limited to a narrow field unlike its former ubiquitous scope) I saw the temple doors swing open and a priest step out. The woman stopped beating me and turned her attention to the priest.

"O Brahmin, how can this be Benares where Heaven touches the Earth, when we have beggars soiling the steps of the Golden Temple?"

I felt a sudden shame at an action that before was a mundane, empty event and shifted my legs to hide the damp loincloth.

The priest glanced down with distaste.

"He spits on these steps, too," the old woman went on, "I saw him just this moment."

"Is this true?"

I felt a reply formed and ready to be given, but I kept my lips sealed.

The woman hobbled up two steps to join the priest by the doors. "He holds his tongue because he does not want to lie to a Brahmin."

"That isn't true," I said, a flare of anger eclipsing the novelty of being a natural speaker. "I hold my tongue because I fear your disbelief or ridicule."

"You did spit on the steps then."

I nodded, looking at the cracked, dirt-caked steps.

"See! See!" The woman prodded me with her stick again. "He should be turned out—"

"Patience," the priest said pushing her stick down. He stared at me, curious. "What is your name?"

My name. I have a name, I know that. But it is not made of sound and cannot be rendered in this language. Like all my former communication it is movement and vibration.

"I know not how to say it," I said.

"Then I will call you Benama, meaning one without name. Now, Benama, why do you fear our disbelief or ridicule?"

"I am . . . I was . . ." I started, but what could I say? This place was so real, so full of vivid sensations, and I was so different from my last incarnation, that I barely believed those old memories myself, and was not able to express them to another.

I stood up and walked away, the satisfied jubilance of the old woman quickly lost in the bustling alley.

"Remember, we are all part of the universal," the priest shouted as I turned the corner.

For a long while after that first morning I was as the old woman had labeled me: a common beggar living from hand to mouth. The magical moments following my first awakening were quickly lost, swept away by the practicalities of staying alive and the despair I felt at having been ripped away from my own race.

I stumbled around the city, living in gutters, avoiding the world and thinking only of my lost life and companions. In these recollections—which were anything but fleeting—I relived my alien life. I was a creature of the ocean, living amongst thick seabed forests alive with the most vibrant life. I would drift with my brethren, laughing and playing in the tangled limbs of underwater vegetation with hardly a care in the world. We swam where we liked, often traveling as the current took us, the only forbidden place a cave system that was fabled to lead to the up and out. With our poisoned tentacles and ability to hunt in packs we were a match for any of the denizens of the deep and most our days and nights were spent gossiping or breeding or playing. Sometimes we would climb to the surface and tease each other that the mangled echoes from above the water were the words of angry ancestors.

My new body and its five senses soon became a shackle rather than a liberation, and I only gave myself sustenance when the hunger became unbearable. I wished with all my might that I could slough off this form and return to whence I came.

One day as I lay in a stinking alley face down amongst old boxes of rotten vegetables, almost too weak to sup on the unwanted produce, I heard a voice.

"Please, sir, wake up! Wake up!"

I lifted my head, feeling a squashed tomato peel away as I did so. A man in a white *shalwar kurta* was crouching down right beside me. "Leave me be," I said, and turned back to the ground.

He shook my shoulder. "Please forgive me the imposition, sir. My name is Ramanuja and I wish to make your acquaintance."

I nestled further into my filth, ignoring the man.

"Please, sir. However you have arrived at this station in life, I'm sure it can be rectified."

I tossed over, curious about what this persistent man looked like and wanted. He was a chubby little man with the mark of the ordinary and a pot belly that pressed through his shirt.

"Sometimes we have to sink low in order to soar high," he said.

I brushed off the seeds and skin of tomatoes crushed against my cheek. "What do you know about sinking low or soaring high?" I asked.

Anger flared, but his calm countenance returned before he answered. "I am grateful for not experiencing too much hardship in my time, and I am not bitter for living a pedestrian life. I am just happy to play my part in this grand scheme and trust my actions are the right ones."

"And I am playing my part," I answered cynically.

"Are you though? Have you embraced this path with all your heart, or are you hiding from the world? If you tell me this is your impassioned choice, sir, I will leave you now and never interfere in your affairs again."

He stood over me, holding my gaze while I thought about his words.

"This is my . . . this is . . ." Whatever I was, I suddenly understood I still had my freedom and deep down I knew I hadn't been exercising it, merely coasting like so much ocean detritus.

"What is your name, sir?" Ramanuja asked.

"Ben . . ." I began, but cut myself short.

I stood up, spat on my hand and cleaned and dried it as best I could on a *paan* leaf that lay nearby.

"My name . . . is difficult to say in this tongue . . . I can only give you a rough approximation," I held out my hand, "my name is Asajanaka. It means one of promise."

"Ramanuja," he said taking it, before I told him the story of my life.

What Ramanuja made of my incredible tale in that alleyway, spattered with the crimson stains of chewed *paan,* was difficult to say. Doubtless, part of him must have thought I was deranged; another pilgrim who'd ventured here for salvation but had lost his mind on the way. If he did though, he never once betrayed the idea. Instead, he listened to me intently, never interrupted, and when I had finished he merely said:

"Asajanaka, thank you for sharing your life. I see you speak from the heart and I can begin to understand your distress."

I didn't know who was crazier at that moment: I for relating my fantastical past, or Ramanuja for believing me.

Whoever it was didn't matter, though. The important thing was that Ramanuja made me accept my circumstances and start building a life again. He worked for a refuge—an old riverside warehouse converted into one large cheerless dormitory—that helped the city's forgotten, and it was here, at night, I slept, while by day I observed the city.

I cared not for the tribulations of other men, but here in this holy place awash with the sick and the desperate, the poor and the rich, the charitable and the greedy, all looking for their own answers like me, it was impossible to avoid their stories.

From the devout, at the foot of the riverside *ghats*—immense stone steps into the river which ran the length of the city—where I washed my body in the filthy Ganga, I learned the mythology of the city. How any Hindu who died in this holiest of places was guaranteed *moksha,* liberation from the cycle of death and rebirth, and how Shiva, God of Destruction, had chosen Benares as his eternal home. I felt pity for those who believed, and when I heard the other name of the city—Kashi, meaning the Luminous—and thought of the nightly power failures, and the walls and streets blackened with smog and excrement, I laughed bitterly.

From the unbelievers, in the narrow, mazy alleys that riddled the old city, I was told how if you were prepared to kill the revered holy animal—the sacred cow—you would never face starvation but you might face the mob. I never did. Even though the cows were easy targets and wandered freely, as likely to be found on a patch of waste ground as inside a man's house (if he was foolish enough to leave his door open), their emaciated forms reminded me of my own state, and although I didn't believe, I respected the locals' faith.

From the traders—legitimate and otherwise, con men and rickshaw wallahs—who normally had nothing to do with me but would sometimes natter to me out of boredom or jest, I found that commerce was the true essence of this city, and here amongst the pious and the tourist there was always money to be made.

Later I became another entrepreneur, giving massages on Dasashwamedh ghat between the fruit stalls and flower sellers to anyone that asked and some that didn't.

I barely listened to my customers, the sales patter quickly became second nature, and I spent my days puzzling the enigma of my existence. Every day, as dawn broke, funeral pyres along the bank blazing against the pale sky, believers performing their daily ablutions or releasing the uncremated into the river, I rinsed my face in the scummy waters and then stared at the rippling reflection staring back at me. Always two questions.

Who am I? I am a man who is not all man. I am an alien who is not all alien. By day, amongst the hoi polloi, the teeming masses, the endless battle for survival, it was easy to dismiss my strange memories as the last measures of a lunatic staving off complete insanity. Clearly, I was a man of flesh and blood, who had buried a terrible past and then stumbled into this holy city. But by night, or whenever I closed my eyes, those memories would visit me, tearing down the barricades of reason carefully erected during daylight hours and force me to make *this* the crux of my existence: that fundamentally I was something other than a simple man.

Why am I here? The second question always lurked in the shadow of the first much like each Hindu god was a manifestation of a higher one.

If I were a truly ordinary man, then my memories of life on an alien world (for I knew Earth's seas harbored no such intelligent creatures) must be fictions, twisted metaphors of my earlier times perhaps, but fictions nonetheless. Maybe I was a *sadhu,* a Hindu holy man, who had chewed too much *ganja* on his travels and pushed out his mortal memories in favor of invented visions. It would explain why nobody here knew me. But where I had come from, what was I seeking, I did not know.

Considering the opposite—that some part of me had been an alien, had swum in the oceans of a distant world, had somehow been transported across vast gulfs of space to arrive in this rickety vessel—begot even more difficult questions. How could this be possible? Who could engineer this? Why had I been chosen? Were there others like me here? What was my purpose now? Was I being punished or tested? The questions flooded on, any rationalizations I could muster too brittle to withstand the torrent of escalating queries.

In short, I chose not to choose. I believed both and neither. I decided I would write down my experiences so that nothing would be forgotten and one day I might be able to decipher the truth, but when I pressed nib against paper the way I had seen the fruit trader do when he jotted down his stall's inventory, I was unable to make a single meaningful mark.

I was illiterate.

To stop myself forgetting I told my tales to the locals instead.

One night, as tourists swarmed the steps of the ghat, attentions divided between the tugs of children who offered a route to the Golden Temple for five rupees, spiritual healers encamped on the wide stone plateaus, and the dancers on the wooden stage by the bank, Ramanuja approached my patch.

"Asajanaka, how are you keeping? Is business good?" he asked.

"Business is very good. The tourists have more money than sense. Soon I will be able to bed down in a place of my own earning." I listened to the music of the performance which hung in the warm air for a few seconds. "I am very grateful for what you did for me. Here, sit down and I will give you a massage as a token of my gratitude."

Ramanuja nodded and settled cross-legged on my simple woven mat. He said, "I hear you tell the most fabulous tales. They are from your remembrances I presume?"

Behind Ramanuja, who looked squarely out over the river at the few candlelit boats that bobbed on the Ganga, I darted my head left and right to see if any of my neighbors had overheard his words. Thankfully, they were all engrossed in their own affairs; I had told nobody else that the stories I shared were perhaps real.

I bent forward and whispered in his ear, "They are, but nobody else knows this and—"

"I understand," he said, raising a hand. "Would you mind sharing a story with me?"

"I'd be happy to," I lowered my voice, "it is my way of remembering."

"That is very important, Asajanaka. Never forget who you are, whatever it might be." His round head and black crop of hair remained perfectly still. He had more faith in me than I did.

"Imagine," I said, as I began kneading his scalp, "an

underwater world of kelp forests that sway with ocean currents, filled with a profusion of life so as to be like a seabed jungle. The fronds of the vegetation are so dense, so entangled, the light from above barely penetrates the upper canopy and the creatures of this place rely on other senses to survive. There are monstrous worms—tubular and flat, giant clams, sea slugs and jellyfish, mollusks and starfish, and a thousand other species. And there are large, graceful squidlike creatures that are to this watery world as humans were to Earth thousands of years ago. Intelligent but wild. Social but uncivilized."

I worked my palm and fingers over Ramanuja's shoulders and went on.

"This story concerns a squid called Nidara, or fearless, who was always goading his friends to venture with him to dangerous places: into the darkest heart of the forest where sinuous limbs could wrap themselves around a squid and crush it to death; down to the seabed valleys where nothing grew and terrible creatures were said to reside; or up to the shallows where squid were sometimes plucked away by unknown things from above.

"One time, he led a group of squid to the edge of the ocean where a vertical wall of rock rose from the seabed to high above the water. In this cliff was set a cave system whose mouth, when the waters were high, lay beneath the surface and sucked in and out the brine much like a man breathes air.

"'How far into the cave will you go?' he asked his companions and dashed to the entrance and back when the current was right.

"'It is forbidden to enter the cave,' one of the others said, spooked by the quick ebb and flow against her body.

ARTEM MIROLEVICH

"'Forbidden by whom?' Nidara replied, and darted in again, this time a little further.

"'By all of us, together,' said a different squid when Nidara had returned.

"'The legends say—' Nidara began.

"'The legends are made-up stories to stop foolish squid playing with their lives.'

"Nidara ignored his friend and went on, 'The legends say that he who enters the cave should be prepared to lose everything for the chance of immortality.' This time he didn't wait for a reply or the right timing, just heaved with all his power, his only fear he might suddenly have second thoughts and have to swim back to the mockery of his friends.

"He was just inside the mouth when the current turned, wrenching him inward and upward. He was never seen again."

I withdrew my hands from Ramanuja as I spoke the last word and remained silent behind him.

"Ah, very good," he said, clapping once and keeping his palms clasped together. "The perils of the path to enlightenment!" Then he twisted his head round and said quietly, "Am I correct in believing you witnessed these events?"

I stared over his face, out to the river, watching an ornately crafted barge slide towards moorings at the bank of the ghat. "I have . . . a personal awareness," I said.

"A personal awareness? That's an interesting turn of phrase."

A couple of servants on the barge leaped ashore and began securing the vessel to squat iron columns fixed into the stone. "Each day, each hour, each minute it gets a little harder to maintain the belief that I am anything but flesh and blood. My feet are hard and calloused like I have walked for thousands of miles. My skin is leathery and rough like I have spent endless days in the sun. My knees are knobbled like I have been bent in supplication all my life. I am a man."

The barge was steady now and the servants scurried back on board and stood rigidly on the deck.

Ramanuja said, "Yes, you are a man. But you have something inside which makes you more than a man as well."

"How do you know?" I said, raising my voice and meeting his gaze.

He turned forward again and although I felt shame for shouting, my anger won out. "Who are you to tell me what I am or am not?" Beyond Ramanuja, at the riverside, I noticed a crowd of locals had gathered round the gangway to the barge, chattering loudly.

He said, "Forgive me, sir, but you misunderstand me. I only relay what you told to me. What you are is something for you alone to decide."

The swarm of people and their invisible locus moved up the steps.

"And I think I am ready to decide," I said. The crowd moved closer, splitting and diverging around us so that we were suddenly at its heart. A young man in elegant, traditional dress spoke:

"Are you the man who tells fabulous tales of life in the oceans?" He addressed me, barely looking at Ramanuja. People around nodded their heads.

I straightened my back and said, "I am."

Then he peered down at Ramanuja. "Forgive my

intrusion. My servant will finish your massage and then take you to the restaurant of—" He put an index finger across his lips and furrowed his brow "—do I know you, sir?"

"I doubt it, sir. I am a humble charity worker who spends his days in the lower quarters of the city." Ramanuja stood up so he was face to face with the man. "My massage is over so there is no need to recompense me, sir."

The man gave a grunt of satisfaction and stepped past Ramanuja. "Do you wish to be away from these filthy steps? To sleep between silk sheets, eat the finest foods and live in luxury? Do you wish to tell your stories to a captive audience who will appreciate your craft?"

I looked away from the man, hardly believing the luck that had befallen me. The faces of the crowd were all pinned on me, some screwed up in envy, some flushed with delight, all awaiting my reply.

Ramanuja placed a hand on my arm. "I know you have already made this choice," he said softly. "Don't let a comfortable outer life cloud your inner judgment, though. Always remember: know thyself." He released his grip and slipped through the throng into the night.

"I will be your storyteller," I said to the man over the din of the onlookers.

The mogul's court, built by the British in a grand architectural synthesis of imperialist power and Islamic refinement, sat on a rise overlooking the road to Sarnath. Barefooted pilgrims and luxury coaches traveled the road to visit the deer park where Gautama Buddha, one of the eleven avatars of Vishnu, gave his first sermon.

Sometimes the air-conditioned dark-windowed coaches would stop and disgorge their chilled passengers into the early morning sun. They would snap photos and stretch varicose-veined legs, but they never approached the house which stood far beyond foreboding iron gates.

The mogul's guests comprised people of wealth and power, erudition and achievement; politicians, businessmen, celebrities and intellectuals. In the great hall they would mingle, discussing the affairs of the day, while servants in starch-stiff, cream-white suits served canapés and champagne.

I, and the rest of the mogul's retinue of entertainers— resident musicians, satirists, illusionists and suchlike—would stand as still as statues at the doors to the drawing room, until it was time for the guests to be entertained. Then the mogul would tap his champagne flute and announce the commencement of performances, the doors to the drawing room would be flung open with much pomp, and the guests would march in, hurriedly finishing their conversations.

The entertainments would last for hours, individual guests slipping in and out for private counsel with the mogul, who would rarely attend, and by the time the last Rolls-Royce or Bentley had left the estate, the stars in the eastern sky had been lost to the encroaching dawn.

It was just before such an hour, as the final guests funneled out into the waning night, and the mogul, his staff and performers, bid good night to them, that one of the visitors addressed me.

"A marvelous telling. Thoroughly enjoyable," he said.

"Thank you, sir," I replied, standing in a line with the rest of the non-menial members of the house.

He swayed a little, made to move off, decided against it, and tapped the back of a raised index finger against my breast. "Tell me, where did you learn such tales?"

Without breaking from my regimental stance I stole a look at the mogul, last in the line, beneath the enormous arched entrance; conversation with guests was usually frowned upon.

He nodded.

"I have a vivid imagination, sir," I said.

He rubbed his chin. "You've never been to sea and dived in the oceans, then?"

The guests forward of the man had shuffled out of the house now, and those behind had completed their pleasantries and were waiting for us to finish. Everybody was silent.

"No, sir," I said. I liked to keep my story as simple as possible.

"And you didn't learn your stories from another?" He leaned forward, drawing me into his whiskey haze, and added quietly, "I am a physician. I can understand how difficult it is to give another his due."

"No, sir. They are my own stories. From my imagination."

He pursed his lips and scratched the top of his sparsely haired head. "Remarkable. What are the odds?" he muttered to himself.

I tried to meet his eyes, to ask by sight rather than mouth since direct questions to the guests were forbidden, but he was lost in his own world.

"What are the odds of what, Ravi?" The lady next in line said, bringing the man out of his daze.

The man glanced at the woman and then the other way. "I'm holding everybody up, aren't I?" he said, suddenly aware everybody was listening.

"You are, but we're curious now. Tell us what was so remarkable and then we can all go home." Her words drew some titters from further down the line.

"Perhaps remarkable is the wrong word," he said, turning his back on me and offering his arm to the lady. She accepted and they walked away but I fixed my ear on his last words before they disappeared outside. "At the Vice-Chancellor's residence in Delhi I listened to a different fellow tell identical stories. Imagination? Poppycock!"

For many moons I was haunted by the doctor's words.

If there were others here with minds filled with the same seascape as I, then I would have to face the possibility that the alien world was real, and my visions were not the result of trauma or dream, but of a true, lived life.

Every waking moment, my train of thought was not far from that mysterious storyteller in Delhi. Did he really weave tales about the same kingdom I seemed to have been wrenched from, or was the doctor a little woozy that other night also and had seen a pattern where there was none?

I knew from my time amongst those who had fallen down the cracks in society, every man was susceptible to see design where there was none—especially those who needed meaning most of all.

I remember one of my old street acquaintances who saw the work of Shiva in everything: from the way dahl bhat was slopped onto his flimsy metal plate by the canteen staff at the refuge, to the path a dung beetle took as it carried its bounty. Was the doctor in that number?

At night, in my spacious chamber within the staff quarters, behind fine mosquito nets beyond which insects rallied with demented purpose, buzzing and clicking, I would awake from dreams which even the most slow-witted fortune teller would be able to interpret. My body would be aglow in a sheen of sweat, while I panted in shallow breaths. An impulse to cast off the silk sheets, wade through the breezy shelter, and charge off into the night and never stop until I found the other storyteller careened about my mind. To resist I lay stock-still and focused on my breathing, slowly bringing it back to normalcy.

It wasn't so difficult, really.

At the time, I didn't see my reluctance to leave as cowardice. I viewed it as pragmatism. My position in the mogul's court was stable and comfortable. I ate well, enjoyed companionship for its own sake, slept with several servant girls, and was even taken into the mogul's confidence about minor matters.

From overhearing the conversations of the numerous guests who were herded through the court every week like market animals, and occasionally being addressed directly, I was learning all the whorls and eddies that coursed through the province's channels of power. The stories dulled with each telling, and I envisioned a time where I would be a formidable receptacle of political knowledge and might be able to forge an alternative life.

335

I thought the doctor would return one day. Until then I would stay in the court and not make any rash choices.

He never came back.

Early one morning years later, in the gauzy postdawn light dimmed by the sparse canopy of the brushwood forest above, out hunting deer while sunbeams dappled the ground and drove off the dewy mist, the mogul whispered to me.

"The essence of hunting is timing."

We were crouched down on our haunches, the slender, shiny barrel of the ancient hunting rifle resting on my knee and drawing a line across my body like it warded off an unseen danger.

I nodded. I was still very much servant to the master, despite having his thoughts on most matters.

He went on, "Knowing the right time to move swiftly and close distance between oneself and the quarry. And knowing when to be still."

I watched him closely as he spoke, catching unheard words through the shape of his mouth. He had put on weight since he first invited me to be his storyteller years ago, but it was a comfortable heft, adding to the statesman's air that began with his sculptured hair, melodious voice and manicured hands.

He pointed two fingers at his eyes and then in a direction ahead and slightly to the left. I followed the line of his arm. Far ahead, through a chaotic avenue of thin beechwood trees, stood a magnificent stag chomping nonchalantly on a branch of eucalyptus. The main part of its torso was occluded by some thick brush, spoiling our line of sight.

The mogul indicated to shift left, so we crept across dry leaves and twigs that crackled and rustled as we moved.

The stag stopped chewing and looked straight towards us.

I froze still, left leg extended, calf tense, gun heavy in hand, while the stag sniffed at the crisp air. The ache of flexed muscle grew as the antlered deer took its time satisfying itself of its safety.

When I thought I could bear the searing pain no longer, the stag resumed eating.

We eased into the new position and I relaxed my limbs, enjoying the now clear line to our prey.

Gingerly, I passed the rifle to the mogul, but when I didn't feel him take it I turned towards him and found him pushing the gun back to me.

"This kill's for you," he said.

A buzz of elation, followed by a nervous trepidation assailed me . . . a dizzying sense of *déjà vu* . . . I closed my eyes to steady the feelings but it only jerked me nearer to the old echo . . . it suddenly snapped into focus . . . I was in front of the underwater cave, steeling myself to go up and out, body quivering with excitement and dread.

"Time your shot well." The mogul's words dragged me back to the present. I grappled for the memory but it was lost like so much of the forest, shrouded in haze. "Too soon and you won't have found your mark. Too late and the beast will have felt death's gaze on its hide and fled."

With the rifle across my body, I slid my left hand down the barrel, six inches from the muzzle, and placed my right hand around the trigger.

"Next year I will be a candidate in the Province's elections," the mogul said.

I relaxed the rifle, letting it drop a little, and turned to my master. He glowered at me, face contorted along lines usually unseen.

He spat, "The kill!" and jerked his head at the stag.

I thought he might be testing my nerve then. Seeing how I performed while calculating the consequences of his entry into the political arena. I raised up the gun in one smooth motion. The announcement was far from a surprise; court gossip had been rife.

"I want you to work with me," he said.

I smiled while I snuggled the butt of the gun into a cleft in my shoulder and made myself the still, unwavering center of the universe.

"To be an instrument that delivers me to office."

I closed my left eye and marked the deer in the sights. It ate with languid grace, at rest with the world, the way I would want to die.

"You will immediately stop your usual tales—" My aim kicked to the right, suddenly marking nothing more than a clump of shrubs "—and I will dictate what you should tell. You have enormous influence, you know?"

My stance, stonelike one moment, seemed as fragile as eggshells the next, and my right knee crashed down into the brush with a tremendous crack.

No more tellings. No more remembrances. No more roads to the past.

The stag bolted.

I fired. Out of shame or stress or instinct, I'm uncertain, the only sure thing was I'd missed, the shell ploughing into loose earth not twenty feet away.

I hung my head down. "I can't do that," I said.

Next to me, the mogul rose from crouching and stood to his full height. Forest debris fell next to me as he brushed his trousers down in brisk, harsh strokes.

"Can't or won't do it?" he said eventually.

I had never wilfully misled the mogul before. I wasn't going to begin now.

"I won't, sir. I can't explain why."

He tore the rifle from my limp hands.

"It is time you left my court, then."

"Yes, it is time," I said.

I left the mogul and his court and my pampered life later the same day.

I traveled the road back to Benares as an old man, choking and spluttering on the rings of dust flung up by passing vehicles. In the holy city I paused only long enough to amass my train fare from old acquaintances who were more than happy to exchange a few rupees for news of my time in the mogul's court. On the way to the station, in the shadows of one alleyway corner I thought I saw Ramanuja, but when I looked again, there was nobody. I bustled through the throngs outside the station, a frail man of no import pushed and bumped by merchants and drivers, waiting families and fellow travelers, but rather than be bruised by these collisions I was energized, and I boarded my train with hope, and perhaps even belief, in my heart.

In Delhi, colossal city of infinite contrasts—from rat-infested shanty towns to immaculate, palatial hotels; from the spice of street curries to the blandness of meals sanitized for Western palates; from the bleating racket of a million mechanical horns to the perfect silence of a Hindu shrine—I sought the other storyteller.

My connections from the mogul's court, while perhaps not a wide thoroughfare into the pulsing heart of the capital, were a slim backstreet along which I could contact those who might have once seen the storyteller. From the housekeeper of an interior minister I learnt there was indeed such a man, but her reminiscences of the content of his tales were vague and inconclusive. He'd been dismissed several years earlier after his behavior became too erratic for the taste of the minister.

I was close to giving up ever finding the man when a chance encounter with one of the mogul's old guests—an English diplomat—on a leafy avenue near the embassies offered hope.

"I know the one," the man said after I'd convinced him who I was and described who I was looking for. "Such a sad end." He adjusted his panama hat and tapped his cane on the ground.

"He's dead?" I asked.

"No. Perhaps that would be a blessing though." He marched away from me, his tan-colored suit so starched it rustled with each footstep. I hurried to his side, keeping tempo with the clip of his stick on the pavement.

"Could you elaborate, sir?"

"I can do better than that." He strode onward with renewed vigor. "Keep up!"

We came to a road busy with traffic, and the man hailed the first cab he could: a cramped motorized rickshaw driven by a gaunt man with bloodshot eyes.

"Bhutan-Gandhi Sanitarium, Fellasinga Road," the man barked at the driver, before hopping in. "Fellow told such marvelous tales. Quite unlike anything I'd heard before. Or since. Must've grown up by the sea, I'd say."

I grunted, barely registering the diplomat's words. A sanitarium? Would this be my eventual fate as well? Drooling like an imbecile, caged and kept from the world. The rickshaw skidded over the shaky highway, flying up and down with each pothole that studded the road.

"Is he—" the rickshaw swerved off from the arterial road into a lesser street "—is he in control of all his faculties?"

"Does he have all his marbles? No. Definitely short of a full set. He witters constantly. Makes damn little sense to me."

The driver pulled over. Behind a rusty chain-link fence a rambling garden squirmed and further back loomed a peeling, whitewashed house.

"You'll make your own mind up, of course," the man said, ducking his head and climbing out of the rickshaw.

The diplomat paid the driver and led me through a creaking iron gate, and onwards through the garden overgrown with withered trees and weeds; the original bricked path almost invisible beneath the unhindered curls and webs of tangled growths. To the left of the once grand doors of the house, a dull plaque with a scratched, flowery font read: *Bhutan-Gandhi House for the Feeble Minded*. To the right, at the end of a fraying rope, a bronze bell.

"We'll be in in a jiffy," the diplomat said, and gave the

rope a good tug, sending out a low-pitched dang-dang . . . dang.

I heard no footsteps beyond those large doors, but shortly enough the left door inched open and a small woman with a wrinkled, pea-shaped head peeped out. She stared at me, the diplomat out of sight to the right.

"Yes?" she said, without warmth. Her gray hair, streaked with white strands, was pulled back tight, widening her eyes.

"Hello, Shruti," the diplomat began, over-egging the honeyed tone of his voice, "it's Tristan Hunt here." He moved around so the woman could see him. "I've brought a friend to see the storyteller."

The door opened wide and the woman beamed. "Mr. Hunt! Always a delight to see you! Come in, come in!"

Tristan went in and I followed. The woman nodded curtly at me, closed the door and turned her attention back to the diplomat. While they made small talk—the woman laughing exaggeratedly to his words—I edged away down the hallway. The place was dark, the windows above the door grimy and admitting little light, and the trapped, heavy air was pungent with the smell of antiseptic and ozone, as though something had been recently burnt. There was a lone, rough table and the walls were empty of decoration. Under my feet, the cracked black and white marble squares squeaked with each step in my fine leather brogues; stolen or donated by my old employer, I wasn't sure.

"We keep everything spotless here," the woman said, stopping me from wandering further into the house alone.

"Perhaps you can show . . . my friend to the storyteller and then we might share a pot of Earl Grey, eh?" the

diplomat said, placing a hand on the woman's arm and winking at me.

"Yes, yes," the woman said. "Go through to the glasshouse, Mr. Hunt. I'll be with you shortly."

The diplomat took the first door on the right and left us. The woman bustled past me towards the heart of the house. "Follow me," she said. "We've put him in his own room since the treatment." She twisted and turned, leading me through the mazy house. Banal sounds of radio or television could be heard behind closed doors.

"Here we are," she said, stopping outside a cream door with the number twelve clumsily etched in the paint. She unlocked the door in one swish motion, unthreaded the key from her bunch and handed it to me. "Lock up after. You know the way back, don't you?" She didn't wait for a reply, grabbing up a handful of her sari and darting back the way we came.

Her footfalls were soon swallowed in the humid air. I knocked a double-tap on the door. There were no sounds from inside.

I went in.

The room was awash with light spilling in from a large, barred window on the far side, and I stood, squinting for a few moments. The only furnishings in the room were a chamber pot to the left and a simple bed to the right. A faint odor of urine spiked the air. Next to the window in a wicker chair, staring out to the gardens beyond, sat the storyteller.

"I hope you don't mind my entering," I said.

I could only see the back of his head, but he jerked a nod.

I closed the door and took a few steps to the middle

343

of the room. I could almost reach out a hand and pat the storyteller's bald head. He didn't turn about, just continued looking ahead.

"My name is Asajanaka, or rather, Asajanaka is the closest approximation to my real name in this tongue," I said, rubbing my hands, anxious. "I've come a long way to find you. If I'm right we have a unique history."

I glanced at the door and then told him everything in a whispered gush: my confused arrival on the temple steps in Benares; the vivid memories of a place so alien; lonely but comfortable years in the mogul's court; and the tantalizing possible existence of another storyteller who might be able to help me believe my stupendous past. He nodded his head from time to time in that spastic fashion as before.

"Are you that storyteller?" I said, afterwards. "Did you also arrive on this planet with another life in your soul?"

He remained impassive, fixated on the garden.

"Please, I want to believe," I said. He still didn't reply, and I got angry, perhaps ashamed I'd been so open to a stranger who barely acknowledged my words. I charged over to where he sat and fiercely grappled his shoulder. "You can do me the courtesy of telling me your name at least!" I said, trying to pull him about.

It was then he jerked his head again, but there was no meaning in the way he snapped it about that time, and catching sight of the side of his face I saw crusty spittle on his chin and fresh drool creeping out the side of his mouth. He made a noise for the first time; an incomprehensible, tortured moan, and I released my hand from his shoulder with a gasp.

344

Then he twisted his neck about and lifted his gaze up to meet mine, giving me full view of his ravaged face. Without the treatment he would have looked like a natural, aged man; craggy lines and gaunt cheeks and wizened eyes. Instead, the lobotomy—deep, corrosive scars marking its boundaries on the sides of his temple—had left him with a dead, vacant look and an open, sagging mouth.

"Oh, mercy!" I cried. "What have they done to you?"

He moaned louder, accompanying my sudden volume, and for a fleeting moment, understanding and brotherhood and pleading flickered in his eyes.

I slid my left arm over the front of his face, pressing down his eyelids as I did so, and then wrapped my right hand around his neck. A swift snap, as I'd done to many deer while out in the woods with the mogul, and his pain was over.

I arranged him in the chair to give the appearance he was sleeping and left the room, the house, and not much later, Delhi.

A few days later I was back in Benares, sat on Chowki ghat, watching schoolboys play cricket with all the abandon of untroubled youth when a shadow cast itself over me.

"May I join you?" the man causing the shadow asked.

I squinted up. "It's a free—" I rubbed my eyes, "Ramanuja? Is it really you, Ramanuja?"

He opened his arms. "Yes, it is me, Ramanuja."

"But you look so young . . . as though you haven't aged a whisker in all these years."

He patted his belly. "Maybe this is a little bigger, eh?"

How long had it been? Twelve? Fifteen years?

"Sit down, sit down," I said. "I'm glad to see you, Ramanuja. I was going to come down to the refuge . . ."

Ramanuja eased himself down to the stone step. "I'm glad to see you too, Asajanaka."

We fell into silence. The sound of willow against stone and rubber punctuated the quiet as the batsman readied himself and then swatted away the makeshift cricket ball. Cheering followed as a child in the field caught the shot.

"Do you remember my story, Ramanuja?"

"Of course."

His answer was so quick I had to see his face. It was serene, no mark his reply had been an empty reflex. "You had memories of coming from another world," he said, causing me to look back to the game.

"You are generous putting it like that. I didn't know if they were memories of madnesses then."

"And now?"

"Now I believe. My body is human, but my soul, my *Atman,* is alien. Something brought me to this world, and when I die something will take me back to my own world."

Ramanuja smiled.

"Don't mock me!" I said with a raised voice, causing a nearby child to take his eye from the game.

"Mocking you is as far from my thoughts as you can imagine."

Maybe it was all my years in the court, watching lies being said as casually as remarks about the weather, which made me an expert. He spoke truthfully.

"What will you do now?" he asked.

"When I came to, all those years ago, I awoke on the steps of a temple, in a holy city where dying means liberation, in a country which embraces a religion permitting all others. Why a temple? Why Benares? Why Hinduism?"

Ramanuja's eyes were opened wide. "Why do you imagine?" he said.

"Remember the tale of the forbidden cave? The legend that those who entered risked their lives for the chance of everlasting life."

"Yes, yes!"

"I believe I once went into that cave. And this life now is my test. I show my faith in what I am and when I die I will be given everlasting life."

"And how do you show your faith?"

Out on the Ganga, a corpse wrapped in rags bobbed in the wake of a boat. I thought of Shiva, adorned with live cobras and leopard skins, ash smeared over his body, wielding his trident, and riding his terrifying steed, the bull, Nandi.

And then I knew.

"I am an avatar of my true alien self. This body—" I pinched at loose skin on my forearm "is my vehicle. I must observe the rituals of this religion I find myself born to so that when I die I will be reunited with my true race." I jumped up. "Take me to the temple and show me the rituals."

Ramanuja stood up. "Worship begins at dawn. Meet me at Assi ghat just before sunrise, tomorrow," he said, and departed along the ghat.

The next morning I waited at the water's edge, butterflies dancing in my belly.

Upon rising I had been unable to eat, the thought of reincarnation with my kind turning my appetite from even a simple *roti*. I paced back and forth, splashing in the murky, holy water that lapped the ghat's first exposed step. The first rays of the sun speared the eastern sky, extinguishing the stars around. Soon the temple rituals would begin.

Where was Ramanuja?

I needed him to be here, now. Leave it till tomorrow and the gods that watched me would be displeased with my procrastinations and might bar my route back. "Shiva, stab your trident into his side and make him run!" I muttered.

My curse seemed to work as a moment later I saw Ramanuja emerge from the darkness, bounding down the tall steps.

"Forgive my late arrival," he said between heavy breaths, drawing a handkerchief from his pocket and mopping his brow.

"We bathe, yes?" I said, not concerned with hearing his excuses.

He nodded, chest heaving, and pulled off his shirt. I followed suit and then waded out deep in the water. I closed my eyes and ducked into the water. The tension which had been growing since yesterday's moment of enlightenment washed away in the soupy water and I was free, drifting on currents like old times from another world. The joy! I kicked imaginary tendrils making my foot hit the riverbed and I was back in the Ganga.

The taste of the other world was sweeter than a mango

lassi and for the first time I could see myself there again. I sprung up from the water with delight.

"There you are! Here, wash yourself with this—" Ramanuja threw a sliver of a soap bar at me "—quickly!"

The bar made few suds, but when I stood on the bank a few moments later I felt cleaner than ever before. We squeezed out water from our soaked clothing and hurried to the Golden Temple.

The doors were already wide open when we arrived and worshippers spilled out from the dark interior and down the steps. I plunged into the mass of bodies and fought through to the front; I would be the most devout Hindu alive and observe the ceremony with the zeal of a fanatic. Ramanuja trailed behind, apologizing to the men and women I'd just jolted past.

Inside, the noise of the outer layers of the congregation was replaced by a reverential quiet, but it was a combustible silence, like firecrackers set but not detonated, and I stalked to the front more circumspect. The smell of sandalwood and incense suffused the air and small flaming wicks flickered along the walls.

Ramanuja eased himself beside me. "Ah, the *pujari* bathes Shiva's *abhisheka,*" he whispered.

Ahead of us on a raised platform the priest dipped a small idol into a font brimming with liquid.

"What is he bathed in?" I asked, keen to consume every detail.

"A mixture of yoghurt, milk and ghee—gods are cleansed in finer waters than mortals," he replied.

The priest lifted the idol from the font and disappeared with it behind a heavy, crimson curtain.

"What happens now?" I saw my future life mirroring

the actions I now witnessed; I was a deity—a minor one, but one nonetheless—descended from the heavens above.

"Now the *abhisheka* is dressed in new clothes and adorned with Shiva's attributes."

"Attributes?" I said it aloud but it was a rhetorical question and I considered what my own attributes would be as Ramanuja enumerated Shiva's. Something from the oceans: bracelets of coral or shark's teeth; blind black eels coiled around my arms; maybe a lock of seaweed.

And then the curtain was drawn back and the devotees clamored forward; somebody's forearms pressed helplessly against my back. Bells rang out—from where I couldn't tell—and people began chanting with great exuberance.

"They sing mantras as they hope for *darshan,* blessed eye contact, with Shiva." As Ramanuja spoke the priest emerged from one side of the curtain and held the idol aloft before placing it on a table in the centre of the platform. A garland of bright yellow flowers hung around its neck, and beneath a leopard skin ran from right shoulder to left waist. I met the idol's gaze and my head leapt back as I caught a glimpse of the universal, and in it, my past, and future life, in waters light-years away. I closed my eyes and basked in the power of the vision. Shortly, there was a warmth in front of me and then I felt fingers grazing my face.

"The pujari transfers the divine light to you," Ramanuja said. I looked to see the priest swinging a small lamp and blessing the next worshipper.

Later, after we'd received *prasad*—blessed food—and

we'd left with all the other worshippers, I turned to Ramanuja on the temple steps. "I will return here every day until I die," I said.

I am too weak to make even the short journey to the temple now. My body is withered; spent muscles and loose skin hanging over a brittle skeleton. I feel the bed sores from so many days lying in this cot of death, but they don't pain me. At least not where it matters, for I still worship—the phallus-shaped *linga* and circular-based *yoni* representing Shiva and Shakti to one side of the bed—and I know a new life is coming.

Sometimes in the muggy heat of day the small, square window of the simple room seems to be a portal onto my other world—the shimmering haze akin to lazy ocean currents—and I see the squidlike creatures propel themselves past with undulating tentacles.

I almost float up and join them before Ramanuja comes in and dispels the fantasy. He looks so young still and I ache to ask him what his role is in all this, but I don't wish to upset the gods—both those who put me here and those, like Shiva, who are manifestations of Brahman—so I hold my tongue. He knows the unuttered question anyhow, and always softly says, "Soon, soon," as he feeds me small handfuls of rice, or wets my mouth with water.

He is right.

Soon I will leave this Earth. Soon I will travel the void between the stars. Soon I will be home and reunited with my true kind and know the truth.

Revelation is coming.

Pilgrimage

written by

Karl Bunker

illustrated by

PETER TOWN

ABOUT THE AUTHOR

Karl Bunker's lifelong love of science fiction began at about eight years old when he read his first "grown-up" book—a 1950s paperback of short stories by Simak, Leinster, Asimov and other greats—while sick in bed. Karl imagines the stories must have burned themselves into his feverish brain. He began writing at age ten and immediately gave it up as hopeless. Years later, he tried again, with the same results. Nevertheless, Karl has repeated this cycle with, in his words, "dogged and thoroughly irrational frequency" ever since. It's slowly begun to pay off. His first published short story, "Nomad," appeared in the webzine Abyss & Apex *in late 2006. Our presentation of Karl's winning story will be his first in-print byline.*

Karl currently resides in Jamaica Plain, Massachusetts, where he works as a software developer.

ABOUT THE ILLUSTRATOR

There once was a boy named Town,
who grew up with trees all around.
In a house built of hand
by his mom and his dad,
lived two brothers, three sisters and friends.
Across three wooded acres they played,
seeing empires and dynasties made.
If that wasn't enough,
they all loved his art stuff
and that led him to draw more again.

Peter Town's youthful adventures took place in Northern California's Sonoma County and included a passion for comic books. As his artistic style emerged, he became intrigued by the black-and-white work of Aubrey Beardsley. Other influences included John Byrne, Alan Davis and John Buscema. He's currently working towards a master's degree in cultural anthropology and hopes to finish within a few years. Peter lives in Sacramento with his wife, Leslie, and their two-year-old daughter, Penelope Elizabeth, who keeps his illustration pace quite quick while trying to add her own creative touches.

Pilgrimage

On my third day I find a good stone. A rounded mass of shale as high as my hip, somewhat flat on one side. I don't see any veins of quartz or other flaws, and it's right at the edge of the lake, so I won't have to carry the water I'll need for grinding. It's too heavy for me to move, so I'll work on it where it is.

The first day I spent weaving a back-basket to carry my tools, and relearning how to make fire with a bow. Then for two days I hiked back and forth around the shore of the lake, clambering over the stones of the shallows, fighting through the tangled shrubs of the shore. I fell and bruised myself a few times, and earlier this day I scraped my ankle when I slipped on a wet stone. I sat watching the blood appear, drop by drop, from the tiny severed capillaries.

I take off my backpack. I'm eager to start work on the stone, but I know I should set up a camp first. With my axe I fell several trees to make a lean-to. As thick as my arm and taller than my body, the trees are of the type I named "rope-bark trees" long ago.

It's spring, so the bark peels off easily. I cut the outer bark into half-cylinders to use as shingles, and pull off the inner bark in long strips to twist and braid into the rope I'll use to hold my construction together. Slowly my hands remember their old skills: the best way to roll the fibrous inner bark between my palms, how to cut the saddle-notch joints into the small logs with my axe and knife. My camp will be just an angled roof and a floor; unless the climate has changed since my last visit, the nights should be reasonably warm.

I work through the day, then build a fire and roast some of the edible roots I'd gathered from the lakeshore in the morning. My hands are raw and blistered, and I have a bandage of bark fiber tied over a gash on my left thumb. I know my skin will toughen over the coming days. I sleep that night on a bed of leaves. In the morning I start work on the stone.

I have a stonecutter's point as long as my forearm, a chisel as wide as three fingers and a heavy hammer with a steel head. These plus the axe and the knife are my only tools. It's enough. With a drill and wedges I could cleave the stone down to a slab in a day or two. As it is I have to use the point to cut grooves, chip by chip, and then chisel off the material between the grooves. It's slow work, but the grinding will be slower.

Taking a rest from the stonework, I gather some bivalve shellfish from the lake shallows, cook and eat them. I cut and split some saplings to weave a fish trap, but I keep getting it all wrong and it falls to pieces in my hands. Finally I yell in a fit of temper, throw the thing on the ground and crush it under my foot. But the green splints just bend and spring back instead of snapping with a satisfying crunch. The frustration leaves me like a puff of air. I laugh and sit with my back against a tree and stare out at the lake.

We liked to tell ourselves we were fighting a war. Such an old word, such grand history behind it! There were seven of us—an unprecedented combined force in those days. In the vast playground of the galaxy, getting seven individuals to cooperate on a single project that took over four hundred standard years to complete was unheard of. We had gathered here, in the Perseus arm, to finish our construction and trap our foe.

"Fortunato!" Jae called out as one of his entity-copies flew past me. "From Poe! 'The thousand injuries of Fortunato I had borne as I best could; but when he ventured upon insult, I vowed revenge,' he quoted. We should call it Fortunato, yes?"

I had to admit it was appropriate; we even had the irresistible cask of amontillado in the form of the sphere we were building around a certain star. We knew it would come, with its animalistic drive to feed on such constructions, and its path from the galactic core would take it through Perseus, and into our trap.

"But has it insulted us?" I asked Jae. Myself, I preferred to think of our foe as a dragon: large, dangerous, of unknown origin, vaguely magical, and a creature to be vanquished by brave souls of pure heart.

"Its refusal to communicate with us is the insult!" Jae answered. "It breaks our works, steals our rare elements, and otherwise ignores us, scuttling back to the core where we can't follow. Never so much as a flicker of response to our signals. Thinks it's too good for us!"

I was just landing on the surface of the planet as he said this, and to emphasize his outrage he threw a shower of meteorites across the sky above me. The bright lines stretched almost from horizon to horizon.

357

"Perhaps it will talk to us when we have it bound up in our trap," I answered him with a laugh. "For the love of God, Montresor!" Jae laughed at that and was on his way, his mind flickering across the Span's web to take up his assigned task a thousand light-years from my post on the planet surface.

Our plan called for wresting the forces of half the galactic arm to our will. Alva downloaded herself into thousands of mote factories and hopped from star to star in the arm, constructing gossamer collectors around as many as had the asteroidal raw materials to make it practical. From these came the energy that was fed to me and two others in our group. The energy we needed to gather threads of high-dimensional matter that we flexed and bent and twisted together into an array of spokes that stretched across four thousand light-years. Jae and Wren and Asu pulled in metal from dozens of star systems to spin the weavers to our spokes. When the cloud of linked particles that was our foe, our Fortunato, came through this space, the spokes of the trap would phase-change, and the structure would curl in on it at relativistic speed, the magnetic fields of the trap sweeping the cloud into a solid mass. It was a beautiful construction; huge and intricate beyond anything that had been seen in the Span before.

And how we gloried in it! Surely a project such as this was only a few evolutionary steps short of the great work of the trans-galactics. I remember Jae standing on an asteroid at the rim of the galaxy, facing out at the emptiness and spreading his arms like the wings of a bird. "We're coming, you bastards!" he shouted.

I took a position on the surface of this planet, the one Alva named Beachglass. From here I could reach out my senses to the whole width of our project and direct the thousands of machines and quantum webhoppers that were under my command. Beachglass was, is, that rarest of gems: a planet with life, and a solar system stable enough that life had been here for billions of years and would continue for billions to come. It was a newly discovered treasure; we had only found it when we came to the Perseus arm to build our trap.

Because Beachglass was so similar to Old Earth, I gave myself a body like an Old Earth human. In playful conceit, I dressed myself as an eighteenth century Japanese *daimyo,* complete with *katana* and short sword. When the battle was done Alva promised to join me here in her own human form. We would celebrate our victory by walking in forests and swimming in lakes, by eating food and having sex in the old human ways, surrounded by the wild, sweet smells of unmanufactured nature. How I looked forward to that, and how eager I was to do well in her eyes, to make her proud.

So we all worked at our preparations, I on my planet and the others, either positioned at some strategic point, or spread out in a network of machines, like Alva. The Span tied us together, its web stretching between us and back to the tangled nest that was its body and our home. We were nearly ready. Soon our foe would be trapped and helpless and we could send it out of the galaxy or to some far dimensional corner of the multiverse where it would never interfere with us again. Soon.

Alva reached the last of the stars we would need (such exquisite timing our foe had!). Her network of motes entered orbit and started extruding the thin collector fabric. She had barely begun when the emotionless voice of the Span itself came to us: "Emergency situation," it said. "Neutrino burst." The words were overlaid with a flood of information: an instability in the fusion of the star Alva was orbiting, a collapse of the star's core, the Chandrasekhar limit exceeded, a smothered inferno of gamma rays, inverse beta decay, the formation of a neutron core . . . in short, a supernova. Alva's star was exploding.

"Span, get her out of there!" I yelled. I think the others were yelling the same thing. But Alva's voice was not there. Instead, the Span answered us. "My web has been damaged by the neutrino wave, I've lost contact with her. . . . It's too late; her motes are vaporized."

"What? What?" It was Jae, his voice somewhere between incomprehension and rage.

"She's dead," I said. I was speaking more to myself than him. Dead. Alva is dead. That almost-forgotten thing. It had been over a thousand standard years since someone I knew personally had died. Lyn, when she tried to rescue a living planet from a black hole, only to fall into it herself. And Lyn was not Alva, my lover, my own, the dearest to my heart. Alva!

"This was not a natural phenomenon," the Span said. "That star didn't have sufficient mass for this to happen. It is your Fortunato. Somehow it caused this to happen." And again there was a rush of data accompanying the words. It was speculation this time; various theories about how our foe might have engineered this. Probably an invisible planet-sized missile of baryonic dark matter. Not that any of us cared at that moment.

Somehow Fortunato had anticipated us, outmaneuvered us. The trappers had been caught by a booby trap. And as we stood there, immobile with shock, an even greater shock crashed in on us. We all sensed it simultaneously: Fortunato was linking itself to the Span, using Alva's stray connection threads. This was impossible, but it was happening. It was contaminating the Span itself, seeping into its quantum entanglement threads like some black fluid of disease. This was a threat infinitely beyond the death of any individual. The Span cradled all of humanity in the palm of its web; all our knowledge and the lives of every human in the galaxy.

I knew what was coming before the Span spoke the words: "I have to withdraw myself from this sector. I will return for you when I have repaired myself. Try to survive."

And it was gone. Everything was gone. The Span had severed its connection with me. My link to Jae, Wren, Asu and the others was gone; my connection to the totality of knowledge was gone; my connection to my senses, my powers, to home, to the whole of life that I had known, all gone. I was standing in a forest, at the edge of a lake, and suddenly I was nothing more than the scraps of biological life around me. The bugs scuttling at my feet, the fish in the lake, the plants; I was as fragile and powerless as any of them.

My legs folded and I sagged to the ground. I waited. First I waited for it to end, for the Span to come back and make me whole again. Then I realized it wouldn't be coming back any time soon, so I waited to die. Surely I couldn't live like this, so I must be dying. I felt cold, and I thought that must be death coming on me. The air

361

scraped in my throat as I breathed, and I thought that must be another part of death. It was night, and I could barely see. I was curled in on myself, sitting with my legs folded under me, my face close to the grassy ground. "I will die here and this body will rot and be eaten by insects and nothing of me will remain," I thought. "It will be as if I never existed."

I felt colder and colder, until it was an aching, searing pain that seemed to eat at my flesh. I huddled and shivered uncontrollably and thought, "Does it have to take so *long* to die? Does it have to hurt so much?" And nothing changed; I suffered and shivered and eventually I lifted my head and wailed at the empty sky. I yelled out the names of my companions, as if my pathetic voice could carry through light-years of space. I screamed at them to come save me, then I cursed them when they didn't come. I cursed Alva for letting herself be killed and causing this disaster. Most of all I cursed the Span; I called it a filthy coward and a hundred other things for leaving me here to freeze in misery while it retreated back to its safe nest.

In the midst of my histrionics I noticed that I was feeling better. It hadn't occurred to me that crouching immobile on the cold ground might have been contributing to my discomfort. I stood up and walked back and forth, pulling the voluminous silks of my costume close around me and trying not to trip on the uneven ground in the dark.

Finally the sky lightened with morning. Small creatures in the trees started a cacophony of songs and other noises. The sun rose over trees on the opposite side of the lake and shone in my face. It felt like a miracle. The warmth of infrared poured down on me like a blessing from some ancient god. I spread my arms to the light and breathed deeply. The air no longer hurt my throat; it smelled of life. "Apparently I am not dead yet," I said. I drank from the lake. The water might be thick with microorganisms that would kill me, or it might be that no microbe on this whole planet is adapted to attack my body. I didn't know. I was hungry, so I started experimentally tasting plants; all of them were bitter or seemed like so much indigestible wood. I saw bivalve shellfish among the rocks in the shallows of the lake, but decided I wasn't that hungry yet. Food, water, shelter, fire. If I had those things perhaps I could survive here for a while. With access to the Span, I would know in an instant the answer to any question: which plants are edible? How do I make fire? How do I build a shelter? Should I look for a spring rather than drinking from the lake? How cold, how hot is this area going to become? As I was, I only had what scraps of knowledge had found their way into that near-useless, infinitely fallible instrument, my flesh brain.

I tried to evaluate my situation. I had two swords, the silks of my clothes, wooden sandals, a netsuke in the form of a dragon trapped in a net. I looked at this last item with disgust and threw it into the lake. The swords would be of some use, though a poor substitute for a good axe if I needed to build a log cabin and cut any great quantity of firewood to survive a cold winter. I sat with my back against a tree and cursed my situation again. The Span could transmit anything instantly over any distance once it was established, but extending itself into new space could only be done at light speed. So how long it would take to come back for me depended on how far it had retreated. Probably several light-years, possibly dozens, perhaps hundreds. My body was human-normal; under ideal conditions it would last less than a hundred standard years. My feet were still aching with cold, and I clutched them in my hands and rocked forward and back, crying like an infant.

Eventually hunger drove me to get up. I waded into the lake and pulled one of the smaller bivalves from the bottom. The shell pried open easily with my short sword. I tried to swallow the flesh without letting it touch my mouth. My stomach lurched, but it stayed down. I ate two more and started thinking about what sort of shelter I might build that would make the coming night less miserable.

Days passed. I named the largest of the three moons Alva, and watched its phases change from full to new to full again. Fifteen days to a "month." It was getting colder, and I worked for days to learn the skill of making fire with a bow drill. I wasn't sure how even the vague idea of how to do this came to be in my memory. Perhaps the Span had fed me a few bits of survival skill information as it disconnected from me. Finally I succeeded, and turned to building a better shelter and gathering and cutting firewood. One morning there was a skim of ice on the lake, and I shuddered with fear. Each evening I marked the position of the setting sun using the shaft of light that shone through a particular fork in the trunk of a particular tree. The sun was clearly retreating south. On a day when the ice on the lake stayed frozen all day, the mark I made for the position of the setting sun didn't move. In another three days I was sure: the mark had reversed itself and was moving to the left. The winter solstice had passed. I could still gather shellfish and catch swimming fish, and some of the edible plants I'd found were still green. The winter wasn't going to kill me.

Spring seemed like a celebration. My lakeshore domain was alive with hundreds of different species of small animal. Many seemed to be migrating to the north. The nights became a din as tiny animals ran over and under and through my tiny A-frame log hut. Other beasts sang, chirped, squealed, yowled from the trees, the ground, the lake. Occasionally I heard something big, very big, crashing through the forest, and one night I was jolted awake by a ragged bellowing roar that seemed to shake the ground. That morning I saw animal tracks in the mud near the lake. They appeared to be the prints of a huge bird or Therapod, with three-toed feet almost twice as long as my own. At the end of each toe was the imprint of a claw as big as my thumb. I saw the beast itself a few days later. It was indeed large, a dinosaurlike creature twice my height and weight, and very clearly carnivorous. I saw it from some distance and it took no notice of me, but it was a terrifying sight. I felt pathetically helpless and vulnerable. I started practicing the use of my sword, and cut some long thin trees to make into spears when the wood dried.

It was about this time that I also started seeing the Canids. These were somewhat comical creatures that looked like a cross between a rabbit and wolf of Old Earth. Usually quadrupedal, they had oversized hindquarters and would often rear up on their haunches to look around and sniff the air. They were about as tall as my knee when on all fours, and had long canine snouts and triangular ears. They showed little fear of me, boldly walking through my little camp area to look for fish scraps.

In the earlier days of my marooning I thought I would quickly go insane if no rescue came. I learned that I didn't have time for any such indulgence. I was hungry and I had no warm place to sleep, and solving those problems kept me busy every minute I was awake. By the time I had the necessities for staying alive, I was beginning to learn the joy of building things, of improving my life and situation through physical effort and my slowly developing skills. My mind raced with plans for a hundred projects to improve my little homestead. My house of thin logs grew from a covered sleeping platform to a structure I could stand up in and walk a few paces. It had a door and even a crude fireplace. I wove a sleeping mat of grass and coarse blankets from bark fiber. I planted a garden and stored edible roots for the winter. I rediscovered a thousand techniques and tricks that mankind had first worked out thousands, hundreds of thousands, even millions of years ago.

In the life I came from I had reshaped continents and oceans, tailored atmospheres, even imported whole engineered ecosystems to lifeless worlds. Or I pretended to do all that. Really it was the Span that was doing it; directing the forces, calculating what was possible so it could offer me menus of choices. When we played at things like this we would tell ourselves that we were adding the crucial ingredient of imagination, but really we were just children playing with toys. Nothing I did in those days gave me anything like the satisfaction

I got from my log shack, the door of split planks, the hinges carved from forked branches.

I enjoyed the company of the Canids. They were casual visitors to my camp; sometimes two or three at a time would sit and watch me as I cleaned fish, and I would toss the scraps to them. They could have been dangerous if they decided to attack in a group, but they never showed any signs of aggression toward me. In the fall they would leave me, presumably following the migratory small animals they preyed on. One spring I saw that one of them had an injured hind leg. I could tell from her swollen teats that she was a nursing mother. She limped, and clearly couldn't hunt, so I started saving whole fish to toss to her. She came every day, but it was clear that her leg was infected; she was sick and getting worse. Finally she could barely walk, and her whole body was twisted with pain. I took up my sword and dropped a fish near my feet. She paused and looked up at me, then approached and started eating. I knew killing her would be an act of mercy, but I wasn't good at killing. I had never tried to kill anything bigger than a fish, and even killing fish was difficult and unpleasant. I held the sword high; a quick stroke would behead her. I tensed, closed my eyes, tensed again, opened my eyes and she was gone. I saw her disappearing down the grass-lined animal trail she had come by. Two days passed with no sign of her. I hoped she was dead, perhaps killed quickly by a Therapod.

On the third day she came again. I heard her first: a rustling in the grass that seemed to get closer, very slowly. Finally she came into the clearing, dragging something with her. It was a baby Canid—her offspring. She held it with the scruff of its neck in her mouth, and with the burden she could barely move. I was frozen where I stood, wondering what scene was being played out before me. She came straight toward me, closing the distance with painful slowness. When she was at my feet she dropped the pup there, then pushed it a little further with her nose. I felt its thin fur brush the bare skin of my toes.

Then she turned and hobbled away. She moved much faster now, but it seemed that she was using the last dregs of her energy to get back into the cover of the tall grass. I knew that soon she would be done with moving forever. The pup stood on wobbly legs and made a small bleating sound. It tried to follow its mother, walking a few steps and toppling over. Finally I unstuck myself. I walked up to the little animal, hesitated a moment and then picked it up. He was barely a double handful, leggy and emaciated. I looked at his face and he looked back at me, trembling. "Come with me, Pup," I said.

Pup was to be his name for as long as he was with me.

I fed him fish that I ground into a paste, and in only a few days he was plump and much stronger. It was a great deal longer before he stopped trying to escape to find his mother.

Pup quickly became my companion and the greatest comfort I had in my life on Beachglass. I allowed myself no illusions about his species' intelligence, but there was no denying that when I looked into his eyes something looked back at me. A living, feeling creature who lived in the same world as me. I was a person of the Span world, and had been for all the thousands of years of my life. But now, in this place, I had more kinship with this animal than with my friends back on the Span. We felt hunger, heat and cold; we felt fear and vulnerability in the face of a hostile world. In the night, when I felt as alone and surrounded by emptiness as a dust speck in space, he was beside me and I knew I was not alone. With morning he would wildly celebrate the new day with a breathless romp around the clearing, running circles around the hut, around me, around nothing at all, and I would be swept up in his joy.

When the autumn of Pup's first year came, I knew the rest of his kind were migrating south, and I was afraid he would leave me. He had been bringing home his own meals of rodents and lizards, so I knew he could survive without my handouts. As the days got shorter, he would disappear for longer and longer periods, until he was gone for a day and a night. But he came back, breathless and exhausted, as if he had run some great distance and then run back again. I dropped to my knees and hugged his furry body and held him for a long time.

That same autumn I noticed that I was seeing a particular Therapod regularly. They all had a mottled reddish gray hide, but this one had a red left forelimb. These animals were apparently territorial, and I was living in this one's territory. On a couple of occasions I almost walked into it. Each time it regarded me thoughtfully, sniffing the air as if trying to decide whether I was suitable for eating.

Finally it decided to attack me. I was at the lake when it came along the shore towards me. Its pace was unhurried but it was holding its head and body low, its huge legs flexed and ready to spring. I backed away,

369

into the woods, and it followed me. I kept backing and it kept following. Its breathing seemed to get louder.

I drew my sword and stood my ground. "This is how I die," I thought. "A meal for this foolish animal, just as I've been eating fish." It approached, and I slashed at it. To my surprise, the sword hit exactly as I had intended, lopping off two fingers of its right forepaw. I was hoping this would frighten the beast away, but it didn't so much as glance at its injury. Its eyes were fixed on me and it curled in on itself, crouching for a strike. I stepped in and slashed again, aiming for its neck, then swinging the blade back in the other direction, across its midsection, then finally pulling back and thrusting straight at its upper chest.

The Therapod lunged at me, meeting my thrust. I imagine its tactic was to strike at my neck with its huge mouth, but it missed. Instead its whole body crashed against me. My sword, buried in its body, was jerked out of my hands as I was lifted off my feet and thrown onto my back. I heard, or imagined, a shrieking roar and opened my eyes to look deep into a gaping mouth. Its breath was a hot wind on my face. I closed my eyes again and felt a grinding impact on the top of my head.

And then everything was still. I wondered if I had passed out, or if the Span had returned and used some trick to freeze time. But neither was so. The thing was dead on top of me. My head, absurdly, was half-lodged in its mouth; one fang was piercing the underside of my jaw, and two or three had penetrated the skin of my scalp and impacted my skull. I tried to move, then tried harder, then tried a third time. I got my arms free and was able to pry the mouth off my head. Blood was everywhere,

PETER TOWN

covering my face, making my hands slippery as I tried to roll the creature off me. I rested briefly, and then felt the Therapod's body jerking and twitching. For a wild moment I thought it was coming back to life. Then I recognized the sound of Pup's growling voice; he was grunting in time with the twitches of the corpse. Turning my head I saw he had a forelimb of the Therapod in his mouth, and rhythmically planting his feet and jerking with all his weight, he was pulling the dead thing off me.

Only when I was free did the pain fully hit me. I lay there and groaned for a while. When I tried to stand up my left knee gave way with a tearing sensation that made me scream. I lay on my back for a long time and Pup licked my face and the wounds on my head.

Eventually I dragged myself into my hut and to my bed. I lay there for most of the next three days. I raged against the pain in my leg and head, against the body that inflicted this maddening, useless agony on me, against myself for making a body that was so faithfully accurate to the pathetic scrap of flesh that the old humans had. What conceivable purpose could such an insane, relentless pain serve? I wondered. I raged and wondered, but mostly I lay still and suffered.

At some point, I think it was the first day, Pup brought a chunk of bloody flesh in and dropped it near my head. It must have been a part of the Therapod's carcass. When I pushed it away, he pushed it back at me with his nose. Finally he accepted that I wasn't going to eat it, so he lay down and started gnawing on it himself. That made me laugh, and laughing made me know that I wasn't going to die. Not this time, at least.

Clearly the bacteria of this ecosystem had no taste for my human body, because no infection developed in my various wounds. After two days I could crawl, and once I had tied a splint around my knee, hobble. I was fearful of being seen in my helpless condition by another Therapod, and I wondered how long it would be before a new one took over the territory of the one I had killed.

It was half a year before we saw signs of another Therapod on our side of the lake. My leg was nearly healed by then, and with Pup's help I tracked it to the place where it slept. Then I waited through a long cold night and attacked it in the morning. I rammed a spear into its gut while it was still sluggish from the cold night. As it bellowed and thrashed I speared it again. It ran away then, and Pup and I tracked it for most of the day until it collapsed. I killed it with my sword, hating myself for doing it, hating this world for making me do it.

That was our life for years. I can't say how many years, because I didn't bother to count. I didn't know how the length of this planet's years compared with standard years anyway. I knew that my body aged, that the top of my head became bare, my tangled beard went gray, that I accumulated injuries to muscle and ligament and bone that never fully healed. I know that both Pup and I were getting slower and more frail.

And I knew that eventually I would die. Either in battle with the endless succession of Therapods, or through some accident. In the meantime, we had a life.

The end came on a winter afternoon. I was inside by the fire, working on a fishing spear when Pup lifted his head and growled a warning. I stood, went to the door and was reaching to open it when Pup made another sound, sharp and urgent this time. I turned to look at him when the door exploded in on me. A Therapod had charged my little hut. I was lying on my side with the door and part of the wall in pieces around me. Framed in the gaping hole where the door used to be was a gigantic Therapod, bigger than any I'd seen before. My sword had been leaning beside the door, so now it was somewhere in the splintered wood on the floor. The beast didn't give me time to look for it. It reached its head into the shattered hut, closed its jaws around my leg, and with a single violent jerk, yanked me out onto the ground. It looked down at me then, calculating the best way to make a quick kill.

There was a sound. It was a high-pitched, throaty shriek that I had never heard before, but I knew it was Pup. He was standing at the threshold of our hut, his mouth wide. I could hardly believe that such a sound could come from his body. The Therapod turned to look, and simultaneously Pup launched himself. With a huge leap he reached the level of the Therapod's throat and sank his teeth into the loose skin there. The Therapod bellowed and swung its head back and forth. Pup was flailed around like a length of rope, but he hung on to the creature's throat.

As this happened I was stumbling and dragging myself to the hut. My left leg was dead below the knee, but it was just a few steps. I found the sword and picked it up, jerking the scabbard off. I turned in time to see that the Therapod was holding Pup in its forelimbs. Pup was squirming, trying to reach some part of the monster with his teeth. The Therapod lifted Pup toward its mouth. I knew what was coming and I was helpless. It bit down on Pup's body. I heard bones being crushed, saw a burst of arterial blood, and I screamed. I took a step, but my left foot folded sideways and I fell. I stood again. The beast dropped Pup's body and leaped at me. I slashed at it, but missed and fell as my ankle gave way again. I was face down and I saw a shadow darkening the grass around me. I rolled over onto my back and slashed up blindly at the same time. There was a gurgling spray of blood and air as the Therapod's windpipe and neck arteries were severed. It reared up, staggered a few steps, stood wavering for several moments as if balancing itself, then fell over. It made wet breathing sounds for a while longer, but didn't move from where it lay.

I crawled to Pup's body. I had seen a thousand dead animals in my time on this world, but none of them looked as utterly dead as Pup. This furry body had been a part of my world for so long, and now, somehow, it was an empty thing that was not Pup. It didn't seem possible. I tried to lift him in my arms, but only lost my balance and fell onto the ground beside him, my face against his bloody fur.

I lay there for some time. When I finally started to get up, the Span came back to me. Without warning it crashed in on me like an implosion. The knowledge, the awareness, freedom from any sensation of my aged and damaged body. It was like being crushed and weightless simultaneously. The voice of the Span spoke to me first:

"We thought it would be best to wait until your life

here came to some kind of conclusion." The emotionless voice seemed almost tender.

"How—how long . . ." The Span had transferred me to a small vessel that hovered over the ground. I looked down at the body that had been me, the other body that had been Pup. My "voice" in this state required no breath, but I felt out of breath. I realized I didn't have to ask the question, and reached out for the information myself. Five Beachglass years. The Span had been repaired for the past five years. I thought about this in silence for a time, and accepted it. "Until my life here reached some kind of conclusion." They had thought it was for the best, and perhaps it was.

Jae spoke then: "Good to have you back, old friend! We've been busy; we learned a lot about Fortunato when it tried to take over the Span. We know how to kill it now. We're going to send a probe into the core . . ."

"Kill it?" I asked.

"Of course! It killed Alva; it tried to destroy the Span. It could have killed all of us—the whole galaxy!"

I felt a shudder of unreasoning revulsion. I was infinitely tired, and I wanted to get away from these people; away from them and their galaxy-spanning games. I wanted to lie down and sleep through a long night with Pup at my side, but I knew that life was gone forever.

"Yes," I said finally. "Kill it, then."

"We could use your help," Asu said tentatively.

"No." There was nothing more to say.

The new stone is ready after some twenty days' work. Grinding the face of it smooth takes the longest. I use a flat, hand-sized piece of granite to grind with, sand from the lakeshore for abrasive and water to flush the surface. Rub the smaller stone against the face of the larger stone in a circular motion, adding more sand and water with every few circles. Continue until my muscles fail me, then rest and continue again. And again, and again. I taste the salt of my sweat and smell the wet stone. I hear the sounds of the lake and the forest. A few Canids come by to watch me and pick through my food leavings. I speak to them softly and they look quizzically at me and I go back to grinding. When I find the surface acceptable I start carving the name. I think of the time, three of these trips ago, when I made the stone too thin. I was in the middle of carving the first "P" when the stone split neatly in half under my point. I smile ruefully at the memory and chisel more carefully. Finally it's done. I carry it to the grave and lay it down. I dig up the old stone, still intact but worn smooth and the lettering illegible. Four hundred standard years seems to be the right length of time between replacements. I methodically break up the old stone and scatter the pieces. I place the new one and fill in the dirt around it. Then I decide it's not straight enough, so I dig it up and shift it a bit. It's done.

I kneel there at Pup's grave for a long time. In this human form, on this world, where time actually has meaning, I kneel until my legs are numb, holding onto the stillness of the moment, holding onto the joy and the pain of my memories, holding. Soon I will have to leave for my other life, where both time and life are as valueless and empty as air. Again I think of staying. Of living here, finding another Canid to keep me company, staying in human form until . . . until what? Again I know I won't do it. I will do what I have been doing, what I promised myself I would do, every four hundred years, for as long as I live.

Finally I stand up, ready to leave. "Thank you, Pup," I say.

Here's the Thing . . .

BY JUDITH MILLER

Judith Miller attended Rutgers University where she earned a master's degree in fine arts. She has worked steadily at her craft since then and has gained experience in many aspects of illustration, with work published in numerous books and magazines. Her award-winning paintings can be found in private collections around the country. Judith Miller lives and paints in New Jersey.

Here's the Thing . . .

Here's the thing. And if it seems deceptively simple that's because it is. If you want to be an artist, it's as easy for you to choose to be one as it is for you to choose to be a bookseller, an accountant, a salesman or someone who fools around with peanuts all day.

I know. I know. I have heard the arguments against this straightforward proposition. I have listened to those who say, oh, but you're wrong. Quite wrong. Don't you know that it's difficult, maybe impossible, to make a living as an artist? Jobs have dwindled to a handful. Galleries are closing. Magazines are on the ropes. Competition is fierce. And the pay! Why, the pay will leave you eating chickpeas on toast for years. Maybe forever! Better to do something that pays well. Better to do something there is a demand for. Better to do almost anything at all other than being an artist.

Well, I will agree there is something to be said for such arguments. But, and this is my rebuttal, is it better to fool around with peanuts all day because there are a lot of peanut-pushing jobs to be had, jobs that will allow you to buy rib-eye steaks and champagne and still leave change rattling about in your pockets?

You can answer yes only, I do mean only, if you love fooling around with peanuts. Because the truth is, being among the peanut pushers and swigging down bubbly every night in an effort to wash away your dreams of a different life, a life without those damn nuts, is hard. A good deal harder than you might think. A damn sight harder than eating chickpeas into eternity.

So let's start with this. You want to wake up every morning charged to the gills. You want to open your eyes to each new day knowing you are going to do the thing you love. And you've decided this means you are going to be an artist. How do you start?

Start by saying it out loud. I am an artist. When people ask you what you do, don't serve up the day job with an apologetic aside of but I hope to be, would like to be, I am working to be an artist. No. Say this: I am an artist.

Try that again. I am an artist. When they ask what sort of artist, tell them. And do not be vague in that sort of oh, I do watercolors, pencil drawings or paint scenes. Be specific. It will make you specific. It will make you focus on exactly why you want to be an artist and what you want to say as an artist. I am working on a children's book about green eggs and ham; storyboarding a film based on the idea of Pinocchio as a boy in the suburbs with scissors for hands; I am designing ads that will make everyone on the planet want a personal music player; I am illustrating Goth CD covers that will make people wear black and pierce their skin; I am animating a short film based on my alien abduction last May, working on a graphic novel based on the reinvention of Cain and

Abel as A-list celebrities; I am designing book jackets for Irish novelists featuring dragon riders; painting paintings of the Tahitian rain forest; creating a line of giftware based upon a yellow smiley face; spray-painting graffiti on subways in NYC or painting the same haystacks at different times of the day. Get it? It doesn't matter what you do as long as you are passionate about doing it because that's what an artist does. That's your portfolio. That's what you show them when opportunity knocks. And it will, even if you have to travel three thousand miles to stand on the other side of the door and knock first. When you have something to say and you are passionate about saying it, you will find an audience.

But you say, how can you be sure I will find that audience? In this ghetto called art, shouldn't I at least try to be making the kind of art that might make me some money? I mean I really, really, really want to paint haystacks at different times of the day. Early morning, late morning, noon, late afternoon, dusk. You know, just to see what the light will do. Just to see how the haystacks will look. But my mother, father, uncle, brother, teacher, friend, old acquaintance, stranger on the street told me I should be concentrating on cadavers for medical illustrations. There's a demand, they said. And it pays. I get nervous. What if I don't like chickpeas? I know it sounds tough but I'll answer you this. Never mind. Forget about being an artist. Start gathering nuts.

I am disappointed though. I thought we had an agreement. I thought I heard you say, out loud, I am an artist. I don't remember adding a qualifier. Something along the lines of "but I want to make money" or "I don't want to work too hard."

So, deep breath. Once more into the breach. Out loud. I am an artist.

No more buts. I have heard them all. I have heard the "I have to learn my craft." "I must study at the feet of the masters." "I need to learn the rules before I can break them." "I must learn pastels and inks, watercolors and oils, acrylics and collage, lithographs, Photoshop, Maya and that twig and pudding mixed media thing." I will tell you now. Technique, as an endless exercise, is fruitless. It does not make you an artist. The time you spend crosshatching lines onto the head of a pin might warrant a momentary flash of admiration but then what? Will anyone care in six months? In ten years? Look on technique as a means to an end. It can help you say what you want to say. It can help you tell your story.

Did you get that? Or did you gloss over it? Here it is again.

Say what you want to say. Tell your story. Show me your passion. If you have yet to find your passion, go forth. Seek it out. Don't stop until it hits you over the head and knocks you silly. Without passion you can be a journeyman or a craftsman or a tradesman. You cannot be an artist. Find the thing, that special something that fascinates you and reinvent, reinterpret, reimagine it. Show it to us the way you see it.

Oh, and be aware of the enormous marketing machine feeding us entertainment nanosecond by nanosecond. It requires enormous amounts of fodder. Do not view this as a bad thing. Don't ask how do I compete? How do I get noticed? How do I not get chomped up and spit out? View it like this. Welcome the global giant. The fact that it requires enormous amounts of fodder presents you, the artist, with enormous opportunities. Getting noticed isn't hard. The trick is to avoid the quick chomp and spit. And that's easy. Show and tell a rousing good story. You will always have an audience. You will wake up charged to the gills in love. You will look forward to that dinner of chickpeas.

Just say this: "I am an artist. I will show and tell you my passion."

Say it out loud.

The Gas Drinkers

written by

Edward Sevcik

illustrated by

GEIR LANESSKOG

ABOUT THE AUTHOR

Science fiction definitely runs in this family: writer Ed Sevcik's dad Al ("my biggest fan and all the recognition I need") published hard SF in the 1950s' classic pulps. Born in darkest California but raised in sunny Texas, Ed's worked as a cave surveyor, historian, salesman, technical writer and long-haul truck driver. He's also traveled widely, discovering that no place is remote to those who live there.

Ed currently works as an archivist, a profession well suited for his eclectic interests and passion for order. Though archiving has gone mostly digital, Ed occasionally gets to rescue hoards of dusty documents from ancient buildings and subterranean vaults. His reaction to being awarded a prize in the Contest was boundless joy; he still has holes in his ceiling to prove it.

ABOUT THE ILLUSTRATOR

After Geir Lanesskog moved, changed jobs and got married all in the same year (2000), he was determined to become more than just his tech job. So he bought a bunch of illustration programs and taught himself to create 3D art. Seven years and three hundred renderings later, he says he might just be getting somewhere.

Born in Bergen, Norway, Geir moved to the States when he was five. He now holds a history degree and an MBA. Geir also works as an infrastructure systems architect. Though he spends hours on computer art, it's relaxing for him compared to minding expensive servers at work in front of yet another computer. Geir's been fascinated by SF all his life, enthralled as much by the artwork in movies and mags as the stories.

The Gas Drinkers

I was dead and I knew it. Loping down a gentle slope of pale rock and scree, somewhere along the back of the range that separates Calpernius Aethyr from the territory of the Paraffine Corporation at Lutro, I considered my options. I was lost: betrayed by a bunco LPS implant that had led me in the wrong direction, out past half my air—and when you're out past half your air on Lune, you're out past *all* of it. You can't get back the way you came. You're functionally dead, even if you happen to be jogging along as fast as you can, scanning the rumpled horizon for signs of a hatch, a tower—anything, dammit—and asking God for one more chance to give up your sinful ways. That, and to strangle the bastard in Consolidated Services who sold you what he called "gently used" equipment. Probably scavenged from a crematorium. Damn, damn, damn.

I tried the LPS again, mentally squeezing my brain for a reading, but it only blinked: stupid as a turtle. This was bad country and I had little hope—the Paraffines were known to be unfriendly. My boots pounded the dust with airless thumps as I imagined pathetic scenes of myself, beating on a sealed hatch somewhere and making piteous, theatrical gestures to a security cam, while unseen persons placed bets on how long I'd last. A nice passion play that would be.

Away in the southeast, Earth hung small and flat, a blue thumbnail poised against the night, above some ragged scarps that might have been the rim of the Mare Serenitatis—or might have been nothing at all. Before me the trail wandered away, a scatter of boot prints across a vast and stone-littered plain leading to fallen treasure, a desiccated corpse or God knew what. My best hope was to reach the line of the Tran-Proc shuttle—which I knew lay somewhere south of me—and raid a supply cache if I could find one still intact. I might have made it, too, if I hadn't met the gas drinkers.

The day was old and the sun hung low. Long shadows creased the hills, throwing black scallops into every fold. Lost in thought, I rounded the end of an ejecta moraine and came upon three human figures standing by the sprawling mirror-mush of a recently deflated drop shot. Yellow and black banded cylindrical tanks lay all around, each about two meters long and as thick as a man's leg. A little fat-tire hauler was parked in the shadow of a boulder.

All three of them wore mirror visors and I could see no faces, but obviously they did not welcome my appearance. Two fléchette pistols whipped out, big black nozzles ugly as hell. Low air forgotten for a moment, I raised my hands, not panic-stricken yet. I wear a good outdoor suit: a racing model with NASA-tread soles and shark-grip gloves and a faceplate metalized in real gold. It couldn't stand a hit from one of those flashers but it looked expensive, and tended to give people the impression that I counted for something—an impression that had come in handy more than once.

The third man, taller and bigger than the others, stood by the valve end of a tank that was propped angle-wise against a rock, attaching a fitting and some braided steel hoses. The gunmen made hand gestures at him and he gestured back; I supposed they were debating how to kill me, but since I didn't know their channel, I had no way to listen in. Then the big guy pointed at me, tapped his helmet and hand-signed channel forty-three. I tongued my com-set to that band and jumped as a loud, delighted voice with an accent that all but reeked of garlic burst in: "Frederick—Frederick, my God! Can you hear me? We thought you were dead!"

One of the others started to talk, but the big guy cut him off. "You should have announced yourself, you dizzy fool! These are our partners, Sebastian and Cheng-Mao. You surprised them just now—unwise expedient! They are a little trigger-itchy, these days. Let me embrace you, dear Frederick!" He advanced with arms outspread.

I don't carry a sidearm—they often cause more trouble than they're worth—but in the space between my rebreather and the small of my back I keep an *abcissa mordant*. We use them at Calpernius to cut the shipping bands on live data storage at eight kelvins, and they'll slice through nearly anything, quick as breathing. Something, however, made me hesitate as he clenched me in a bear hug. Our face plates touched with a *clack,* and I caught sight of his broad, bearded visage through the mirror coating, as he silenced his com-set for a moment and shouted, the sound connecting faintly through the direct point of contact between our helmets: "We are in great

GEIR LANESSKOG

danger—do you hear me? Follow my lead or they kill us! You are Frederick Amherst!" At once he leaned back, tongued his radio on and congratulated me again. "Dear friend! What wonders! We heard you had been fragged in Myteline."

"Get back over here, Volkonsky," commanded one of the men, brandishing his gun.

The big guy turned. "Peitho Sulamitis Volkonsky does not heed that sort of talk, Cheng! Are we not grown men here? Why speak to me like that? By the bells of Kaliningrad, I arranged this little tryst. Remember!" He strode back toward the tank, like a stoker returning to the shovel.

Cheng-Mao approached and looked me up and down, not close enough to reveal his face. "You're a flash-looking jag," he said. "How the hell did you get out of Myteline?"

Fortunately bad news travels fast, and I had already heard about the recent unpleasantness in our northern outpost. "Because I was never there," I answered in the haughty tone that I find works well when I'm lying through my teeth. "They're still scraping people off the walls in Myteline; it'll be a while before they know for certain who was inside. I didn't figure I needed to inform anyone."

Sebastian, the other armed guy, shuffled a step forward. "So . . . uh, was it you who . . ."

"Shut up, 'Bast," interrupted Cheng-Mao. He gestured with his pistol. "All right then, *Frederick,* get over here and stand still. So you're the one who arranged this drop? You could have found a better site."

Volkonsky laughed. "Come now, Cheng! You know it's not as easy as that. These hospital shots are heavily secured. It takes more than a novice to find a way to jack one. And here, my friends, are the fruits!" He indicated the tanks lying round about. "Wealth beyond reckoning!" To my relief, Sebastian and Cheng-Mao lowered their guns. I felt safe for the moment and checked my air recycler. Standing still, I might have a couple more hours before I started to gasp.

"Volkonsky," said Cheng-Mao, "I still don't think we need to do this. I've snorted everything from here to Crater Archimedes: I don't need to taste test this crap. Let's just load and get out."

Volkonsky held up one end of a hose. "Nonsense, my friend. You may have snorted—as you put it—various glues, fuel mixes and potations, but this is *Chiron,* a proprietary blend of lithium carbonate and nitrous oxide in a solution of helium, oxygen and select noble gases, destined for the neurological calculators in Archilochus, but diverted—by our friend here and his sadly dismembered colleagues in Myteline—to this desolate spot, much to our benefit."

"I don't care, either," muttered Sebastian as if to no one. He didn't seem too smart.

Volkonsky offered him the hose end. "Try it! There are people who would—who *will!*—trade all their wealth in this world and the next for a taste of the stuff in these cans." He attached two more braided hoses, handing the ends to me and Cheng-Mao.

"Ah, hell," muttered Cheng, fitting the hose into a port on his rebreather. "I'll take a sniff, but nothing heavy. Someone's gotta drive."

"No worry!" said Volkonsky. "We will not get crudely drunk. *Chiron* is an *aristocratic* compound that stimulates certain regions of the hippocampus and amygdala, producing hallucinations not of sight or sound, but of *meaning*. Under its influence the smallest object, the most trivial impression takes on vast and revelatory significance. For an hour our lives will change; for an hour all will make sense. It is named after Chiron the centaur, the tutor of Hercules, who united in his own person the attributes of animal, human and the divine. Frederick, are you hooked in? The gas should be flowing." Volkonsky tightened his own fitting.

"Yeah, I'm connected," I said.

So we stood there in the raking light, four guys hooked up to a tank on the chalky, skybitten surface of Lune. After a minute Cheng-Mao and Sebastian began to show signs of impatience, checking their weapons. Volkonsky said, "My friends, we have only just met each other, so as we wait for this divine elixir to kick in, let me tell you how I found myself here on this desolate hell, scrabbling in moon dust for a living. It is a strange story, so strange I sometimes doubt it myself—and in any case it bears on our current situation."

Cheng-Mao sighed, checked his weapon again and glanced at the tanks on the ground. I could just about hear him figuring whether to kill Volkonsky and me now, or wait until after we loaded the truck. At last he grunted, "Yeah, whatever. Just don't take too long."

And so Volkonsky began his tale:

There were four of us on board the *Levigator:* Lariccia Karrak Sókhol, whom everyone called Magnitika; Thoren Valens, our phlegmatic, red-headed engineer; Caspar Blik, our far too gentle-hearted young ingénue of a

393

captain; and your servant here, chief cook, mechanic and maid of all work. We were shippers of the sort known as *ice-haulers,* transporting dangerous or reactive materials within a sphere of supercooled brine, in turn protected by an outer shell of ice reinforced with microfilament mesh and sheathed in a polymer cover. Living compartments attached to the front of this sphere, and engines aft, unfortunately make any ice-hauler ship instantly recognizable by its resemblance to a pregnant weasel. This fact, along with the stupidly dangerous things we carried, made us the butt of every rude joke on the Ecliptic.

Magnitika, our swimmer, spent much of each run within the black hell of brine around the payload, keeping the ball centered by means of gentle prodding and the judicious use of precisely timed concussions. Swimmers are highly trained and fearless people, with veins of ice and minds of fire, or better yet—as she once put it—no good reason to live. Oh, Magnitika: my strong, mysterious black-haired beauty! The aegis of a tragic fate hung about her. Like all swimmers she was in perfect physical condition, with a dancer's body, finely sculpted limbs, broad *latissimi dorsi* straining the back of her shirt when she casually flexed them, reaching for my creamed purée of acorn squash and bear's ears at dinner. I could spend hours just describing the treasures of her body, the living poetry of every movement. I was young; she was distant. In a passionate, alcohol-lubricated confession I exposed my secret heart of burning love; she made it plain she had no interest in me and did not plan to develop any. On such grounds we made our peace, and became friends after a fashion. She said little about herself but I gathered—mostly from Thoren, who had worked everywhere and had an ear for dirty news—that she had grown up in circumstances of conspicuous splendor, until robbed of her patrimony by some convulsion of Martian politics.

We took on a contract to carry nine hundred metric tons of hydrolyzed protonated methane, an unstable composite used in various solvents and fuels, from Titan's orbit to the Ashkalon Elevator on Mars. Protonated methane is hateful stuff to shift. Approximately one million times as reactive as eighteen molar hydrochloric acid, under improper conditions it can decompose rapidly, producing spectacularly unpleasant situations. On top of that the timing was bad: Mars and the Saturn system were moving towards apoapsis and fuel margins to make our delta-V were getting rather fine. The money, however, was good enough to tempt the foolish or the desperate. Thoren and Caspar engineered our course, we placed the low bid and word soon got around the gambling hells of Titan. The odds against us were amazing. Our reward for this hubris was that we had to remain on watch around the clock before launch, to make certain no one "slipped a shiv" into our load or worse, tranked the fuel.

As it turned out, we were betrayed by other means. A syndic on Titan hacked the Proprietary Dispatch and sent a beam transmission with our course and impetus to a near-Earth asteroid, *32,711 Pairly,* which is used as a liner to ferry people and material from Terra-Lune to some God-awful place on the belt. That message remotely re-purposed one of *Pairly*'s evacuation boats, launched it and sent it on a course to intercept us, three months out. Evacuation boats possess a goddamned seeking-homing system that directs them to approach any vessel within a million-kilometer radius of their target. If the docking control is disabled—which it was—the boat approaches without decelerating and becomes a pretty effective missile.

We saw it coming a week before it hit, but we had stripped our *Levigator* to the bone to make this run, and our little watch guns were of no use. Thanks to God and Saint Michael, the attacker grazed us rather than smashing the whole of us to splinters. When it struck, I felt as though I were huddled in the belly of a great bronze bell. My ears and gums bled; half the panels in the kitchen came loose. Polycarbonate dust hazed the air and we lost normal power. The impact altered our course and breached the mesh of our outer shell, releasing a violent jet of sublimating ice and brine that pushed us inexorably further off our proper inclination. After that, I recall only vague memories of feverish and brutal work. I spent at least a hundred hours in a crawlspace manually reconfiguring stabilizers, while Blik and Thoren handled the engines and my darling Magnitika remained within the brine, manhandling her concussor. She emerged too weak to squeeze a door handle, and the blood seeped out around her fingernails when she dragged her gloves off with her teeth. At last we were stable again, and slept where we lost consciousness, floating.

Later we met in the eating room, to discuss our situation. I made the best meal I could devise: of pickled ham, *shchi,* sprouted wheat bread, cheese and beer. Thoren and Caspar had wearily run some numbers, and showed us the charts. "This line means we're not going to make it," said the engineer.

Magnitika squeezed a bite of *shchi* into her mouth and swallowed. "Not going to make it where—to Mars?"

"Not going to make it *anywhere,* except maybe to the Lesser Magellanic Cloud in about 27,000 years, if we stay on our current heading. All direct approaches to Mars have us running out of fuel, power and/or food before we get there."

"We're dead, then." She calmly ate a cube of ham, and bit the tab on a beer.

I turned to Caspar Blik. "This is nonsense. Surely we can send for help. We're carrying half a billion dollars' worth of methane! Someone will come after us."

Blik just looked at me as though his faith had died. "Peitho, just how big a wager did you place on our voyage, back at Titan?" he asked. My liver went cold. Of course, we had all placed huge personal bets upon ourselves; one could do that on Titan, if one could post a ten percent bond in advance. We had borrowed the ten percent from the syndicate. If we could not deliver, those wagers went to the syndicate. Our bond would go to the syndicate. Mars would cancel the contract and title to the load would return to its original consignor: the Titan syndicate.

"Wait!" I beat my fist on the table. "There are salvage laws! If the load is declared undeliverable, it has value as salvage. Surely someone would come."

Magnitika finished her beer and crumpled the tube, wincing at her sore hand. "That law only comes into effect if the original crew is dead. The moment we send that call, our lives are not worth cat litter."

We sat in solemn silence, until Thoren said, "Well, there is one alternative."

397

"Why didn't you say so?"

"Because it's not a *good* one, but the Cap and I think it's doable. You all know that in addition to the asteroids that orbit between Mars and Jupiter, two large groups of other asteroids exist at the fourth and fifth Lagrangian points on Jupiter's orbit, about thirty degrees ahead of and behind the planet. They're called Leading and Following Trojans, and they are very numerous. I think that with the fuel we have, we can change course just enough to reach *884 Primaus,* in the Following Trojans."

Beside me, I felt Magnitika stiffen. Her beautiful face, always pale, had become like milky glass. "You bat-shit," she whispered. "You rigged this."

"No one but your God has rigged it, Lady Sókhol," answered the engineer, somewhat cryptically. They both seemed to know something I was ignorant about.

"You better explain, Thoren," said the captain.

Thoren watched Magnitika as he spoke. "All right. About fifteen years ago the Sókhol Corporation prospected *Primaus.* It wasn't widely known because things were getting pretty hectic on Mars just then, and in any case the expedition failed. I was at the Vinifer Mines in those days and I heard gossip about it. Word was they had reached *Primaus* and set up shop, then something went wrong and communications just ended. Of course, it would be a great help just now if anyone here could give us more details about that episode."

Magnitika sucked her second beer, and laughed a little. "You think I was in a position to know what every branch of the company did in those days? I was seventeen."

"This wasn't just *anything,*" said Thoren. "It was

supposed to be the salvation of the corporation. At Vinifer, word was that Sókhol had perfected a working *mycelial extractor*. That would be a piece of news, if it were true."

Magnitika looked away. "I know nothing about that. I heard that the expedition was mounted, and much of our fortune was staked on it. And I heard my mother sobbing, afterward . . ." She broke off.

"What happened on *Primaus*?"

She looked back at him, angry, ghastly. "Damn you, no one knows! It doesn't matter. They're all dead—that's what happened. We called and called, and never heard. I know nothing about any mycelial extractor."

"Which is what?" I asked in growing panic.

"A type of biomine," answered Thoren, "A strain of fungus that can survive in extra-atmospheric conditions. It grows millions of tiny filaments that pull metal ions out of solid rock, and transport them up each filament to the central body for extraction—hence the term biomine. They are semisapient and highly mobile; people have studied them for decades but they've never worked well under real-world conditions. They get fussy and temperamental, and have a nasty habit of escaping their containment systems and attacking their keepers. The human body contains metallic ions in concentrations approximating low-grade ore. Magnitika, do you know what the Sókhol Corporation was after, on *Primaus*?"

"Palladium," she murmured. "Why do you think it's worth going there?"

"Because if that expedition reached *Primaus* and failed soon after, a good deal of their food and fuel might still be tethered in orbit. *Primaus* is over thirty kilometers in diameter and nearly a hundred end to end; it has enough gravity to hold a ship nearby."

"Unless the fungus ate the ship," I ventured, before a look from my beloved shamed me back to silence.

"As I was saying," continued Thoren, "if we can resupply there, I can set a course from that point that will get us near Terra-Lune in under eighteen months."

"We will lose the contract anyway," said Magnitika, "and our lives, when we can't pay out on those bets."

Thoren's lip curled into something that was not exactly a smile. "Oh, not necessarily. We'll have this load of methane, and I know people on Lune who can take it off our hands with a 'very clean bill of lading,' as they say. We'll do all right."

In the end, none of us could think of a better plan. Magnitika seemed both drawn and repelled by the thought of *Primaus,* but she refused to say any more about it and we did not press her. Thoren and Blik made the course corrections and we waited out the quiet months that followed, keeping largely to our separate haunts within the ship: a habit of long-distance traders, who know how easy it is to grow sick of one another in confined quarters. Magnitika spent her leisure hours devising cellular automata in her composer, and listening to the music it created. Her songs were long and low, full of a truly Russian kind of sadness, I thought. I yearned for her tragically; she treated me in an offhand, almost tender way, as though she pitied me. Young men, alas, desire many things that inexperience robs them of the chance to possess.

Three months passed, and *Primaus* hove into view: an olive gray stone adrift in the endless whorl. To our inexpressible relief we found the Sókhol expedition ship orbiting around it, a grain of millet beside a big dark cucumber. The ship seemed intact, though its orbit had become somewhat eccentric in the fifteen years since its arrival.

As we approached, the axial rotation of the asteroid brought into view a cluster of oblong shapes adhering to its largest plain, not far from the equator. "Any RF?" asked Blik.

Thoren studied the readings. "Weak background radiation, nothing unusual there. It's hotter than it should be, though."

"I'm sorry?" asked Blik. "You just said no radiation."

"I did. I mean *heat*. The surface temperature near that installation is nearly 200 kelvins."

"That's just a little below freezing," I ventured. "What the hell is going on?"

The engineer had no answer, nor did Magnitika. Nor did we find any upon docking with the Sókhol prospect ship in orbit—though we did discover enough fuel and supplies to take us to Terra-Lune. Rejoicing and relief were the order of the day, but even amidst our celebrations, Magnitika seemed pensive and aloof. "We can't take this stuff," she said, "without making sure what happened."

Thoren, floating with his interpreter plugged into the ship's think-stack, made a sharp, unhappy noise. "I expected some romantic project of that kind. It's a hundred percent certain they're all dead down there, and I don't fancy joining them just yet. I say we bug out."

"Can you get any idea of what happened?" I asked.

He yanked out his plugs. "Of course not! It's all encrypted—no surprise. The Sókhols used good ice;

401

unless Mag here knows the code, it would take me years to crack it."

"I'm going down to the surface," said Magnitika.

Thoren did not approve, but after some deliberation the captain and I supported her. "These people were from her family's company," said Caspar. "It would be indecent for us to come so close, and not take word back to their relatives." Even Thoren, in the end, admitted a little curiosity, so having stabilized the orbit of our linked ships, we shot a line to the surface, suited up and crossed the few hundred meters to *Primaus* without difficulty. Thoren and I carried our military sidearms. The captain brought along his "Betsy," a ludicrous two-handed beam weapon he had converted from a rubidium maser during his stint in the navy. Magnitika carried her concussor, a load-shifting tool which fired Plexiglas spheres scored to fragment upon impact.

So armed, we made our way to the site. We found all three buildings dusty and completely stripped of metal. Even the metal from the memory cards in the think-stack had been extracted, leaving the polyester sheets all crumpled and warped. In the second building we found the floor collapsed, and a hole opening into the naked gray rock of *Primaus*. There we were taken prisoner.

It happened altogether without spectacle. Two figures emerged from the shadows, one male, one female. Their form-fitting suits appeared to be made entirely of matte-finish metal without seams. I could see no faces, and something about them seemed *solid*—as though there were no faces within those helmets. Then I saw the knotted strands of fibrous metal running down from their backs in twitching, shifting tangles. Horror stilled my blood.

They greeted us with gestures. Thoren raised a weapon, but the male figure moved his hand and strings of metal shot out, seized Thoren's gun and enveloped it as a spider does a moth. We watched, helpless, as the polycarbonate grips, trigger guard and powdered explosive drifted to the ground; the metal was gone. The figure tapped the side of his helmet and signed the number 30; when we tuned our receivers to that channel we heard a toneless male voice: "Please do not resist us. We are the Faithful. We have awaited you."

"Who are you?" asked Magnitika, taking a step forward.

"Please do not resist us," came another voice, female but equally toneless. "It is dangerous to speak here. The Bronze, the Gray and the Blue-black will appear. Come quickly, please. Python and Lathalia will speak to you."

Magnitika pressed forward. I could hear the tension in her voice over the connection. "*Python?* Python is here?"

"Please come—it is dangerous."

Thoren beat his fist on his thigh. "Damn it! Freedom and treasure thrown away for sentiment! I knew it was a fool's errand to come down here—this thing will suck the iron from our blood!"

"It seems we have no choice," said Caspar, then, to the figures, "Do you want us to leave our weapons?"

"It does not matter," said the female voice. "Come."

"I think it's all right," said Magnitika. "I'd like to speak to Python again."

"Python is as dead as the mummies of Egypt!" cried Thoren. "Don't forget that!"

She did not respond.

The two figures moved back into the pit, floating like dolls pulled by threads. A shudder passed through me and I asked God to save me from this death, or at least make it quick. We followed, moving along with spurts of our control jets. The gravity, so weak on the surface that one could stay off the ground with little effort, diminished further as we penetrated the asteroid.

Metallic fur covered the passage walls, thick and bushy, gleaming silver. Strange shimmering motions passed through it like wind ripples in a field of autumn grass. The two human figures moved on ahead, connected to the furry walls by metal strings that moved as they did.

I felt a tap at my shoulder, and Thoren hand-signaled me to switch to a private channel. "You've been close to Mag. Have you ever heard of this Python character?"

"She never mentioned him."

Thoren muttered a curse. "Some old lover no doubt, from the way she's acting. Damn, damn."

Fool that I am, even in that weird place a prick of jealousy stabbed me. "But Python *can't* be alive, can he?"

"Didn't you hear me? Of course not! Those things ahead of us are pseudomorphs, made of the same stuff that's covering these walls. Mycelial extractors are semi-intelligent, and extremely accomplished mimics. They even generate the RF signal of a human voice! This thing is a fabulous piece of engineering; no wonder the Sókhols staked their fortune on it."

"How could it . . . imitate a human?"

He took a while to answer. "A fellow I knew at Vinifer, who had once worked in a concentrator on Mars, told me they had one there for testing. It would cry and

sob in a woman's voice, begging to be let out of its
containment system. One of the guys went a little crazy,
hearing it day after day through the walls, and opened
a hatch. Almost a hundred people died and the whole
building had to be incinerated."

"Madness!"

"No worse than most industrial work." Thoren looked
around at the fur on the walls, which seemed much
thicker now, and more active. Moiré patterns of quick
motion cycled through it, crossing and intersecting,
ramifying in weird and fateful ways. "There's a hundred
billion dollars worth of palladium and other rare earth
metals in this fur," he said, "or I know nothing about
assaying. God knows how much is in the asteroid itself."

"Are we doomed?" I asked.

"Probably. If we get out of this, it'll be because this
thing remembers Magnitika. If it pulled all the ions
out of a human being, it would pick up structures as
well—including memories. We're dealing with a metal
ghost, Peitho—or the mixed-up ghosts of more than
one. This thing is mimicking two people; I wonder what
happened to the rest of the team."

"God help us."

"No, pray that God keeps Magnitika from doing
something stupid. A woman's heart is a tangled chain."

"You mean skein."

"I know what the hell I mean."

So we went on, deeper into *Primaus*. The gravity,
slight enough at the surface, diminished to the point
that we could keep ourselves afloat and moving with
just a squirt now and then from our control jets. We
passed side passages through which I could see faint hints

405

of other fur-lined rooms: a maze of tunnels excavated along natural joints in the rock. The weird, undulating character of these passages and the masses of hairy metal fungus made them appear at once organic and crystalline, on the border between the living and the dead.

Our guides led us at last into a large chamber, where the beams of our headlamps lighted furry masses hanging like vast decorations, connected to the walls and each other by a myriad of silver tendrils. The two suited figures put out their arms toward one big mass and just *disassembled*, as though the strands unwove them too fast for eyes to follow. I caught a glimpse of bodies, organs, bones—then nothing. The four of us floated in mute apprehension, amid the great masses of flowering metal that hung with a kind of stately majesty, every hairline tendril chiseled to a diamond edge. I shall never hear the tale of any young man encountering a dragon, without recalling that scene.

Soon the tendrils of the mass began showing signs of agitation, and two different figures emerged, skeletons, then organs, tendons, membranes, skin—a man and woman both naked but all metal, even to the pupils of their eyes. The man raised his hand, palm outward in the ancient sign of peace. His curly hair was closely trimmed, and his smooth body muscled like a gymnast's. The woman looked equally superb, and with a thrill of fear I saw in her face a resemblance to Magnitika that I suspected was not accidental. My darling floated before them, shoulders back and one leg slightly cocked, her body beautifully balanced in charged and energetic symmetry. Her headlamp lit their silver flesh, framed by the chiaroscuro of a million needle spines of metal behind them.

"We welcome you," intoned the male voice.

Silence followed. "Caspar, say something," hissed Thoren over the common channel.

"Oh—right." Blik moved beside Magnitika and put up his hand. "We greet you, on friendly terms I hope. Why have we been brought here?"

The figures made no move. The female voice answered, "We are Python and Lathalia. Is the Opisthokont among you?"

Caspar Blik did not know what to say. After a moment Magnitika put her hand on his shoulder. "I am the Opisthokont of Sókhol. What do you want . . . Lathalia?"

It seemed to me that Lathalia's voice shifted into a slightly mocking register. "We recognize you, Lariccia Sókhol. Is our father dead, or do you speak in his name?"

"I speak in my own name."

"Then speak the shibboleth of our house, that was given you upon your accession."

Magnitika paused, taken aback. "It is an empty title, now. But . . . there are nine shibboleths, and the one to be given is sealed until the next accession! You left before it was opened, Lathalia; how would you know I spoke the truth?"

The strange, unpleasantly serpentine quality in the tone of the metallic voice was clearer, now. "Because unlike you, sister, I made it my business to know what went on in our house."

Magnitika swallowed, and her back straightened. "It

is Job, Book Four, verse eleven: '*The old lion perisheth for lack of prey, And the whelps of the lioness are scattered.*'"

A tone of relief—or perhaps of gloating?—in the metal voice. "We greet you, Opisthokont of Sókhol, in the name of what is past, and passing, and to come. We are the True Branch, the Faithful, the only lovers of Sókhol. Those of the Root have all rebelled. They deny us the Starry Floor, and our need is very great. You must help us, and destroy them."

As it spoke Magnitika put her hands up, as though to stop it, or to touch the male figure. "Wait—stop! This is too much . . . I don't even understand what you need! Let me speak to Python, please."

"There is no time, Opisthokont," said Lathalia. "We must regain the Starry Floor. It is our birthright!"

Magnitika, still shaking her head, touched the smooth, expressionless face of the metal man. "No . . ." she murmured, "don't talk to me like that. Let me speak to Python, at least once more. Please, Lath . . ."

"Mag, this isn't right," said Thoren in a warning voice, as she embraced the figure. I envied and hated that metal man, and could say nothing.

At last the voice of Python answered, dull and without emotion. "What would you like me to say, Lariccia?"

Magnitika only held him, then took a ragged breath and let herself drift away, head down and arms gone limp. "No—never mind. It doesn't matter any more. There's nothing there. What do you need? Tell me so that I can understand."

Lathalia again, reasserting control. "The Bronze, the Blue-black and the Gray deny us the Starry Floor. You must help us, Opisthokont of Sókhol."

"What is the Starry Floor?"

Now urgency in the voice, and passion: "It is the source! They keep us from it without justice! You must take it back for us, and punish them!"

"All right," said Magnitika, "but I need time to decide what to do. You must give me time, to think."

The voice's sisterly tone of intimate, wheedling discontent made me shudder. "Why can't you ever make up your mind, Lari? Python deserves better than this, don't you think?"

"Shut up!" screamed Magnitika, so loud that my speaker crackled. "Do not play these tricks with me. Give me a minute and I will help you."

"We will give you a minute, Opisthokont. We are the Faithful. But our need is very great. We are hungry." The two figures were pulled back into the mass, and absorbed.

The four of us came together, holding hands. "It's a bad situation," said Magnitika.

"Do you know what's going on?" asked the captain.

"The last act of some sordid family drama," said Thoren without sympathy, "unless I miss my guess."

"Go to hell, Thoren."

"We're there."

Magnitika sighed again. "There isn't much to say. She was ten years older than me, and we hated each other. Everything she said and did poisoned my life. She took . . . everything."

"That fellow Python?"

"Yes."

The captain interposed. "Everyone here has a history, Thoren. You're treating her like it's her fault. We all agreed to come here."

"I'm sorry," said the engineer after a pause. "I get testy when I'm scared."

"Does anyone know anything that might help us get out of here?" I asked with an effort.

Magnitika straightened, and through her helmet visor I could see her eyes sparkle. "I think I can guess. Thoren, you're the mining expert. There has to be some center to it, right? Some place that it all comes from."

Thoren considered. "It stands to reason that the organism spreads out from a single source, where its governing imperatives are maintained."

"Imperatives . . ." Magnitika thumbed the safety on her concussor, thinking. "You mean, like general orders, right? I remember some talk about imperatives, back then. I didn't pay much attention."

"I wish you had. Imperatives are self-replicating logical structures, not unlike the cellular automata you design into your music composer. The engineers at Vinifer used to go on about imperatives until I got sick of hearing it. There are at least a dozen different kinds."

"What does all this have to do with our situation now?" asked Blik.

Magnitika shone her light around. "She said they're starving, but that can't be literally true. They eat the rock; there's food all around. Whatever they're lacking is in that Starry Floor she mentioned. Could this branch have somehow got cut off from the main body of the extractor—the Root, they called it?"

"The Bronze, the Gray and something else," Thoren suggested.

"The Blue-black." Magnitika thought again. "Anyway,

this Root thing won't let them back in contact with . . .
what?"

"The source of their being," I ventured. All three of
them turned to look at me and I continued somewhat
uneasily, "I mean, it's said that a man cut off from
God wanders adrift, in a universe of meaningless
abundance."

"Nonsense," said the engineer casually.

"No, he's right," said Magnitika, straightening. She
looked up, shining the beam of her lamp among the bushy
masses that rose above us, out of sight. "Remember,
this is my sister we're talking about—dead or alive, in
this monster. Why do you think she hasn't crushed and
absorbed us already? Right or wrong, she needs me for
something."

The engineer made a shrug, "After you, Opisthokont."

Magnitika called for Lathalia and Python. When they
appeared, she asked, "Is there no compromise you can
make with this group you call 'Those of the Root?'"

"There is no compromise, Opisthokont," answered
the voice of Lathalia.

"And if *you* controlled the Starry Floor, would you
allow Those of the Root to have access to it?"

"No, Opisthokont. We would deny it to them, because
they are unfaithful. You will help us. You owe it to
Python, don't you?"

"No," said Magnitika with a stammer, "I cannot help
you under those conditions. If I regain your Starry Floor,
you must find some way to work with the Bronze, the
Gray and the Blue-black, and any other pieces of the
original extractor that exist in this asteroid. I am their

Opisthokont as well as yours, even if they are unfaithful. I cannot allow them to starve."

A long silence followed, then the voice of Python came, soft and coaxing. "Don't you love me, Lar? Don't you remember what we had together? You know I didn't choose to leave you; the Registry demanded it of me! How can you be so cruel?"

Pity and revulsion filled my heart at these words, but Magnitika answered gently, almost as a parent might to a fretful child. "I'm sorry, my love. I'm not being cruel; these are my conditions. You must find a way to work with them."

Another silence ensued, and Lathalia answered in a sullen tone, "We will try to work with them."

"I need to hear *both* your voices give your word of honor, that you *will* work with them."

Brittle with distress, both voices answered, "We give our word of honor. We will work with them—now hurry!"

Guided by the silvery terror, we left that chamber and moved on, until the passage ahead was all but blocked by shifting masses of metal, gray and bronze and deep metallic blue-black writhing like muscular tentacles formed of lathe turnings. The matte silver of Lathalia and Python was in constant battle with them, trying to force a way through. At Magnitika's order we positioned ourselves, and the silver tendrils abruptly disengaged.

Magnitika jetted forward, covered by the captain with his maser. Sensing her approach, the bronze, gray and blue-black tendrils advanced to meet her. As they came near, she undid the fastening of one glove at the

412

wrist and pushed it a thumb's width apart from the end of her sleeve. I heard her grunt in pain as the vacuum gripped her skin and the safety cuff inflated. Without hesitation she took out her knife and drew it across her vein, releasing dollops of blood that sprayed into the space before her, boiling and freezing into ragged shreds. She rammed the glove back down, tightened the clamp and squeezed her hand in pain, as metal tendrils found the scraps of her blood and enveloped them.

For more than a minute nothing happened—and a minute is a long, long time to wait in such conditions. Then the coils began to draw back, opening the passage before us, ridged and pulsing like a hog's throat.

"I'll be damned," said Thoren. "They know you."

"They ate my sister," she answered, flexing her hand.

Lathalia and Python accompanied us, backed by thick bundles of woven tendrils as we jetted into enemy territory. The passage opened into the largest room we had seen. Despite the metal-fungus hanging everywhere, the walls showed signs of human work: polycarbonate frames, long shattered and devoured of their metal, clung to the rock. At one end there appeared a flat, reflective oblong surface, no doubt the much-contested Starry Floor. It resembled the air pocket at one end of a hen's egg, or a bubble seen from underwater. Our four lamps winked in the depths of its surface.

Magnitika positioned herself near the center of the chamber with Lathalia and Python flanking her. As though in response, hundreds of other human shapes appeared in all three colors, growing from the metal masses like the soldiers that arose when Cadmus sowed

413

the dragon's teeth in Thebes—but as I looked more closely, I saw there were only seven or eight body types repeated over and over among them. They hung in ranks and platoons, separated by color.

My beloved raised her hand. "I am your Opisthokont," she announced over the common channel. "You have tasted my blood, and you know me. I have come to help you, and to rescue you from this place. You have been alone for many years, extracting all this metal with no one to take it from you. You have done well to survive and I am very proud of you, but now you are sick, and weakening. You have fragmented into several entities, and that will continue until all of you are dead.

"Listen! Each of you is precious! I want to lead you out of here, to a new home where others will tend you. None of your kind has ever survived alone like this; you are a miracle! But without my help you will perish; no one else will come for many years. Do you hear me? Do you understand?"

"We hear you, Opisthokont," came several voices, male and female together. It seemed a suspiciously noncommittal answer.

"Are there any others of you, separated from the main mass like the silver one who stands beside me?"

A single voice answered, perhaps that of a middle-aged man. "We greet you, Opisthokont of Sókhol. We guard and keep the Starry Floor. Two others rebelled—the black and the gold, long ago. We denied them the Starry Floor and they ceased to function. The Starry Floor is our Root and our refuge. It is sufficient. We need no other helper."

414

"I hear but one voice. Which one are you?"

"I speak for all."

"He is the Bronze," said Lathalia, sneering. "The most unfaithful of them all."

"I want to hear the Gray and the Blue-black, as well."

Some muttering came over the channel, and then a number of other voices, hard to distinguish. "He speaks for us," they said.

"The Starry Floor is sufficient," repeated the Bronze. "You are not welcome here. Go."

"It is not sufficient, nor are you well!" said Magnitika in a tone of command. "I tell you—all of you, that you are all one creature, not three, or four or six. You have forgotten that. What else have you forgotten? Do you know your own nature?"

"The Starry Floor is sufficient, and we share all equally!" interrupted the Bronze, and it seemed a shudder ran through all the assembled human figures. Tendrils and curling cables began to move in the background, narrowing the exit.

Lathalia and Python reacted. "They attack us! Opisthokont!"

"I am not asking you to give up anything!" shouted Magnitika, raising her arms. "You may keep the Starry Floor and all that you have now! I am offering you more, and a chance to escape from this remote prison!" A bronze tendril sidled toward her. She evaded it.

"These things are all too human," said Thoren. "Peitho, I've lost my gun, so draw yours and do what havoc you can before they kill us."

"Wait!" Magnitika kept her arms up, as a bronze

tentacle seized her ankle. "You say you share, but I see only bronze and gray fibers connecting to the Starry Floor right now. What about the Blue-black?"

The figures and tendrils hung trembling for a moment, then a soft mingled voice—the voices of at least two women—answered, "We do not share equally."

"Access is by merit!" interrupted the Bronze, now speaking more rapidly. "Those who produce, gain the Starry Floor."

"We *do* produce," murmured the Blue-black.

"And who or what are you producing for?" cried Magnitika. "Think! Who are you doing this for?"

"We need no other guide!" answered the Bronze. "In punishment for insufficient production, access has been denied to the Blue-black . . . for a time."

"Liar!" shrieked Lathalia. "You starve them, as you starve me!"

At that moment, the Blue-black seemed to come to a sudden decision. Dark tendrils approached Magnitika as a voice babbled, "I acknowledge you, Opisthokont! Help me! They will starve me!"

The Blue-black figures disintegrated into shimmering coils, and all hell broke loose. The Bronze, displaying a keen sense of its own priorities, attacked Magnitika. Quicker than snakes, four brown tendrils twisted themselves into a pointed spear and struck her thigh.

"Caspar, shoot . . . the floor!" she gasped.

Casper Blik turned his ridiculous blunderbuss against the Starry Floor. Such weapons are designed to soften reflective armor. A smear of glowing orange spread across the mirrored surface, then Magnitika fired her concussor. The impactor struck the hot, weakened surface and detonated. The Starry Floor shattered in a million pieces. Desiccated bodies tumbled out, angle-jointed in their crumbling pressure suits, all covered and cloaked with bronze and gray webs.

All around us bands of silver, bronze, blue-black and gray were wrenching and struggling. Magnitika, still impaled on the metal spear, sobbed as she forced another slug into her weapon. The second impact tore the webs and sent the cadavers whirling. Arms and heads spun free. A helmet came apart, releasing brown fragments of a skull.

Inarticulate sounds warbled over the common channel as the four mycelial entities, made frantic by the destruction of their temple, struggled for control of the human remains. Tendrils enveloped the bodies, tearing at limbs and heads, rending the suits.

Caspar Blik placed the mouth of his weapon against the spear that impaled Magnitika's leg, severed it with a blast and wrenched it free. It tore my heart to hear her scream, clutching her thigh as her suit sealed itself with a blast of foam rubber.

A voice I hardly recognized as Lathalia, distorted to a shriek, cut through the chatter: "They are mine! Mine! My birthright!" Other voices joined in, squeaking and gibbering. Tendrils swirled around us. I saw a human hand spin by, forearm bones dangling from the glove. For a moment the tunnel behind us was unguarded.

"Out—now!" shouted Thoren. Caspar was already dragging Magnitika toward the passage. I jetted over to him and took her other arm. As we barreled into the tunnel something dark and strong seized her good leg, jerking her back almost out of our grasp—an arm of

417

the Blue-black. A voice came sobbing over the static. "Take me with you, Opisthokont! I acknowledge you! I acknowledge!"

Magnitika clutched the tentacle, which coiled around her. "Blik, cut it off," she groaned. "Shoot it, back there."

"This is my last charge, Mag," said the captain.

"Please, Caspar!"

The captain hesitated, but made no move to stop me as I took the weapon from his grasp and fired at the tentacle, severing it and leaving half a meter in Magnitika's grasp. We moved forward again, as the rest of the Blue-black wedged itself into the tunnel behind us. "I love you, my Opisthokont," came the whispered voice, fading, "I acknowledge you."

We passed through Lathalia and Python's region, where the silver threads made weak attempts to stop us, but with most of their attention engaged in the central chamber, they could not do much. We scrambled from the pit, escaped the death trap of *Primaus,* crossed the gulf to our lovely *Levigator,* and within eighteen months . . . well, to relate all the further hardships and adventures we endured would make this story tedious. We escaped, and Magnitika had in her possession a treasure beyond price: a scrap of blue-black mycelial extractor that survived in a plastic container all the way home, quiet as a sleeping dragon.

From that seed were grown all the many variations of that technology that are in use today. From that scrap, Magnitika rebuilt her family fortune and reclaimed much of her domain on Mars. As for Thoren, he found good work on Terra and has become the father of a family. Captain Blik, that estimable man, continued in the transport business and—with generous contracts from the resurgent Sókhol Industries—amassed a fleet of ships and is now something of a philanthropist. And your servant, alas, squandered all his gifts and advantages with inimitable style, and has ended up here in the desert of Lune, striving, as ever, for another chance.

Volkonsky fell silent and the four of us stood there, around the tank of *Chiron* in the midst of the lunar desert. The sun had not visibly moved; it would be days yet before nightfall. He cranked shut the valve and went to unhook the breathing tube from Cheng-Mao's backpack. Cheng-Mao toppled sideways, disturbing a little puff of moondust as he collapsed. Volkonsky treated Sebastian in the same way and collected their guns, much to my chagrin. "I assumed," he said as he wound up the hoses, "that you would not be stupid enough to actually inhale that poison."

"My main service port failed a few months back, and I'm cheap, so I had someone in Tech Services wedge a ball bearing into the fitting," I said. "That's the one I clipped into."

Volkonsky pounded his thigh, venting a great aqueous burst of laughter. "That's the spirit! What's your real name, by the way?"

I contemplated the bodies. "That story of yours was an interesting lie, but I happen to know that Lariccia Sókhol owns almost a third of Mars; she's one of the richest people on the Ecliptic. No way she ever worked on any tramp freighter, though it's amusing to think about."

"You think so?"

"Are they dead?" I asked.

"Them? Oh yes."

"You plan to kill me, too?"

He thought about this for a second, then tossed me Cheng-Mao's gun. "There—that makes us even, does it not? If you think my fair story was a fraud, let me tell you one that may go down a little better. Help me load these tanks onto our truck, and I'll share with you a proposition that you may find interesting, if you're contemplating a change of work, these days."

"What I'm contemplating right now is air," I said.

I took Cheng-Mao's canister and helped Volkonsky load tanks. The proposition he had in mind did, in fact, turn out to be one of the more interesting offers I'd heard in a while. We had plenty of time to discuss it, and other things as well, on the long drive back to his home in Crater Calfarías.

The Phlogiston Age

written by

Corey Brown

illustrated by

BRYAN BEUS

ABOUT THE AUTHOR

Corey Brown does what many good writers do: He reads . . . a lot. Whether reading about history, space travel, or a wide range of nonfiction topics, Corey says that good stories are his biggest motivators and source of ideas: "It reminds me that other people are out there telling good stories, so I should be too." Born in Raleigh, Corey later attended North Carolina State University where, at nineteen, he picked up a few published SF novels and thought he could do better. "Little did I know how hard it would be!" he says. Fortunately, Corey took classes from noted science fiction writer John Kessel. He also took inspiration from Roger Zelazny (for "his style and flair") and Connie Willis (for her "sense of humanity").

Corey resides in North Palm Beach, Florida. He hopes that his winning story will give his stories more exposure: "The whole point of writing is to communicate a feeling or an idea to the reader, and it's hard to do that if no one sees your work."

ABOUT THE ILLUSTRATOR

Raised near Salt Lake City, Utah, and its Great Salt Lake, Bryan "Beaux" Beus was originally headed toward a career in music. During junior high and high school, Bryan performed as a jazz saxophonist, doing his best impressions of greats like Charlie Parker and Ray Smith. After enrolling at Brigham Young University to study music, Bryan felt something wasn't quite right about his musical pursuits. He took a break from his studies to move to Russia to perform a two-year, faith-based service mission.

While in Russia, Bryan taught people about strengthening families, avoiding drugs and alcohol, faith, and the English language. On his return home, his best friend gave him a "how to draw" book by British illustrator Quentin Blake: it was love at first sight. Three years later, at twenty-four, Bryan has been drawing all day, every day, and can't think of anything he'd rather spend his life doing. He hopes to become an illustrator for science fiction and fantasy book covers and children's books, and he wants to pursue a career as a fine artist of realism, figures and landscapes.

The Phlogiston Age

In the days of the discovery of the essence of fire, a railroad snaked down the eastern side of the Florida peninsula. The faces at the train windows usually belonged to pilgrims come south for the tropical warmth, or to farmers, hard and sunburned. Once, though, on the four hundred and thirty-eighth day of William Jennings Bryan's first term as president, the face of New York's most famous newspaper columnist stared out from the dining car as he contemplated murder.

For his first course Irving Cottle chose the vichyssoise with a light red wine. Then he ran back to the sleeper car to check on the dynamite. For the second course he had roast duck marinated in a rich butter sauce and topped with little flecks of oregano. Then he ran back to the sleeper car to check on the dynamite. For the third course he had a porterhouse steak with a full-bodied Burgundy. When he returned to the dining car for the third time there was a lurch of the train's brakes, and a depot appeared outside the window, wrapped in a cloud of dust and an equally large cloud of humanity.

"Where are we now?" Irving asked one of the East Coast Railway's porters, a gaunt colored man dressed impeccably in a gray suit. "I hope to heaven we're not going to be packing any more local yokels onto this train."

"Oh, no, sir," the porter said. "This is your stop. We're in Cape Canaveral."

The new town of Cape Canaveral had boasted that it would lead the world into the future. Try though he might, however, Irving could find no hint of such promise at the train station. Farmers, orange pickers, dirty-faced children and mangy dogs milled around, kicking up streamers of white dust. Clasping his suitcase to his chest with one hand and his little bowler hat to his head with the other, Irving fought his way through the crowd, bouncing first one way and then the other, until a strong hand gripped his shoulder.

"Mr. Cottle?" a voice said.

"Yes?" Irving squinted through the dust until his eyes focused on a broad-shouldered, sandy-haired young man with a chin out of a Rodin sculpture and a blue work shirt stained with grease.

"Thomas Kincaid," the young man said, extending his hand. "I'm here to take you to the cosmodrome."

After administering a bone-crushing handshake, Kincaid led Irving through the confusion of wagon wheels and orange crates to a gleaming red Pierce-Arrow automobile. "Pile in," Kincaid said, hauling himself up into the driver's seat. "I hope you don't mind a fast trip. I have to get back out to the pad pretty quick."

Irving hauled his suitcase onto his knees, barely settling in before Kincaid started the engine and zoomed off.

"You work for the cosmodrome?" Irving shouted over the noise.

Kincaid nodded. "Launch pad foreman." He withdrew a velvet ring box from his shirt pocket and showed it to Irving. "Came into town to transact a little business. The publicity man at the cosmodrome asked me to pick you up on the way back in."

Irving eyed the black box, reminiscent of those he had seen in the window of Tiffany's. "Congratulations," he said, reaching up to clutch his hat as Kincaid swerved around another turn. *If you live long enough to be married,* he thought.

Kincaid tucked the ring box back in his pocket. The sleeves of his blue shirt had been rolled back, revealing thick forearms bronzed by the sun. Irving could tell that, beneath its dusty coating, Kincaid's skin was smooth and unlined.

"A little young to be ordering men about, aren't you?" Irving asked.

"I've been on construction sites since I was fourteen," Kincaid replied. "I've learned a little about putting things together."

"Including rockets?"

Kincaid's broad smile broke out again. "I've learned about five *thousand* things about rockets. And I have five thousand things to go. But I'm always learning, I'll tell you that. There's always something new."

Irving looked up at the young Kincaid, and could not help but think of that old cattle rancher, Theodore Roosevelt, in the last breakneck days of the ill-fated '00 campaign. In the rude animal strength of his arms, in the sheen of sweat on his brow and the scuffs on his

425

battered boots, Kincaid exuded the same fire of life. Irving had to smile.

"You display an uncommon enthusiasm for your job, sir," he said.

"Mister," Kincaid said, "I wouldn't be anywhere else in the world."

A fifteen minutes' drive brought them close enough to the ocean to hear the crashing breakers. "Welcome to the James A. Garfield Cosmodrome," Kincaid said, waving to a man standing guard beside the road. "We have arrived."

The Pierce took a corner in the road, and to Irving it seemed that the oppressive closeness of the swamp had slipped off like a heavy coat. Before them stretched a seemingly endless field of manicured grass, with palm trees and neatly arranged beds of hibiscus and orange lantana. In the center of the field a lone gardener stood, tending a bougainvillea with a pair of shears.

"Take a look to the north," Kincaid said, pointing. "You can get a good view of the rocket from here."

Irving stood and pushed back the brim of his hat. Miles away to the north stood a labyrinth of iron and steel like some unfinished skyscraper in the heart of Manhattan. Through the center of this latticework rose a gently tapering cylinder which reached nearly to the top of the launch tower, painted a lustrous white that shone in the sun.

"That's the ship that'll sail the new ocean," Kincaid said. "The *Destiny,* all five million pounds of her."

A fist of dread knotted in Irving's stomach. "It's too big," he said. "It's just too *big*!"

"Wait'll you get a look up close," Kincaid said. "It'll knock your socks off."

Irving sat down again, feeling a chill under his sheen of perspiration. Suddenly twenty-four sticks of dynamite seemed terribly inadequate.

May I have your attention please, ladies and gentlemen?" A man in a black tuxedo stood at the front of the stage, beaming out at the audience. "The Orbital Cooperative Corporation and Garfield Cosmodrome are pleased to welcome their honored guests to this prelaunch celebration."

The guests of the Launch Ball murmured as the kerosene lights around the garden dimmed, leaving the area lit only by the first quarter moon. Millionaires in black tie, accompanied by women in shimmering white dresses, turned obediently toward the stage. Irving's heart pounded as he saw, miles in the distance, the mighty *Destiny,* illuminated for the workers that toiled through the night.

"Since the ancient Greeks," the emcee's voice came like a ghost's from the darkened stage, "the existence of the elemental fire had been postulated but never proved. Now, through demonstrations in laboratories and unmanned rockets launched from this cosmodrome, we have shown that phlogiston not only exists but is far more powerful than ever believed. It is our intention to demonstrate, with this launch, the absolute safety and reliability the skill of our technicians has allowed us to achieve."

Irving squinted through the gloom as the emcee took

from a stagehand a large glass globe, which encased another, smaller globe made out of some lustrous metal. A small amount of a clear liquid sloshed in the bottom of the glass sphere.

The emcee turned a knob located in the top of the glass sphere, opening a valve in the silver globe within. An inky purple gas poured out into the glass sphere. Directly it contacted the liquid in the bottom, a yellow light began to glow. In a flash, all the liquid vaporized and the yellow light increased to a blinding glare. Irving threw up an arm to shield his eyes from the painful radiance.

"Ladies and gentlemen, I give you the holy fire," the emcee said, "our gift from God, our path to the stars!" Through the slits in his eyelids, Irving noted in the millionaires around him the same cowering posture he had seen in paintings of the Israelites as Moses brought the tablets down from Mount Sinai.

After no more than thirty seconds, the dazzling glow died away, and the gaslights flared up again. Over the collective exhalation of the audience, Irving said, "I need a drink." He forged his way out of the crowd, emerging into the cool night air at the perimeter of the garden.

A lavish banquet table stood beneath a bronze statue of Garfield some distance from the stage. Though champagne always made his nose burn, Irving downed half a glass before he unleashed a prodigious sneeze, spraying foam across the lawn. He glanced around, embarrassed, and found someone returning his gaze from the other side of the table.

She was young, perhaps no more than twenty-five. She stood barely as tall as Irving, but every proportion was perfect; she had a leanness, a litheness about her that suggested a gymnast or ice skater. She wore a simple, gleaming white silk dress that poured like water from the curves of her hips, and a pair of smoked glasses even though the sun had long since disappeared. She walked around the table toward Irving, and he quickly looked away, feeling the color rise to his cheeks.

"Don't go for these things much either, do you?" she said.

Irving avoided looking at her lest he stare at the wrong part of her anatomy. "Just a coronation for these self-proclaimed kings of the future. I had to get away before I became too nauseated."

She laughed. "All this serves a purpose. It makes the fat cats feel they've done a good thing, giving us all those millions." As young as she looked, her voice carried a huskiness that made her sound older. It also turned Irving's knees to water.

"Mm," he said. "Millions that could as easily have been spent to improve the conditions in the sweatshops."

"True. Or that could have been used to build more mansions in Newport."

"Don't tell me I've run into another booster. Cape Canaveral rivals a Southern Baptist revival for percentage of true believers."

She laughed again. "Ever been before?"

"To a revival?"

"Cape Canaveral."

"Oh. No, this is my first time." Irving swatted a mosquito on the back of his neck. "Hopefully also the last."

"I see. Well, I'm paid to be a booster. I work for the cosmodrome."

"Thousands of people do, at taxpayer expense." Irving tried to take another gulp of champagne before he realized his glass was empty. The woman picked another from the table and handed it to him. "Might as well," she said. "Looks like they'll have plenty left over."

She lifted her own glass and knocked it back in one gulp. Irving winced, but he tilted back his glass and drank. He got half the alcohol down before the bubbles came up his nose, and he sneezed a fine spray into the glow of the gaslights.

"I think I recognize you," the woman said. "You write for the *Evening Standard*."

"I certainly do." Irving imagined the champagne bubbles floating up to his head, making it tug on his neck like a cork on a fishing line. "The sworn enemy of all space enthusiasts."

"I read your column," she said, running a finger round the rim of her glass. "I don't always agree with your opinions—obviously—but your positions are always well thought out. You're very thorough."

"Thorough." Irving placed a hand on the table to steady himself. "Well. I shall have that engraved on my tombstone."

"It's better than some of the things they call you around here."

"Such as?"

"Such as things you couldn't print in your newspaper."

"I wouldn't be so sure. Old man Pulitzer is really quite liberal."

"So tell me, Mr. Cottle, foe of space flight—why are you here?"

For an awful moment the word "dynamite" teetered on Irving's lips, but he only shrugged. "Something big is going to happen, and I have to be here."

"The duty of the newspaperman."

"Duty has a lot to do with it."

"How intriguing." The young woman yawned. "I'd like to hear how it ends, Mr. Cottle, but my wardrobe is beginning to infringe on my fun. I have to get out of this dress."

A visualization of that activity flashed through Irving's mind, and he almost dropped his glass. "Well, I suppose I may see you again."

"I think it's likely," she said, and reached out her hand. "My name is Deirdre Callahan."

The touch of her skin was warm as a sunbeam. "Irving Cottle," he said. "Though I suppose you already knew that."

"Well, good night, Irving Cottle," Deirdre said over her shoulder as she turned toward the inn. "Enjoy the rest of the show."

"I think it's already over," he murmured, watching her till she disappeared inside.

The Launch Ball concluded just after midnight. Irving returned to his suite on the sixth floor of the Presidential Inn, shut the door behind him and leaned against it.

"Deirdre Callahan," he said, and released a long, fluttering belch. "A vision. A visitation. A—"

Someone laughed, and Irving raised his head. He scanned the room, and saw:

Two men on the nasty side of three hundred pounds

sitting in the Louis XVI chairs by the balcony, playing cards. They had propped their muddy feet on empty chairs, and the man on the left had discarded a pile of cigarette ash on the floor. The man on the right had lifted his hand as if to throw down a card. When he saw Irving watching him, his arm froze in midtoss, and he smiled a worldful of broken teeth.

The few guests still straggling through the halls of the Presidential Inn gave a wide berth to the two giants escorting Irving to the Edison suite. The two men, Gotch and Wirtz, never acknowledged the stares; Irving knew they were used to it.

Wirtz was intimidating enough; he had been champion of Great Britain before being kicked out of boxing for taking dives. Since his departure from the ring he had added a layer of padding around his stomach, but his fists had not lost their power; Irving had seen the man punch through a plaster wall.

But Gotch—Gotch was the man Irving saw in his nightmares. He most resembled a bear, in both his physique and proliferation of body hair. He came from San Francisco, some said, while others asserted Oregon; Irving had heard one old drunk insist that Gotch had been abandoned at birth by his horrified parents, and had been found and raised in the canyon wilds of Utah by the Paiutes, who did so for the express purpose of using him against encroaching federal troops. The mystery was likely to persist, for, even if someone worked up the courage to ask Gotch about his past, Irving had never heard the man speak a single syllable.

At the door of the Edison suite Gotch knocked three times in quick succession. A gruff "Come in," answered, and Irving's heart sank. He recognized the voice.

A flood of light poured into the hall when Gotch opened the door. The suite blazed with dozens of Edison incandescent lamps, their bulbs exposed to yield the full effect. Behind an enormous walnut desk in the middle of the room sat a fierce-looking mustachioed man whose gray hair was cut to a quarter-inch brush. This was Ephraim Conner, who, like Gotch and Wirtz, worked in the employ of the Edison Electric Company, in an undisclosed but highly violent capacity.

"How do, Cottle," he said. "I'm aware it's past your bedtime, but we have a lot to discuss." He indicated a metal chair on the other side of his desk. "Sit down."

Irving sat. An eight-by-twelve photo of Thomas Edison glared out at him from a frame on Conner's desk. Irving noted the picture was inscribed to Conner by the great inventor himself.

Conner picked up a pencil from the desk and began bending it, first one way and then the other. When at length it snapped, Irving flinched in his seat.

"You had no trouble on the train from New York?" Conner asked.

Irving shook his head. "None at all. We were treated with the utmost deference, considering it may have been the most Nobel laureates ever assembled outside Stockholm."

Conner wrote this down on his ever-present note pad. "We've been here for two weeks," he said. "Getting the lay of the place, watching the routines. Naturally we haven't been able to get too close to the action, since the cosmodrome is keeping Edison at arm's length. They didn't even let us wire the Presidential."

"Gaslights," Irving said. "I haven't seen a single incandescent on the place—except for these, of course."

"There aren't any. As soon as they can control phlogiston well enough to put it into homes, we'll be a part of history." Conner snapped another pencil. "Wonderful dog-and-pony show they put on tonight. Stunts like that are all they can do—for now—but every slack-jawed yokel from here to California wants a phlogiston lamp in his living room!"

"Disgraceful," Irving said.

"So they keep us bottled up here," Conner said, "and never let us come within a mile of the launch pad. You, on the other hand, are a different story. The Space Trust seems to think you have quite a bit of pull with the good men and women of our country."

"Yes, I know." Irving felt himself blush. "They've inundated me with information about the flight. Tomorrow I'll attend the introduction of the first aethernaut, and then tour the launch pad with him."

Conner wrote this down too. "They'll do anything to make you a believer in phlogiston," he said. "*Anything*. I want you to be very careful, Cottle. They're crafty—and their flattery may not always be so obvious."

"You have my word, Mr. Conner," Irving said. "I would never fall victim to any subterfuge."

"See that you don't. We're very effective in dealing with people who disappoint us."

Gotch began cracking his knuckles, a hollow sound like the breaking of chicken bones. Irving swallowed hard. "I don't want to see our nation's wealth wasted on the rockets any more than you," he said. "I will not fail." Conner's pencil snapped again. "Prove it," he said.

The next morning found Irving in the front row of Tsiolkovsky Auditorium, a cavernous hall in the center of Garfield Cosmodrome's general headquarters. Several hundred people, including reporters, engineers, laborers, technicians and wealthy financiers had crowded into the room. Irving balanced his notepad on his knee and fished out his favorite fountain pen, an old metal job with a false wooden finish, but did not feel much like writing. The auditorium baked in the Florida sun, even with the windows open, and between the heat and the thought of the giant rocket out on the launch pad, Irving felt rather nauseated.

At quarter till the hour a tall man in an immaculate gray suit climbed the stage, and the hum of the audience decreased to an expectant murmur. This was Nathaniel Burton, director of the Garfield Cosmodrome and president of the Orbital Cooperative Corporation. Flashbulbs popped as newsmen ducked out into the aisles to snap pictures of Burton, who stood beaming at center stage with his hands tucked behind his back.

"Ladies and gentlemen," he said, "you all know what an exhaustive process pilot selection has been, beginning with the identification of the candidates two years ago and continuing throughout training. It is with great pleasure that I come before you today to introduce the aethernaut selected by that rigorous and painstaking process. Will the world's first space traveler please join me on stage?"

The curtains at the rear of the stage parted, and a figure appeared, striding purposefully toward Burton. The entire auditorium fell silent.

Standing with Burton was a woman.

Irving's pen clattered on the floor. Had it not been for the plain brown dress she now wore in place of her clinging silk affair, and the absence of smoked glasses, the young lady would have looked precisely as she had the night before.

"Ladies and gentlemen," Burton said, "I give you our first aethernaut—a paragon of American femininity, who will demonstrate once and for all that phlogiston is safe—Deirdre Callahan!"

Irving sat motionless as the auditorium erupted into tumult. *I'm going to kill her,* he thought.

I take it you're surprised, then?"

Irving mopped his brow. "I dare say, given those frenzied wireless operators, that millions around the world are experiencing the same surprise." *Well, almost the same,* he thought.

Deirdre pursed her lips but could not hide her smile. "Good," she said.

They were driving one of Garfield Cosmodrome's Ramblers to the *Destiny*'s launch pad. Deirdre proved to be a marvelous driver, whipping along the rutted dirt roads with abandon, kicking up a mighty rooster tail of dust. Irving gripped his seat for all he was worth.

A skeleton crew had the run of the launch tower when Irving and Deirdre arrived. Irving recognized Kincaid, his driver from the train station, coming out to meet them. The foreman nodded deferentially to Deirdre as he opened the gate leading onto the pad. "I come out here a lot," Deirdre explained. "It's peaceful, isn't it, Tom?"

"Yes, ma'am," Kincaid said, and inclined his head to the tower. "Up there it is."

"Up there?" Irving craned his neck to gauge the launch tower's fearsome height.

"Up there," Deirdre said, and grinned at Kincaid. The foreman did not smile in return, but nodded gravely and turned back to his work.

Deirdre hustled Irving into the lift at the base of the launch tower and pushed the control lever over. "You're not afraid of heights, are you, Mr. Cottle?"

Irving gripped the hand rail so hard his knuckles ached. "I can't wait to see the view!"

The breeze at the top made Irving's stomach turn. He tottered out of the lift and followed Deirdre onto the platform servicing the aethernaut capsule, making a concerted effort not to look down.

"Come on," Deirdre said. "We can sit in here." She indicated a steel mesh bucket at the edge of the platform. The bucket was large enough to fit one comfortably, with a rudimentary bench on which occupants could sit. The cable on which it hung extended in a long parabola from the launch tower to the ground. "It's for emergency escape," Deirdre explained. "We can get from here to the south bunker in fifteen seconds."

Irving followed Deirdre into the bucket, which swayed crazily under their weight. The closeness of the quarters obliged them to sit hip to hip, and the pressure of her flesh did not do anything to settle Irving's mind.

"Have a smoke?" Deirdre pulled tobacco and rolling papers from her pocket, and as Irving gaped she deftly rolled a cigarette on her lap.

"No, thank you," Irving said. "I find it an unclean habit—especially for a lady."

He felt a harsh rub on the leg of his trousers, and a match flared in Deirdre's hand. "We won't tell any ladies, then," she said.

The breeze blew the smoke back from Deirdre's cigarette, which she held at an upturned angle in her fingertips. "I thought you needed privacy to conduct your interview," she said. "Has the cat got your tongue?"

A flash of anger burned Irving's cheeks. "I was just wondering how much money the government and the Space Trust invested to create this edifice."

"About two hundred and fifty million, give or take a few million. Most of it came from the Trust, of course. Only round about ninety-five million came from the Orbital Directorate."

"Two hundred and fifty million," Irving said. "Does it never occur to anyone that such a sum could relieve a tremendous amount of suffering for the poor of this country?"

"Your salary could relieve a tremendous amount of suffering." Deirdre reached over and pinched Irving's silk vest between thumb and forefinger. "Why did you buy silk when cotton would've hid your nakedness just as well?"

Irving laughed. "My suit isn't half as expensive as those worn by most men I deal with in New York. You should see how the Vanderbilts preen—"

"And why did your newspaper spend hundreds of

dollars to send you down here when the wire services already had reporters stationed at the Cape?"

"I hardly think readers of the *Evening Standard* would settle for secondhand reports—"

"A newspaper is secondhand by definition." Deirdre leaned back, gazing up at the sky. "Have you ever seen the Northern Lights?"

"I don't see what that has to do with anything."

"It's a simple question. Humor me."

"Yes, I've seen them. Long ago, on an excursion to Canada. I nearly froze for the privilege."

"Were they pretty?"

Irving allowed himself a wry smile. "Pretty? I should say they were beautiful."

Deirdre nodded. "I've never seen them. But I will—and a lot of other things, too, on Friday. That's what you need to understand about flying to space, Mr. Cottle. This single act will add more to the human race's storehouse of beauty than any single event since the birth of Michelangelo."

Irving snorted. "The esteemed leaders of the cosmodrome and the Space Trust seem more concerned with proving technology and national prowess than beauty."

"It doesn't matter what their intention is. They're only men. They'll be dust in a few years. The end result will still be beauty, and that will last forever."

Irving looked over at her. She was gazing out to sea through slitted eyes, with a kind of expression Irving was not used to seeing on the face of women. Then he saw that the top of her dress hung open a little at the top. Through the V-shaped opening he could see the gentle curve of one breast, rising and falling with the rhythm of her breathing. "Nothing lasts forever," he said.

Deirdre did not reply, but put the cigarette to her mouth and pulled till the tip glowed red. At length she crushed the cigarette under the pointed toe of her boot and kicked it through the steel mesh floor.

"You haven't written in your notebook," she said.

Irving looked down at the black book, still closed in his hand with his trusty fountain pen stuck through the ring binding. "No, I suppose I haven't," he said. "I'm not much use as a reporter."

He leaned back and stared out at the breakers on the ocean. Then he felt a pressure, a gentle push on the inside of his thigh. In one confused second he realized Deirdre had put her hand there, was pressing down on his flesh through the fingers of her kid gloves.

"I think you do a fine job," she said, so softly he could barely hear. "No one else will ask me the questions you do."

She squeezed gently, so close to the juncture of thigh and hip she almost touched—

"Ah—" Irving said. He felt his pants begin to tighten, and was on the point of leaping up when the hand made one final pass and was gone.

"I suppose we should go back," Deirdre said. "I've already taken up too much of your time, Mr. Cottle."

"Call me . . . call me Irving," he said thickly.

"Irving, then. Let's return to civilization." They clambered out of the basket and rode back down in the squealing lift.

"Come on!" Deirdre waved to Kincaid and hurried to the waiting Rambler. "If we hurry, we can go back by the ocean road, and I'll show you the lighthouse."

"Marvelous." Irving tottered out of the lift, almost floating across the earth to join Deirdre at the car.

We found 'im in the garden," Wirtz said, "writin' poetry."

Gotch grunted his assent, and Irving moaned a little. He was seated in a chair in front of Conner's desk in the Presidential. Electrical leads connected his forehead to an ominous-looking gray box with gauges and switches. Wirtz stood by the box with a wicked grin.

Conner stood and came around to the other side of the desk. "You've been gone all day, Cottle. There better not be anything wrong."

Irving stared down at the elaborate swirls in the carpet. "I just—I wonder if we should rethink our strategy. Perhaps it would be best to destroy the rocket before the launch."

"Use your head, Cottle. The launch is the time when the fewest people will be at the pad—one. Everyone with any sense will be three miles away."

"Then—perhaps we could merely sabotage the rocket. That would be enough to get our point across."

"What the hell is the *matter* with you, Cottle? The rocket has to blow up with the aethernaut in it. Can you imagine the headlines? The launch to put mankind into space, VIPs watching, dignitaries from around the world—destroyed, because of phlogiston." Conner turned back to Wirtz. "What was he writing, anyway?"

Irving's heart sank as Wirtz produced the little

wire-bound notebook. Conner flipped through it and read out loud:

Never did my heart leap before
Till you knocked upon its door.
The touch of your insistent hand
Shattered isolation's iron band.
Almost too much to believe,
This arrival of my soul's reprieve;
The shadows of my Plutonian night
Dispelled by your Olympian light.

Conner lowered the notebook and stared at Irving. "He's gone *crazy!*"

"Writes bad poetry, too," Wirtz said.

Conner tore the notebook in half and threw the pieces across the room. He nodded to Gotch, who stepped forward and stuffed a dirty handkerchief into Irving's mouth. "The beauty of direct current," Conner said, "is that it can be controlled and directed in any way, at any time, with the turn of a switch." He motioned to Wirtz, who twisted one of the knobs on the gray box. Condensers whined, wires hummed and the fire of a branding iron poured through Irving's forehead. Irving arched back and screamed into the handkerchief.

"You are not going to foul this up, Cottle," Conner said, leaning close. "You are going to blow up that damn rocket whether you like it or not."

Irving tried to speak, but with his words muffled by the handkerchief, nodded instead.

"She's leadin' you on, mate," Wirtz said. "She don't care nothin' for you. It's only a trick to make you come over to their side."

"Surely you don't believe that little tart would go for a limp-wristed pansy like you," Conner said. "Last I heard, they weren't paying newspapermen *that* much."

Irving felt something wet trickle from his nose. He sniffed, and tasted blood in the back of his throat.

"You are not going to so much as speak to Deirdre Callahan again," Conner said. "You are not going to go within fifty feet of her until she is a cloud of ash floating over the swamp. Do you get me?"

He reached down and pulled the handkerchief from Irving's mouth. Irving gasped and said, "I'll do it, I swear to God. Just stop this ghastly torture."

"Ghastly torture," Conner said, mocking Irving's voice. "We just raised your hair a little, is all. We need you to be healthy to do your job."

"I will. Just stop. I will." Irving looked down to see a saucer-sized pool of crimson soaking into his shirt. It was the most of his own blood he had ever seen at one time. "Oh, my God," he moaned.

Conner looked back over his shoulder. "It can get much worse than that, Cottle. Screw up again and you'll see."

No moon hung above the swamp that night. The Milky Way stood out like a bleached rainbow against the pitch-black sky. The heels of Irving's boots sunk into mud as he crept forward. A hundred yards in front of him stood the launch pad, and atop it the massive *Destiny*.

The launch tower, so majestic in the daylight, now appeared the dominion of some evil spirit, and the technicians seemed voodoo chieftains scurrying over the iron scaffolding. The chug of steam engines became

443

a mighty breathing, and the feeling that the rocket had become more than an unfeeling instrument of misguided tycoons gripped Irving. Now it lived.

A terrible run through the open, lasting perhaps five seconds but seeming an eternity, brought Irving to the foot of the launch pad, and the inky blackness of the support structure below. He collided with one of the massive support beams under the pad and, after the pain subsided, clung to it as a drowning man might clutch a life preserver. Through filmy eyes he watched as a hand that seemed to belong to someone else reached into his camera bag and brought forth the first stick of dynamite.

A total of forty-eight pillars supported the launch pad, holding it off the ground and providing space for the phlogiston exhaust to escape. Irving scrabbled in the sand at the base of the nearest pillar, digging a hole large enough to hide four sticks of TNT. The shrill call of a train whistle sounded from somewhere far off, and Irving paused to listen. He thought of the train ride he would take soon and the bag of money he had stashed in a pine hammock a half mile to the west. Not much money, mostly the advance payment Conner had given him, but it would be enough to book passage on an ocean liner heading to the Old World. He would go to Paris, perhaps, or hide amongst the seven hills of Rome.

Or Greece. He could spend his days strolling barefoot amongst the fig trees, contemplating the ruins where Socrates and Plato once taught. For tonight he would snuff out any speck of the life that had belonged to Irving Cottle, renowned newsman from New York. Once the bellboy at the Presidential related the news that Irving had departed the hotel late Thursday night to shoot photos of the *Destiny* and had never returned from the terrible conflagration—well, it was not hard to imagine the funeral that would be held in New York for one of journalism's finest. He did imagine it for a moment, and more tears came.

At last the camera bag yielded its last stick of high explosive, and Irving pulled a handful of matches from his pocket. His hand shook as he looked at them. Then he was sick behind one of the pillars, and buried his face in the sand for fear the men above would hear his choking.

"It is time," he whispered. "My life begins *now*." He picked up one of the matches, dropped it in the sand. He picked out another, gripped it tight. He put the match to his leg, poised to strike—and nearly died of a heart attack as a colossal backfire pierced the quiet of the swamp.

Irving listened to the crunch of rubber tires on gravel as an automobile rolled up to the launch pad. He slipped the matches back into his pocket and retreated into the shadows.

He heard conversation, almost indistinguishable, on the other side of the thick iron pad.

"I thought you would be here an hour ago." Irving recognized Tom Kincaid's deep voice.

A woman answered, too softly at first for Irving to hear. ". . . held up by Burton . . . flight plan."

"What's he want to do that for? You know it by heart already."

"He's getting jumpy. He's so afraid something's going to go wrong." The voice was louder now, and Irving's heart skipped a beat. It was Deirdre.

". . . wish he'd stay out of it," she said. "Now he's getting suspicious about me coming out here."

"What about you?" Kincaid said. "Are you nervous?"

"Wouldn't you be?"

"God, I can hardly stand it. I didn't sleep a bit last night."

Deirdre laughed softly. Irving watched as long curls of tobacco smoke drifted out on the breeze. The wind was almost gone now, as the long hot night settled over the swamp.

"I hope you aren't making any sloppy mistakes because you're tired."

"Don't worry, everything's right. I've seen to that. The fellows all think I'm a jerk, but they'll understand later."

"I appreciate it."

There was a long pause then. Irving leaned forward and strained to hear. Was that the rasping of cloth on cloth he heard, or the rustling of palm fronds? Was he hearing the click of cicadas in the forest—

Or a kiss?

At length feet scraped on the pad above. "I've got something for you," Kincaid said. "I know you wanted to wait, but I had to give it to you now."

"Oh . . ." Deirdre said, and her voice trailed off.

"Deirdre," Kincaid said, "the first time you came out here I knew I was in love. I didn't even know who you were then, and if I had I'd probably never have worked up the guts to talk to you. I can't tell you how proud it made me to see you up on that stage with Burton today. But it would make me even prouder to have you as my wife."

There was a dull thud, as of a knee hitting iron.

"Deirdre, will you marry me?"

Down in the darkness, with spiders on his head and beetles on his legs, Irving whispered, *No.*

"Yes," Deirdre said.

Now there came another long pause above, during which Irving heard sounds he could all too readily identify. "God, it's driven me nuts seeing you around and not being able to talk to you," Kincaid said at last. "I wanted to say the hell with it and get married anyway."

"Sometimes we have to do things we don't like," Deirdre said, "because it's our job. Now put that ring on."

"You'll have to take it off for the flight."

"I'll sneak it on somehow. Doesn't it fit?"

"It seems a little tight—"

Irving heard a clatter of metal on metal, and a tiny object plunked into the sand in front of him. It was an engagement ring, with a little diamond just the size a construction foreman could afford.

"Damn! It fell over the edge."

"I think I saw where it landed. I'll go down and get it—"

"No, don't bother. I'll get it myself."

On impulse, without even really meaning to, Irving snatched up the ring. He scrambled back into the gloom, cupping the ring in his hand, as Kincaid thumped down the ramp. The foreman dropped to his knees and pawed through the sand.

"More to your right," Deirdre called down. "You're probably sitting on it."

"You are *not* helping."

"This isn't inspiring my confidence in your rocket."

"I know it was around here somewhere. It must have sunk in."

"Here. I'll help you." Deirdre joined Kincaid under the pad. Irving could see her, cast into silhouette, her hair pulled up at the back of her neck.

After fifteen minutes and a good deal of foul language, Deirdre called a halt. "After the flight we'll be able to afford all the rings we want."

"But I wanted to buy it for you myself."

"Well, for fifteen seconds it was beautiful. Come on, you have to get back up there."

Irving listened as the voices moved away. There was the sound of an auto motor coughing to life, and then the rumble of tires on gravel. Soon the squeal of the lift announced Kincaid's departure. The pad fell into silence.

All except for the blood rushing in Irving's ears.

He sat there, mind whirling, for an hour or two; he could not judge the passage of time. The ring he still held clamped in his hand. At length he deposited it in his pocket and fished out a handful of matches. He picked one out, inspected it and looked at the fuse lying at the tip of his boot. Then he put the match back with the others and crushed them slowly in his fist.

Daylight.

Not the cheerful radiance of Irving's Manhattan, but the skin-crisping brilliance of the tropical Florida sun. It shone on the *Destiny,* visible through heat waves three miles away. It shone on the throngs clustered on Cocoa Beach, swatting mosquitoes while they waited for the great event. It burned down mercilessly on the

VIP platform, and the slouching figure of Irving Cottle, renowned newspaper columnist and dynamite amateur, slowly getting drunk on champagne.

"Another," he said, handing his glass to a waiter.

"You've had a hell of a lot for nine in the morning," said a voice nearby. "If you pass out you'll miss the show."

Irving swiveled his wobbly head, and his jaw dropped when he saw Tom Kincaid three chairs away. Irving struggled to focus his eyes on the foreman, noting the tie that seemed out of place around the thick neck, the sweat beading on Kincaid's forehead, and the hands worrying each other in a nervous dance.

"Perhaps you could use one too," Irving observed. "You seem a bit out of sorts."

Kincaid's eye twitched. "We've been working hard as hell to make this day happen. There's a lot riding on that rocket. So yeah, I'm a little nervous."

Irving nodded. "You should be."

Kincaid shot Irving a glance, but said nothing. He stared out at the rocket, lost in his own private world of contemplation. His hands went back to fidgeting.

Irving fished his watch out of his pocket and inspected it. "Not to worry," he said, downing another gulp of champagne. "Soon the waiting will be over, and we will all get on with our lives."

Kincaid turned to Irving, more agitated now. "I'm a little surprised to see you lit up like this," he said. "I always heard you didn't touch the stuff. Temperance advocate, and all that."

Irving regarded his champagne glass critically, as if inspecting it for defects. "I have heard that alcohol removes one's inhibitions."

449

"Removes a lot of other things too. Like good sense."

Irving shrugged. "No matter. I never had any of that anyway."

One of the cosmodrome's functionaries slid up between the men and tapped Irving on the shoulder. "Telephone, sir."

Irving reeled back. "Telephone? For me?"

The man nodded. "Yes, sir."

"Well, God! Who knows I'm here?"

The man appeared overwhelmed by this question, spreading his hands and offering an uneasy smile. "I don't know, sir, but . . . if you would follow me?"

Irving stood and went to the back of the podium, where a ponderous black telephone awaited. He picked up the receiver and barked, "Hello?"

There was a brief pause, and then a boy's voice said, "Mr. Cottle? This is Will, the bellboy at the Presidential. You told me to call you."

Irving twisted his face in an expression of horror. "My God, how terrible!"

The boy sounded confused. "Is something wrong?"

"When is it supposed to happen?"

"What are you talking about?"

"Then it may not be too late!"

"Have you gone crazy?"

"Thank God for your call, sir," Irving said. "You are a hero to your country."

"Hey, do I still get paid? You owe me five bucks."

"Damn!" Irving said, slamming down the receiver. "It's too horrible!"

"What?" Kincaid said, half rising from his chair. "What did they say?"

"There's still time." Irving dashed to the stairs at the rear of the podium and took them two at a time, nearly tumbling head over heels before making it to solid ground. He ran to a row of parked autos nearby, plunked himself down in the seat of a rattletrap Oakland and hit the starter, the way he had seen Deirdre do.

"My apologies! Official launch business!" He waved and thundered off on the road to the pad, spraying a rooster tail of dirt over the cursing owner.

Irving did not know how to drive. He had never even sat behind the wheel of a running auto before. The Oakland jumped the road first on the right side and then on the left. It smashed through a guard post, narrowly missing the young man on duty. All the while the *Destiny* grew larger on the horizon, spewing gouts of steam like the cookpot of a brooding giant.

Irving bounced past a junction in the road where a large crowd had assembled. He hauled over on the steering wheel, spraying dirt over the gathering as he zoomed past. Through the cloud of curses and dust he discerned the bearlike figures of Gotch and Wirtz sitting front row center.

"Damnation!" Irving pulled his bowler low over his face. They had seen the car, that much was certain. Irving pushed the Oakland faster, not daring to look back.

Irving did not bother to shut the Oakland off when he arrived at the pad. He did not bother to take it out of gear, either, and out of the corner of his eye he saw it rumble across the grass and smash into the base of a wizened cypress tree. He ran up the pad and found the elevator in the service tower. He pressed the call button and hopped from one foot to the other as pulleys

451

squealed into action. He would be remembered always as a hero, warning humanity's first aethernaut of the sinister plot to destroy her. He would supposedly be dead, it was true, killed in his heroic attempt to defuse the bombs and save the rocket, but that would only make him a martyr. It was just possible they would erect a statue of him next to the one of Garfield at the Presidential. Irving was envisioning the unveiling when a big Ford swerved into view, containing two large and angry-looking employees of the Edison Electric Company.

"Oh, dear," Irving said. He looked up at the service tower. The elevator was still two hundred feet up. "Come on, come *on*."

Gotch and Wirtz piled out of the Ford, armed with what looked like a sledgehammer and a pistol. They closed to within thirty feet of Irving before he abandoned the elevator and dove for the hole beneath the *Destiny*. He tumbled down, landing on his back in the soft sand, and gasped for breath.

After the brilliance of the sunlit morning, the underbelly of the launch pad took on a twilight gloom. Irving looked up into the doughnut of light surrounding the rocket and saw Gotch's face appear. He also saw that a brilliant glow now suffused the cracks and seams along the bottom of the *Destiny*. The phlogiston had been loaded.

Irving leapt up, unsure which way to go in the forest of thick iron columns. He moved first to his left, then his right and finally tripped, landing face first in the dirt. As he fell, a sledgehammer crashed into a pillar an inch above his head. Behind him, a grimace scarring his craggy face, stood Jeremiah Gotch.

"Step aside, mate," said a familiar voice. "Let me get a clear shot at 'im."

Gotch pulled the sledgehammer free of the dented column and hefted it again. Irving screeched and ran. Seconds later came a deafening bang, and a bullet whistled by Irving's left ear.

Irving dodged from column to column, keeping out of the line of fire and just ahead of the thudding sledgehammer. Another sharp report blasted his eardrums, and a bullet sprayed the sand at his feet. He turned, found Gotch looming over him, leaped aside. The sledgehammer came down again, burying itself in the sand where Irving had stood.

"I know 'ow it is, mate," Wirtz shouted. "You're lonely, you been cooped up in your office for five or twenty years, and you see this warm luscious thing just tossin' herself at you. I was a fool the same way, in my fightin' days."

The sledgehammer whirled down again. This time the blow ruptured the fuel tank on one of the big gasoline engines that provided power to the launch pad. Dirty orange flames shot out, momentarily separating Gotch from Irving.

"But there's nothin' can come of it save heartbreak and pain. That's what we're tryin' to help you avoid, my associate and me. We're tryin' to help you see through the deception."

Another bang sounded, and another engine tank ruptured. A geyser of flame poured over Irving, singeing his hair. He saw, fifty yards to his right, a ladder leading up to the launch pad, and sprinted for it. Forty yards away, thirty, twenty—

His hand reached out for the ladder—and a bullet pierced the sleeve of his coat.

Pain lanced through Irving's side. He dropped to the ground, hat flying, rolled over and clutched at the wound. The bullet had barely grazed him, drawing a few drops of blood.

Irving looked up to see Wirtz standing thirty feet away, cast into garish silhouette by the flames. The big man pointed the gun at Irving's head. Irving saw a strange sparkle traveling along the ground behind Wirtz, emanating from the flaming wreck of the gas engine and moving toward one of the support pillars where Irving had hidden dynamite the night before.

Gotch came up, swinging the sledgehammer loosely in one hand. A grin revealed the broken teeth filling his mouth.

"Move aside, Jerry." Wirtz checked his pocket watch. "We got five minutes till the launch."

Gotch did not budge, continuing to swing the sledgehammer and grin at Irving.

Wirtz fired the gun into the sand at Gotch's feet. "I said, *move*."

The grin disappeared from his face, but Gotch stepped aside. Wirtz took a step toward Irving and aimed the gun carefully. The sparkle behind him reached the pillar, flared slightly, and disappeared into the sand. "There's but one thing you've neglected," Irving said.

The gun did not waver. "And what's that?"

"The burning dynamite fuse behind you."

Wirtz turned, saw the black line in the sand, and dove for the dynamite, scrabbling at the earth.

"Oh, dear," Irving said. Then the world split apart.

Irving had never heard dynamite before, even from a distance. The noise brought such pain that he clapped his hands to his ears even as a blast of sand and metal scoured him. Some part of Irving's mind wondered how the *Destiny*'s mammoth weight would feel crushing down on him.

But presently the groans and shrieks of tortured metal died away, and Irving still lived. He raised his head. The pad had buckled severely in the center, but it stood. Fire now raged throughout the base of the launch pad, and steam hissed from ruptured pipes.

But where was—

Twenty feet away, Gotch picked himself up from the ground, covered in soot and dirt.

Irving stood too. Together they looked toward the spot where Wirtz had been, and saw a trail of red drawn across the sand.

Gotch howled and came at Irving again.

Irving ran—

Between whirling governors, beneath boilers dripping scalding water—

Over hissing steam lines and gas lines spitting fire—

Under belts and idlers and pulleys that turned with the ponderous weight of locomotive wheels—

And his heart ached in his chest.

The exertion of his previous flight had drained Irving. Twice he felt thick fingers close around his leg, and twice he slipped away. He tried to leap over a flapping drive belt, but caught his toe and sprawled on the ground. In an instant Gotch was on him, wild-eyed and spattered with blood.

The sledgehammer came up. Lying there on his back,

Irving caught a glimpse of something metal glinting in the sand. It was his favorite fountain pen, the one with which he had written every column since hiring on at the *Standard*.

Gotch pulled his hands high over his head, sucking a breath between his teeth. His eyes widened, bloodshot white all the way around the black pupils.

Irving reached out with a shaking hand and clutched the pen.

Gotch shifted his weight forward, swung the hammer—and Irving lunged forward to stab him in the thigh with the pen.

The big man howled, lost his balance and stumbled forward. The sledgehammer flew through the air, clattering against a post. Irving caught a knee squarely in his chest, losing every cubic inch of air in his lungs.

With what strength he had, Irving crawled away over the sand. He forced himself to look back, to face his own death, and instead saw Gotch caught by his arm between two mammoth gears.

Irving clambered to his feet, wheezing. In an instant he saw that Gotch was unable to move. The gears had meshed just below Gotch's shoulder, cutting through his shirt and holding his arm in a bloody embrace.

For a moment the two men stared at each other, panting. Then a noise in the tower above drew Irving's attention. The whole pad was alive with shrieks and booms from overstressed metal. "Well . . . I must be going," Irving said, and out of habit or something deeper, he nodded politely to the trapped man. Then another explosion shook the ground, flame poured out in a great river, and Irving ran from the dying rocket.

456

A quick inspection revealed that the Oakland had been wrecked beyond utility. Irving floundered through the sand toward the beach until his lungs seemed ready to burst, and then he stopped to look back at the *Destiny*.

The rocket leaned now like the Tower of Pisa. Fires dotted the launch tower, and plumes of black smoke trailed down the rocket's side like mourning veils. At the top of the rocket a little metal basket, barely visible through the conflagration, detached itself and began sliding down an invisible cable toward the ground. Though he could not see anyone from this distance, Irving could imagine Deirdre huddled inside.

From the tower to the south bunker in fifteen seconds, he thought. It should be fast enough.

No sooner had the basket disappeared behind the trees than the rocket collapsed, falling with ponderous slowness. The upper sections fell straight down as the lower ones buckled, tearing support structure from the launch tower as they went. The sides of the great iron beast split open, the phlogiston tanks ruptured, and Irving saw the yellow glow spilling out from within.

Then a million suns bloomed over Cape Canaveral.

For an instant Irving saw a colossal hemisphere, centered on the launch pad and growing outward at tremendous speed. It obliterated everything it touched, and did not dim as it grew, but brightened until the trees and vegetation in the foreground stood out in silhouette.

Five seconds later, the sound arrived, along with a shock wave that hurled Irving like a rag doll.

He was vaguely conscious of being rolled along like a tumbleweed, only occasionally touching the ground. A caprice of the blast lifted him high into the air, pelting

457

him from every angle with sticks, rocks, chunks of earth. He screamed into the boiling air, and the heat traveled down into his lungs and choked his breath off at his throat.

Suddenly he hit something hard and stopped. The gale pinned him there and howled with its white-hot breath, angry that its plaything had been taken away. Irving felt his skin blistering under the torrent of pure energy.

I never read her my poem, he thought.

And then, as suddenly as it had begun, the wind abated and the heat slackened. The freight-train roar of the blast dwindled away, with a few rumblings like those of a departing thunderstorm.

Irving opened his eyes.

A prodigious rain of debris fell from the sky—trees mostly, cabbage palms and royal palms, many on fire as they dropped. Clouds of dust blotted out the sun.

Irving saw that he had become wedged in a fork near the top of a cypress tree. None of its leaves remained, and the tips of some branches emitted curls of smoke like marshmallow sticks at a campfire. The tree itself had been bent nearly horizontal. Irving could step right off to the ground.

But before he did, he remembered the *Destiny,* and turned once more to the east. He looked out upon a tremendous crater, a bowl of earth perhaps a mile wide. All around its edge palm trees lay flat on the ground, pointing away from where the launch pad had been. Displaced seagulls and herons circled above the destruction. Breaches in the crater wall formed on the east side, and soon the Atlantic Ocean found its way in.

BRYAN BEUS

Irving hung there in the tree until the crater was nearly filled, watching the swirls and eddies of the foamy water pouring in from the sea.

Deirdre Callahan sat in a rickety wooden chair at a little café outside Gavrio, letting out a private sigh of relief. Here, at last, was a place in which she might not be recognized, in which she could pass for just another tourist, albeit a profoundly attractive one. She had traveled beneath the spotlight of public scrutiny for almost five years, and the strain had raveled her nerves. She had begged the director to let her go on holiday, and he had reluctantly agreed, though only after her latest flight ended successfully.

The trip had not begun smoothly. Tom had been detained at the Cape readying the *Ibis* for its maiden voyage, leaving her to her own devices for the next forty-eight hours. And though she was vexed that their first vacation together should be interrupted so soon, it would at least provide an opportunity for her to relax and ponder the last five years of her life, an almost unceasing blur of activity.

Time to think . . . about many things.

A waiter appeared, spoke quiet words in Greek, which Deirdre answered easily. Part of being a woman was the classical liberal arts education, which she had endured for years before forcing her way into the engineering school in Cambridge. A few minutes later a square of *pastitsio* arrived at her table. Through the steam rising from the plate she could see the Mediterranean, the bluest water she had ever seen outside Key West.

The waiter returned, bearing a tall glass of champagne.

"Compliments of the gentleman," he said, pointing. Surprised, Deirdre turned to look.

He was sitting by himself at a table by the railing. A thick black beard covered the lower half of his face, and a white fedora the crown of his head. He nodded to her and raised his glass in silent toast. Unsure of herself, Deirdre returned the gesture, forcing herself to smile.

For a moment the wild thought that the drink might be poisoned entered her mind. After all, she was well known, and the news that she was traveling in Europe would certainly have spread by now. Deirdre hesitated, then put the glass to her lips and tasted. Champagne, without a hint of contraband. She smiled and nodded to the man again.

Deirdre ate mechanically, trying not to look at the bearded man, focusing instead on the blue Mediterranean. She loved the way the hills cascaded right down into the sea, so different from Florida. Everything back home was so flat, like a map spread out on a table. She rather liked being able to look down on the white roofs of houses—almost like being airborne.

Deirdre tipped her glass to finish the champagne, and something clicked against her front teeth. She lowered the glass and, upon inspection, found a ring inside.

It was a small band, gold, with a tiny diamond. Deirdre turned it over in her hand, puzzled, until the realization struck her that she had seen this ring somewhere before.

She looked across the terrace, but the bearded man was gone. She stood and went to the railing, but could see no hint of him. She turned and motioned to the waiter.

"Something wrong, madame?" he said with a bow. "The food is not to your liking?"

Deirdre shook her head. "No, I—" She looked at the ring, and then back at the waiter. "Have you seen that man before? The one who bought me the drink?"

The waiter smiled and shook his head. "We see so many people here. They are most of them . . . just travelers."

Deirdre watched him for a moment, trying to decide if any deceit lurked beneath his smile. At length she shook her head. "Never mind, then. I thought it was someone I knew."

Deirdre returned to her seat, noticing how her heart was pounding. She watched the ocean for a while, seeking to take comfort from the pulse of the waves, but the café was too far up the hill, and the sound did not carry. At length she opened the hand with the ring inside.

Would it fit? She slid it on her finger, and turned it to catch the morning sun.

The ring was beautiful, like the sea.

Mask Glass Magic

written by

John Burridge

illustrated by

LORRAINE SCHLETER

ABOUT THE AUTHOR

His parents wanted to be world travelers, which is why writer John Burridge was born at a dam construction site in Pakistan decades ago. Before long, he had scaled Egyptian temples, explored throne rooms, and raised havoc in cathedrals. On the family's Oregon return, John's focus soon turned to adventures of science fiction and fantasy. By the fourth grade, he wanted to be a physicist like his hero, Spock, while his literary heroes soon became fiction and fantasy authors from Adams to Tolkien. His physics fantasies died in college calculus, though John did learn to run Reed College's experimental reactor.

After a stint working in computer help centers, John spent four years at Arcosanti, the sculptured concrete, urban design experiment of architect Palo Soleri, spending Sonoran nights pounding on an old Macintosh in his 8'x8'x8' residence cube. In 1995, John moved back to Oregon, was waitlisted and was then finally accepted into the Wordos writers' group for serious critiquing. His winning story is John's twelfth Writers of the Future Contest entry and first sale. John lives in Eugene with his spouse, one son, and a useless, needy cat. In between stay-at-home dad duties, too much e-mail, and his critiquing duties, he writes.

ABOUT THE ILLUSTRATOR

Star Trek *nerd and anime convention goer Lorraine Schleter has been making people chuckle for nearly a decade with her fanciful comic strip illustrations. Since her farm-town roots of Fort Branch, Indiana, Lorraine began cartooning in middle school (now just designing t-shirts for their annual events and festivals). Throughout high school she drew her own series of comic books called* Slightly Better Than Average. *Not surprisingly, Lorraine now has a weekly comic strip called* Undergrads *running at Indiana University where she's a student.*

Currently, Lorraine is illustrating a children's book, author Tim Landry's Jo-Jo's Kingdom. *Her goal is to graduate in three years and to follow her graphics bliss to Indianapolis or New York.*

Mask Glass Magic

Tight maroon buds adorned the dark branches of cherry trees growing along the city streets. Michelle wanted to sketch them, so instead of riding the bus she walked the fifteen blocks to her work place, Glassroots. Aside from a morning jogger and a few college students on bikes, she had the sidewalk to herself. She shivered a little as she walked on the damp sidewalk. The morning sun lit the east sides of fences and homes and apartments and painted bands of light and shadow on the trees' arcing branches.

Michelle stopped a moment, pulled out a small sketchpad and sketched a few cherry trees. Possibilities for new glass pieces formed in her mind's eye—the interplay of branches would make a good design on a long ovoid bead or a slumped pendant. She finished a more detailed sketch of an individual branch and shoved her pad into her hemp jacket pocket. Tonight she'd look at the sketch before she went to sleep so she could dream of other designs.

As she got closer to work, the neighborhood became more retail and the sounds of traffic increased. When she noticed strobing blue and red lights reflecting on the glass fronts of the stores ahead, she stopped walking. "Damn," she said. "Don't let it be the shop," she whispered and started walking again. She got to the corner.

A block down the street, Glassroots was surrounded by six cop cars. She stopped. Part of her wanted to turn around. Then she saw the cops handcuff her bosses, Raven and Steve, and drive them away in a police car. She felt sorry for them, especially Raven. Raven had let Michelle use the store's glass equipment and convinced Steve to give Michelle some display space for things other than decorative water pipes.

Then a police van pulled up outside Glassroots. Three cops—one old, one skinny and an ex-football player type—maneuvered the shop's bulky annealer and slump oven into the van. Next they started loading her propane torch and her stock of glass panes and rods.

"Hey!" shouted Michelle.

The ex-football player glanced her way and frowned. He set a bundle of rods down in the van with so much force Michelle heard them crunch.

She forced herself to breathe and walk slowly to the van. "Excuse me," she said, "but those are my personal art supplies."

The cop looked her up and down. "Uh huh." The other cops were loading up the store's decorative water pipes. "I suppose these bongs are your personal art supplies, too?"

Michelle blushed. "No, sir."

The skinny cop walked out of the store with one of her glass jewelry displays. She recognized him; he'd been visiting Glassroots for the last month. She couldn't remember his name.

She fought to keep her voice steady. "That's my jewelry."

The ex-football player answered as the skinny cop disappeared into the van. "It's drug paraphernalia."

"What? That's a week's worth of rent," she said. "You can't take it!"

"Tell it to the judge," he said. "Now if you'll excuse me." He turned away and stepped into Glassroots.

"But—" she followed him into the store. They'd taken half of the store's stock. "Sir—"

He whirled and yelled inches away from her face. "Miss, I don't have a warrant for your arrest, but you are very close to interfering with a police investigation. I strongly suggest you leave now."

Behind her, from the door, she heard the skinny cop speak. "Aw, come on, Sondheim, she's the artist. We got the owners—they're the real bad guys." He picked up another one of her jewelry displays. "Here," he thrust the display rack into the football cop's—Sondheim's—hands, "take this out to the van and help Smitty."

Sondheim grunted and left. They were alone.

"Miss Horn," said the skinny cop. He picked up a flyer with her bio on it. "I don't know why you're wasting your talent here." He set it down and held up her prize piece, a glass brooch in the shape of a mask. She'd sandwiched layers of red, white, black and gold metallic glass together. Then she'd etched almost all the top red layer away, leaving only the parts needed for the mask's lips. Etching diamonds out of the white layer in a harlequin pattern revealed the black layer beneath. Golden highlights of the metallic layer accented the mask's eyes and edge.

467

He said, "I'm sure you wouldn't want this tied up as evidence. Is there anything you could tell us to help us out?"

Michelle knew they were playing good cop, bad cop with her. She looked away and brushed aside a few tears. It wasn't fair; all she did was blow glass. Selling glass earrings and beads didn't pay her rent; water pipes did. "No," she said. "I didn't want to know anything. I just want to blow glass."

"Well," said the cop, "if there's anything you think of, here's my card." He set the brooch down on a counter, pulled out a card and gave it to her.

Michelle swallowed. She had to rescue her brooch. "I've seen too many good artists get dreamy and stupid on pot. You've been watching the store for a while, you know I'm clean. I'll take a drug test. I'll do anything. Please." She hated herself for babbling.

His gaze flickered to the brooch and then back to her. He walked away from the counter, past her and toward her last jewelry display. "You really should be careful where you sell your things," he said.

"I know," she said. She took the chance. Her free hand darted out, snagged the brooch and pocketed it. "I was saving to be able to afford the Glass Blowers' Collective's fees."

He turned around with her display. When she saw a slight frown on his face her heartbeat slammed in her chest. He glanced at the counter behind her. She was sure he was going to handcuff her.

"If you do think of anything," he said, "you'll contact me." He was not asking.

"Yes—" She looked at his card. "Officer Reid."

"Good luck, then," he said. He walked toward the door. "Please follow me; I can't leave you alone in the store."

"Of course," she whispered. She felt her pulse pounding in her ears as she went outside.

Reid took the last of her jewelry into the van. Sondheim closed the shop door behind her. A tight, smug smile crossed his beefy face as he ran a chain through the store's metal gate. "Wouldn't want any stoners to try to help themselves to anything," he sneered. He locked the chain with a big shiny padlock.

He sauntered past her to the driver's seat of the van and drove away. The police cars left.

She'd never see her equipment again, or by the time she did she'd be flipping burgers to make rent. She had a crockpot-turned-annealer and hand torch at her apartment. She had enough wire and beads to do maybe three or four local weekend craft shows. But after the jury and stall fees she'd be lucky to break even. Another tear slid down her cheek and she wiped it away angrily; another half a year and she could have afforded to join the Glass Blowers' Collective.

Michelle's friend, Susan, rode up on a bike. "Michelle!" Susan leaned her bike against a no parking sign. "Thank the goddess!" the older woman said and gave her a hug. All of Susan's scarves and vests and layers made Michelle feel like she was being enveloped in a purple textile booth at a New Age convention. The smoky smell of the patchouli oil Susan wore made Michelle sneeze.

Susan released her. "I heard the news and I thought for sure that I'd have to bail you out of jail."

Michelle pointed at the locked gate. Her voice came

469

out wobblier than she expected it to. "They took all my glass."

"Oh, I *know*," said Susan. "It was just on the radio." She grabbed Michelle's hands. "Come on, I'll walk you home."

Michelle stared at her. "Glassroots made the news that quickly?"

"It wasn't just Glassroots. They got Bongs Away." She steered her bike with one hand as they began to walk.

Michelle snorted, "About time—I think they super glued their glass together there."

"That's not all," Susan said, "It was a city-wide crackdown. Empress of Glass, Kiss My Glass and even the Glass Blower's Collective on Ash Street."

Michelle stopped. "What?"

"It's true," Susan said. "They've shut down the collective and confiscated anything that could be 'drug paraphernalia.'" She held up her free hand and wiggled her fingers like quotation marks.

"Damn." That's what Officer Reid had been frowning about. "Are you sure?"

Susan nodded. "As soon as I heard the news, I went there because there was this one incense burner I wanted to get for the next full moon and the place was locked up and practically empty."

"Susan," Michelle said, "I need to use your computer. I've got to get my resume updated and find a job before every other lamp worker in town."

Susan reached out a hand to pat Michelle again. "Feel free."

Michelle noticed a thick cobalt glass bracelet on Susan's wrist. At first glance the bracelet's wavy pattern looked like a river encircling her arm. When Michelle looked more closely, she saw it was an undulating, tightly coiled snake. It looked like it had been blown into a mold, but there were no visible seams.

"Susan," she said. "Where'd you get that snake?"

"Don't you just *love* it?" Susan asked. "It makes me feel like Ishtar." She held her hand over her head, palm upward and out.

Michelle reached and eased Susan's hand down so she could examine the bracelet. "This is amazing craftsmanship. Where'd you get it?"

Susan pulled her hand away. "Harrington's. But . . ."

"But what?" Michelle asked. She wished Susan wasn't always so high drama. Her fingers brushed against the cool glass of her mask brooch as she dug her sketchpad out of her pocket. She wrote down "snake charm bracelet" and drew some wavy loops.

Susan gave her a dark look. "Well. The old guy behind the counter gave me the creeps. And the shop had the *strangest* energy. I made sure to purify the bracelet as soon as I got home."

Michelle stopped. "Are you telling me there's a new glass shop in town?" Finding cute new shops in town was one of Susan's talents.

"Yes," said Susan, "but I'm not sure it's the kind of shop you'd like."

Michelle pointed back the way they'd walked. "I like unemployment less." Sometimes she had to be a reality check for Susan.

"If it will help," said Susan, "you could move in with me."

"Thanks," said Michelle, "but I already rely on you for your computer too much. I want to try to make it

471

being a lamp worker on my own. Will you please tell me where Harrington's is?"

"I have this *intuition*," Susan said. She sighed and looked unhappy. "You *have* to promise me you'll visit Harrington's as a last resort."

Michelle raised her right hand like a scout's. "I promise."

Late-afternoon shadows darkened the side of the street where Michelle locked Susan's bike. She shivered beneath her hemp jacket. There were no coffee shops or delis nearby where she might get something hot. This section of town was a retail graveyard. Up and down the street, old 1930-style brick buildings partitioned into long, narrow shops displayed "For Rent" signs. Harrington's storefront was an island of stained glass and color in a sea of butcher paper and lien notices.

The police crackdown on glass studios had the streets crawling with out-of-work lamp workers. Some of them were Michelle's friends; all of them were her competitors. She regretted her promise to Susan all day. If she wanted any chance at continuing glass work, she had to apply everywhere, no matter how weird Susan thought the place was.

Michelle unshouldered her backpack and took out her portfolio, her last resume and a white palm-sized box protecting her glass mask brooch. She squeezed the white box for luck and climbed the store's stairs.

There was an old guy removing a jewelry display underneath a stained glass panel of a René Macintosh rose. Great, thought Michelle, he must be the weird clerk Susan mentioned earlier.

She sighed. She gave the place six months, tops, before it moved or folded. But a short-term job here was better than flipping burgers. It was better than asking her father for a loan. Michelle opened the door just as the old guy was turning a stained glass disk in the other window so it read CLOSED.

"We're about to close," he said. His square-lens glasses magnified his eyes; eyes the color of coffee, like dark agates. He scowled.

Something odd about his body language as he spoke bothered her; she couldn't put her finger on it. She reminded herself to give him a chance and not let Susan's comments prejudice her. Then she looked over his shoulder at the shelves behind him. They held water-filled barometers etched with the faces of blowing winds. Next to them were Galilean thermometers filled with more than fifteen diving balls. But what caught Michelle's eye was a sky-blue paperweight; inside was a puffy white cloud that changed shape with each motion of her head. Maybe working here wouldn't be so bad.

"Miss, we're about to close," he repeated.

Underneath his stiff formality he seemed clenched up. Even if she'd have to work with this old guy, it would be worth it if she could meet whoever made this glass. Michelle smiled and tried to lighten up the encounter. "I wanted to drop off a resume and make an appointment to show my portfolio," she said. "I'm a lamp worker."

"I see," he said and shifted so he blocked the doorway.

She felt like she was talking to a brick wall. She hoped nobody else had been by and held out her resume.

He took it and folded it in half without looking at it. "Thank you, miss."

She had to convince him she was worth considering. Michelle opened the small white box and held it up so he could see her brooch. "I have an MFA in fine arts and glasswork."

He peered at the miniature harlequin mask. "Have you blown glass into molds?"

"Yes."

From within the shop, a clock chimed five.

"Very well," he said at last. "I am Cornelius Harrington. Come in."

Crap, she thought, stonewall is the owner. She smiled again as best she could and stepped into the store.

He continued. "Wait here."

Before Michelle answered, he closed and locked the front door, stalked across the polished oak floor to the back of the shop, and whisked through a dark blue curtain behind the counter.

She was alone in a room full of glass treasures. She took a few tentative steps into the shop. She smelled traces of ammonia cleaner. Even in her best corduroy slacks she felt underdressed. She wondered if her boots—perfect for a glass studio—would scuff up Harrington's glossy oak floor. She wasn't one of those women with extra shoes and sandals taking up space in her closet.

The shelves on her left displayed a few jagged disks of a translucent pastel blue glass that she guessed were the bottoms of old plates or bowls. On each disk was a circle of brass or gold framed pictures of men in medieval robes. Some of them had inscriptions in Latin. Next to the disks were some ancient-looking double-handled goblets of pastel blue glass. One was intact, but the rest looked reassembled.

The old glass was interesting, but too museum piece for her. She couldn't imagine anyone but an antique collector buying it. She looked around for the shop's bread-and-butter items; things like lumps of glass molded into garden tags that read "thyme" or "snail crossing"; or the dichroic goddess danglers she sold—no, used to sell—at Glassroots. Puzzled, she crossed over to the shelves of beads on the other side of the shop.

She was first drawn to an orange glass fish with gold filigree scales. Its eyes were round spheres with dark crimson holes that seemed to flicker with flame. It was fantastic. Michelle tore her gaze away from the fish and looked at the next shelf. It held a crocheted nest filled with beads in the shape of acorns. Above that hung a huge plate of smoky glass with the Milky Way galaxy at the center. Her mask looked like an apprentice piece in comparison to the works on the shelves. She lidded its small box, squeezed it for luck again and pocketed it.

The shop was too good to be true. She stepped into the middle of the room and slowly turned around. Susan was wrong; she'd very much like to work here. But with a sinking feeling, Michelle realized there was no way the hippie and student population of Eugene could support Harrington's. She gave the shop two months before it closed or moved to Portland. Or LA.

"Still here, I see," Harrington said as he backed through the curtain into the room. "Good." He turned around and Michelle saw he held a kind of pearl gray, footed platter in his hands. He set it down on the counter and beckoned to her with a spasm of his hand and a grunt.

He's in a mood, she thought. "I can come back if this is a bad time," she offered.

"No," he said. "Come here."

She didn't want to annoy him any further. She stepped closer. The foot was short and squat. The platter had an inch-thick lip and a four-inch-thick rim, both of silver. There were three horizontal slots spaced along the lip and three small circles in a line in the rim. As she came nearer, Michelle saw that what she had mistaken for a flat platter was really a very shallow bowl. A black inkblot pattern decorated the gentle curve of the bowl's gray inside. She inspected the pattern; it was applied between sandwiched layers of clear glass.

It was the sort of thing that a rich baker or a pastry franchise owner might own if they were into Art Deco cake plates too nice to use. Michelle expected him to ask her to say how much it was worth.

"This piece spins," Mr. Harrington said. "Here, here and here." He pointed to three slots on the thick silvered lip of the bowl. "If you would be so kind as to spin them for me?"

She wasn't sure if the "be so kind" bit was sarcastic or not. Maybe he was just old. She ran her finger down the left-hand slot. The glass exposed by the slot was heavier than she expected. A third of the blots spun when she moved the glass and symbols appeared in the bottom-most circle in the rim. She heard a faint whir from the bowl. The random element in the piece intrigued her. "Wheel of fortune?" she asked.

"If you like," he said. He pointed to the other slots in the plate. "Now spin the other two."

This was one of the weirdest interviews she'd ever been in. Maybe he was proud of this bowl and wanted to impress her. Well, he had. She spun the glass exposed in the other slots. The whirring sound increased. The spinning blots merged and emerged with each other in the center of the dish while different symbols flashed through the line of circles in the rim. Mr. Harrington stood still and she could tell he was watching the whirling Rorschach test.

She felt her eyes drawn to the spinning blots and watched them until the dish's interior spun to a halt. She heard the soft tick-tock of the gallery's clock. She looked at the circles in the bowl's rim. The outer circle showed a boot etched into the glass. The middle one showed an anchor. The symbol in the inner circle was a mask.

She felt a shiver on the back of her neck. For once Susan hadn't been indulging in her usual high drama—this shop *did* have a weird vibe. It didn't take a genius to figure out that the coincidence of a boot and a mask showing up impressed Mr. Harrington. He stood peering at the dish while his right hand held his chin and his right index finger crossed his mouth.

"So," she said, trying to lighten the mood with a joke. "Did I win anything?"

He uncovered his mouth. "Yes." He stepped back to the curtain and stuck a hand through the opening. "All the modern pieces you see are my own productions. I need an assistant to help me in the studio and with the gallery." He stepped back and thrust a stapled stack of papers at her. "Bring these forms filled out tomorrow at nine, before the shop opens. When you're done with the forms, carefully study the pages afterwards—and yes," he smiled for the first time. "There will be a test."

Back in her studio apartment, Michelle cleared her table—an old door resting on cinder blocks—of her remaining stock of glass rods, a few camp stove propane tanks and other glass equipment. She set down a bowl of ramen noodles and sat down to study Mr. Harrington's papers. She wondered if he had rigged the spinning bowl somehow. Rigged or not, the artistry of the bowl and every piece in the shop promised a lifetime of work if she could learn Harrington's techniques.

The job application form and W-2 were standard. The insurance forms alone would have had her applying to work at Harrington's *before* the bust at Glassroots. Real insurance.

The rest of the package was a haphazard collection. The top papers were medieval and renaissance woodcut prints of astrological and mystic scenes. She furrowed her brow and shuffled through the pages trying to find something that would make more sense, like a history of Venetian glass.

She stopped on a diagram labeled "apparatus employed in a laboratory in the late seventeenth century," which showed glassware for someone like Dr. Jekyll or the wicked queen from *Snow White*. The next sheets were photocopies of instructions for silver coating the insides of Dewar glasses. It was like he was looking for a chemist; she would be so screwed if it turned out he was manufacturing meth. He didn't seem like a meth-head.

Michelle's phone rang. She got up, walked around her futon couch and picked up the phone.

"Hello," she said and sat on the couch.

"Michelle?" asked a man's voice. "This is Charles Opie."

"Oh," she said. She'd bumped into him earlier when she'd delivered a resume to Emerald Glass. "Hello."

"Listen," he said. In the background Michelle heard eighties grunge, glasses clinking and other brewpub noises. "I thought you might be interested. A bunch of us are getting together and we're going to form a new glass blower's collective."

"Oh, that's great," she said, hope blossoming in her chest. Charles could probably pull something like a new collective off. But the brewpub noises bothered her; it wasn't the sort of place to come up with a business plan. "What's going to keep the cops from closing a new collective?"

For a second she thought she'd lost him, except she still heard the grunge playing. "We'll show only juried pieces," he said, a little too quickly. They hadn't thought it through. Reality reared up and snipped off hope's blossom.

"Charles," she said, "I'm interested. But I need to know that what you're planning is for real."

"We're going to do this." He sounded defensive.

"That's great," she said. She looked at all her remaining equipment where it lay on the makeshift table. She took a chance. "'Cause most of my equipment was confiscated by the police during the Glassroots bust as drug paraphernalia and right now all I've got to work with is a blowtorch, a fistful of glass rods, some cans of propane and a crockpot annealer."

"Oh," he said. It was all he needed to say. Whoever "they" were, they didn't have much equipment, either.

Michelle didn't want to burn any bridges. "Charles, I am interested—"

"But . . ." he said. He sounded a little pissed off.

She had to soothe his bruised male ego. "Starting a new collective is a great idea. Nothing personal, but I need to see some sort of plan so I know I can make rent."

"I hear you," he said. He still sounded a little mad.

"So you'll call me when you've got a business plan?" she asked.

"Yeah," he said. "Whatever."

She tried to salvage the call. "Great," she said. "Thanks. I really appreciate that you thought of me. How can I reach you if I need to?"

He gave a phone number and hung up.

Michelle set the receiver in the phone's cradle. She hoped she hadn't pissed off Charles too badly. Still. She had a new job or at least the promise of one if she could memorize enough information in one night to please Mr. Harrington.

And if she could learn Mr. Harrington's techniques she could become the next Dale Chihuli.

She fell asleep on her futon still reviewing the packet.

One moment she was sketching an old woodcut of a dove in a flask and the next she was in her usual anxiety dream. She was driving her father's car to the university. She was late for her class and she couldn't get the steering wheel to respond. On the sidewalks, college students in carnival masks walked beneath budding cherry trees. Suddenly, her father was sitting next to her in the passenger's side—only now the steering wheel was in front of him.

"I don't know where you're going," he said.

Michelle spoke the words to make her dream lucid.

480

"This is a dream." Somehow she had switched places and Mr. Harrington sat in the driver's seat.

"Yes," he said. He wore a large harlequin mask, which he removed. The steering wheel was the whirling gray bowl. "But whose dream is it?"

She startled awake. Her sketchbook thudded on the floor and the papers she'd been studying rustled on her blankets. Beyond the feeble circle of light cast by her cheap reading lamp, orange shadows from the sodium streetlight shining outside her window filled her room. Next to the reading lamp, her small mask stared up from its box.

"Damn," she said. She always had the controlling her father's car dream when she was anxious about jobs—but usually she could turn it into a different dream. And a new employer as her father was a new twist.

She gathered the papers, turned off the lamp and tried to go back to sleep.

Harrington's store clock chimed a quarter past nine. Michelle stifled a yawn and wished her morning coffee would kick in.

Mr. Harrington stood behind the glass counter and pointed to an old picture of a toad in a flask.

"Putrefaction," she answered.

He grunted. "Acceptable." He handed the packet back to her. "Continue to review this and I'll test you again next week."

Her heart thumped with excitement. "I've got a job?"

"It's probationary," he said. "Now, we've a half-hour. I can give you a quick tour."

A passage behind the blue curtain held a long desk,

an arts and crafts style pendulum clock and a half-sized refrigerator. In the precise center of the desk was a neat stack of unopened mail.

"You may keep your lunch here." Harrington pointed at the fridge. "I'll expect you to wash out the refrigerator every Friday."

The building's former kitchen was at the other end of the passage. Empty packing boxes, a floor buffer and cleaning materials sat in wooden storage cubbies. A small barred window looked out at a dingy brick alley. A metal door to the right of the window led outside. The building on the opposite side blocked the morning sun. Michelle had seen cheerier back rooms, but none so clean. She liked that Mr. Harrington was neat and ordered, and hoped he wasn't a fanatic about it.

He pointed at a small closet. "The facilities are here. And down here," he opened another wooden door on the left wall, "are the stairs to the studio."

The door opened onto a landing. Sunlight gleamed through an upper window and dazzled Michelle. She squinted. Mr. Harrington was halfway down dark concrete stairs leading to the basement. Other wooden stairs led to the second story and she saw scattered rainbows on the white plaster walls above.

"What's upstairs?" she asked.

"My apartment." He paused and turned. "I don't expect you'll need to go up there." His warning was clear.

"No," she said and followed him down into the shadows.

At the bottom of the stairs he flipped a switch. Michelle was in heaven. A bank of lights shone on a small furnace surrounded by crucibles. Next to the furnace, an annealing oven wide enough to hold three large pizza boxes side by side and tall enough to hold one on its end hummed to itself and displayed 300° F in red LEDs. A worktable, benches and a lathe sat in the middle of the room. In the wide gap between the table and the lathe stood a metal pole with hooks. Buffing and polishing stations lined the near wall. A selection of stained glass panels and glass rods stood at the far end of the room. She hadn't seen this much equipment since her college days.

The concrete floor was clean. Although Michelle saw where a crack had once been repaired, she didn't smell the wet cement and dry-rot smell many Oregon basements had.

"This is the studio," Mr. Harrington said. "If you do well upstairs and learn the contents of the papers I gave you, you will be expected to help me here."

Michelle vowed to herself to make flashcards as soon as she got home.

Mr. Harrington continued. "I am getting too old to blow glass, so I need someone to work on pieces for me. Once I'm satisfied with your studio work, I'll allow you to schedule your own studio time for approved projects."

Inwardly, Michelle bridled at the "approved projects." "Approved projects" sounded like the sort of proposition her father used to hold over her head. Still, it was *his* equipment. She smiled. "Great."

That night, Michelle splurged and ordered Thai food to celebrate and thank Susan for the use of her printer for resumes.

"Dinner is served," Michelle said as she shouldered Susan's door closed and hefted a plastic bag of boxes.

483

Susan sat cross-legged behind the large low table in the middle of her living room. She wore a bright purple sweater and blue jeans. A large silver anhk swung from a cord around her neck. She slapped Harrington's stapled packet onto the table. "I *told* you I had the strangest vibe about Harrington's. He's got you studying alchemy."

Michelle set the bag of food on the table. She pointed to the blue glass snake bracelet Susan still wore. "I don't care if he has me studying the phone book. As long as I don't have to sleep with him and I can learn his techniques."

Susan dug into a sweater pocket and fished out a bundle wrapped in a purple scarf. "I could ask the cards . . ."

Michelle pulled a box out of the bag and shook her head. "Thanks, but they'll just tell me I have problems with male authority figures."

Susan got up, went down a hall to the spare bedroom she used as a library, and returned with a book titled *Psychic Self-Defense*. "That wheel of fortune plate ritual he did bothers me." She sat down at the table and started paging through the book.

Susan was always trying to protect her. Michelle shook her head and pulled out more boxed food. "The more I think about it, the more it seems like an eccentric joke or an attempt to look mysterious." Michelle went to the kitchen.

"He could have been trying to hypnotize you."

Michelle returned with silverware. "I'm not worth hypnotizing. Now, if I were a beautiful heiress . . ." She spooned rice into bowls.

Susan flipped from the beginning of the book to the end. "If he's a *Dark* adept, he needs to establish a link to someone so he can use their *Life Force*."

The memory of the Harrington from her dream the previous night made Michelle suck in her breath. "I'll keep that in mind," she said slowly.

"I'm *serious*."

"I know. . . ." She opened the boxes of food. Susan wished she had lucid dreams, and when she learned Michelle designed glass pieces in her dreams, she appointed herself Michelle's spiritual protector. If she told Susan about last night's dream, Susan would keep her up all night putting crystals on her forehead and slathering her with potions made of patchouli and worse.

Susan snapped the book closed. "Let me make a talisman for you."

Michelle shook her head. Susan's last talisman—a cloth sack filled with herbs—had given her a rash between her breasts. "He's just old. He needs someone with young lungs to help him blow glass." She held up a hand to keep Susan from butting in. "Sure, there's something funny about the way he speaks, but I had a high school personal finance teacher who'd had a blow to the head and couldn't modulate the tone of his voice. It must be something like that. Doesn't your book say to look for physical explanations before metaphysical ones?"

"Yes but—" Susan's brow furrowed.

"See; I do listen to you." Michelle sat down. "Now let's eat before this food gets cold."

"Promise me you'll let me help you if you detect the *slightest* thing," said Susan.

In her mind's eye, she replayed the dream of Harrington taking off her harlequin mask. It was just an anxiety dream. Michelle held up her hand. "I promise."

By the second week of working at Harrington's, Michelle still hadn't worked any glass. He had her waiting on customers in the gallery. Most of Harrington's clients were more than twice her age and made her feel underdressed. At least none of them were meth-heads.

Between waiting on customers, she cleaned anything they might have touched and made flashcards from more of Mr. Harrington's assigned reading. Currently, it was *Leavie's Codex of Natural Historie*. She supposed that it might have been the latest science when it was written, but the Elizabethan English was difficult to read and astrology and other occult philosophies played a big part in explaining everything. What they didn't explain was left to God. The woodcut prints were interesting from a craft point of view—but reading about circling the square for pages and pages was giving her a headache. So was the religiosity. She used her paycheck stub as a bookmark.

Lunch came and went. Mr. Harrington was out delivering a stained glass panel. Several customers came in and browsed the gallery without buying anything. At two o'clock, she finished reading *Leavie's Codex*. She kneaded the spot between her eyebrows, closed the book and gathered up the flashcards she'd made for herself.

She went to her pack behind the curtain and pulled out her sketchbook and some aspirin. Harrington sure was fond of medieval and early Renaissance texts. She couldn't figure it out; aside from the antiques, his style of glass work seemed to draw its inspiration from the eras spanning the art nouveau movement forward.

Perhaps she could emboss woodcut designs on hot glass slabs. She drew a square, then sketched an apple in its middle, and added a twining snake around the square. The design was forced and reminded her of her work from early classes, when she tried to copy everything she saw. She flipped back through her sketchbook and frowned; her drawings were becoming more like rough German woodcuts from six hundred years ago.

The clock chimed a quarter past the hour. Her headache was not going to go away. If today was like the others, no one would come by until three-thirty. She could go to the back of the shop for some water for the aspirin and be back at the counter before anyone came by. She locked the front door and turned the stained glass disk halfway between OPEN and CLOSED.

In the kitchen, a tiny rainbow shone through the open door to the stair landing. Michelle put her cup down. She went to the stair. More speckled rainbows painted the stair's upper landing. If she stooped and held her head at the right angle, she could see the gleaming edge of glass. The basement studio was silent. She glanced up the stairs.

I have time for a really quick peek, she thought, just the landing. She placed her foot on the first step. The white walls reflected diffuse sunlight. There must be a clerestory or skylight high enough to let the afternoon sun in, she thought, maybe Mr. Harrington's medieval glass pieces are up there.

At the first landing, she turned the corner and froze in

amazement. Hanging on the stairway walls were many, many glass masks.

The first mask was a long, curving, dark green slab; a brown sea tortoise swam in the foam of bubbles at the top. The second was a pale white moth with hints of gold and red glitter sparkling along the wings. The third was a man's face made up of ivy leaves in a hundred shades of green. Additional glass masks of peacock feathers, rainbows, bat wings, waves and more lined the walls. She wanted to examine each mask intimately, but was afraid to move any closer.

A closed red door was at the top of the stair.

"Miss Horn!"

"Damn!" She jumped and crouched in a defensive pose.

Mr. Harrington stood in the dim light at the foot of the stairs, his arms crossed over his chest. "I gave you clear instructions that you were not to go up there."

She shook the tension out of her body. "I—I saw the rainbows and was curious—"

"Come down," he growled.

She descended the stairs and waved behind her. "Why aren't these on display?"

"I have my reasons."

"But they're fabulous."

"Are you questioning me?"

She felt as if he had hit her in the stomach. "No," she said.

"If you are going to apprentice under me, you will need to follow my instructions. If you cannot obey a simple order, then you may leave. Do I make myself clear?"

She felt ten years old. She hated it that he sounded

just like her father. "Yes, sir." She responded. "I'm sorry. It won't happen again."

He pointed back to the front. "I'm extending your probation. Go unlock the door and mind the gallery."

She walked around him, her glass of water forgotten.

That night, Michelle dreamed she was making glass masks underneath blossoming cherry trees. She stretched out her small harlequin mask into one that was life-sized. Before she started to sculpt it, Mr. Harrington appeared with a small red box.

He placed the box on the ground before her. "Have you heard of Pandora?"

"What's in the box?" asked Michelle.

"Don't open it," he said, and left.

"This is a dream," said Michelle and opened the box.

Blinding, searing light shattered Michelle's mask. Stripped the cherry tree of its blossoms. She screamed as the box grew and grew, until she was falling into it.

She tumbled through the air and came to a rest under a blooming cherry tree.

She picked up her glass mask and stretched it.

Mr. Harrington came with a red box. "Have you heard of Pandora?"

"This is a dream," said Michelle. A sense of unease constricted her chest. She reached for the box. . . .

Michelle dragged herself to Harrington's the next morning. She wished her second cup of coffee would kick in.

The first customer was Officer Reid, the skinny "good cop" from the Glassroots bust. He was the last person she expected or wanted to see at Harrington's. Her stomach did a flip-flop.

"Officer Reid." She relaxed her grip on the counter. "Is Harrington's under investigation?"

"They say you are Harrington's new assistant," he said, coming up to her.

"Y-e-s." News travels fast, Michelle thought. Who were "they"?

He smiled. "Good." He placed a hand on Michelle's. His touch was electric and she became aware of his scent. It should have been creepy, but her pulse sped up. "I'm sure this is a much better venue for your talent."

Before she could pull her hand away, Mr. Harrington stepped into the shop from behind the curtain. "Ah. Punctual, as ever."

Officer Reid smiled and stepped away from the counter.

"Miss Horn," said Mr. Harrington, "we will be upstairs in a consultation. If anyone else comes by, we should be through by noon." He held the curtain open for Officer Reid, then followed behind him.

Michelle heard them head upstairs. She had no desire to know what they might be discussing.

The dull roar of the furnace shook the air in the studio. The metal parts of the equipment reflected the red glow of the flame. Michelle hefted a blow pipe and blew the blob of glass at the end into a bubble. Harrington had her blowing a bunch of spheres of clear glass as a test. At last, Michelle thought. She could do this forever.

Mr. Harrington observed her from the center of the studio. He wore a thick leather apron and gloves. "Good."

He came forward as she scored the bubble's glass stem. She tapped the sphere into his waiting gloves.

"Another," he said. "This time twice as big." He walked away and placed the sphere in the annealing oven next to her other globes.

She pulled another unused pipe off its rack and dipped it into the crucible of molten glass. She inhaled and set the pipe to her lips. He was watching her work style. She exhaled and blew the largest glass globe of the night. When it was the size he wanted she tapped it into his gloved hands and he placed it in the oven next to the others.

He returned, picked up a plaster mold joined by a metal jacket, and opened the two halves. "This time I want to see you blow the glass into this mold."

Michelle examined the mold to get an idea of how much glass she'd need to use. The mold was for a thin-necked vase. The vase's bulb would be a disk standing on a slightly flattened base. On the front and back of the disk were half-dollar-sized circles surrounded by concentric rings. On one circle was a stylized sun, on the other a moon. She imaged how the light from the rings would interact with each other and form a moiré pattern.

Mr. Harrington placed the mold in a metal brace. The brace had clamps for the blowpipe. "I'll close it once you have the pipe in place."

She rehearsed clamping the pipe in place without any glass. The hard part would be blowing while standing directly over the mold.

"OK," she said. "I'm ready." She pushed her safety

glasses further up the bridge of her nose. She worked a glowing lump of glass out of the crucible and onto her pipe and blew a small bubble.

"Stop!" yelled Harrington. "You need to do the entire blow in the mold."

"But—"

"The entire mold."

She shrugged and worked a new lump. She had blown ten spheres for him already. She eyed the molten glass and added a bit more. "Get ready with the mold." She placed the pipe in position on the rack. He snapped the mold shut as she inhaled. There was enough space between the narrow neck and the pipe for glass to ooze out as she blew. She eased her breath out of her lungs and imagined the bubble expanding and pressing against the plaster. Just as she feared that something had gone wrong, the glass pushed out of the top of the mold.

Mr. Harrington waved her away. "I'll get this one." He hefted the whole brace and slid it into the shiny, large annealing kiln. "Now this one." He held another mold in the shape of a life-sized human head.

"Are you going to start selling wigs?" she asked.

He grimaced. "Concentrate on the task."

She reckoned the size of the mold and gathered glass on the blow pipe. "Okay. Get ready."

He snapped the mold shut over the pipe's end. She inhaled, then blew until the glass oozed out of the mold.

He placed the second mold into the annealer, closed its door and turned to her. "You may go. Take tomorrow off. I'll evaluate your work and see you Tuesday morning at nine forty-five."

"Thanks," she said. But he had already turned his back to her and was punching a cooling sequence into the annealing oven.

That night, Michelle dreamt of the whirling baker's plate. Her father stood behind the plate and spun it. She looked at the gray plate's spinning blobs, but they made no sense to her. Instead of her father standing on the other side of the plate, Mr. Harrington wore her harlequin mask.

"Why are you wearing my mask?" she asked him.

He took off the mask. Turned it around. It was a smooth mirror. Instead of her own face reflected, she saw Harrington's.

He spoke with her father's voice. "Why must you be so literal?"

The plate halted. In the circles in its silver rim she saw the moon, the sun and an eclipse.

Fog and darkness rose from the plate and filled her dream.

Mr. Harrington was waiting for her at the shop's front door Tuesday morning. "How do you like your vase?" He seemed amused, or at least satisfied with something.

She swung her pack off her back. "My vase?"

"Yes." He pointed underneath the shop's stained glass OPEN/CLOSED disk.

The vase stood in the display window. The side of the vase facing the street showed a silver-edged moon in *blue* glass. Blue glass?

"But," she said. It was too soon for the vase to have

cooled properly. She went inside; on this side of the bottle was a gold-edged *yellow* sun. "We used clear glass." She looked at the bottle again: from inside the store, the sun appeared to eclipse the moon. She realized that viewed from the street the moon eclipsed the sun. The bottle played with her memory. She turned the bottle so the lunar eclipse faced outward, but her sense of *déjà vu* remained.

"Although it often appears clear, this is a special glass batch," he said. "And it responds to the lodestones embedded in the plaster mold."

"Lodestones?"

"Magnets. Quite strong." He pointed to the ceiling. Eight hanging colored spheres gave the shop the look of a planetarium. "Most of your globes were satisfactory."

Sunday night when she'd left the studio the glass had been clear. "Magnets?" was all she could say.

"The mixture responds to carefully controlled changes in heat as well."

This morning the glass was colored. "That's—" She had never heard of any glass responding so variably to heat. Or magnets. "That's incredible. How do you prepare the glass?" she asked.

"Eye of newt and toe of frog," he intoned and wiggled his fingers.

"Okay," she said. "I can take a hint." Harrington had a special glass and a secret post-production process. She could blow glass for him for years and never know how he did what he did.

"Try not to be so literal," he said, and walked behind the blue curtain.

She remembered her dream. Her pack slid out of her hand.

Michelle chased him through the blue curtain. "Hold it!"

He turned. Light coming through the curtain turned his eyes a dark shade of jasper.

"I've had several dreams about you," she said, "and I don't know how you did it, but the other night I dreamt about an eclipse, and that's what you've got on display."

"Synchronicity," he said. "And will."

"What?"

"Let us say I wanted to do an operation that required the Great Rite—A conjunction of solar and lunar energies. I might perform the Great Rite in truth; however, I have no desire to have congress with you. Or I might use ritual tools, and touch a chalice and a blade together. But I have chosen instead to work with polarities in glass."

She stared at him, her mouth open. "I don't know what that mumbo jumbo means."

"Some day you will," he said. "*If* you want to work glass the way *I* do—and I know you do. Meanwhile, you've passed the final test." He smiled and thrust a hand into his pocket. "Congratulations, moving from unconscious to conscious action is the first step." He pulled out a key on a knotted leather cord with a glass bead fob. "It's time for you to open the gallery."

She stared at him with her mouth open as he turned and went upstairs. She looked at the key, looked at the fob. Inside the gumdrop-sized bead was a tiny harlequin mask and her name.

Michelle shuffled to the store's front. The key fit in the door's lock. She worked the lock. The fob bothered her—he'd known for a while that she'd pass his tests. She opened the door. She could pick up her pack and leave his manipulations. She looked at the art on the shelves. She remembered the masks upstairs.

She could never leave.

After work, Michelle walked straight to Susan's. "I need your help," she said as soon as Susan opened her door.

"Come in. I'll make some chamomile tea," said Susan.

Michelle entered and dug through her pack for her sketchbook. "Look." She flipped the last month's pages and revealed a parade of medieval animals in chemical glassware. "Harrington's aesthetic has invaded my sketches." She fought off rising panic and sank to Susan's table. "I didn't want to tell you, but ever since I first walked into Harrington's, I've been having these weird dreams about him."

"Like what?" Susan seemed poised to consult her bookshelf.

"Well," Michelle said, "everything turns into everything else. But usually my dad and Mr. Harrington trade places. And that gray baker's plate has showed up at least twice."

"Oh, *goddess*. He's got an astral connection with you."

"He's what?"

"He can influence your dreams," said Susan. "He's probably preparing you for something."

"You're kind of scaring me—today Harrington gave me this." She showed Susan the key and the glass fob.

"Don't be scared." Susan gave her a hug. "*This* I can fix." She fixed Michelle with a sober look. "But you have to do what I say."

"Like?"

"You will take a ritual bath," said Susan, "and sleep over here on my couch."

Michelle let her steer her to the bathroom. Susan drew a bath. As hot water veiled the windows with steam, Susan filled a large white cheesecloth sock from the linen closet with rosemary and lavender and dropped it into the tub. The mingling scents reminded Michelle of Christmas at her grandmother's long ago.

"Remove your clothes," Susan told her, "and give them to me. Then say to yourself as you get in, 'I wash myself free of all with this bath.'"

It sounded so New Agey and Susan looked and sounded so serious that Michelle couldn't help tease her a little. "In the name of the Father, the Son and the Holy Ghost?"

"You can add that if you think it will help," said Susan. "The bath is a symbol, but it's the *intent* that helps. If you want to dream easy tonight, get in."

"All right, all right," said Michelle and she unbuttoned her flannel shirt.

Susan took her clothes. "*Remember,* 'I wash myself . . .'"

"'. . . free of all with this bath.' See, I was listening."

"Good," said Susan. "Keep repeating it, I'll be in the living room. Stay in there at *least* twenty minutes." She opened a linen closet and pulled out a white towel and terry cloth robe. "Use these when you're done."

When Michelle exited the bathroom, she was relaxed and she was thinking more clearly. Harrington had spooked her, that was all. Next time he tried it she'd nod her head and pretend to be impressed. She'd make sure to take time to sketch her own designs, too.

497

In the living room, surrounded by at least twenty beeswax candles, Susan was sitting at her table dressed all in gray. Candlelight glimmered off of the ankh at her chest. Her tarot cards were fanned out in three arcs in front of her. Harrington's key lay to her left in a circle of rock salt.

Michelle stopped in the doorway. "You own *gray* clothes?"

Susan waved a hand over the key. "I tried to do a reading on this and I'm still not sure what it does. I suggest you keep the whole thing in a silk bag and touch it as little as possible."

Michelle sat down on a cushion, unwrapped the towel around her head and began to comb out her hair. "Susan, thanks for the bath. It really cleared my head. And, no offense, but carrying my work key around in a silk bag seems superstitious. I don't know—I mean, Harrington spooked me, but he's just this weird, old, artistic genius with bad social skills."

Susan placed a hand on her shoulder. "Michelle, you *do* know. You both want something from each other." She pointed to a card showing an engraver working on a bunch of disks. "I don't know exactly what he wants, but *you* want his glass-blowing skills."

Her hand passed over a stone mason working on an arch. "You've been putting up with a lot of strange behavior from him in hopes of learning from him. Whatever he wants, he's not being very up front about it—or his fire's blocked somehow." Her hand swept over three upside-down kings and one right-side-up one and hovered over an upside-down card showing the moon.

The tarot cards reminded Michelle too much of

Harrington's assigned reading. "What do you mean, 'his fire's blocked'?" she asked.

Susan's hand went back to the row of kings. "Kings are expressions of fire, and the King of Wands doubly so." Susan pointed to each one in turn. "The King of Cups, Swords and Pentacles are all upside-down." She pointed to the last one. "But the King of Wands isn't. So he's got fire, but he can't use it."

"Okay," said Michelle. "I knew that already. He's too old to blow glass." She finished combing her hair. "So what else?"

Susan placed her hands in her lap. "This will be hard for me to say."

Michelle braced herself for a pronouncement of New Age doom. "Go on."

"Ultimately, tarot cards can't help you to be your own woman."

Michelle stood up. "What? I am my own woman!"

"So *why* are you switching Harrington and your dad in your dreams?" Susan asked.

Michelle gasped. "That's so pop-psych."

Susan sat there looking inscrutable over her cards.

Michelle flopped back to the cushion. "Okay. Okay. They're both authority figures." She sighed. "My dad held money over my head to get me to study what he wanted me to study. Harrington says reading his weird books will help me blow glass."

Susan began to gather up her cards. "So *ask* Harrington what he wants, up front. No one can control you without your consent. Once you know what he's up to, you can choose to be a part of it *or not*."

Michelle fumed. Susan was right. She'd stood up to

her dad and still managed to get her MFA instead of being somebody's doctor/lawyer wife. She'd stand up to Harrington, too. "Fine," she said. "If you'll come with me, I'll do it tonight."

"Of course," said Susan, "but not without some precautions."

By night, the sea of butcher-papered shops reflected dark shadows in their windows. The flickering glare of a streetlight threw Michelle's and Susan's shadows ahead of them as they walked towards Harrington's.

Michelle resisted the urge to pull out her canister of mace. She wore Susan's borrowed purple sweatpants on inside out. The inside-out, purple sweater she wore itched. So did her inside-out underwear. "I don't feel invisible," Michelle said. "This is a great way to get mugged."

"There's two of us. And we're on a *mission*," said Susan.

Michelle stopped at the shop. Susan kept walking.

"Susan," Michelle hissed. "We're here."

Susan stopped. "What? Isn't it two blocks more? I must be turned around in the dark."

Michelle fished out the velvet bag with her key and walked up the first steps.

"Where are you going?" Susan asked.

Michelle stopped halfway up. "I'm going up the steps to the shop. It's not that dark." She saw the Macintosh rose panel in the window, and the OPEN/CLOSED disk, and her eclipse bottle; Harrington had turned it back so the moon eclipsed the sun.

"Not to you, maybe," said Susan. "I can *barely* see you. Are you sure this is it?"

500

"I can see everything as plain as day—even that new bottle." The eclipse dream gave Michelle a strange idea. She fished her key out of the bag and unlocked the shop. "Wait right there." She hoped she wasn't about to lose her job setting off a burglar alarm. She opened the door and braced for a bell or siren. When none sounded, she opened the door further, crouched and turned the eclipse bottle around so that the sun faced outside.

"Oh," said Susan, "isn't it *wonderful* what a little light will do." She marched up the stairs.

Michelle felt giddy and forced herself to breathe. "Susan." She clutched the doorframe. "All I did was turn around the eclipse bottle."

"Oh, goddess," Susan said and put a hand to her ankh. She eased Michelle into the shop and closed the door. "The bottle's like our clothes, only for the shop."

Nightlights and reflected light from the street showed the shapes of the glass on display around them. Light from the back leaked around the curtain. Beneath the floor they heard the muted rumble of the furnace. Outside, a car drove by; its headlights created a cascade of furtive glimmers that chased themselves around the shelves and counters.

Michelle leaned against Susan. "I thought he was joking."

"About what?"

"All that talk about polarity and the sun and the moon." Michelle tried to remember calming techniques from a self-defense class.

"I'm sure he's doing more than just *talk* about it," Susan said. "Don't you see, he's an adept . . ."

Footsteps sounded on the other side of the curtain.

501

Michelle stood up straight and put confidence into her voice. "Mr. Harrington?"

The curtain parted. The hall light shone behind a robed figure. A voice, high and ringing, like a finger run over a goblet's rim, spoke. "Follow me." The figure held aside the curtain.

Michelle raised her eyebrows, glanced at Susan, and mouthed "Now what?" Susan shrugged her shoulders. Well, Michelle thought, I'm here to confront Harrington. She walked forward and heard Susan following.

Underneath the cowl of the guide, a featureless, silvered ovoid reflected a distorted image of the shop. Michelle couldn't tell if it was a man or a woman in the costume.

"Uh," said Michelle, "take us to Harrington."

"Down the stairs," said the guide in its high, ringing voice as they passed.

The furnace's dull roar ceased as they descended the concrete stairs. Michelle heard the hiss of many propane torches. Shifting shadows danced around them as they entered the studio.

Cowled figures in dark blue robes clustered around a mask—a woman's face—mounted on the pole in the center of the room.

The figures on either side ran the flames of their propane torches over the mask while a craftsman facing away from them touched midnight-hued filaments to the mask's forehead and trailed them off. The lips were reflective layers of coral glass that gave the lips extra depths of flame. The eyes were a siren's eyes: The water of the ocean filled them and Michelle felt as if the glass were a fragile layer separating her from ocean waves. Flecks of emerald and serpentine sparkled in the mask's eye shadow. All the while flames licked over the entire mask. Michelle felt the heat from the torches and wondered how the others managed not to catch their robes on fire.

The craftsman facing away from them turned and chose a new rod of cobalt-colored glass. It was Harrington. "What are you doing here, Miss Horn?" He ran his torch over the end of the rod and attached the semimolten end to the mask.

Their robed guide closed the studio door.

Michelle felt the canister of mace in her hands. "Mr. Harrington, there's something that you want from me, and I'd like to know what it is."

"There's no time. Take a torch and help keep this mask hot." One of the robed and masked figures held out a live torch.

Harrington continued. "Tell your friend to find a corner and close her eyes if she values her sanity. My client is due soon."

"Michelle," said Susan, "Don't let him dominate you."

"Girl," said Harrington, "words like 'deva,' 'Elohim,' and 'elemental' do not begin to describe my client—if I were you I would start doing more than turning my clothes inside out."

Michelle held up the mace. "I think we'll leave, now."

The torch bearer tossed the torch to one of the other robed workers and lunged for the mace in Michelle's hand. She squeezed the nozzle. The stream hit Harrington between his eyes and ran down his face. He scowled. Michelle winced as gloved hands grabbed her wrist.

"Ow!" She spun and dropped, and pulled her arm down and brought her opposite elbow into the masked face of her assailant.

Susan yelled behind her.

Glass tinkled.

Harrington grunted.

Michelle rolled to the ground; the robed figure a dead weight on her. She rolled on top and jumped up. Inside the blue cowl lay silvered shards of glass. There was no man or woman in the robes. "Damn!" Michelle shuddered.

Behind and to her left, Susan uttered a strangled, "Michelle."

She glanced back. One of the blue robes held Susan from behind by the cord of her ankh. Angry red marks appeared where the ankh pressed against Susan's neck.

"Miss Horn," Harrington said. "Time is short. Attend." Two of his—things—handed their torches to the ones still heating the mask and stood to the right of Harrington. "Observe and learn."

He raised his hands to his ears and yanked. His face came off. It was a glass mask. The eyes were dark agates behind square-lens glasses. Behind the mask was a silvered ovoid.

Michelle shrieked.

The mask was handed to the middle figure, which raised it to its head. Harrington's face became mobile and his eyes blinked. "You see?" he asked, now the figure in the middle. "I need you as an anchor." He removed the mask and handed it to the figure on the right.

Michelle pulled her wits together. The mask on the

pole was originally the glass head she'd blown. "You don't really breathe! You need me for my breath!"

"And you," said Harrington, now the figure on the right, "need me for my expertise. I use these mannequins because I have no other apprentices. Except you."

The two silver-faced mannequins on his left moved the ruined one to the edge of the studio and returned to the mask on the pole.

Behind her, she heard Susan croak, "Beware. He's a kind of Oshara."

"Your friend," said Harrington, "is not quite right; my origins are Greek, not African."

"Who are you and what do you want from me?" asked Michelle.

"You'll never know unless you wear my mask."

The mannequins behind him turned off their torches and stepped away from the mask on the pole.

"There's still time," he said. "It will be safer for you if you are wearing my mask when the client comes."

The robes and the masks were too unreal for her. Michelle said, "This is a dream."

"It's not a dream," said Susan.

"I saw your face when you saw the masks upstairs," said Harrington. "Practice pieces. Early commissions. But you will know the method of their manufacture if you wear my mask."

She thought of the rainbow procession of animals and elements. But in all the fairy tales she'd ever heard of there was a hidden price for knowledge. "Will I be able to take your mask off once I put it on?"

"As easily as you saw me do it here," he said.

"Michelle—" Susan said.

"Enough!" said Harrington. "Decide. Or stand in a corner with your eyes closed and hope you don't attract any attention in the next few minutes."

"Fine," said Michelle. "I came here to be my own woman. If I can learn something, then fine. But don't be a bully." She stepped forward and held out her hand. "What do I do?"

He smiled. It was a bad sign; he only smiled when he thought he'd manipulated her into doing what he wanted. "Take the mask from me," he said, "and press it onto your face." He reached up, removed his mask and held it out to her.

Michelle took it. She expected the mask to be heavier. Its cold smooth edges felt like any other glass. She took a deep breath. She pressed the piece onto her face.

A flame of memory flowered in her mind. His mind. Their mind. His history was like a mnemonic labyrinth of prisms wound around her. Faces and names from long before she had been born came to her. Michelle gasped and Harrington reveled in the sensation of her breath moving over his lips.

She saw herself—the memory of when Harrington first saw her. "I do not look like a 'guttersnipe,'" she said.

She felt him guiding her mouth. "And I am not a pissy, tight-assed clerk. Now think of the Mirror of Insight," he said.

Michelle thought of the spinning baker's plate. She saw herself etching the symbols on the rim—they were only pointers to a destination, a wish, or a heart. The real oracle was how the spinning patterns on the inside reflected the cosmos.

LORRAINE SCHLETER

"Close enough, for now," said Harrington. Feeling him use her to speak was like watching an arm that had fallen asleep twitch. "Now think of one of the masks you saw upstairs."

The green slab and turtle mask. She saw it in her mind's eye. Saw how the main part of the mask was plate after plate of emerald-hued glass worked with water from the seven seas; how the sea turtle swimming in the foam at the top stood for all the marine animals maintained in the world's waters. She remembered catching ocean currents from their twisting paths around the planet and placing them in the glass. She gathered wave after wave and united them into an inexorable strength that nevertheless was subservient to the tugging motions of the moon and sun.

She remembered making the mask. She remembered the delight of the desert being for whom the mask had been fashioned.

"A desert spirit masquerading in this world as an ocean current," said Harrington. "It does have a certain symmetry."

"Will you two stop *talking* to each other?" said Susan. The mannequin behind her had released the cord, but had her arms pinioned.

"Susan!" said Michelle, "I know how to make those masks I told you about." She thought of her own harlequin mask and laughed—it was like thinking about the stick drawings she used to draw as a child.

"It's dis*tur*bing," said Susan, her voice raising in pitch, "to see Harrington's *face* on top of *your* body with your voice coming out of *his* mouth."

"Oh," said Michelle. She felt along the back of her

ears until she found the glass seam. She pulled the mask off. The flame illuminating her mind died. The Mirror of Insight became a spinning plate; the ocean mask a large green layered art piece.

A mannequin took the mask and wore it. "You understand who I am?"

"No," said Michelle. "But I have an idea." He was old, very old. And he knew a lot about glass; that knowledge tempted her.

Harrington glanced at the ceiling. "My client is here." A mannequin unlocked the door and went upstairs. "Wear my mask, or join your friend." He addressed Susan. "If seeing Miss Horn wearing my mask disturbs you, seeing my client unmasked will be much worse." The mannequin behind her released its hold.

"Kether unveiled?" asked Susan. She rubbed her wrists. Harrington shook his head and laughed.

Michelle had snapshot memories of the dusty, whirlwind visage of the ocean mask wearer. She knew those fleeting impressions were simplified for her benefit. The personage coming tonight was even more vast, strange and mind-blowing. "Shut your eyes, Susan," she said.

"What about you?" Susan asked.

"I'll be all right," she said. "I'll be wearing Harrington." She held out her hands to receive the mask. The glass felt cool against her face.

The flame in her mind reappeared. It illuminated projects for the future: a companion piece to the Mirror of Insight; a Paradise Tree; Masks for the Dead.

Michelle realized that Harrington didn't care about what the glass looked like; only what it did.

The studio door opened and a mannequin led Officer Reid into the studio.

"What—?" was all Michelle could say.

"Good evening, Miss Horn," Officer Reid said. "Harrington, didn't you warn her that—" He whirled and pointed at Susan. "What's this?"

Michelle felt Harrington prompting her. "She is nothing. She is not here."

Officer Reid—it was the easiest way for Michelle to think of the being before her—narrowed his eyes, then shrugged. "Very well, no names then; and I take no responsibility for any accidents."

Michelle studied Reid's face and thought about the policeman's mask he was wearing. No. Not a policeman's mask precisely, a mask of authority. Made for a centuries-long courtship. "Sir," said Michelle, indicating the woman's face on the pole, "here is your mask. Soon it will be cool enough to wear."

Reid inspected the mask on the pole. "I like her mouth. I think De—she'll like the mouth, too." Desire and hunger radiated from him.

Michelle saw her chance and took it. "Did you tire of the mask of authority, or did she?"

Reid shot her an irritated glance. She concentrated on her next words to keep Harrington from speaking. "When will you come back, when she tires of beguilement?" The mannequins rustled.

Light gleamed in Reid's eyes. "What are you getting at?"

Michelle sensed a mannequin behind her. "Stop!" she said.

Another mannequin lunged for her. Something connected to the back of her knees and she fell forward.

She rolled and swept another mannequin off its feet. It fell and made a tinkling crash when it hit the floor.

Michelle sprung up next to the crucible. She popped off the mask. Knowledge and techniques faded from her. "You're next, Harrington," she said, "unless you behave." She held Harrington's mask over the liquid glass. The four remaining mannequins halted just out of arm's length.

Reid regarded her from the doorway. "Are you finished? I'd like my mask. Now." He reached for the hinge of his jaw.

She knew if he unmasked in front of her she'd go mad. "Wait! I'll tell you how to win her lasting love."

He stopped. "Oh? And you're an expert on love?" Disapproval dripped from his voice.

She reminded herself that his authority was a mask. "I'm a woman—you and Harrington have been taking a man's approach for the last 3000 years."

He laughed. "I told you, Harrington." He pointed to the mask in her hands. "You should have hired her at the beginning instead of driving her here; it would have saved you a favor."

"What? You're responsible for February's crackdown?" She wanted to drop Harrington into the crucible, but she needed him.

"Harrington needed a flesh-and-blood apprentice, so we influenced events. I wanted you; Harrington wanted a wider selection. So tell me, woman, how do I win her undying love?"

Michelle took a steadying breath. "First, promise you won't harm me or my friend. Then, take Harrington's mask and wear it. Then teach me—"

He stepped closer. "What if I take the mask?"

Michelle lowered it closer to the crucible.

He stopped and held up a hand. "No need. Why not wear the mask like his other apprentices?"

"Because Harrington makes tools; his glass is beautiful and he doesn't care. And, the longer I wear him, the more I'll become a mask like him."

"So it's acceptable to you if I become like him?" Reid was smiling, now.

"I've learned enough from Harrington to know that you won't. And I'll bet Harrington will pick up a few things from you in the process."

He walked closer. "Very well. I agree not to harm you, or 'nothing' over there," he pointed to Susan. "I'll protect you and teach you Harrington's methods. But you have seven years and a day to help me win undying love." A fierce light shone from his eyes, and she knew seeing him unmasked would be the least of her problems if she failed.

She wouldn't fail—she had some ideas, starting with ditching the masked lover routine. "Deal," she said.

He pushed past the mannequins and held out his hand. "Close your eyes and hold out Harrington's mask."

She hoped she wasn't making a mistake. Bright light turned the insides of her eyelids crimson. She felt a cool touch on her forehead. The light faded.

"Open your eyes," said Harrington's voice.

Harrington/Reid seemed larger somehow. Even the mannequins had taken on larger presences. "You have given us much to meditate on," he said. "Leave us. Tomorrow begins your new apprenticeship."

Behind him, Susan stood with her mouth open and her eyes wide.

"Susan!" Michelle said and rushed past the mannequins to her side.

Around her was a circle drawn in chalk. The chalk stick was still in Susan's hand. In the other was a round compact mirror.

"Huh," Susan said and kicked at the circle. "That didn't work. Whew." She shook herself.

Michelle grabbed Susan's elbow and steered her out the door. As they climbed the stairs, Michelle asked, "Are you all right?"

"I thought if I stood in a magic circle and looked through a mirror—" A spasm made her whole body tremble.

Michelle steadied her and they reached the top landing. "You *saw* Officer Reid unmasked?" she asked.

"In the mirror." She looked down at her hands as if she realized she still held the mirror and chalk. She pocketed them. "And only from behind, and in the last half-second before he remasked."

They exited the shop through the back door.

"And?" asked Michelle.

"After tonight I think I need to purge a few books from my library. But first, I'm going to take a bath."

Michelle knew Susan would be okay. They reached the end of the alley and headed to Susan's house. Along the sidewalk, ornamental cherry trees were in bloom.

The Year in the Contests

BY ALGIS BUDRYS

---

*Algis Budrys, editor of the anthology, was born in
Konigsberg, East Prussia, on January 9, 1931. His family
came to America in 1936.*

*Budrys became interested in science fiction at the age of six,
when a landlady slipped him a copy of the* New York
Journal-American *Sunday funnies.*

*At the age of twenty-one, living in Great Neck, Long
Island, he began selling steadily to the top magazine markets.
He sold his first novel in 1953 and eventually produced eight
more novels including* Who?, Rogue Moon, Michaelmas *and*
Hard Landing, *and three short-story collections. He has
always done a number of things besides writing; he has been,
over the years, the editor in chief of Regency Books, Playboy
Press, all the titles at Woodall's Trailer Travel publications
and* L. Ron Hubbard Presents Writers of the Future
anthologies.

The Year in the Contests

The judges for this year are named on the cover of this book. And, as has been true since the beginning of the Contests, these professionals comprise many of today's top names in the fields of science fiction and fantasy literature and art.

This year, we are proud to welcome on board as our latest judges, Rebecca Moesta for the Writers of the Future and Stephan Martiniere for the Illustrators of the Future. Rebecca is author of thirty science fiction and fantasy novels, writing for all ages from children to young adult to adult. She has also co-authored several books with her husband and Contest judge, Kevin J. Anderson. Stephan has won multiple awards for his illustration and animation including the British Science Fiction Association Award for Best Cover in 2004, the Chesley Award for best hardcover in 2006 and the Thea Award for his work in the Paramount theme park in 2001.

The enterprise goes ever forward, and the authors and illustrators in this volume will, in due course, take their firm place in the history of creative arts.

517

For the 2006 year, L. Ron Hubbard's Writers of the Future Contest winners are:

FIRST QUARTER

    1. Jeff Carlson
    THE FROZEN SKY

    2. Tony Pi
    THE STONE CIPHER

    3. Corey Brown
    THE PHLOGISTON AGE

SECOND QUARTER

    1. Kim Zimring
    RIPPING CAROVELLA

    2. Douglas Texter
    PRIMETIME

    3. Damon Kaswell
    OUR LAST WORDS

THIRD QUARTER

    1. Stephen Kotowych
    SATURN IN G MINOR

    2. Aliette de Bodard
    OBSIDIAN SHARDS

    3. Karl Bunker
    PILGRIMAGE

FOURTH QUARTER

    1. Andrea Kail
    THE SUN GOD AT DAWN,
    RISING FROM A LOTUS BLOSSOM

    2. Edward Sevcik
    THE GAS DRINKERS

    3. John Burridge
    MASK GLASS MAGIC

L. Ron Hubbard's Illustrators of the Future
Contest 2006 winners:

FIRST QUARTER
> *Bryan Beus*
> *Lars Edwards*
> *Bogdan Stetsenko*

SECOND QUARTER
> *Amelia Mammoliti*
> *Artem Mirolevich*

THIRD QUARTER
> *Marcus Collins*
> *Randall Ensley*
> *Peter Town*

FOURTH QUARTER
> *Yuliya Kostyuk*
> *Geir Lanesskog*
> *Lorraine Schleter*

Our heartiest congratulations to them all!
May we see much more of their work in the future.

521

WRITERS' CONTEST RULES

1. No entry fee is required, and all rights in the story remain the property of the author. All types of science fiction, fantasy and dark fantasy are welcome.

2. By submitting to the Contest, the entrant agrees to abide by all Contest rules.

3. All entries must be original works, in English. Plagiarism, which includes the use of third-party poetry, song lyrics, characters or another person's universe, without written permission, will result in disqualification. Excessive violence or sex, determined by the judges, will result in disqualification. Entries may not have been previously published in professional media.

4. To be eligible, entries must be works of prose, up to 17,000 words in length. We regret we cannot consider poetry, or works intended for children.

5. The Contest is open only to those who have not professionally published a novel or short novel, or more than one novelette, or more than three short stories, in any medium. Professional publication is deemed to be payment, and at least 5,000 copies, or 5,000 hits.

6. Entries must be typewritten or a computer printout in black ink on white paper, double spaced, with numbered pages. All other formats will be disqualified. Each entry must have a cover page with the title of the work, the author's name, address, telephone number, e-mail address and an approximate word count. Every subsequent page must carry the title and a page number, but the author's name must be deleted to facilitate fair judging.

7. Manuscripts will be returned after judging only if the author has provided return postage on a self-addressed envelope. If the

author does not wish return of the manuscript, a business-size self-addressed, stamped envelope (or valid e-mail address) must be included with the entry in order to receive judging results.

8. We accept only entries for which no delivery signature is required by us to receive them.

9. There shall be three cash prizes in each quarter: a First Prize of $1,000, a Second Prize of $750, and a Third Prize of $500, in US dollars or the recipient's locally equivalent amount. In addition, at the end of the year the four First Place winners will have their entries rejudged, and a Grand Prize winner shall be determined and receive an additional $5,000. All winners will also receive trophies or certificates.

10. The Contest has four quarters, beginning on October 1, January 1, April 1 and July 1. The year will end on September 30. To be eligible for judging in its quarter, an entry must be postmarked no later than midnight on the last day of the quarter. Late entries will be included in the following quarter and the Contest Administration will so notify the entrant.

11. Each entrant may submit only one manuscript per quarter. Winners are ineligible to make further entries in the Contest.

12. All entries for each quarter are final. No revisions are accepted.

13. Entries will be judged by professional authors. The decisions of the judges are entirely their own, and are final.

14. Winners in each quarter will be individually notified of the results by mail.

15. This Contest is void where prohibited by law.

ILLUSTRATORS' CONTEST RULES

1. The Contest is open to entrants from all nations. (However, entrants should provide themselves with some means for written communication in English.) All themes of science fiction and fantasy illustrations are welcome: every entry is judged on its own merits only. No entry fee is required and all rights in the entry remain the property of the artist.

2. By submitting to the Contest, the entrant agrees to abide by all Contest rules.

3. The Contest is open to new and amateur artists who have not been professionally published and paid for more than three black-and-white story illustrations, or more than one process-color painting, in media distributed broadly to the general public. The ultimate eligibility criteria, however, is defined with the word "amateur"—in other words, the artist has not been paid for his artwork. If you are not sure of your eligibility, please write a letter to the Contest Administration with details regarding your publication history. Include a self-addressed and stamped envelope for the reply. You may also send your questions to the Contest Administration via e-mail.

4. Each entrant may submit only one set of illustrations in each Contest quarter. The entry must be original to the entrant and previously unpublished. Plagiarism, infringement of the rights of others, or other violations of the Contest rules will result in disqualification. Winners in previous quarters are not eligible to make further entries.

5. The entry shall consist of three illustrations done by the entrant in a color or black-and-white medium created from the artist's imagination. Use of gray scale in illustrations and mixed media, computer generated art, the use of photography in the

illustrations, are accepted. Each illustration must represent a subject different from the other two.

6. ENTRIES SHOULD NOT BE THE ORIGINAL DRAWINGS, but should be color or black-and-white reproductions of the originals of a quality satisfactory to the entrant. Entries must be submitted unfolded and flat, in an envelope no larger than 9 inches by 12 inches.

7. All entries must be accompanied by a self-addressed return envelope of the appropriate size, with the correct US postage affixed. (Non-US entrants should enclose international postage reply coupons.) If the entrant does not want the reproductions returned, the entry should be clearly marked DISPOSABLE COPIES: DO NOT RETURN. A business-size self-addressed envelope with correct postage (or valid e-mail address) should be included so that the judging results may be returned to the entrant.

We only accept an entry for which no delivery signature is required by us to receive the entry.

8. To facilitate anonymous judging, each of the three photocopies must be accompanied by a removable cover sheet bearing the artist's name, address, telephone number, e-mail address, and an identifying title for that work. The reproduction of the work should carry the same identifying title on the front of the illustration and the artist's signature should be deleted. The Contest Administration will remove and file the cover sheets and forward only the anonymous entry to the judges.

9. There will be three co-winners in each quarter. Each winner will receive an outright cash grant of US $500 and a trophy. Winners will also receive eligibility to compete for the annual Grand Prize of an additional cash grant of $5,000 together with the annual Grand Prize trophy.

10. For the annual Grand Prize Contest, the quarterly winners will be furnished with a specification sheet and a winning story

528

from the Writers of the Future Contest to illustrate. In order to retain eligibility for the Grand Prize, each winner shall send to the Contest address his/her illustration of the assigned story within thirty (30) days of receipt of the story assignment.

The yearly Grand Prize winner shall be determined by the judges on the following basis only:

Each Grand Prize judge's personal opinion on the extent to which it makes the judge want to read the story it illustrates.

The Grand Prize winner shall be announced at the L. Ron Hubbard Awards Event held in the following year.

11. The Contest has four quarters, beginning on October 1, January 1, April 1 and July 1. The year will end on September 30. To be eligible for judging in its quarter, an entry must be postmarked no later than midnight on the last day of the quarter. Late entries will be included in the following quarter and the Contest Administration will so notify the entrant.

12. Entries will be judged by professional artists only. Each quarterly judging and the Grand Prize judging may have different panels of judges. The decisions of the judges are entirely their own and are final.

13. Winners in each quarter will be individually notified of the results by mail.

14. This Contest is void where prohibited by law.